A Hussar's Promise

A tale of chivalry, love, and betrayal in 17th century Poland

(BOOK 2 OF 2)
BY GRIFFIN BRADY

ISBN 978-1-7354558-7-7

Cover design by Jenny Quinlan, Historical Editorial
Maps by Cathy Helms, Avalon Graphics LLC
Edited by Jenny Quinlan, Historical Editorial
Proofread by HippoCampus Publishing
Printed in the United States of America
Trefoil Publishing

Dedication

To Tim, Kyle, Matt, and Ryan

Contents

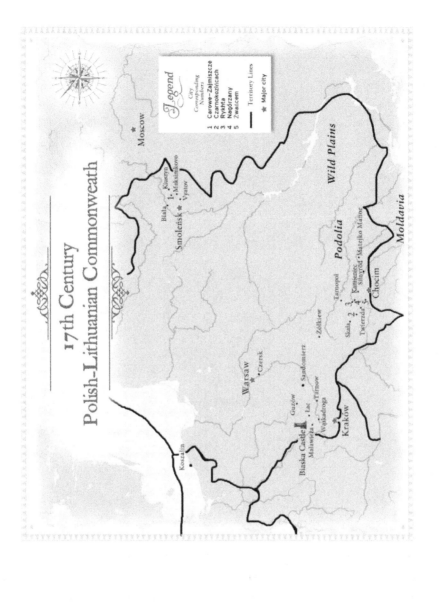

17th Century
Polish-Lithuanian Commonweath

Legend

City
Corresponding
Numbers

1 Carowe-Zajmiszcze
2 Czarnokozinicach
3 Rykhta
4 Nagórzany
5 Zwaśicem

—— Territory Lines

★ Major city

Moscow

Biała
Kusym
1 Maksimkowo
Vyatow

Smoleńsk

Wild Plains

Podolia

Tarnopol
Kamieniec
Silnyród · Matejko Malloc
Skała 2 3
Twierdza 4 5
Chocim

Moldavia

Żółkiew

Warsaw
· Czersk

· Sandomierz

Guzów
Błaska Castle · Łac · Tarnow
Malewirża · Waskadroga

Kraków

Koszajn

Chapter 1

Beginnings

The thunder of pounding hooves and billows of dust engulfed Jacek, stinging his eyes as he rode behind his four outriders. The landscape they traveled was an unending expanse of tawny grasses, resembling a great suede cloak tossed over the earth. He squinted into a late-day, azure October sky streaked with filaments of white, but nothing moved along the flat horizon. Today's journey was no different from yesterday's, or the day before, or the day before that, and it jabbed at his raw nerves. But instinct told him the Tatars still roved, searching for human treasure, and he could not let down his guard.

He blew out a breath. Since he'd been assigned command of the border outpost at Silnyród months ago, his life had been one long series of skirmishes with the cunning raiders. Jacek chuckled wryly to himself. *Assigned.* Banished was a more apt description. Banished to a decrepit fort in Podolia for loving the wrong woman.

And now his days were spent hunting. But it wasn't for venison or pheasant among other noblemen as he'd once done. No, he hunted Tatars, small bands splintered from a thousands-strong army pushing into Muscovy for the sole purpose of carrying off Slavic slaves. The devils! They had no trade but slaving. It was these harriers his undersized garrison scouted and fought. In the last few weeks, they had scattered like autumn storm clouds—which prickled him all the more. The Tatars were sly, and they were quick. Would they slither through border patrols, past spies, unnoticed? Where would they come from next? Would they strike at night as villagers slept? Or now, over the next swell of ground?

The enemy had devastated harvests and stores of food to keep its army going. Would they leave when none remained? Or grow so fat with plunder that they would return to the warmer climate of their Crimean homeland? The time wasn't here yet. Maybe never. They might remain and raid throughout the long winter, and if they did, the outpost Jacek commanded needed more shoring up.

Of late, daily patrols and scouting missions turned up nothing. No raiding parties to kill, no captives to save, no enemies to question. Not even signs of the damned Zaporozhian Cossacks, whose unlawful forays into Ottoman territory sparked vengeful counterattacks against defenseless folk. Folk he was resolved to safeguard.

For now, he and his limited force chased ghosts across the plains.

Waning golden light signaled the end of the day's scouting, and the party turned for home. As they approached in the gloaming, Silnyród's fortress walls loomed like an enormous galley on a deserted sea. The surrounding flat ground was broken up by breastworks bristling with wooden spikes, a ditch, and stone barricades stacked the height of two men. Though not tall enough to prevent a determined enemy scaling the walls, the stone was more solid—and more defensible—than the rotting wooden palisades he'd found when he'd first arrived. To the right, on the fortress's eastern flank, smoke from sprawling cooking fires blanketed the village.

Guards on the battlements hailed Jacek and his troop as they clattered across a bridge spanning the ditch. Behind them, men secured the fortress's giant doors against the night and lit torches braced to the thick walls.

"Has everyone reported?" Jacek dismounted, tossing his reins to a stable lad.

"Yes, and they saw nothing," his second, Lesław, replied.

Jacek nodded and pulled off his plumed helmet, ruffling his short brown hair to cool his sticky scalp. Another lad began unfastening his gorget, breastplate, and vambraces as something clamped on his heel. He jerked his leg, but the vice held—and growled.

"Jesus, Tymon! What in blazes is wrong with your devil of a dog?" Jacek shook his ankle, but the small beast held.

"Damn it, Statyw! Release the lord!" bellowed a stocky man heading briskly for Jacek.

Jacek lifted his boot, and the dangling mongrel attached to it, and let the stable master at it.

2

"Keep that blasted thing away from me." Jacek scowled as Tymon unclamped the offending mutt and dropped it to the ground. Jacek sprang back as the fiend lifted one of its three legs to wet his boot.

"My apologies, Captain Dąbrowski." Tymon erupted in a string of oaths and chased after Statyw. The mongrel was Jacek's most spirited adversary of late. How good it would feel to be rid of the damned thing!

Jacek stalked through mud to the log manor house, reminded by its sadly hanging thatch that its roof needed repairing. He flung the front door wide, setting a few serving maids to squealing. When they recognized him, the young ones smiled and the old ones scowled. He ignored them all, save one.

That one, Bogna, the capable commander of his household, accosted him as he navigated the hall. "My lord, your boots?" She pointed behind him at lumps of muck in his wake.

He shrugged. "It's all off by now."

"Tchah!" She threw up her hands, her wizened face pinched in a scowl.

Men crammed tables, slurping and grunting their way through their servings. Jacek wended his way round them, nearly grinding his hip on a table corner. The men stopped to acknowledge him, and he waved them back to their meals.

"Bogna, why are the tables this way?" he asked as he pulled off his gloves.

With an eye-roll, she said, "Lately, you have brought on so many soldiers, my lord, all of them hungry, that we needed more seats. This was the best arrangement." Leathery hands on her hips, she added, "Your meal is ready, m'lord."

He nodded. "I shall wash first." He thought he heard her mutter, "Take off those boots."

The smell of *bigos*—hunter's stew—filled his nostrils, setting his stomach to growling. Stepping through a doorway off the main hall into a low-ceilinged room, Jacek smacked his forehead on the frame—again—and cursed. *Jesus, damned door!* As he rubbed his head, he paused before his makeshift shrine that held a candle, the wooden rosary his mother had given him, a crucifix, and a depiction of the Black Madonna—Our Lady of Częstochowa. Here he crossed himself and mumbled a quick prayer to be forgiven his incessant blasphemies, a habit he'd never broken and likely never would. Then he threw his gloves on one of two trunks and glanced at the painting of his beloved mare, Jarosława, suspended above it. The piece had been given him by Oliwia four years ago at Christmas when he'd been twenty-two and she sixteen, and though he hadn't fallen in love with her until the following year, he had treasured the picture even then. He still did despite everything. It was one of two remembrances he allowed himself of Oliwia.

Just as he sank into the furs covering his rough wood-framed bed, there came a rustle. In the doorway stood a beaming serving maid with a pitcher of water.

"For you to wash up, Pan Jacek," she said sweetly.

"Leave it there," he grumbled and jerked his chin toward a rickety washstand as he rose.

She poured water into a cracked porcelain bowl before setting down the pitcher, then held her hands out to him. "May I take your cloak and *kolpak*, m'lord?"

"No." He dropped the fur cap beside the gloves and whipped off his cloak and pegged it. She stood still, watching him as he began unbuttoning his mud-spattered *żupan*. With an exhale, he said, "What is it?"

She fumbled and reddened. "I merely … I wondered if there is aught you need, m'lord."

"Yes. To be left alone." He closed the door on her crestfallen countenance, then dipped his hands in the bracing water and scrubbed his bearded face. After pulling on a fresh garment, he trudged out the door and took his seat at the head table among his fellows. Materializing from the shadows, the same maid hurried to fill his tankard with *piwo*, then painstakingly placed a full trencher before him. It was a wearisome routine, and he had scant patience for the fawning tonight. Even if he were to find himself in a moment of weakness, he knew better than to seek pleasure in his own house. *No entanglements.* Entanglements had always proved messy, and he'd avoided them—save the one which had shattered his heart.

Before Oliwia, he'd always found women wanted far more of him than the lone tryst he wanted of them, and he'd rarely fancied lying with whores. After Oliwia, even trysts held little appeal, for she became the measure by which he judged all women, and they could not compare. She'd ruined him. In the end, it was far easier to forgo intimate encounters altogether and focus on his prime objective, which was to build his reputation as a commander and gain the king's notice—and an estate. If he had to do it in this godforsaken place, then so he would.

He shoveled spoonfuls of bigos into his mouth amid the soldiers' good-natured jibing directed at a young, dark-haired garrison soldier.

"Anyone see Florian trip over himself today when Luiza brought out the slop?" a soldier mocked. "Never seen a lad so eager to feed swine before."

"No," another replied, "but I saw him trip when he ran to pull up a water bucket for her."

Florian's curls twitched as he shook his head. "You lot are jealous."

"You stole my favorite tavern maid, you cur," the first soldier complained.

"She wasn't yours to steal," Florian retorted, pointing his eating knife at him. "Jaromir promised her to me at the first, soon as he saw I'm the best man for his daughter." Florian turned to Jacek. "Luiza told me to be sure you will come to the wedding, Captain."

"I will not miss it," Jacek replied.

The first soldier hooted. "'Luiza told me.' You're already whipped, Florian."

"Florian, you are *not* invited to come with us to Milda's tonight," said a different soldier.

"Milda has nothing I want." Florian grinned. "Take Benas," he added, jerking his chin toward a young Lithuanian soldier. The lad had just arrived from a nearby village to train with Jacek and Lesław.

"Benas, you may accompany us tonight to Milda's, but don't think you're getting a go at the new girl," the first soldier chortled.

"Why not let the pup have a go?" said an older soldier as he sucked on a pipe. "He'll be done before he starts, and you lads won't have to wait." The men exploded in guffaws and pounded hands round the table. His face red, Benas stared hard at his platter.

Thank the saints for the new girl! Jacek had added men to the garrison, but brawling had become all too common among those vying for the hand of any unmarried maid or the services of the overworked Milda and the few whores in the village. Though he was pleased to add the soldiers, Jacek begrudged the fact that to keep them he needed the whores too—or rather, he needed to help Milda recruit them any way he could. It wasn't that he minded whores, but Jesus, he had better things to do! Nonetheless, the new girl's novelty had so far distracted the men from fighting each other while giving Milda a much needed rest *off* her back.

Florian piped up, interrupting Jacek's inner grumbles. "Captain, with harvest over and the Feast of St. Hedwig upon us, surely Bater Beg's army has turned for home by now."

Jacek grunted and reached for the bread, tearing off a hunk before the maid could do it for him. "We've had no new reports of their movements. Crown Hetman Żółkiewski's patrols have uncovered little, and his spies cannot predict when the devils will be done ravaging Muscovy and go home. And then there are the damned Cossacks."

"Which ones?" asked Benas.

"The Zaporozhians." Jacek washed down the dry bread. Bogna shooed the maid away and refilled his cup. He thanked the old woman and took a swig.

Benas wore a puzzled expression. "But they are with us, yes?"

"Most times, but if they smell opportunity, then hang alliances," Jacek replied.

"Do you mean they fight against us?" Benas's growing confusion deepened the creases between his brows.

"No, but they cause problems for the Commonwealth when they raid Ottoman territory. They break the truce between our countries, and the Turks strike back," said Florian.

"An eye for an eye?" asked Benas.

"Usually, they send the Tatars to do their dirty work, though," one soldier added.

Finished with his meal, Jacek dropped his napkin on the table. "Żółkiewski's duty-bound to enforce peace with the Ottomans. But the Zaporozhians don't follow rules and raid anyway. So Żółkiewski apologizes to the Turks and pleads with the Cossacks, and when the Turks retaliate, guess who has to defend?" Jacek pointed from his chest to Benas's and back again.

A soldier's son burst into the hall on a gust of wind and hurried toward Jacek.

"Captain, I was told to give you this!" He thrust a bundle in his hands. Jacek scanned the packet, recognizing the seal belonging to his master, Lord Eryk Krezowski. The one who had stranded him here.

6

"Bogna, see the messenger gets something to eat," Jacek mumbled as he rose. He crossed to his chamber and barred the door. Seated on the edge of the bed, he unfurled the bundle in the glow of the bedside lantern. What he unwrapped was a dagger with a letter penned by Lord Eryk. Puzzled, he inspected the dagger and recognized it as his own. Then he read the note twice before tossing it aside.

The missive delivered only cheer. Or so Eryk asserted. Deputy Witold Bilicki had concluded Jacek was not responsible for the brutal murders of two women. One had been a tavern maid he'd argued with—whose mutilated body had been found beside his stolen dagger—and the other a whore who'd taken him in later that same night when he'd passed out in a drunken stupor. Both had been alive when he'd left them, and neither had deserved her fate. But now someone had been arrested and had confessed, and Bilicki had returned Jacek's knife. The other bit of "good news" stole Jacek's breath like a well-placed fist to his stomach.

Jacek lay back, his arm folded under his head, and stared at the hewn ceiling. Reaching into his żupan, he extracted a bound lock of sable hair and drew it over his mouth, under his nose. The scent was long gone, but he rubbed it against his cheek, the silky strands catching on his beard. His mind unexpectedly jumped to the maids in his kitchen, in the tavern, and the wenches in the village. But thinking of them stirred not even a modicum of desire.

Why is it the ones you don't want make nuisances of themselves, while the one you do want …

"The one you *do* want belongs to someone else and now carries his child," he muttered aloud. It was one thing to fool himself into believing no intimacy took place between the woman he desired and her husband, but it was quite another to be slapped with the evidence that his self-deception was utter fantasy. He tucked the precious tress back in its place against his heart.

As he looked up at the ceiling, he tried to focus on one point, tried to lock out all the commotion in his head, but he could not expel the disturbing images of Oliwia in Eryk's bed. His mind wandered backward, along a familiar path, to Oliwia before she married Eryk, when Jacek had believed she was his. He grew more agitated, berating himself for losing her.

If only I'd secured her promise before leaving on campaign. Or returned when I said I would instead of chasing my dream. She would be mine now.

He imagined never seeing her again; he was destined for battles, and she now for childbirth. Would she survive its perils? Fear chilled him, and in that moment he cared little that his own fate might lie at the point of a Tatar's scimitar. It was a long while later when fatigue finally claimed him, and he drifted off, quite alone.

Yelling startled him awake in the dark hours. He flung off his covers and began pulling on clothes while his door rattled in its frame.

"Captain! Captain!"

Bootless, Jacek shot to the door, unbarring and opening it in one motion. Benas stood in the frame, his eyes wide, his breathing rapid.

"We're under attack! The village and part of the fortress are in flames."

"Tatars?" Jacek grabbed his boots and weapons. His retainer, Marcin, materialized out of the main hall murk.

Benas shook his head. "Uncertain. It's chaos."

"Did any villagers get inside the walls?" Jacek asked as Marcin helped him into his armor. Jacek buckled on his sword belt and slid his *szabla* in its scabbard, then gripped his favored weapon, the *nadziak*—his war hammer.

"I don't know, but the tavern's one of the buildings ablaze."

Jacek grasped Benas's shoulder. "Where's Florian?"

"None have seen him."

"Christ! Marcin, roust Lesław. Benas, get to the stables and tell Tymon to start saddling the horses."

Chapter 2

Biaska

Oliwia fell back on the mattress with a groan. Her husband, Lord Eryk Krezowski, lay beside her, stroking her arm while he eyed her. She recognized the look—the hungry look. After exhausting every possible excuse on her overused list, how much longer could she hold him at bay? Soon she would have no escape, but what wife did? Especially one who'd come from nothing, from nowhere, and had found herself unexpectedly, unwillingly, married to a powerful lord. Most women would wish to be in her slippers, wed to this man, carrying his child. Unfortunately, she was not most women. Unfortunately, she burned for another.

Moreover, the luxury and station were superfluous, at times glutting. The only gain that mattered was what she'd secured for her younger brother, Filip: his safety and his heretofore unattainable lofty rank as the lord's kin. For these, she could tolerate her misery and her husband's lust. Most days.

Now Eryk was reaching for her. Even defying the Church's rule against marital relations during pregnancy did not dissuade him. Rolling to the side, she gave him her back. If Oliwia had learned anything during her nineteen years, it was how to deflect, how to adapt. How to protect those she loved.

"My stomach is not right. Perhaps if I rest a bit longer this morning …" she mumbled, hoping he would believe her and leave her alone. Alone to dream of Jacek's tall, sculpted warrior's body; of the way he'd felt when his muscular arms had enfolded her; of the pine-and-leather smell of him; of his gentle hands and mouth on her; of the mildly salty taste of his coarse-stubbled neck; of his beautiful sapphire eyes.

"But you just slept the entire night! Are you feeling as poorly as that?" Eryk tugged her shoulder until she flopped on her back. Propped on an elbow, he pressed his hand against her cheek. "Your face is rosy enough." A frown bunched his dark brows.

She flung her arm over her head. If she tried, really tried, might she conjure Jacek in Eryk's place? But she'd endeavored it, countless times, without success. No, her condition was her best—and last—defense against Eryk's advances, and she clung to the nausea, practiced it, even as it receded.

At the outset of her pregnancy, she'd not needed to feign anything, for she had been overwhelmed with biliousness. Many an episode of retching had given her pause. Was the child within poisoning her? Did it know she fervently wished another man's seed grew there?

Eryk caressed her face, and her emotions twisted and set to dueling within her. He swept his hand down her throat, heading for her chest, and she brushed it away. A little flame of fury flared in her even as a tear pricked her eye.

"My innards churn, and I feel as though my strength leached from me overnight."

He withdrew his hand, hauled himself off the mattress with a huff, and shrugged on a robe. "Can Nadia get you anything?"

She shook her head and let out a silent sigh of relief.

He walked to the fireplace and stabbed at the embers, their glow brightening the morning gloom. "Oliwia, I think it best if you move to your own chamber."

Had she heard correctly? Snatching at the prospect she would not have to sleep with him every night, elation flooded her, and she fought back her giddiness. She turned her head to him. His amber eyes trained on her, he looked every bit his thirty-six years this morning, and she noticed, for the first time, silver strands glinting in his dark hair and deeper lines etching his face.

"As you wish," she replied evenly.

"I don't wish it, but I am concerned for the child. I will take every precaution so that he might grow strong in your womb. 'Tis not too early to begin your confinement."

"Yes, of course, my lord."

"I will speak to Nadia and see it's arranged today, then." He paused. "Oh, and Oliwia? I've more business to attend that will keep me away tonight."

"Do the troubles on Biaska's eastern edge continue, my lord?"

"Yes. While I lament being away from you, I fear this will be the way of it for a while."

"Of course. Whatever time you need."

Just then, Eryk's manservant entered to help him dress. After they left, Oliwia sat up and pulled on a cloak. With a light step, she headed for the marble hearth and its warmth. Though it was a mild fall, the stone walls trapped the night's chill and slowly released the cold so that no space within felt warm. But inside, Oliwia was as cozy as the fire before her.

Plopping onto a velvet cushion on an oaken chair, she averted her gaze from the flames. Nadia, her handmaid these last three years, had told her many a wives' tale, such as looking at a fire could bring a babe with red birthmarks. Oliwia had heeded her, for what could it hurt?

Now she ruffled her hair. It had grown enough since her wedding to skim the tops of her shoulder blades and give her the pleasure of twisting it once more. The blaze fired off a raucous pop and a sizzle of embers. Oliwia brushed one from her shoe, then tucked her legs under her. As she stared at a corner of the Turkish carpet, her past danced within its whorls. Filip had been one and she ten when their parents had died in bleak, frozen Muscovy—so far from England, so far from home—and her existence had transformed to naught but safeguarding her brother. Then Jacek had rescued them from their ruined village and they'd come to Biaska, where they'd built a life from the tattered remnants of their childhood. How things had changed!

She closed eyes, remembering Jacek speaking her diminutive in his deep timbre. Besides Filip, he was the only one who used it, and she loved hearing it. "Liwi," he would say, his eyes twinkling as he smiled at her.

With a disgusted "pah!" she discarded her foolishness. Were she not married, Jacek still wouldn't want her. He hated her.

After Nadia helped her dress, Oliwia shambled down the passageways, holding her nose against the oily smell of the torches. Filip sat at a trestle table in the cavernous, tapestry-covered hall, working on a mouthful of something yellow, and she headed for him. He raised his blue-gray eyes

11

and grinned. She stooped to kiss his head, but he dodged her in a familiar move.

"Liwi," he said around a mouthful of eggs, "you must stop doing that. I'm a soldier now."

She folded her arms across her chest.

"You don't believe me, but I am," he insisted. "I spar with the metal blade."

"What did you do with the wooden one Jacek gave you?"

"Pah." Filip flipped his hand with flourish. "Wooden swords are for children."

She bit back a smirk. "Tell me, Master Filip, what have you learned from Pan Henryk?"

Filip could barely contain his glee, launching into the minutiae of the steps and motions of swordplay. Gesturing wildly, he threw about terms like *strike* and *counterblow* as easily as he would shake leaves from his hair. Oliwia watched him as he blathered on, unmindful of most of what he said. She was simply happy to be with him.

A serving maid deposited a plate of eggs and sausage before her, and her nausea came roaring back. She pushed the plate away.

"Not hungry, my lady?" a male voice asked.

Oliwia glanced up to see Henryk standing over her with a dimpled-cheek smile. She looked about furtively, then eased. Eryk had left; Henryk was in no current danger. Despite his womanizing ways, Henryk, who became captain of the guard after Jacek's departure, had been her good friend since she'd arrived four years ago. But when Eryk's jealous nature had flared, she'd avoided him. She'd missed Henryk's cheerfulness dreadfully, so she invited him to sit.

"Perhaps you would care to finish my meal?" she offered.

He twirled his nut-brown moustache. "I've eaten, thank you." He cleared his throat. "I thought you might like to know I received a letter from Jacek."

Oliwia felt a little pang. "Is he … is he well?" *Has he given his heart to anyone?*

Henryk chuckled. "Well enough. The attacks have died down, and he's hopeful the Tatar army is gone. Now his attention is devoted to Silnyród's defenses, though he has little patience for the tedium—nothing new in that. I believe the skirmishes are his only diversion." He winked.

"I wish him well," she said wistfully, her head blooming with thoughts of Jacek. Nowhere was there any thought she betrayed her husband. Instead, she was torn by the belief she betrayed the man she truly loved every time her husband lay with her. Guilt twisted in her like a coiled rope. Silently, she vowed to visit Father Augustyn, Biaska's beloved priest, though she would find no absolution. None existed for sharing a marriage bed with one's husband.

Her thoughts were torn back to the present by the old cook, Beata, waddling toward her with a cloth-covered bundle. "Perhaps this will tempt m'lady?" Unwrapping it, she deposited an apple tartlet on Oliwia's plate. The fragrance set Oliwia's mouth watering. *The mother who desires sweets is sure to have a girl.*

"Thank you, Beata. It smells wonderful."

The woman's droopy face brightened. "Pan Jacek told me how much you like my tarts, m'lady. That he used to sneak them to you."

Unexpected tears sprang to Oliwia's eyes. She swallowed hard, waiting a beat to recover herself and her voice. "Yes, he did." The words came out in a choked laugh.

Filip's hand snaked to Oliwia's plate; Beata swatted it.

"'Tis not for you, young master. 'Tis for your nephew!" she declared hotly. Her eyes suddenly widened, and she covered her mouth.

"It's all right, Beata," Oliwia soothed. *Do not remark upon the pregnancy lest it invite the evil eye.*

A sharp blare of horns sounded, heralding riders. Oliwia darted her eyes to Henryk's just as he pivoted from her. The tart forgotten, Oliwia rose and followed him, Filip on her heels. Soon she stood beside her brother on the ramparts as Henryk and several guards directed a score of men across the drawbridge. They clattered behind a banner depicting a red eagle holding a serpent in its talons against a field of white. The banner belonged to Lord Antonin of Wąskadroga, Eryk's conniving cousin.

"Why the devil is *he* here?" she hissed.

"You do not like Lord Antonin, Liwi?"

"I like him—and trust him—as much as the snake on his flag."

Oliwia stormed down the steps, halting atop the forestairs before the keep. Still mounted, Antonin swept her a bow from the courtyard below, a beatific smile lifting his pitted, fleshy cheeks. "Ah, Lady Oliwia! What a lovely vision you are," he cried.

Hands clenched at her sides, Oliwia called back, "To what do we owe the pleasure, my lord?" *What devilment are you about?*

Antonin shrugged, then waved a hand in the air. "We were riding by, and I told my men we must stop so I could pay my respects to my cousin … and feast my eyes upon his beautiful bride." He leered at her wolfishly.

"Riding by?"

"Yes, yes. Let us get settled, my dear, so I can save myself yelling from the saddle."

Momentarily disregarding her duty as gracious hostess, Oliwia called back, "But Lord Eryk is not here presently." Antonin did not appear surprised; his grin seemed to grow wider.

"No matter, my dear. It is your company I relish."

He leaned over and spoke quietly to a wiry, sandy-haired, sharp-eyed man beside him, then dismounted and handed over his reins. The man headed for Henryk's men-at-arms, Antonin's horse in tow. Antonin raised his gaze to Oliwia expectantly.

"Please. Come in and take some refreshment," she gritted out.

Laughing heartily, he climbed the steps. "Delighted, my dear. So pleased to be invited." He embraced her when he reached her, the smell of his lanky gray hair rancid. He planted his lips on her cheeks far too long for a polite greeting, holding her fast, his bristly beard scratching her.

Once seated in the great hall, Antonin tossed back her finest mead. It dribbled down his chin, and he wiped it on her linen tablecloth. She bit back the urge to ask the real purpose for his visit.

With a sly look, as though he'd read her thoughts, he said, "I apologize for not sending word, my dear. I only today decided to divert here on my way back from Kraków, and a messenger would have arrived at the same time as I. Better to present myself, yes?"

Henryk entered the hall, his brows bunched in a frown, and sat beside Oliwia.

"Ah!" Antonin exclaimed. "The noble captain of the guard. My cousin is lucky to have you, Pan Henryk. Perhaps you would deign to show me your fortifications so I can improve Wąskadroga's defenses. As I recall, my cousin once offered to have his then-lieutenant … Let's see, what was his name?" He snapped his fingers.

"Pan Jacek Dąbrowski," Henryk said in a dark voice.

14

"Ah, that's the one! I'm that aggrieved to hear he no longer serves Biaska." He lowered his voice conspiratorily. "He must have greatly angered my cousin to end up—"

"Lord Eryk once offered a service, Lord Antonin?" Henryk interrupted.

Antonin gave him an amused look. "Yes. He offered to have Pan Dąbrowski inspect my armory and give me counsel. I now offer him the same service."

Before Henryk could respond, Antonin barked, "Radek!" The sandy-haired man from the courtyard hurried from another table where he'd been eating amid Antonin's retinue.

"My lord?"

"Captain Kalinowski," Antonin said to Henryk. "It is captain, yes? You remember my lieutenant, Radek? Radek, tell the captain how eager you are to help him with his arms inventory. One can never be too careful, can one? We must forever be on alert for brigands and help one another defend against those who would steal from us."

In an even tone, Henryk replied, "That will not be necessary. Biaska is well equipped to withstand an enemy attack." He pierced Antonin with a hard, hazel-eyed stare. Antonin returned it. Radek twitched, his eyes sliding from Antonin to Henryk and back again. Oliwia, now seemingly invisible, rode a powerful undercurrent she did not yet fully comprehend.

She *did* comprehend she was powerless to refuse Antonin's plea to stay the night, however. After the evening meal, when Antonin had been shown to his guest quarters, she pulled Henryk aside. "What was that exchange with Antonin about?"

Henryk shrugged. "I merely reminded him he's not in charge here."

"Why do you suppose he has come?"

"I have little idea. I doubt he was simply 'riding by.' He insisted on seeing the garrison, so I indulged him."

Oliwia's eyebrows shot to her hairline. "Was that wise?"

"Do not fret. Kasimir was instructed to give him an abbreviated tour. Antonin discovered nothing consequential, but he was appeased."

Oliwia folded her hands over her belly. "You will place extra guards at the armory and order our men to watch his entourage. And I want guards hidden in the alcoves outside his bedchamber."

Henryk grinned. "I did assign additional sentries at the armory and have Antonin's men housed together where they are being observed. I had not ordered guards to watch his door." Henryk paused. "You've some guile, Oliwia."

She gave him a head dip. "I will do what I must to keep Biaska from Antonin's mischief, though I suspect it will take far more than craftiness to stop whatever scheme he is hatching."

Next morning as he prepared to leave, Antonin bent to embrace her and moved his lips to her ear. Before she could pull away, he whispered, "You're hiding something, my dear. I can scarcely wait to discover it." His tone was playful, but a chill danced up her spine nonetheless.

Oliwia's shoulders eased when Antonin and his contingent rode away. Nothing had happened during the night. Would Eryk be cross when he learned of the precautions she'd taken against his relative? She patted her stomach protectively. Her disquiet over Antonin's words was far greater than the customary worry over envy or witchcraft or the evil eye. He must be plotting something.

Eryk lay on his back, one arm folded under his head as he scanned the darkened bedchamber. He'd seen it several times before, but his attention had always been drawn elsewhere. Now he studied it closely, warmed by its weathered oak paneling and the crimson curtains that allowed in just enough sunlight to remind him it was late afternoon. The exercise kept his mind from the guilt accompanying the delights derived from the naked body beside him as he struggled to reconcile his tarnished moral edge. Instead, he disregarded it.

Zofia propped herself on a slender elbow and tossed her golden brown hair behind her.

"I am delighted to see you again, my lord. All of you." She offered him an impish grin as her soft brown eyes scanned him. Reaching up, he fingered her loose strands and smiled at this woman with graceful lines bracketing her eyes and full mouth—a mouth that, only a short while before, had driven every thought from his mind. He brushed his thumb over her lips, then cupped her head and brought those lips to his, kissing her gently. For now, his cravings were quenched.

She stroked his chest, winding a finger in his mat of curly hair. "To what do I owe the pleasure of your company after so short an absence? Not that I am complaining, mind."

"I missed you," he said simply.

"Yes, I believe you did. I thought you might devour me like a plum tart when you first appeared in my yard today."

He chuckled. "Was I so obvious?"

Her eyes danced. "To me, yes." Her expression grew sober, and she let out a soft sigh. "When I first met you after your wife died, I hoped you and I might become better acquainted. But then I did not hear from you, and I confess I cannot help but wonder why you are here in my bed and not at home with your new wife."

"Well, with the child ... she's been so ill." He cleared his throat.

"Oh. Well, she will recover, and when she does, I am sure she will be eager to have you back in her bed. How could she not? I hope that does not keep you from mine."

Warmth shot through his veins as Zofia's words soothed his battered soul. Maybe it was because she had been raised a gentlewoman, or maybe it was because she had already buried two husbands she'd loved. He cared not the reason, only the way he felt when he was with her—important, esteemed. As if he were her whole world.

Oliwia has never been eager to have me in her bed. I am doubtful that will change soon, so yes, Zofia, I shall return.

"She is young, yes?" came Zofia's gentle voice. "She does not yet understand, my lord. Perhaps she requires more seasoning."

Eryk laughed and gave her a quick peck. "She is young, yes. But I believe I have given her ample 'seasoning.'"

"I understand she is comely and was sought after before you wed her. Has she a lover?"

An image of Oliwia's flawless, unclothed body floated through Eryk's mind. An unsettling jolt of jealousy flared. "No, it is quite impossible," he said brusquely. *Because I sent him to the border's wasteland.*

Zofia lightly ran her fingers along his jaw. "She may be young and beautiful, but she is also foolish," she whispered.

She leaned into him, and Eryk kissed her. When they broke apart, she lay back. He trailed his fingertips over her breasts, down her body. Closing her eyes, Zofia let out a soft moan and languidly arched her back. He bent his head to her, and for a moment he imagined this was his wife murmuring his name and writhing seductively under his touch.

Romek Mazur, Antonin's other lieutenant and the true leader of his troops, stood in a pine thicket under cover of night. To get any closer risked alerting the dogs in the yard. His eyes were fixed on a lit window on the second floor. He'd waited for hours, curious if Krezowski would head out. But everything about the manor home looked quiet, as if those within prepared for bed. The gates had been secured, and he made out shadows in the guards' quarters where Krezowski's detail remained. The light in the widow's window dimmed, then winked out. Krezowski would be staying until morning. While it was too early in the affair to make out a reliable pattern, the preceding visits had also fallen on a Thursday night, and the time between had shortened. Romek began wagering with himself as to how soon the visits would occur at regular weekly intervals. *Men and whores—so damned predictable.*

Chuckling, he returned to his horse tethered in the shadowy recesses of the copse. Pleased with his discovery, he decided it was time for his reward. He'd been patient, letting several months lapse since the last time he'd carved up a woman. On the far side of Sandomierz, several villages distant, waited a tavern maid who had little idea she was his next prey. She'd made it clear she wanted him, and it was time he paid her a call and showed her his hunting knife. Hopefully, she'd give him a livelier chase than the last one had.

Chapter 3

The Wild Fields

J acek burst into the yard, where a line of guards wound from the well, swinging buckets of water into each other's hands, trying to douse flames in one corner of the fortress. Around them dashed panicky people. Jacek ran up the ladder to the battlements and was greeted by a flaming flight of arrows. He ducked as they whizzed past him and slapped impotently into the dirt below. In a crouch, he ran along the walkway, brushing past soldiers firing muskets into the night and artillerymen wheeling light cannon into position.

"Hold your fire until you can see what you're shooting at!" he barked.

He reached the eastern wall and peered over top of it. Lurid flames writhed on the outer edge of the village amid cottages, barns, and sheds. Fiery bursts from a toppling structure told him the tavern and its contents were lost.

Christ! Where the hell is Luiza? Jaromir? They must be inside the fort. Florian has them.

Just then, he spotted Lesław below and yelled at him. "Get the men mounted! We're going to sally out."

"Yes, captain," Lesław called back.

A guard standing a horse's length away said, "Commander, what are your orders for us?"

"I want six bowmen up here. Tell them to hold their fire until they can see what the devil they're shooting at. Make sure we've extra guards at the postern gate. Keep the big gates shut after we ride out. If the bastards come at them or start climbing the walls, throw boulders on them." He pointed to one of many rock piles stacked about the ramparts.

Within minutes, Jacek's wheel-locks nestled in their holsters on either side of his saddlebow. His broadsword hung from saddle straps. He swiftly mounted his warhorse, Jarosława, and yanked his helmet on. With Lesław, Marcin, and a handful of cavalrymen, he raced out of the gates. He gripped his sabre and headed for a cluster of buildings in the village. No flames rose there. Yet.

They haven't gotten this far. Or this is their escape route. Either way, we cut them off, then we cut them down.

Amid dark cottages, his exhales a rapid cycle of steam, Jacek's eyes sharpened, and he took hold of the nadziak. The smell of smoke was everywhere, and out the corner of his eye, he spied the fiery glow rising from the village square. Jarosława stomped a hoof and chuffed. Digging his heels into the mare's flanks, he spun, scanning, scanning, searching for movement behind closed shutters, but he saw none—until a bolt flew from the dark, glancing off his breastplate and skittering off his pauldron. He jerked, startled.

"Arrows! There!" he hollered just as a small flight slung through the air.

He accelerated into the duskiness where the arrows had come from, where shadows moved like dancing demons. Behind him, his fellows shouted and peeled away in a thunder of hooves. *Christ! Where are they going?* Before he could turn and follow, a light caught his eye. *Torch!* He raced at it, raising his sabre. The crackling of fire and men's cries reverberated in his ears, muffling his charger's hoofbeats. A horseman poised to loft the torch, turning as Jacek was on him. Jacek took in the narrowed eyes, the flattened nose, the black hair, the foreign tongue as the man yelled. He could smell him.

Tatar!

Bastard!

The foeman's eyes grew wide as Jacek slashed at his raised arm. The torch sizzled to the dirt. Jacek backhanded the nadziak as he flew by, and he felt it connect, barely, just as his eye caught on a line of wavering light in the dark. More horsemen! His momentum carried him toward a dark tangle of horses and men shouting around him.

How many devils? Christ! How many torches? One, two, three … More I can't see? Go! Go!

He hurtled at them as they loomed, hacking at two before three more spun and encircled him. One tossed his torch in the air, but Jacek swung the nadziak and batted it to the ground. Jarosława whinnied and skittered closer to the offender. Jacek brought the claw down hard on the enemy horse's snout while slashing backhanded, connecting with another foe's forearm. The man's panicked screams rose, drowning out the horse's; both dropped back. Wheeling, Jacek kicked out at the third man, missed him, then swayed, off balance. A blade came at him, its edge glinting in the firelight. He threw his sword arm up in a clumsy parry, recovered, and sliced his sabre downward. It whistled through air. The man retreated, cloaked by dimness.

Damn it!

Jacek lost count of how many he'd injured, how many had escaped, but he'd killed none and injured one horse. The shouting had stopped. He'd moved farther from the village, farther from his men. He fought alone.

A man loped toward him on foot. Hoofbeats sounded, and two horsemen came at him. Dropping his sabre on its sword knot, Jacek yanked a wheel-lock from its sleeve and fired. The flash lit his enemy's face before smoke enshrouded them. Shrieking, then nothing.

One.

The man's horse lurched away. Jacek backed up several steps and arced the nadziak at the man on the ground, striking sinew and bone with a solid crunch. The man cried out and thumped under Jarosława's hooves. She trampled him with a crack of bone.

Two. Where in blazes did the third go?

Christ! I'm fighting ghosts in the mist!

A chill raced up Jacek's spine, and he pivoted in time to glimpse the outline of a drawn bow. *How many paces?* He dug his heels into Jarosława's flanks, wielding the war hammer. She leapt toward the mounted bowman as Jacek hooked the war hammer's claw on the bow, sending the shot on a harmless path. Then Jacek crashed the nadziak down, digging the claw into the man's ribs. The foeman juddered and howled, doubling over, gripping the haft, still in his saddle. His mount began to pull away. Jacek released the war hammer, clutched the enemy horse's reins, and took up his sabre. He hacked until the man quit thrashing, then released the panicked horse.

Where's Lesław? Where is everyone?

Smoke filled his nose and stung his eyes. Fire roared behind him. Gasping in caustic air, he looked around. Firelight illuminated four bodies on the ground. He pushed a jittery Jarosława toward scrambling silhouettes outlined against the flames.

"Jacek! Here!" Lesław's voice rose as he drew near.

In the otherworldly orange glow, his men were laying out bodies. He scanned the faces of the dead, and his heart dropped when he recognized Milda and Luiza's mother among them. He crossed himself and bit back his rage.

"We got those we could, Jacek, but some fled with captives. They can't be moving fast. Do you want a detachment to pursue?" Lesław asked.

"No. We don't have enough trained men, and the few we send would be targets for the Tatars' arrows." Jacek swallowed the knot in his throat. "Where's Luiza, the rest of her kin?"

"Haven't seen them. Only Jaromir. He brought his wife out," Lesław said grimly, lifting his chin toward the woman's corpse.

A howl rent the air behind him, and Jacek swiveled. Florian leapt from his horse and flew toward them at a dead run. Jacek dismounted and caught him.

"Luiza!" Florian wailed, straining against Jacek's hold.

Jacek dug in his boot heels and held him back. "She's not there!"

Florian seemed not to hear him and continued fighting Jacek's restraint.

"Florian, this isn't going to help Luiza!" Jacek yelled.

"Jacek, look!" Lesław cried. Jacek followed Lesław's pointed finger.

While Jacek gripped Florian, a man staggered out of the flames, reeled, and collapsed. *Jaromir.* A beam crashed down, landing on Jaromir's legs, shaking his body with the impact. Jacek released Florian and ran toward Jaromir, who lifted his head and tried to crawl away. Jaromir flopped back down, pinned, letting out a mournful wail that rose above the crackle and rumble of the flames. Lesław shouted at Jacek. A shower of sparks, like flaming raindrops, hit Jacek. He crouched, throwing his arms over his helmeted head.

Christ Jesus! No turning back now.

He dragged in a breath and dodged more raining fire as a wave of heat nearly knocked him flat. Jaromir lay just beyond his reach, menacing flames licking at his ankles. Fire seared Jacek's skin as he vaulted toward his prone friend. Hair burned—maybe his, maybe Jaromir's—as he kicked at the beam. It didn't budge. He kicked again. And again. Someone else was beside him, kicking and hefting. *Florian.* Together, they dislodged the weight and dragged Jaromir out of the smoke. His lungs on fire, Jacek stumbled to the ground, coughing. He raised his head, tore off his helmet, and pulled in sweet air.

"How is he?" Jacek gasped.

"See for yourself," Lesław panted.

Jacek looked over his shoulder. Jaromir testily pushed Florian away even as he hacked up smoke. His trousers below the knee were gone, but his boots remained intact. Jacek sat up and looked at him.

"Jaromir, where are your children?"

Jaromir's face twisted in anguish. "They took them! Both my girls and my little boy!"

"Luiza?" cried Florian.

"All of them."

Jacek's eyes stung as they swept the southern horizon from Silnyród's battlements. The sun kissed the eastern horizon in a fiery line that resembled a glinting knife's edge, transforming the morning sky pale yellow. He was getting his first clear look at the wreckage wrought by last night's raid. Most of the fortress had escaped destruction, but the blackened village was half gone. The smell of char and smoke clung to his clothes, his hair, everything. Worse, over three score villagers were also gone, either kidnapped or killed during the raid.

Below him in the yard, a detachment of warriors prepared to ride out; he would soon join them. First, he turned to a grizzled soldier beside him, a man who would act as garrison guard after the detail rode out. Jacek held out two letters.

"You know what to do with these if I don't return?"

The man nodded dourly. "A messenger carries this one to Biaska," the soldier said as he pointed, "and that one to your family."

Jacek handed him the missives. "With God's grace, I'll be back and fetch them from you myself."

As Jacek clambered down the ladder, his heart seized at the sight of Jaromir seated on a wagon, his damaged legs swathed in linen strips. A group of soldiers was clustered round him, Florian among them.

"Jaromir!" Jacek called. "What are you doing?"

"I want to find my children, Captain," the older man growled.

Jacek laid a hand on his shoulder. "I understand, Jaromir, but to find them, we must move fast, and you won't be able to keep up." He pointed to Jaromir's bandaged legs and stopped himself from reminding Jaromir he had a wife to bury. "Besides, the people of Silnyród need you here. Leave the hunting to us." Jacek nodded at Florian.

"We will bring them back, Jaromir," Florian said, his clenched teeth white in his smoke-smeared face. "And if not, I will avenge them." His nostrils flared, and his dark brown eyes smoldered like the ruined village.

Jacek stared at the riot of tracks leading from the village as he considered his plan. *Find them, kill them, bring back the captives.* The party of raiders couldn't have been much larger than his squad of two score; it was even possible his warriors outnumbered theirs, for they'd killed twelve foes during the attack. But the Tatars would be wary, anticipating Jacek's detachment on their tails, and they would move fast. He prayed they would not join up with a larger force.

It took little time to separate the captors' trail and discover they weren't covering their flight—which made him nervous. He sent scouts ahead and continually swept his gaze over the flat, exposed steppe as they rode. *Hard to mount an ambush on us here. Still ...*

The first body they came to caught him by surprise. He thought he looked upon a glistening black rock, which was peculiar in this barren land. As he stared at it, the rock broke apart and became five ravens making a great beating of their glossy wings. They didn't take flight but hopped and flapped as they pecked at one another and fought for space to resettle themselves atop the body splayed in the grass like a cloth doll.

Florian leapt from his mount and ran to the corpse before Jacek could order him to stay put, scattering the black birds, who cawed at him belligerently. He kneeled and turned the body over. Jacek held his breath. Florian looked up at him, his face drawn and ashen, his eyes hard. He shook his head and picked himself up.

"Who was it?" asked Jacek.

Florian trudged back to his horse and, without looking at Jacek, replied. "A girl, maybe nine. I didn't recognize her."

She must have slowed them down. Maybe she cried too much.

Jacek wanted to stay, wanted to bury her in the ground where nothing could tear her frail body to pieces. He wanted to mark that grave with a cross and say a prayer over it, but they had to move, had to keep going. He crossed himself. A lump in his throat dissolved and sped to his belly, where it flared white-hot. He raised his arm, and his men fell in.

The scene repeated itself throughout the day. With each grisly discovery, Jacek held his breath, waiting and watching as Florian ran to the corpse, knowing he couldn't stop him, wondering what the young man would do if the body were Luiza's. Sometimes it was someone they knew, and other times not. Had other settlements been terrorized by the brutes? Whether man, woman, boy, or girl, each had had their throats slit, their bodies left like rubbish for the wolves and carrion birds. The waste was heart-wrenching.

After a brief stop to water the horses, one of the scouts galloped toward them as though the very wind carried him. He reined his horse before Jacek and, between panting breaths, told him they'd found their people and their captors. Jacek's heart lifted for the first time that day.

"They've joined a large contingent of Tatars."

Jacek's heart dropped. "How many?"

"At least four hundred, and more than that in captives. Hard to be sure because we could only get so close."

"How many prisoners are men?" *If we add their number to ours, maybe we stand a chance against their captors.*

"Few. Mostly women and children."

Christ.

"And the terrain?" asked Jacek as Jarosława bent her neck and tore a clump of grass from the ground.

"What you'd expect. Flat. Exposed. The camp is surrounded by wagons and sentries," the scout replied, "but we saw no other fortifications."

"The bastards are taunting us," Jacek exhaled. "They know we can't counter them in time." *Jesus, if only I had two score hussars. Then we'd cut those whoresons down like ripe wheat and—*

"Can't we attack when they begin marching their prisoners?" pleaded Florian.

Jacek looked around at his small detachment. "With what? We are two score, and only half are battle-ready."

"We can't just give up!" Florian tossed his hand to the sky. A vein at his temple pulsed.

"I didn't say we would give up."

Time for a new plan.

First, he needed more information.

Jacek hunkered in a shallow gouge in the earth he shared with his small scouting party. They were a half-dozen men. The prickly stubble of dead grass, brittle with frost, poked his face as he peered at the Tatar camp forty paces away. His muscles cramped with cold, dampness saturated his bones, and though his body was hollow, he would have heaved any food he took in.

Night had settled in. His companions' dulled armor betrayed no telltale gleam. Heavy clouds blotted out starlight, and though Jacek couldn't make them out, he continually glanced upward, praying they would bring the snow he smelled in the air. The only light came from the camp, which sprawled over a rise, illuminated with torches as though a merry feast took place there. But women screaming and pleading, children bawling, their wretched howls punctuated by the raucous laughter of their captors, were a cruel contrast to the warmth of the dancing amber flames. Jacek gritted his teeth, locking out images of people he knew, people who were his friends, people he was meant to protect. Desperately, he looked for any weakness in the camp, anything he could exploit. But he was too far away.

An anguished wail pierced the air and raised the hair along his forearms. Florian's fingers dug into his shoulder. "Luiza!" he hissed and sprang up.

Jacek grabbed him and hauled him back into the shallow depression. Florian thudded beside him.

"You don't know it's Luiza!" Jacek hissed. Florian's muscles were coiled, taut, as Jacek restrained him. Suddenly, they slackened, and Jacek let him go. Florian slumped beside him.

Planting his hand on Florian's shoulder to prevent him bolting, Jacek slowly raised his head, bringing his eyes level with the ground. Sentries, only their silhouettes visible, were turned away, facing a fracas in the camp. *Good.*

"I'm getting a closer look at their defenses," Jacek said. "Florian, with me. Lesław, Marcin, cover us." He would have preferred taking either man with him and leaving Florian behind, but Florian would not have stayed put.

Jacek slithered out of the ditch, and Florian followed. They crawled on their elbows, crunching over dry grass, to a rock little wider than Jacek's shoulders and no taller than their raised heads. Jacek narrowed his eyes and glimpsed a flash of bare legs running within the camp. Several pairs of black boots followed at an amble.

"Mary, Mother of God!" Florian choked. "She'll die from the cold!"

"Quiet!" Jacek squeezed his eyes shut. *She won't last that long. And when death comes, it will be a mercy.* He flicked his eyes back open and scanned the ground, the girl's screams echoing in his ears. Florian tensed beside him.

"We have to find a way in," Jacek breathed.

"You mean now? Just us?" Florian almost sounded eager.

"No, that's suicide. We look for places we can penetrate when we're at full force."

Jacek crawled for the meager cover of a twiggy shrub, Florian right behind. Two distracted sentries who elbowed each other beside a wagon came into sharper view. So did the victim struggling in the camp. Jacek stiffened when he recognized her. Milda's new girl.

As her cries rent the air, Jacek tried to shut out ghastly images of the once jolly young woman now terrified, beaten, stripped, a cord wound round her neck, being made to run a gauntlet of warriors who pummeled her with lances and whips.

"But that's …" Florian rasped. His body shook. Whether from fear, sorrow, rage, or all three, Jacek could not tell. He squeezed Florian's arm hard.

The girl went down, out of Jacek's sight. But he glimpsed a man come forward, a man whose face and carriage would be indelibly burned in Jacek's brain. Jacek swore the man smiled.

A pitiful keening rose up, a plea to stop. It came from the girl. The Tatar commander wielded a flesh-eating whip that he brought down viciously. Her cries stopped, replaced by a chorus of wretched sobs from captives Jacek barely glimpsed. Impotent, Jacek and Florian bore witness as that man, that beast, handed off his whip and fell on her while his men cheered. When he was done, he stood and spat on her. With a flourish of his hand, he invited the others to her, like a sated wolf relinquishing a carcass to the rest of the pack. And they laughed.

Beside him, Florian whispered a desperate prayer. "Lord Jesus and Holy Mary, Mother of God, please hold my love, my life, my Luiza in the palm of your hand and let no harm come to her. I beg you …" The rest was lost in a choked cry.

Jacek stepped out of his tent and pulled his cloak tightly around him as a weak dawn approached. His men were rousing from their short rest, save Florian, who had worked the edges of his blades since their return from the Tatar camp. He said nothing as he scraped the stone back and forth, back and forth. Anguish showed in his haunted eyes and in every line on his young face.

Jacek pulled a hand through his hair and glanced to the southwest, where slate clouds sagged with their loads.

Marcin appeared beside him and looked in the same direction. "It's coming, yes?"

Jacek's eyes fixed on the fluid gray mass, and he nodded.

"How soon do you reckon before it's here?" asked Marcin.

"Midday." Jacek cast Marcin a sharp look. "Now let us pray it's a blinding snowstorm."

Jacek looked at the bleak faces gathering round. Some looked at him in disbelief or as if he were angry, and a few stared blankly. Others, like Lesław, gave him a head bob. The small action lifted his spirits.

"Any questions about the plan?" Jacek called out. His audience shifted and coughed while the wind carrying the storm buffeted tent walls and whipped their flaps.

"If that storm brings the weather I think it will, our enemies will stay in their tents. While they ride out the storm, we become part of it, disappear into it. The blizzard is our cover—just like a dark wood—and the wind will mask our noise as we approach on foot. The sentries will not see us."

He paused and looked each man in the eye, waiting for one to ask what they would do if they *were* spotted, but no one did. *We'll take them down quickly, before they can alert the entire camp. If necessary, Leslaw's men will release Tatar horses to divert them, to prevent them coming after us.*

"We infiltrate in five teams and head for the tents housing captives. We kill their guards *quietly* and lead the captives out before the enemy discovers they're gone. Stealth is everything. The Tatars outnumber us ten-to-one. None can know we're there. The captives must be made to understand; they must remain quiet."

And how many captives would they recover? Again, no one asked. *If we're lucky, we'll get fifty out.*

I need a blizzard, Lord. Time is running out.

They rode at the leading edge of the blizzard, as though unfurling an enormous gray-and-white flag across the expanse behind them. They would stop just out of the enemy's sight and wait for it to catch them up and engulf them. As Jacek rode, he replayed his strategy yet again, trying to quell his doubts and the fear in his belly. What had seemed marginally sound at the outset now blared madness. Added to his misgivings were Florian's possible actions and their outcomes. What if Luiza wasn't among the first captives they found? The young man had nodded his agreement to uphold the plan with a set jaw, but in the end would he abandon it all, abandon them, to rescue his beloved? Jacek flashed to what he would do were it his beloved, then quickly pushed the thought away.

Regret that no sweetheart, no wife, no children would mourn him if he never returned stabbed at him, the thought so swift and covert that he'd no time to deflect it. He gave himself a mental shake.

The small band arrived at a cluster of bushes roughly twenty paces from the gouge in the earth where they'd lain just hours before. They dismounted, handing their reins to two servants who would picket the horses.

"You know what to do," Jacek said, biting back the urge to tell them once more what that was. *Don't be seen. Don't be heard.*

Flakes driven by the howling wind grew fatter, layering their saddles and mounts in white. Jacek could not make out the farthest men on the flank. *Good!* He crossed himself. Beside him, Lesław kissed the cross on his swordhilt.

He nodded at Lesław, who tapped the man beside him with the flat of his blade. Though Jacek couldn't see it, the signal went down the line. Like wraiths, they dispersed in different directions and vanished in swirling opaqueness.

Sabre in one hand and nadziak in the other, Jacek crept over ground now dusted white. Wind whistled through the earholes of his *szyszak* and noisily whipped the snowflakes in spirals, dulling their footfalls. To his right, Florian's silhouette was barely visible against the blizzard's curtain. To his left, no shapes. Pushing aside his fear, he focused on his target as he took one cautious step after another.

A wagon came into view, then two more, forming a wall. The camp lay just beyond. Dropping onto his stomach, he crawled and stopped, listening for the enemy. Hearing nothing save the storm, he dragged himself under the wagon and nearly ran into a white canvas tent. It was large, its long sides blending with the swirling snow. Had his other squads found their tents yet? He stopped again, straining for any sound beyond the keening wind. Was that a cough? Cocking his head, he thought he caught a fleeting sob.

Pressing his cold cheekpiece to the ground, he painstakingly forced up a sliver of the tent's edge and brought his eye to the gap—only to have his view blocked by a length of fabric. Fishing his fingers into the space, holding his breath, he carefully pushed the bit down. The tent's interior was dim, but he caught a glimpse of a woman's arm—and enemy soldiers.

The soldiers were spread out, with several clumped in the center. One, two, six. How many more lurked where he couldn't see? Could they take them out before the Tatars sounded a warning?

A firearm touched off, its report reverberating in the storm.

No, no, nooooo!

He watched helplessly as Tatars exploded from the tent flap, pouring through it and shouting an alarm. Doubtless all four hundred were doing the same in every tent, in every part of the camp. Now came yelling so loud it rose above the gale's racket. Around him, the camp sprang to life with the blare of a horn. Jumping to his feet, he took a step back and looked for his men in the swirling white, but he saw no one. He hissed out their names. Nothing. He edged his way along the tent's perimeter. *Where's Florian? Benas? They should be here!*

He saw the body just in time and caught himself before tripping over it.

Christ Jesus!

Someone loomed out of the blizzard, coming at him in a blur.

He gripped his weapons and braced himself.

Two men advanced on him. Stepping into one's path, Jacek thrust his sabre into his belly, twisted, and yanked it through soft tissue. Before the man's first scream had left his lungs, Jacek crashed the hammerhead down on another's crown. He swiveled his head, looking for the next attack. He needn't wait long. Two more appeared from behind, and he retreated, stepping backward with short, quick steps, feeling with his boot. Just as one foeman lunged at him, Jacek found what he sought and, without looking, cleared the bodies. He sprang back. The man tripped, and as he did Jacek darted forward, hacked his blade down, catching the enemy's shoulder, his neck. The second man fell over the first, and Jacek caught his chin with an underhanded swing of the nadziak. A head jerked back and snapped. Shrieks rose and were torn away by the wind.

Now more came, gray shadows out of white. So many more.

Right for him.

Where the hell is everybody? Are they dead?

He was dimly aware of scuffles muffled by the snow, of panicked shouts. Time seemed to slow, and he relinquished conscious thought, trusting in his body's practiced, reflexive motions. He brought his szabla and nadziak down, across, up, thrusting, sweeping in slashes and swipes, taking small steps back, ever back, between grunts and cries. Metal thudded, its usual clangor muted by the veil of snow.

And still the enemy came.

He was breathing hard, and his arms began to feel heavy. And then it came—from behind, where he never saw it. Something cracked across his shoulders and the back of his head, and his helmet thudded to the ground. He went down hard. The strike had cleaved his skull—it must have.

Take my soul, oh Lord.

Agonizing pain radiated from his head to every nerve in his body. He braced himself for the follow-up blow, but it didn't come. He rolled over heavily, as though lead lined his żupan. A Tatar lunged for him and, oddly, dropped at Jacek's side, a lance in his back. Everything blurred. Whether it was the snow or his vision, Jacek couldn't say, but beside that foe another groaned and crumpled. A figure seemed to be fighting Tatars, flashing in and out of swirling white snow, uttering foreign whoops and growls.

What the devil?

Gathering his legs under him, dragging himself up on his fists, Jacek lumbered upright. His head hammered. A shadow lunged at him, and he sluggishly parried a blow by whacking a hand, then struck with a slash across a sinewy neck. Blood sprayed, turning white snowflakes red. Something turned over in Jacek's brain, as if a bright candle had been lit, and his head no longer thumped. Around him, the whoops and growls grew louder, fiercer, until they rose in a strange, exuberant animal chorus.

Lightning shot through him, enlivening his limbs.

By the saints, I will die a warrior's death, and I will take as many of these bastards with me as I can.

He continued swinging, slashing, but soon his sabre only whistled through air. He was the only one standing. A voice cut through the din.

"Commander! Stop!"

Confused, he squinted into the blizzard where the voice had come from. *Is that God?* He wheezed, trying to catch his breath, and his arms dropped to his sides, numb.

If I am dead, should I be breathing this hard? And would God not call me by my Christian name?

He dropped to his knees and vomited, then pulled himself up again. *I am sorry, God.*

A familiar form loomed.

"Henryk?" he asked the figure.

I am dead … but that must mean so is Henryk. Nothing made sense.

Henryk grasped his shoulders, his face coming closer. "Commander! 'Tis I, Benas. The Cossacks have joined the fight!"

Jacek looked into the young man's eyes, dark against his frosted face. "Are we captured, then?" Jacek gasped. "How many dead?"

The man shook his head, and his face seemed to light up despite his white-coated cheeks. Another figure emerged out of the murk, his thick black moustache frozen with icicles. This man grabbed Jacek and hugged him, pounding his back. Jacek's head reported each pat.

"Pan Jacek! We are forever fighting Tatars, yes? 'Tis good to see you again, though I could wish for better circumstances," a distinct voice, familiar yet not, echoed in his ears.

Jacek pulled back, scanning the man's face. His head throbbed once more, and his vision blurred; consequently, he did not believe what his eyes told him.

"Pan Matejko?"

Battered, exhausted, queasy, his head pounding, Jacek stepped inside the tent and was immediately enveloped in its warmth and the chatter of reuniting captives and soldiers. Folk bustled to and fro as they sorted themselves out, and Jacek shambled out of the flow and looked around. This tent bulged with Silnyród villagers. He peered into small clusters of people, and relief swept through him when he spotted Florian's dark curly head. The young soldier sat on the ground, Luiza in his lap. She nestled against his chest and stared vacantly while Florian cradled her and stroked her tangled hair; she appeared unharmed—on the outside. Tears glistened on Florian's cheeks. Beside them sat her little brother, who looked about curiously. Jacek's heart squeezed, reminded they had not yet found Luiza's younger sister, Adriana. When the boy saw Jacek, he broke out in a smile; Jacek waved him over.

"Pan Jacek?" the boy said when he reached Jacek's side.

"Have you had anything to eat?" Jacek bent over so he was eye-level with the child.

"Yes, sir, some hard bread just now."

"Good. I want you to do something for me, yes? Tell Florian to find me outside in ten minutes. I need his help."

Jacek pulled out a few strips of dried meat and pressed them into the boy's hand. The child grinned. "Yes, sir."

Reluctantly, Jacek left the tent's warmth and entered a cold, white world. He'd traded his bashed helmet for his fur kolpak and pulled it tightly over his ears with a wince. Fat snowflakes dropped like a waving curtain. Through them moved shadowy soldiers, herding captives gently and prisoners none too gently. The air was heavy, damp, and tamped down the smell of woodsmoke and death.

Thank you, Lord, for sending the blizzard and Klemens Matejko.

Matejko had briefly been Jacek's commander when they'd defeated a large Tatar army at Twierzda on the border three years prior. Jacek had liked him and respected him immensely. He was a colonel who had overridden Jacek's insufferable superior, Mateusz Czapski, a ruthless man who had relished abusing Jacek.

When Jacek had gotten his wits back and realized Matejko was real, he'd been overjoyed to see him—and Matejko's estate troops, together with a hundred Zaporozhian Cossacks from the Wild Fields who hunted the same Tatars. It was these men Jacek had heard whooping and growling as they invaded the camp and helped defeat the enemy army. And now, even as the Cossacks recovered their own kidnapped people, they carried out the grisly task of finishing off the enemy with savage pleasure.

Today, the Zaporozhians were on the Commonwealth's side, and Jacek was grateful. In the end, he had saved no one with his desperate plan. Had it not been for God inserting Matejko and the Cossacks, he'd be dead or worse: on his way to Crimea. Jacek shuddered.

He was searching for Lesław when he came upon a snow-covered jumble of bodies. He peered more closely; several were fair-haired. *Not Tatars.* Seated on his haunches, he turned one over. A boy with a blue-gray face and blond hair, about ten. Jacek continued turning, laying the bodies out as he uncovered them. At the bottom of the heap lay an unclothed girl with long brown hair. He gently rolled her onto her back and drew in a sharp breath. Adriana. Luiza's younger sister, stiff, cold, ashen. A memory of the girl's sparkling smile hit him square in the chest, nearly choking him. He yanked off his cloak and covered her, then made his way to Jarosława to retrieve his caparison.

Later, as he stood beside a tent, Lesław materialized out of the snow. "How's the head, Jacek?"

"It'll do. Have you found that devil of a commander?"

Lesław shook his head. "No. The few living Tatars insist he escaped. I've looked over the bodies and the prisoners, and he's not among them."

"Keep looking. And if you find the son of a bitch, I want him alive." *I want to hear him scream and watch him twist when we impale him on a log as thick as his thigh.*

Florian surprised him when he growled from behind. "I want to be the one who kills him, Captain."

"How's Luiza?" asked Jacek.

Florian dashed his gaze to his feet and said nothing.

Jacek put a hand on his shoulder. "Come. You and I must attend Silnyród's dead."

When they reached the line of wagons, Jacek walked to where a row of corpses were laid out. Amid them lay one frail body, shrouded in rich red cloth under a coating of snow.

"Who is that?" asked Florian.

"Adriana. I wrapped her in my caparison."

Florian stared hard, then sniffed and cuffed his nose.

Together with Florian, Jacek hefted each body carefully into the bed of the wagon until only Adriana's remained. She was so light as they placed her on top of the others. He could have lifted her by himself with scant effort. Beside him, Florian dropped his head. His lips moved in prayer, and Jacek dropped his head too.

The next day's dawn revealed a brooding sky and a crust of snow that nearly crested the tops of Jacek's boots. The haphazard army of Jacek's mostly intact squad, Matejko's estate troops, and the Zaporozhian Cossacks left mounds of dead enemy in their wake. The previous day's blizzard had howled about them for hours, scouring all tracks and any hope of finding the Tatar commander or his remaining men. At least two score had escaped. *May the cold carry them to the depths of hell.*

Wagons rolled slowly over the rutted landscape, laden with both liberated captives and the fallen; others held what scant booty they'd scavenged from the decimated Tatar camp.

Matejko soon fell in beside him. "How is your head this morning, Pan Jacek?"

Jacek snorted and immediately regretted it. "As though I consumed an entire barrel of *wodka*, passed out, and smacked my head on a stone floor." He ran his gloved fingers over the mass at the back of his hammering head and flinched.

Matejko grinned, his bushy black moustache twitching. "Without the amusement of having done so. Good thing you had your helmet on. It was quite a blow you took. We were all surprised when you stood up. The Cossacks are calling you 'Kapitana Kamen-holova.'"

"Captain Rockhead," Jacek muttered.

Behind them came raucous laughter and voices shouting, "Kapitana Kamen-holova!" Gingerly, Jacek turned in his saddle and waved to a cluster of kaftan-cloaked, baggy-panted, long-moustachioed warriors pointing and nodding at him.

Well, damn me!

"How did you come to ride with them?" he asked Matejko.

"One of our scouting parties crossed their path, and we decided to help them hunt those who'd taken their people. It's been a while since we've had a good fight, and my men needed practice. And, should I need *their* help one day, they will return the favor."

"The Tatars," Jacek said, "were they Bater Beg's men?"

Matejko shrugged. "We didn't stop to ask. Now they're all just carrion—the best sort of Tatars."

"Not all are carrion," Jacek snarled.

Scanning the caravan, his eyes landed on Florian, his arms wound tightly about Luiza seated before him in his saddle. She hadn't spoken; she just stared blankly. That night as he lay down in his tent, Jacek sent a prayer heavenward for Adriana's soul—and for Luiza's.

He awoke to light illuminating the tent and men calling back and forth. He stood up, woozy and nauseated. Recovering, he stuck his head out the flap.

"Marcin?"

When he got no answer, Jacek set out, shading his eyes against the white-diamond brilliance of the sun's reflection upon the snow. Someone called, "Kapitana Kamen-holova," and he squinted in that direction but couldn't make out who it was in the dazzling light.

"Come, Kapitana," the voice boomed, accompanied by laughter.

As he walked toward them, a confusing scene came into view: a group of Cossacks clustered around a table fashioned from barrels and boards. Among them sat a priest who was writing. The priest mouthed words as the men pointed at his parchment and shouted quick phrases amid chortles.

The man who had hailed him stepped to him with a wide smile and bowed with open arms, sweeping a pipe from his mouth and his cap from his head. "Kapitana," he said in thickly accented Polish, "I am the senior of his Royal Grace Zaporozhian Host Ivan Humansky, the *ataman*—the commander—of these men."

Though more than a head shorter than Jacek, his presence commanded attention. Wiry and fit, with eyes so dark they were nearly black, the Cossack leader's head was bald save one hank of hair that sprouted from a patch upon his crown and fell in front of his left ear. One thick golden hoop hung from his earlobe, and burly moustaches flowed from his lip to below his stubbled chin. About his middle was a red sash, different from the other men's black or gold, distinguishing him as their leader.

"We welcome you," Humansky continued, "our most excellent and valiant comrade and brother, and invite you to join us in writing a greeting to Sultan Mehmed IV." Before Jacek could reply, Humansky barked an order and a cup was shoved in his hand, which he promptly shoved into Jacek's.

"Drink! Join us!" the man bid.

Matejko stood among the crowd. "They received a letter from the sultan," he said with a grin, "commanding them to cease their attacks and submit to him. They are composing their reply, which my priest is recording for them."

Humansky exploded in laughter. "And we all have something to say. Perhaps you would add words of your own, Kapitana? Listen to what we have written so far. Priest, read to our good friend, Kapitana Dąbrowski of Silnyród." Humansky clapped Jacek on the back, jolting his head.

The priest cleared his throat. "Thou Turkish Satan, brother and companion to the accursed devil, and companion to Lucifer himself, Greetings!" This brought a round of hoots and head bobs.

"What the hell kind of knight are you, that cannot slay a hedgehog with his bare ass?" Guffaws erupted all around, and men congratulated one another with slaps.

"That was mine!" Humansky announced. "Listen! There's more."

"Thou scullion of Babylon, thou wheelwright of Macedonia, thou goat-fucker of Alexandria, thou swineherd of Egypt." The priest stopped and looked up from the parchment, his cheeks flaming.

"Say his army eats the devil's feculence!" shouted a Cossack.

"That's good." Humansky nodded approvingly, then peered at Jacek. "Have you anything you would add, Kapitana?"

Despite his sore head and the sorrowful events, Jacek smiled for the first time in days, feeling lighter. "Tell him he's a Podolian thief and a catamite of Tatary."

This was met with howls of laughter. As he began to write once more, the priest's mouth quirked.

Once camp was broken down the next morning, forces dispersed in diverging directions. Following long-lasting farewells and pledges of friendship with Humansky, Jacek accompanied Matejko until they reached a crossroad where their paths separated.

Matejko clasped Jacek's arm warmly. "'Tis always a pleasure to scour the world clean of Tatar scum with you, Captain."

"As it is my honor to serve with you, Colonel," Jacek replied.

Matejko looked him over. "What will you do for the Christmas season?"

Jacek shrugged and stole a glance at Florian. "In between fortifying our defenses and attending Mass, I hope to dance at a wedding."

"You must visit my home on St. Stefan's Day. Come feast with us, dance with us—you and your officers. My wife and daughters cook for weeks, and their dishes are the most delicious in all of Podolia, as I can attest." He patted his round, sashed stomach.

Jacek gave him a small bow. "We would be honored, Pan Matejko. You may count on it."

Chapter 4

Concessions

On the eve of the Feast of St. Barbara, the first feast during Advent's long period of fasting, Oliwia lumbered along the passageway from her quarters, her hand on her swelling belly, savoring the smells of beetroot soup, buttery mushrooms, and baking bread wafting from the kitchens. Still apprehensive of her looming role as mother, she nonetheless celebrated her liberation from her bouts of sickness and her wifely obligations to her husband, whose frequent absences offered a modicum of independence. Her other surprising pleasure was her internal furnace that warded off the ever-present cold radiating from castle walls.

Beyond these, though, motherhood was not something she anticipated eagerly. The thought terrified her. As a girl, she'd only witnessed two women deliver, but she'd heard enough screaming to know the pain was unbearable. Would she live through it? Would her baby live through it? And if she and the baby did survive, then what? Could she love this being planted in her womb even though she did not love the man who had planted it there?

Pulled by the sound of her brother's high-pitched laugh, she paused by a window in the gallery. In the icy courtyard below, Eryk was waving his arms frantically before Filip. Despite herself, she chuckled at the sight of this stately man looking altogether like a flapping crane. Whatever he mimed was apparently amusing, and her brother erupted in a wave of laughter. *Is it possible I will one day feel affection for my husband?*

Whether because Filip needed a new mentor or her husband sought to please her, Eryk had begun to forge a bond with Filip. Only yesterday, the two had hunted together, and last week Eryk had shown him how to prime a pistol—a weapon Filip could barely hold in one hand. As Eryk placed a hand on Filip's shoulder and steered him toward the keep, Oliwia found herself surprisingly grateful for his presence. *Perhaps I will.*

She turned from the window. A strange flutter made her grab her stomach with a loud "Oh!" A round-eyed chambermaid raised her brows and asked if she was all right.

Another flicker, and Oliwia giggled. "I am well."

This must be the quickening she'd heard of. *Either I felt the baby move or else butterflies have taken up residence in my stomach.*

No longer able to deny a tiny being shared her body, Oliwia's trepidation ebbed.

Eryk's anticipation swelled along with Oliwia's stomach. As much as he could, he ignored his fear for her and the child, and when it persisted, his joy usually overcame it. He would be a father. At last.

Marriage to Oliwia was not what it had been with his first wife, Katarzyna, who had loved him as dearly as he'd loved her. He still mourned her. Yet he could not deny his affection for Oliwia. Though they did not share the same quarters, and he frequented Zofia's bed, he sought Oliwia's good company. She still read to him—a remnant of his dark days after Katarzyna's death and a pastime he cherished. In turn, he read to her on the occasions she became nauseated or listless. As he had with Katarzyna, he brought her sweets and small gifts, though for an entirely different reason. It assuaged his guilt.

On a blustery Friday before Christmas, Eryk entered Oliwia's sitting room, where she read from a small book of poems. She slammed it closed when he entered and looked at him wide-eyed.

"I am sorry I startled you, my love. I see you are reading the same book today."

"Um, yes, I ... There are several poems I enjoy very much."

Eryk held out his hand, looking over the volume after she handed it to him.

"Hmm. I believe I have seen this before." He laid it on the table beside him. "Perhaps you will favor me by reading from it later."

"Of course." She cast her eyes to her lap.

He stepped in front of her and leaned down. "But first," he whispered as he kissed her, "I have something for you."

Sitting beside her, he pulled out a deep blue velvet pouch as big as his hand. "Hold out your hands," he instructed, and he gently placed the bag in her cupped palms.

"What is this?"

"Open it," he said.

When she did, she gasped, and her alabaster fingers flew to her mouth. "Whatever is …"

"Here. Allow me." He removed an opulent sapphire-and-diamond necklace from her quaking hand. He brushed her hair aside, draped the jeweled rope around her neck, and clasped it at her nape.

He ran his fingers over her smooth throat and the dazzling stones. "It suits you. Do you like it?"

She touched the necklace with both hands. "Yes, of course! It's beautiful. But I do not understand."

He shrugged. "I meant to give it to you for the Feast of St. Nicholas, but it wasn't ready. Consider it a gift for the season and a gift for a new mother three months hence. Every lady should have gems as beautiful as she. I picked this one to go with your wedding ring, and because the stones are the color of your eyes."

Then Oliwia did the most extraordinary thing. She leaned over and took his face in her hands, and she kissed him on the mouth. Not with passion, but with a tenderness he savored. "Thank you, Eryk," she whispered against his lips. He gazed at her, wholly speechless.

On Biaska's outskirts, Romek waited inside a dilapidated, roofless cabin. Hoofbeats headed his way at an urgent gait, so he quickly nocked an arrow and paced to a window, taking cover behind its ruined shutter. Outside, a man rode into the overgrown yard and dismounted. Sucking in a breath, Romek lowered the bow and removed his hood.

"My lord." He dipped his head as Antonin swept in, a fur-lined red cloak swirling about his fine saffron leather boots. "Does anyone know your whereabouts?"

"No one but my special friend at Biaska, who will cover for me if I am sought." Antonin looked about the space and crinkled his nose as though disgusted.

Romek smirked. "That was a fortunate recruitment on your part."

"Yes, it was. And right under the noses of everyone at Biaska. No one suspects a thing," Antonin said in a self-congratulatory tone. "It is working out better than I expected." He began rummaging in his red silk sash. Soon he hauled out a leather pouch, which he handed to Romek.

Romek opened it and poured coins into his cupped hand.

"It's all there," Antonin retorted.

Romek quickly counted. Looking up, he pinned Antonin's muddy brown eyes. "*This* month's allotment is here, but I understood you would be making up the shortfalls from the last two." Romek kept his voice even. "What am I to tell the men?"

Antonin huffed. "Tell them whatever the hell you please!"

Still holding the pouch, Romek folded his arms and watched him, calculating what the luxurious garments had cost and how much Antonin had spent on his mistresses and whores.

Antonin drew in a breath. "I must return to Biaska before I am missed. I will get you more after I return to Wąskadroga." Then he laughed mockingly. "Perhaps the great and generous Lord Krezowski will give me an advance on the estate I'll be taking from him."

Romek held perfectly still. Antonin heaved out a breath. "Tell them I'll give them a larger share. That should satisfy the greedy bastards."

Arms still folded, Romek shook his head. "That might work for your estate troops, but I cannot bring on new men without paying them, which means we may need to delay. Machjeld continues sending recruits, but I have no way to keep them, let alone train them." Pointedly, he added, "We've come too far to let this slip away."

"It's not slipping away," Antonin snapped. A beat later, he added, "All right. I'll send a purse along in two nights."

Romek grew alarmed. "You will not bring it yourself?"

"I'll send it with Krystiana." Romek must have looked bemused, for Antonin continued, "I brought her with me to take care of my wardrobe … and other needs."

Romek restrained his disgust and kept his bland expression. "Is that wise, my lord?"

Antonin chuckled. "Oh yes. She can be trusted. The girl would do anything for me." His eyes took on a wicked glint. "I do mean anything." Then he straightened his bejeweled kolpak. "You're not overly fond of women, are you, Romek?"

A sudden jolt seared Romek's innards.

Tugging his cuffs, Antonin said absently, "I was sorry to hear of your sister's passing."

"That was nigh on two years ago," Romek blurted, unable to deflect the too-familiar stab of sorrow.

Bella, sweet Bella. She'd raised him, and he'd taken care of her when she'd become ill, but not well enough. He'd tried to get her the cure, but she'd succumbed to the horrible coughing, the spewing blood. And it was Krezowski's fault! That bastard's wealth had been pillaged from Romek's family, leaving them nothing but despair and death.

Antonin brushed his silk brocade sleeve. "Time does pass quickly, yes?"

Not quickly enough. Romek had kept his memories of Bella locked up tight where they couldn't jab him, but Antonin had just ripped off the cover. Watching him ride off, Romek realized the anticipation of Antonin's arrival had been trampled like the bits of clumping wet earth beneath his horse's hooves.

After an evening of entertaining their Christmas guests, Oliwia closed her bedchamber door behind her with a noisy sigh. Slumping against the wood, she shivered with the image of Eryk's wolfish cousin Antonin leering at her throughout the meal or rubbing her arm intimately during the dances. Normally vigilant and possessive, Eryk had not seemed to notice. Instead, he'd devoted his attention to several newcomers, including Pani Zofia, a widow from a nearby estate whose eyes had fixed curiously on Oliwia the entire soiree. Fortunately, other gentlemen guests had paid attention and had made sure she never lacked for a dance partner her, thus keeping her from Antonin's clutches.

Folding her hand fan, Oliwia crossed the room and laid it on her vanity before plopping down. The babe began moving about in her belly.

"Ah, so now you wake up. I see how it is." She rubbed the swell. "Mama needs her rest, and you decide 'tis time to play and turn flips. What a mischief-maker you are."

Continue to be strong, my little one.

She picked up the fan and opened it, staring at the beautiful garden scene painted on its silken folds. Then she unhooked the extravagant sapphire necklace and ran her fingers over the smooth stones. Though the luxury did not suit her—wearing it rather reminded her of an oxen yoke—the gift had been an extraordinarily thoughtful, costly gesture, and she was touched. Eryk had seemed giddy when he'd given it to her. Truth be told, her eyes were much lighter than the stones, but she would never remind him, for she was loath to squelch his delight. Nor would he ever hear from her that when she looked at the sapphires, they brought to mind someone else's eyes.

A hunger pang rumbled through Oliwia's stomach. She walked into her sitting room in search of a tray of food and, finding none, let herself into the passageway and headed for the kitchen. As she passed the guest quarters, she heard a familiar man's voice and a woman's laugh on the other side of a door before everything went quiet again. Pausing, Oliwia put an ear to the wood and hovered before Pani Zofia's guest chamber.

Shock waved through Oliwia.

Her heart thudding, she stole back to her quarters and paced. She picked up the fan and whacked it against her palm. Though emotions wreaked havoc within her, jealousy was not among them. Humiliation, most certainly, and it was firmly linked with anger and disgust.

In my own home!

Oliwia's cheeks stung while her mind spun. Eryk had driven Jacek away, had threatened to kill him if she hadn't agreed to marry him. And there he was, just doors away, with another woman! An *old* woman!

Oliwia sucked in a breath. Maybe she had it wrong. Pani Zofia *was* older, and maybe Eryk was simply … No. There was no mistaking what Oliwia had heard.

Her stomach knotted; she thought she would be sick, and she plopped onto the bed. She began picking at the hem of her sleeve while she caught her breath. Then she growled and twisted her hands in the coverlet as though she might rip it apart, as though she wrapped them about Eryk's neck.

Oliwia admonished herself. Why hadn't she barged in and confronted him? He'd made her a vow, and he'd broken it, made a fool of her. How could he desire that thing over her? *Because I rebuff him.* The thought hit her like a flurry of snowballs. *And if he's driven to her bed, he will not bother me in mine, will he?*

She folded and unfolded the fan—the first gift from Jacek three Christmases back. Her breathing slowed. She dropped to the floor on her hands and knees. From its hiding place beneath the floorboards, she removed the dagger Jacek had given her before he'd left on campaign, before everything had gone so horribly wrong between them—when she had naively believed she was the only woman in his life and he would return to marry her.

Men are scoundrels!

Touching the hilt, she recalled how Jacek had shown her to grasp it and how he had smiled when he insisted she keep it. She had never told anyone of the gift, and she rarely admired it for fear Eryk would discover it. But there was no danger of discovery tonight, for Eryk was busy loving another woman while Oliwia sat amid the fragments of her own love affair. Now she pulled out Jacek's letters and the note he'd tucked into the book of poems he'd given her. She touched her swollen belly, then unfolded the first letter. As she began to read, she wept.

Anxious for a taste of the familiar, Jacek rode with Lesław to Matejko Manor the day after Christmas, on St. Stefan's Day. After disarming in a stark vestibule, they were led to a salon saturated in brilliant light streaming through its high windows. Though the space was not as grand as Biaska, it imbued a feeling of luxury with its arching vaults, vibrant tapestries, numerous portraits, and ornate dark furniture.

The pleasant burble of people talking, punctuated by laughter and a tune being played on a *suka*, lifted Jacek's spirits. Festively dressed people were spread throughout the ample chamber in lively clusters. On one end, near a stone fireplace bright with fire, stood white-linen-draped tables festooned with winter greenery. The smell of roast venison and fowl permeated the air, accompanied by the scent of fresh bread, tangy fruit compote, and mushroom soup. The enticing combination had Jacek salivating.

"Ah! Pan Jacek! Pan Lesław! Welcome, welcome," Klemens called. He embraced each man. "I've thought of our adventures often these past many weeks. Tell me, for I am anxious to know, was there a wedding? Were you able to dance with Florian's bride?"

Jacek smiled, amused by the tough colonel's sense of the poetic. "I was, yes. They were wed just before Advent."

"And how is she?" Klemens asked, his tone now somber.

Jacek darted his eyes to the ceiling, choosing his words. "In time, she will, I believe, recover."

Klemens gave him a knowing nod. Then his expression transformed, and he led them to his wife, myriad family members, and guests. A young woman peeked from behind Klemens with a bashful smile. Her face reddened, and she abruptly ducked behind his broad back. Klemens pivoted and reached for the girl's hand, bringing her face-to-face with Jacek. She kept her eyes down, the smile still curving her mouth.

"Pan Jacek, Pan Lesław, may I present my youngest daughter, Eugenia."

Jacek and Lesław swept her a bow while she dipped in a low curtsy.

"God's blessings on you, my lady," Jacek said.

"I thank you, my lord," she squeaked.

When Jacek found himself seated beside the young woman at dinner, he attempted engaging her in conversation—a titan effort to be sure, for she kept her head down and her answers brief. If he said something even scantly amusing, she tittered nervously. Fortunately, several military men who sat nearby were as anxious as he to discuss those matters most familiar to them.

"So, Captain, apart from the devil of a business with the blasted Tatars …" one guest—a towarzysz, a hussar like him—began, only to halt when his wife placed her hand on his arm. Another cleared his throat. "I understand you were part of the Kłuszyn campaign under Hetman Żółkiewski, yes?"

"Yes," Jacek replied between gulps of mead.

Eugenia, who had been looking elsewhere, suddenly turned her full focus on him.

"How is it such a small force defeated Shuysky's army?" the man asked.

And so Jacek began retelling a tale he'd recounted many times before. After talking for several minutes, the men leaned in while the women began looking around, smiling faintly to hide their boredom or discomfort. It was an altogether familiar experience. Encouraged by a round of appreciative "Ah's!" from the men, Jacek continued.

"We arrived before dawn and fired two villages, then arrayed ourselves against an enemy forty-eight-thousand strong. There were hedges aligned thusly …" He began to scrape lines on the tablecloth with his knife while the restless women fanned themselves.

"First we had to navigate those hedges against their infantry. Because we were so few, we retreated and charged multiple times, making Shuysky believe we were a much bigger—"

One of the ladies stood and clapped her hands. "I believe 'tis time to carol." To a man, Jacek's audience rose briskly; he swallowed his tale and joined them.

They clambered aboard awaiting sleighs. Jacek rode with Klemens's oldest daughter and her husband; she hugged two small children to her. One, a girl of no more than six, crawled into her father's lap, where he pulled her under his cloak and held her. Their display of affection surprised Jacek, for most szlachta—especially men—paid their young children little mind. He was further surprised when the girl smiled at him shyly. Just as the sled pulled forward, the father dropped his arm around his wife's shoulders. A warm smile played on her lips, and he smiled back as she snuggled the other child.

Jacek didn't belong here. He was an outsider, an intruder, witnessing a father's private displays of fondness for his family. As they caroled through the countryside, the snow glittering all around them like a starry white blanket, Jacek could not shake a feeling of hollowness.

Back at the manor, he was beckoned to the cheery hearth by the men urging him to continue his story over a full cup of mulled wine. No sooner had he completed the telling than the musicians began to play, and he found himself dancing one reel after another. He departed the next morning with a warmth thawing his heart—a sensation he'd not felt in a long while.

Chapter 5

To Everything, There is a Season

The winter months passed quietly at Silnyród, though Jacek never idled. Between drilling the small garrison and recruiting more men, he strengthened fortifications, expanded the barracks, and submerged himself in the everyday business of rebuilding and provisioning.

He had not seen Klemens since his Christmas visit, so it was with some surprise that he received a message, followed by the colonel himself. Klemens arrived at Silnyród on an altogether different sort of mission.

With pleasantries dispensed and refreshment delivered by a serving maid, the two men raised their cups with an enthusiastic *"Na zdrowie!"* in Jacek's cramped solar. Klemens wiped the back of his sleeve across his thick-bristled moustache and fixed smoky eyes on Jacek.

"I trust you will not mind my speaking frankly, Pan Jacek, but I wonder if you've settled on anyone for a wife."

Holding Klemens's gaze, Jacek cautiously raised his cup to prevent his mouth dropping open.

"Sir? No," he finally croaked.

With a mischievous twinkle, Klemens said, "I believe you've captured my Eugenia's affection, so naturally it occurred to ask if you've considered courting her. I know 'tis not how things are done, but she is my youngest, so hang tradition. She has not stopped talking of your charm and your dancing—which leads me to wonder what other traits she's glimpsed that have gained her admiration."

Jacek sat upright, choking. "I assure you, Pan Klemens—"

Klemens held up a hand. "A jest only, Pan Jacek. I've never witnessed behavior from you that was anything short of gallant."

Recovering himself, Jacek tried to picture the girl chattering while scouring his head for just what he'd said that she'd found charming. *Certainly not the description of the battle of Kłuszyn.* Before he could ponder the matter further, Klemens plowed ahead with exuberance.

"Many men wish to court my flower, but I've found none worthy." He frowned. "I tell her, 'Patience, Eugenia dear, I will find you a husband— one we both agree on.' She has a generous dowry—a family estate here in Podolia—and I must be sure she and the land pass to a commendable man. Beyond her beauty, she sings more brightly than any songbird. And the way she plays the lute! Brings tears to my eyes. And that's not her only instrument. Furthermore, she sews beautifully and can manage an estate. She has learned well. She will bear many children and be an excellent mother. You can understand why I am so particular. She is a rare jewel."

Utterly at a loss for words, Jacek sipped his mead while he marshaled his thoughts. He respected Klemens greatly, and it was clear how much Klemens loved his daughter. But for Jacek, the girl held no appeal. In fact, she was altogether forgettable.

Klemens tugged one tail of his moustache. "This is … unexpected, so take your time and give the matter some thought, yes? I must say I am hopeful you're amenable for my own selfish sake. Besides my wish to secure my daughter an upstanding husband, I wish to gain your military allegiance as well."

After Klemens departed, Jacek sat at his desk and exhaled through puffed cheeks, dropping his chin in his hand. *Lady Eugenia.* What in blazes did she look like? He remembered two long braids, but what color was her hair? Her eyes? He could not recall.

An enormous snake was unwinding its coiled body in Oliwia's womb, its sharp tail whipping from side to side. She awoke with a start. The bed curtains were drawn against the cold, and she lay in the dark, sweat dampening her brow, willing away the terrifying image and the squeezing in her belly. *No, it cannot be time. I am not ready.*

She had felt spasms come and go for weeks now, but they more resembled mild twinges. This was not the same.

Two long exhales, then another, and the sensation faded. Oliwia began to drift off. The feeling returned, building, rolling through her. It snatched her breath away. And then it ebbed.

She clutched the bedsheets and stared into nothingness, alone with her burgeoning fear. *It will come whether you are ready or not.* Just as she thought the ache had finished with her, a fresh wave swelled, climbing, climbing, until it peaked. She ran her hand over her belly and grew alarmed at its tautness.

Mother, help me!

Fright collided with excitement and washed over her, through her. Her body relaxed. Long minutes passed before more pain seized her, pressing into her lower back. It took its time receding. Pulling herself up, she tugged a curtain open.

"Nadia," she rasped. When she heard no answer, she began to call again, but another surge took her hard, and her call became a cry. She rolled to her side, panting.

Nadia sprang up. "M'lady!"

Oliwia shut her eyes. "I think it is time."

"I will fetch the *baba*!" Nadia squeaked.

The baba. An old woman from the village would attend Oliwia's delivery and care for her and the babe afterward—if they lived. No dear sister or aunt or friend at her side. Though Oliwia had met the woman, she did not know her. The crone's beaky face lent her the look of a vulture, which only fueled Oliwia's fear. What if the baba did something that harmed the child? Abused Oliwia? What if something went terribly wrong? Could Oliwia find fortitude when the pains racked her body? With a prayer, she scooted herself into a sitting position and waited.

The baba arrived as if blown into the chamber by a swirling gust, and she rode that gust as she issued orders to cover the windows and unfasten all locks. The chamber leapt to life. Nadia and several bustling women ran their hands over Oliwia's nightdress, her hair, undoing any knots in the belief doing so would ease childbirth.

"Where are the blessed herbs?" the baba snapped at the attendants. "Get the lady out of her clothing and remove any jewelry. I will help unplait her hair."

Unplaiting the hair was said to hasten the Virgin Mary to a laboring woman's side, but if the Mother of God came, Oliwia did not notice, for she struggled throughout the day and long into the dark hours. She pushed when she was told and sagged each time she descended the crest of a wave of pain. So great was her agony that she imagined her body being torn in two.

Surely she would die.

In the stiller moments, she tried to sleep but could not, and she let the small things flicker through her mind to keep from worrying over the fate of her child. Or herself. The golden flame and the way the candles wavered in the dimness every time someone stirred the air. The sound of crunching straw on the floor, the fizzing wood in the hearth, the sharp smell of its smoke.

Eryk anxiously asked after her, she'd been told. What name would he choose if the child were a boy? If it were a girl, Oliwia would choose Margaret, for her mother. Over and over, she wondered if she would survive long enough to gaze upon the face of her child. Could she love it? She thought of her mother, of all she had sacrificed for the love of her father, of the breadth of such a love. How different it was from her regard for her own husband, the sire of her child. If this were Jacek's child, would she be overwhelmed by joy rather than abject terror and misery?

Bitterness occasionally bubbled in her for delivering an heir to a man she did not love. If Oliwia died, would Eryk marry his mistress and raise their child with her?

Pain ripped through her, and the baba bid Oliwia push once more. "I cannot," she huffed weakly.

The old woman frowned, tutting, "This is God's punishment for Eve's wickedness, and you must endure it like every other mother. Here. Chew these. It will chase away the evil spirits that bring you difficulty." She shoved a pungent mix of chopped onions and garlic into Oliwia's mouth.

Oliwia spat them out and tossed her head to the side, her hair plastered to her face. She thought she would be sick. So repulsed was she that during the next excruciating wave, when it seemed the pain would never subside, she did push. Hard.

"Yes! Yes, that's it! Wait now. Wait until I tell you to push again."

When Oliwia couldn't muster her muscles on the next spasm, the baba rubbed the onions and garlic under her nose, and Oliwia heard a sound that could only have come from a growling bear. It came from her.

"The baby's head is crowning!" the baba cried. "Come. Just one more push, lady. Almost there."

Oliwia gripped the arms holding her and, on a rising yell, bore down. She felt a warm gush, followed by sweet relief. Her chest heaving, she peered between her bent knees as the baba held up a blood-streaked glistening ball attached to a twisted blue-gray cord. The ball began to move, miniscule legs and arms unfurling. An odd little sound, like a mewling cat, escaped it.

Oliwia's exhaustion evaporated. She let out a jubilant cry, tears running down her cheeks unchecked.

Eryk's nerves prickled as he awaited word. He paced his solar, all manner of thoughts bouncing about his brain. Would the child be all right? Would it be a boy? Would Oliwia be all right? And on it went until Henryk found him an hour later, standing at the window, shifting his weight from one leg to the other.

"Henryk? What is it?"

"'Tis Thursday, and I wondered if you would be traveling to … That is, will you require your detail today?"

"Ah! No, of course not. Dismiss them," he said with an energetic flip of his hand. "I must pen a note to inform my … host I am unable to pay a call today. Have a guard collect it shortly."

"Of course." Henryk dipped his head. Eryk absently watched him pivot and go.

Time dragged. Eryk fidgeted with appeals and ledgers covering his desk, reading words and figures repeatedly but retaining none of them. When night fell, he sat before the fire and opened a nameless book only to snap it closed. Repeatedly. Nadia had appeared multiple times to say the child had not yet arrived. He'd even gone to Oliwia's door once, where he'd been stopped by a wail followed by a sound he could only liken to a snarling wolf. His blood had frozen, and he'd hastily retreated to his solar.

He was nodding in an armchair when Nadia poked her head in once more.

He sat up abruptly, rubbing his gritty eyes. "Well?"

"My lady wishes to see you, my lord." Nadia's features gave little away. She just looked nervous, but then Nadia always did.

He flew up the stairs and plunged through the doorway. Daylight was leaking into the chamber, and his eyes caught on Oliwia lying against the pillows. She looked delirious—exhausted, yes, but delirious. Women bustled about the room, cleaning and neatening. The baba appeared before him, a bundle in her arms. Beaming, she handed it to him, and he took it, gazing at a scrunchy face adorned with a thatch of slick dark hair.

"Is it … Is all well?" Eryk sank into a chair beside the bed. Oliwia's eyes sparkled, and she nodded. He kissed the babe's warm, scented skin and passed it to her outstretched hands.

"What is it?" he whispered.

"It's a baby," she teased in a soft voice.

"A boy?" he asked hopefully.

"You have a perfect son, my lord, and a healthy one too, judging by the strength of his lungs," she bubbled like a small child.

With a whoop, Eryk let out the breath he had stowed in his chest, and his shoulders slumped in relief as a huge smile split his face. He leaned over and placed a tender kiss on Oliwia's forehead. His heir had been born.

Weeks passed, and Jacek took up and put away the matter of Lady Eugenia no less than ten times. That he even considered her father's offer surprised him. Of no surprise was that she captured his fancy not at all. Throughout his musings, his mother's words had popped up and bobbed about in his mind relentlessly: "You need a woman to round your sharp edges." On the verge of twenty-six, he allowed the niggling thought his mother might have it right. Perhaps time had come to take a wife.

Far worse choices than Klemens's daughter existed—they'd been paraded before him unendingly by his mother. A union with Lady Eugenia would deepen his ties to Klemens and serve his ambitions well while saving him the trouble of casting about for himself *or* leaving the matter to his parents. And then there was the dowry: the estate Lady Eugenia brought to the union. Not so long ago, he'd fancied himself in control, and the thought of marrying for land had rankled, poked at his pride. Jacek had always meant to earn his own holdings by the time he wed, but his life wasn't turning out as he'd planned; perhaps this was the best he could do. Moreover, the estate would garner his father's approval. It might even lead his sire to deem Jacek worthy of the Dąbrowski name at last.

As for the girl, she was neither overbearing nor shrewish, and she wasn't repulsive—as far as his memory served. She was likely biddable. He'd be gone much of the time, leaving her in charge; she'd be an adequate manager and mother. When home, if he so chose, he could retreat to his own apartments—many married men did not share chambers with their wives. Yes, he could do far worse from a practical standpoint.

And from his heart's perspective? Even if he could revive said lifeless organ, he had no wish to expose it, to surrender it again in his lifetime. In that regard, Lady Eugenia was also a sound choice—she was incapable of tempting him into such folly.

As he crushed on his kolpak and headed outside into a gauzy curtain of rain, he put the debate away yet again and strode through the courtyard. The guards heralded approaching riders. He climbed a ladder to the bright boards of the new fighting platform. Upon the boggy landscape waved Klemens's banner.

"Open the gate."

Soon four guards stood before him; one handed him a sealed note. Waving them toward the kitchen, Jacek entered his solar and opened the letter. Written in Klemens's hand, the scrawled letters asked if he'd arrived at a decision regarding Lady Eugenia. A breathless sentence later, he read that Klemens's granddaughter, the young girl who'd curled up with her father during the sleigh ride, had fallen ill and never recovered.

Jacek dropped the letter onto his desk and himself into his chair. The girl's sweet, shy smile floated before him, and the memory lanced his heart. He stared at a dying fire, thoughts wheeling through his head. That

56

Providence was often brutal and life was short seared him. He'd been leveled by tragedy before; this would not be the last.

During the following days, Easter Sunday came and went. As he tried to cage his despair, he shredded the meticulous wrapping around his life and examined what he'd accomplished thus far. His harsh scrutiny complete, he penned an answer to Klemens.

The day after Jacek wrote Klemens, he received a letter from Henryk. Before he could open it, Lesław burst into his solar. "Have you read it yet? Have you heard the news?"

Jacek shook his head.

Lesław pointed at the letter Jacek held. "Lord Eryk has an heir! He has been christened Adam."

Jacek stared at him, numb. "Is ... is Lady Oliwia ... Does she live?" He held his breath.

Lesław's face lit up brighter still. "She is well, with roses in her cheeks even!" he cried. Jacek felt a burst of relief.

"That is wonderful news," he mumbled. His heart simmered to an even rhythm. It had been frozen for so long that it quickly congealed, and he felt no despair, no joy, no rippling at all.

"Lesław, I leave for Matejko Manor tomorrow morning with a small detail. I may stay overnight. Though we have not yet sighted Tatars, their raids cannot be far off, so extra guards are in order."

"Understood. Going to plot our defenses this year with the colonel?" asked Lesław.

Jacek spun the still-unopened letter between his fingers. "Yes. I won't be gone long."

The next afternoon, Jacek was seated in a salon with Lady Eugenia, her mother, her father, and several siblings, nieces, and nephews. Despite Klemens's presence, Jacek squirmed in his too-small seat as the women chatted. Eugenia, urged by her mother, had plucked a few songs, trilling with a sister or two while Klemens caught his eye and wiggled his considerable eyebrows. In those moments, Jacek realized he far preferred music played while he danced a reel and not while he sat trapped in a strange parlor among folk he barely knew.

He invited Lady Eugenia to show him her garden—accompanied by her mother or another chaperone, of course—but she claimed being outside caused her to sneeze overmuch. When she picked up the lute once more, he feigned fascination to study her. *Not petite, but not overly tall. Lithe, narrow-hipped. Small, orderly bosom. Medium-brown hair, no curls. Faint freckles on a pale, though not sickly, face. Straight, pallid pink lips. A pleasant enough smile.* Though she looked younger, she had turned eighteen soon after the Feast of the Three Kings. He still had no idea the color of her eyes, for she kept them hooded under lashless lids and hairless brows. *Such a strange fashion, removing the hair. Do women really think that makes them attractive?*

Her mother startled him from his thoughts. "You will stay the night, yes, Captain?"

"I, ah, that is, I regret I must hasten back. Our garrison is shorthanded, and I told my second I would return late today," he lied.

Lady Eugenia raised her eyes to him. *Small eyes, brownish. Or is that dark green?* "Will you not stay for supper and a few dances?" she asked meekly.

"I'm afraid I cannot. I must leave before dark."

"The captain has his duties, my sweet," Klemens said indulgently, "but I am sure he'll return soon, yes, Pan Jacek?"

"Yes. If that is acceptable, of course," said Jacek.

A chorus of female voices chirped that yes, of course, he must return and very soon. He glanced out the window. How quickly could he be on his way?

Chapter 6

As Life, So Death

Oliwia sat upon her bed, brushing her thumb over Adam's cheek, marveling at the exquisite feel of his soft skin as he wiggled beside her. His brilliant dark blue eyes stared into hers. *He is the most perfect creature in the world.* Unexpected tears overcame her, and she let out a laugh.

"What, Liwi?" Filip stood by a window, tossing a ball from hand to hand.

She swiped at her cheek. "Nothing. I just thought I saw Adam smile at me. Did you just smile at your mama?" she cooed. "What color will your eyes be, my little love?"

Filip stilled and faced her with a frown. "I don't understand how you can look at him for so long. He does nothing but gurgle and cry."

"I find him fascinating," she said softly.

Adam began to fuss, and she picked him up, snugging his wobbly head. She rocked to and fro, her mouth going from an O to a smile and back again as she gazed at him. She did not notice when Eryk walked in.

"There you are, exactly as I left you, my love." He grinned. "I believe you do naught but hold our son."

Filip rolled his eyes. "That *is* all she does."

"Filip finds his nephew rather dull," she said. "He forgets he was once uninteresting. Ofttimes still is."

"He seems of very little use," Filip huffed.

"It won't be long before your nephew will throw that ball *and* wield a sword," Eryk said. "Beware then, Filip!"

Adam wailed, his bottom lip quivering. Oliwia kissed him and continued swaying, but he would not be mollified. Filip banged out of the chamber just as Anka, the wet nurse, appeared. Reluctantly, Oliwia handed over her precious bundle. *Why does Eryk insist on a wet nurse? I could have—*

"Thank you, Anka," Eryk said crisply. "If you would leave your lady and I in private …"

Anka blinked. "Yes, of course, m'lord." With that, she scurried away, Adam's howls trailing down the passageway. Oliwia pulled in a breath.

Eryk closed the door. "Adam's a fine boy, Oliwia, a lusty, healthy lad."

"Yes, he is."

With a smile, he added, "You've no idea how much I wanted him. I scarcely knew myself."

He drew her up and into his arms and stroked her back. Her shoulders twitched, and she began to pull away, but he held her fast.

"I should be the one to nurse him," she said feebly.

Eryk kissed her mouth, then her neck, murmuring, "Why? He thrives with Anka. Nursing him would only prevent you getting pregnant again." He ran his hand over her waist and massaged her breast as he kissed her jaw, her ear. "Now that your lying-in is at an end," he whispered, "time has come for us to beget another son."

Panic filled her, and she pushed against his chest. "But I just delivered you a boy!" she exclaimed. He gaped at her. "The baba has not told me my lying-in is over," she protested.

Pregnancy had proved her best defense against her husband's advances. And now he wished her to start her wifely duties again? Already? But he'd gotten what he wanted! She'd given him his heir.

Eryk released her, putting several paces between them. "The baba does not rule here," he said harshly. "*I* say it is over, and you will return to my chamber. How many excuses will you offer me this time, Oliwia?"

Her mind churned; she fisted her skirts. "I am … It is … I am not ready, my lord."

He threw up his arms, his brow in a tight knot. "Not ready? You've recovered. Other wives have lying-in periods shorter than yours, and yet *you* are not ready. You are never ready!"

"You have a mistress," she blurted. *Satisfy your lusts with her!*

Eryk jammed his fists on his hips and glowered at her. "Many lords have mistresses. Especially when they have wives who are loath to accommodate them."

Oliwia glared back, her heart hammering. "Your vow of fidelity means so little, your loyalty so easily put aside?"

He tromped to her and pulled her up roughly. Alarmed, she tried to pull away, but he clamped down harder.

"And what of your vow of obedience, Oliwia?" he ground out. "You are my wife, and you understand your duty. I have shown you more patience than any other man would!"

His nostrils flared, and his hot breath fell on her face.

"What have you to say?" he snarled.

She raised her chin and set her jaw. "I find sharing your bed distasteful."

Eryk drew back his hand. She turned her head away, bracing herself. He stood frozen for a beat, then shoved her into the chair, where she sprawled half-in and half-out.

He was seething. "I have never hit a woman in my life, but you push too far!" She had never seen him so furious; fear crept up her spine. He stepped away and paced in choppy steps, then wheeled and faced her again. "You are either more stupid or more brazen than I realized. You overestimate your usefulness to me."

Her elbow throbbed, and she rubbed it as she pulled herself clumsily into the seat. Expressionless, she met his gaze, quelling her roiling innards.

"Katarzyna groomed you. For *me*," he snapped.

Oliwia blinked. *What?*

"From the very first, when you arrived here," he continued, "she shaped you so that one day you would make me a good wife. Well, you were clearly not an attentive pupil, so I will tell you what lesson you utterly missed. A good wife gives her body to her husband willingly. In that regard, you have proven yourself woefully inadequate," he thundered. "Katarzyna always ensured I was gratified, *and* she derived her own pleasure in my bed."

Oliwia caught little of the last bit as truth thumped her. "She *knew* she was dying? And she planned our union all along?"

Eryk pulled in a great breath and huffed it out. Oliwia stood up.

"You owe me far more than a wife's duty, Oliwia." He jabbed his thumb at his chest, disregarding her question. "You owe me gratitude for your life and that of your brother. Think where you'd be if I hadn't taken pity on you in Vyatov! And this is how you repay me? With contempt?"

Jacek had rescued them, but it was Eryk who had brought them from Muscovy to Biaska. His kindness and generosity had made all the difference, for Filip had been safe at last. She owed Eryk so much, but she'd always regarded him as an uncle, or worse, a father. He'd treated her as a girl for years, ignored her for the most part. But then everything had changed. As his grief over Katarzyna's death had receded, he had looked at Oliwia differently. The lust in his eyes, something she'd never seen before, had made her recoil. Shame had not been far behind, followed by guilt over her ingratitude.

She tried to catch her breath, struggling to comprehend Katarzyna's betrayal. The woman she'd loved, trusted, had used her. Had Katarzyna even cared about her? As the truth sank like an anchor, Oliwia's heart splintered. Then a flame ignited within her. Her cheeks heated. She clenched her jaw, narrowed her eyes, and lowered her head as if to charge him.

"Katarzyna *groomed* me for you?" Oliwia's voice, low, dark, surprised even her.

Eryk's chest rose and fell sharply, seeming to deflate with each exhale. "Damn you! That is not what we are discussing here."

"We are *discussing* nothing! *You* are browbeating me!" she stormed, throwing her hand in the air. She took a step toward him; he moved backward. "Has it occurred to you I might respond to you more favorably if you did not treat me as one of your subjects? No? Well, here, you loutish brute, I perform my duty. Take what you want!" She rucked up her skirts, lay on the floor, and flung her legs apart.

Her chest heaving, she stared with unseeing eyes at the ceiling.

"Cover yourself," Eryk said evenly. He reached out a hand to her. "Come."

She glanced at him, unsure. His features had softened.

"Come," he repeated. "This is not what I want."

Still angry, she ignored his proffered hand, covering her legs before lurching upright. She spouted one last bitter barb. "And, of course, my lord shall have whatever he wants."

His mouth hardened for an instant. "Yes, he shall, and the sooner you learn that, the better it will go for you. I would not push my patience further if I were you, Oliwia." He clasped his hands behind his back and rocked on his feet. "Pour me some wine."

The order riled, and she shot him daggers. He dropped into the chair beside hers and waited. Her hand shook, so she bided her time as she poured out a measure. The drumming of her heart finally slowed, but she still stewed when she handed him the cup. She backed up, thumping against the marble mantel. She leaned against it and folded her arms across her chest, fixing her eyes on him. Over a drawn-out sip, he flicked his eyes over her. The fire hissed when it hit a moist spot in the wood, releasing a tiny puff of steam, then continued crackling.

"Sit," he said.

"I do not wish to sit."

"You are a most difficult girl, Oliwia," he exhaled. After a beat, he said, "When I brought you and Filip to Biaska, Katarzyna—bless her generous soul—took an immediate liking to you. She was moved to create a good life for you. So when she learned of your noble ancestry, she undertook to find you a suitor. A *worthy* suitor, she always said. I paid her no mind. I was pleased she had a … diversion."

Recalling how Katarzyna had denounced Jacek as a suitable husband, the lady's scheming came into full view. Oliwia blew out a short, disgusted "Pah!"

Eryk took another sip. "I did not know my part in her plan until the day she begged our oaths, right before I came to search you out. You see, she thought … She knew she would not live long. She'd known for years, but she never told me until that day. Her greatest fear was the lack of an heir for Biaska.

"She struck upon the notion she could solve the needs of two people she held very dear by bringing them together. In me, she saw the husband she wanted for you. In you, she saw a beautiful girl who could save me from sorrow and give me an heir."

He suddenly looked very tired, as though immense sadness drove his shoulders downward and puckered his face with each day of his thirty-six years.

"She was right, you know," he said in a soft voice. "About you. She was right."

Oliwia shifted her weight. "I wanted none of this."

"It matters little now."

She eased into her chair.

"At first, I thought her mad," he continued. "When she passed, I could not imagine honoring the oath. I was … Well, you know how I was. *I* was the mad one, tormented with grief. After a time, I began to see what she saw in you for me; I understood her reasoning. When you began to read to me, it was a wondrous thing, and it brought me back from drowning. The time you spent with me saved my life, truly. I was happy to be in your company, not thinking about the promise, but just uplifted by being with you. And then it all began to change for me. I saw how truly beautiful you are." He stole a glance at her.

"So beautiful that I was blinded to your muleheadedness." He chuckled quietly, and Oliwia felt a little tug on her heart. "After we wed, I knew you did not burn with the same passion, but I thought—I still think—I can convince you otherwise. And we have the best reason, Oliwia—the perfect son we created, our Adam. With God's blessing, more children will come."

They sat in silence for long minutes, both watching the swaying flames. Oliwia had pitched like a drunken peasant, bouncing from horror to fury to loathing—to abject fear over delivering another child.

Now a new emotion took hold: guilt over her own ingratitude. Katarzyna had deceived her, yet she'd arranged for her a comfortable, privileged life of wealth and station. How could Oliwia find fault with that?

She looked at Eryk's strong profile, and a warm tendril emerged and wrapped around her heart. She shared a strange kinship with him; they had both been Katarzyna's game pieces. Could she grow to be devoted to him, to look on him as a companion and not a patriarch? Other women had far less to cling to in their marriages, and they had turned their unions into happy ones. Might she overcome her own aversions? She had to. And what of another child? She'd heard the kitchenmaids talk of some potion or other, or perhaps it was a salve. She'd not paid attention at the time; she could learn now and perhaps, for a little while, postpone the inevitable.

Eryk took her hand and looked at her, his amber eyes moist. "Oliwia, Katarzyna did groom you for me, but I expect she thought she'd already groomed me for you, that I was still the man she'd fallen in love with." He cleared his throat. "I have not done right by you, nor by her, and you both deserve better of me. With all my heart, I wish to show you I truly do love you and that I am deserving of the kindness you've shown me in return. I pledge to sever my … my, ah, friendship with Zofia."

His melancholy pierced her. She was not as sure as he about their future, but in that moment she believed happiness might be possible.

Eryk strode through the castle yard in high spirits after the midday meal. It was an especially fine Friday, and large white poufs tumbled in perfectly spaced intervals against a brilliant blue sky. The fields were fuzzed in varying shades of light green, like newly unfurled, tender leaves, and wildflowers waved jauntily in the countryside. Everywhere he looked, life burst forth. Amid the riotous spring colors were calves, bleating lambs, and fawns.

He had just kissed Oliwia and Adam good-bye and was on his way to the stables, where he met his detail. As he rode between his four guards the scant few miles to Zofia's manor house, he pondered what he was about to do, and remorse lanced him.

When his thoughts turned to Oliwia, his heart warmed. He cringed as he recalled their terrible row, how his normally unflappable deportment had been in disarray, leading him to counter her without censorship. But throwing herself on the rug had hit him as though he'd been doused with a pitcher of icy river water, and his senses had swum back. In a fit of anger, he'd behaved foolishly and revealed far too much. Now all he wished was to smooth over the rancor, for in the end he wanted her to love him. He resolved to woo her as he'd never done, for he longed to possess her—not just her body, but her mind and spirit. He ached to move inside her and see desire in her eyes, make her cry out his name. Oliwia excited him like no other, and he longed to make her burn for him as he did for her.

"You are sure this is where he will be?"

Romek chuckled. "Just as the Vistula empties into the Baltic each day, he goes to the manor house at Małylas every sennight. Each time, it is a Thursday, and he spends the night with his mistress. Sometimes he also goes on Sunday and Monday—not as much lately—but always on Thursday. His schedule has been constant for nearly a year."

"And he takes so little protection?" Antonin asked.

Nodding, Romek continued gleefully. "He only takes four guards. Each time, the same four—for discretion, no doubt. This location is perfect."

"And how do you know this?" Antonin's eyes gleamed.

"One of the manor servants is someone I have known a long time. He records Krezowski's movements and has watched him come and go each time. He knows when the lady and her lover take their meals and what they eat. He knows when they retire to her chamber, and he knows what time he leaves next day. He knows the guards because it is up to him to see they are fed and quartered. Every time it is the same."

Antonin raised his eyebrows. "Every week?"

"Why so surprised? His lady has been with child nearly the entire time."

Antonin's face twisted with a wolfish grin. "Yes, but not the *entire* time. I never knew my cousin was a lecher. How amusing! The arrogant bastard is not as virtuous as he leads everyone to believe. And he's a fool! If that lovely morsel he wed were *my* lady, I would keep the mistress *and* return to my wife's bed at night."

Romek's impatience rose, overrunning his excitement. "But she's *not* your wife."

Antonin sat back, placed his elbows on the armrests, and interlaced his fingers. "No, she is not. Not yet," he chuckled malevolently. "My cousin certainly knows how to pick the beauties, Romek, and this one is more beautiful than the last. I look forward to making her my wife. Unlike those last three sharp-tongued hags, she's young and soft. Ripe. And who knows? If she pleases me, I may keep her a while."

Antonin lowered his hand to his lap. "Just thinking of taking her makes me harder than this table leg."

Now Romek's outrage rose, matching his level of impatience. He bit back his disgust. "It would not be wise to keep her alive."

"I will decide. Not you," Antonin snapped.

Tilting his head back, Antonin closed his eyes. "We are done here. Send Krystiana. I have need of her."

Fuming, Romek stalked from the chamber and banged the door closed. As he stomped down the passageway, he muttered to himself, "He can summon her himself. I will *not* be his procurer. Nor will I be party to what he does with Krezowski's whore. She is no different from the others."

He halted, and a smile spread across his face. "Indeed, she is exactly the same."

Zofia's gentle voice jarred Eryk back to her hall, where he sat transfixed by the twisting flames in her hearth.

"My lord? You look as though you see something of great importance in that blaze." Her eyes glittered with amusement.

"I am sorry, Zofia. My mind was elsewhere."

"Has it aught to do with why you did not come yesterday?"

Eryk ran his finger around the rim of his still-full goblet of wine. He swallowed hard and glanced at her smiling countenance.

"There is something I must tell you," he said.

Her brows began to crease. "What is wrong?"

Eryk cleared his throat. "Zofia, I regret I will not be returning for a while."

"Why?" Her soft brown eyes scanned his.

He took her hand in his, stroking it. "My wife ... Oliwia and I have come to an understanding. We endeavor for another child."

"So you return to her bed to conceive a child. That does not mean you cannot continue to visit mine, yes?" Her voice had risen, surprising him.

"Zofia, we ... She is the mother of my son. She is the mother of my future children. I made her a pledge."

Long beats passed. "You are in love with her, then?"

"Yes," he blurted, instantly regretting the slip when tears pooled in Zofia's eyes and spilled down her cheeks. He had never seen her cry before. He felt affection for her, of course, but he hadn't realized she'd grown to care for him. Unsure what to do, he looked away until she composed herself.

"You must think me rather silly." She regarded him with bright eyes, still moist, but with a small smile now. "I understood our arrangement from the start. But you see, I've grown rather fond of our time together, and I will miss it." She held one side of his face. "I will miss *you*."

He covered her hand with his. "And I you."

Zofia swiped at her nose. "Go. Go to your wife. I wish you much happiness, Eryk."

He rose and pulled her from her seat, then kissed her cheeks.

"Thank you," he whispered.

Before he trotted through her gate, he looked at her one last time. Haloed in morning light, she lifted her hand in a small wave. His guards fell in, and they rode at a steady pace and were soon engulfed in a familiar dark stand of woods. His mind wandered to Oliwia, and he laughed at his own eagerness to return to his wife. *Just like a lovesick lad.*

Jerking its head with a snort, his gelding pulled up, jarring Eryk from his musings. His four guards drew in and surrounded him. Before them stood three riders blocking the path. Eryk placed his hand on the hilt of his sabre and scanned them, but they were hidden in shadow. One walked his mount forward, his gloved hand held up.

"My lord-brother," he called with a cheerful smile. Dressed in hussar garb, the man looked familiar, and Eryk eased.

"Where do I know you from?"

The man shrugged. "Muscovy?"

Eryk squinted to get a better look. Behind him, horses chuffed.

"Smoleńsk?" So many Commonwealth soldiers had taken part in the siege of Smoleńsk. It must have been there.

The man drew closer, his companions advancing with him. "Vyatov."

Vyatov?

The man's horse was nose to nose with his now. "Surely you remember the man whose prize you stole." His smile shifted.

Eryk stared at him, his mind whirring, trying to place him. Hairs on his neck pricked up, and he began sliding his sabre from its scabbard.

"No?" the man mocked. "The ambush? You doubtless remember that. Although I cannot say I am proud of how that endeavor turned out."

"You ride with Lisowski's renegade band." Eryk's alarms began clanging.

Whooshing noises were followed by *thunks*. Eryk swiveled his head as his guards lurched in their saddles. Arrows embedded in flesh. In less than a heartbeat, his sabre was unsheathed, raised, and he wheeled. But he was too late. Even as his sword arm shot forward, something slammed into it. His blade flew from his hand and thumped to the ground.

"I no longer ride with Lisowski," the man said. But Eryk wasn't looking at him. Instead, he was looking at his own arm, trying to understand why he couldn't feel it. Blood, so much blood, was staining his yellow sleeve, growing, spreading. Shouts rang all around him. His dagger was in his other hand, and he thrust it at the man. But in the same instant, his horse crashed to the ground, screaming, thrashing, rolling on him, pinning him. He thrashed along with it, trying to free himself. Pain radiated down his wounded arm.

The horse shuddered, then slowly dropped its head, as if lying down in sweet grass on an indolent afternoon. Still trapped, still struggling, Eryk looked up into the man's face suspended above him. The man leered. "I now serve Lord Antonin."

Eryk drew his arm back and let the dagger fly. The man's head snapped back. He pulled out the blade, then shoved his kolpak's fur cuff off his forehead. A small gash trickled blood. He laughed and wiped the blood away. Others gathered around now, their faces dusky; none were Eryk's men.

"Hold him," the man barked, and soon Eryk's arms and free leg were restrained.

The man leaned down, his face mere inches from Eryk's. His eyes were hard and bloodshot. "Remember me yet?" He looked unhinged.

Eryk tried to wrench himself free. The man clutched his hair and put a knee into his chest, bearing down with his weight, driving the air from Eryk's lungs.

"In case you wondered, your men can no longer help you." With his free hand, the man tossed the knife end over end, catching it by the hilt. "You thought to stick me in the eye with this, didn't you?" His voice had taken on a singsong quality. He flipped the dagger again. "My turn now."

Horror shot through Eryk as the man brought the knifepoint down, gouging, digging into his eye. He tried to yell, but only a desperate grunt escaped. Pain, white-hot, seared him. The man sat back on his haunches and inspected what he held. Still restrained, Eryk gasped, desperately sucking air. His heart would soon gallop from his chest. Bile clawed at his throat. Tears and blood leaked over his face, in his hair.

"Romek Mazur," Eryk finally spat between pants.

Romek jerked his head toward him. A ghoulish grin spread over his face. "So you do remember me. And what you took of mine?"

"I took nothing from you," Eryk ground out, putting his agony into the words.

The grin evaporated, replaced by a dark scowl. "You made me look foolish that day."

"That you did yourself." Eryk twisted, shucking one man's grip.

"What you took from me was the girl. You took her for yourself!" Romek bellowed. "I could have sold her, and I could have saved my sister with the gold."

"You had other chances! Why did you never take someone else, or other plunder, to save your sister?" Eryk snarled. "Because you're a worthless piece of rubbish too pathetic to look after your own." He locked out the throbbing in his ruined eye, his arm.

Romek rose, eyes blazing. He spat a thick gobbet, spattering Eryk's cheek. Cursing, he called orders to someone, and Eryk realized more men were beyond his vision. The men holding him began pulling him up, moving the horse carcass off his leg. He scrabbled. A boot caught him under the chin, and he sprawled backward. They hauled him back up and dragged him into the woods, where they threw him, back first, over something hard. A saddle. They staked his hands and feet to the ground. He battled his fear, trying to focus his one eye on the wavering leaves dancing above him. He couldn't quite make them out for the tears and sweat clouding his vision. *Oliwia. Adam.*

"Leave off. He's mine," Romek growled. The men around Eryk retreated beyond his line of sight.

Romek brandished a hunting knife, flashing it before him, and erupted in a laugh. He cut off Eryk's belt and sash. "Have you ever seen a man drawn and quartered? It looks excruciating."

Eryk felt a tug on his clothing, then cool air chilled the perspiration on his exposed skin. He wrenched, jerked, writhed, but his bindings held fast.

"You son of a bitch," he roared, fighting to keep panic from his voice.

Romek took Eryk's sash and, with deliberate movements, stuffed it in his mouth, then wound a length of it around his head and tied it, forcing the wadding farther into Eryk's throat. As he did so, Romek calmly said, "Doubtless you will soon be begging me to end your life."

Frantic, Eryk pulled for air. His heart hammered. He prayed for it to burst and kill him quickly.

"And think on this while I gut you, you leprous whoreson," Romek continued as he tugged Eryk's chin up, "I will take the lives of your wife and child, slowly, painfully, after your cousin has taken everything you own."

My loves! Oh dear God! I have not protected you from this evil. Forgive me.

Romek plunged the knife into Eryk's other eye, and pain exploded in Eryk's head. He saw no more. As Romek drew the knife tip across his chest, his belly, Eryk prayed and cried. For Adam. For Oliwia. For himself.

His muffled screams, wrenched from him at the point of Romek's knife, were as much from his despair as his physical agony.

His last thoughts were of his wife and son. His last words, their names.

Chapter 7

Another Promise to Keep

Night had fallen at Biaska, and darkness enshrouded the great hall. Candelabra and sconces blazed, bathing furniture and adornments in amber light. Oliwia sat at the main table, staring at the enormous wooden doors that were closed against the night. With every creak, she anticipated they would open and Eryk would stride across the stone floor, hungry and irritable. After their row and reconciliation, she'd expected him to return before the evening meal.

He had promised to give up his mistress, to be faithful, just as Oliwia had promised to welcome him to her bed. He had spent last night, the first Thursday in a long while, at Biaska, but he'd headed out at first light. Had he gone to say good-bye and been tempted by the widow's charms? Had he lied at the outset? Oliwia huffed, pushing away a partial platter of food.

Beside her, Filip perked up, his hopeful eyes trained on her slices of smoked meat. "May I have your meat, Liwi? And your compote?"

She flapped her hand at him. "Yes, yes."

She stood, scraping chair legs across the floor. Henryk, Tomasz, and a handful of guards rose, but she waved them back to their meals. "I am done. Please carry on."

Henryk caught her eye with a sympathetic look. Though they'd never spoken of Eryk's trysts, Henryk knew. He had to.

She made her way to the nursery, and her heart lifted at the sight of her son in Anka's arms. "He is still awake?" Oliwia held out her hands.

"Yes, m'lady. He ate, but it seems to have awakened him." She handed over the boy.

"He waited to see his mama," Oliwia trilled. Tucking him against her shoulder, she patted his tiny back and ambled about the chamber. He rewarded her with a decidedly unchildlike burp. Oliwia bounced him as she walked, cooing, completely lost in the feel and smell of him.

The door banged open. Expecting Eryk, she was startled to see Henryk instead, his eyes wide, his breathing quick. "My lady. A messenger has arrived."

Panic bloomed as she passed Adam to Anka and followed Henryk out the door, along the musty passageway to the stairs. He wheeled when he reached the landing and grasped her arms.

"Henryk, what is it?" Her eyes searched his. "Eryk?"

He nodded. Her hand flew to her mouth. "Merciful God. What has happened?"

"Oliwia," Henryk swallowed, "Eryk is dead."

A jolt sizzled through her. "When? How?"

He glanced upward. "Antonin's men found him a short while ago. He was murdered."

She gripped Henryk's arms, steadying herself, searching his eyes. "I wish to see him."

He shook his head. "No, Oliwia. His body … He is in rather a bad way."

"I will see my husband," she shouted. The force of it took her by surprise.

Unaware where they went as she trailed Henryk, every bit of skin prickled; her innards twitched. He stopped before a door and held it open for her, and she slid inside. The chamber was lit by two candleholders—not enough to chase away the bleak shadows. Her eye caught on a draped mound atop a plank. All was quiet, save the sound of blood pounding in her head. She walked toward the board as if in a fog and reached out, her trembling fingers brushing the coarse fabric. She began to pull it back. Henryk stayed her hand.

"I do not think this wise."

She nodded. "I know, but I will see him."

Henryk began to roll the cloth down. At first, Oliwia could only make out Eryk's dark hair and the pallid skin of his forehead. She stared a moment, not comprehending what she saw, then gasped. Where his eyes should have been were two black holes.

"Keep going," she rasped when Henryk stopped.

Slowly, Henryk lowered the shroud. The body was unclothed, skin smudged with dark streaks. Blood? Dirt? She couldn't tell. She found herself grateful for the dim light, though it could not hide what came next. His chest was split, exposing pale ribs and an unrecognizable mass where his stomach should have been. She turned away and stumbled for the door, heaving what little was inside her. She slumped against the wall. Tears obscured her vision, and she shivered uncontrollably. Arms wrapped around her, cradled her, held her up.

"Come away from here," Henryk said softly. She let him lead her away.

On a windswept plain at the outer reaches of the Commonwealth's border, Jacek sat astride Jarosława and surveyed the broad, flat landscape before him. Armored head to toe among a score of other warriors, he searched the horizon for the telltale sign of riders: plumes of dust, a disruption in the waving grasses, an odd shape in the distance. Klemens's scouts had reported a small band of Tatars moving north, but it had been days ago, and Jacek and his men had seen no sign of the raiders.

"If they veered east, they're in Muscovy by now," he remarked to Marcin, mounted beside him. Jacek kept his eyes trained on the far line where the folds of wheat-colored earth met the steel sky. Though he detected nothing, he braced himself for the onslaught that would be unleashed if the enemy was spotted.

"Captain!" one of the men hollered behind him. Jacek and Marcin turned their heads in perfect time. A shape blurred in Jacek's peripheral vision.

"A rider, m'lord," Marcin said, "racing full-out."

Jacek stiffened and checked his sabre before resting his hand on his pistol grip, then turned his horse and watched for the rider's features to come into view. When he recognized him, he relaxed and waited for Benas to draw up before him.

Benas raised a sealed white square. "For m'lord!" he exclaimed between pants. "From Biaska. Messenger says 'tis urgent. He awaits your reply, sir."

Jacek nodded and accepted the message. "Wait here," he ordered the young guard. He removed a glove and clamped it between his teeth. Hooking his finger under the flap, he tore the seal. He took in Henryk's neatly scrawled words, reread them to be sure, and looked at Marcin.

"Lord Eryk is dead," Jacek said, stunned. "We leave for Biaska." After dispatching orders, he took a small detachment and fell in beside Marcin and Benas, and they tore across the plain. The concern for Tatar raiders settled somewhere in the back of Jacek's mind, replaced by altogether new, overriding apprehensions.

Nearing the crossroads between Silnyród and Matejko Manor, Benas took half the men one way while Jacek led the rest to the manor, where they soon thundered through the gate into the courtyard. Lady Eugenia was running out of the dwelling ahead of her father when Jacek reined in Jarosława. The sight of his betrothed did nothing to lift his spirits—in fact, it rather annoyed him she was there, for she impeded him from his real objective, which was Klemens. He put away the petulant thought. The lady approached with a wide smile, like an expectant child.

"My lord, what a wonderful surprise!" she cried.

He dismounted. "Lady Eugenia." She beamed up at him. He remembered himself and gave her a head bob. Covered in road dust, he didn't bother brushing it from his clothes. "I am here to see your father," he said brusquely as he nodded toward said father. "Pan Klemens, might we speak?"

"Of course, Pan Jacek," Klemens replied, and the two men made for the manor entrance.

Lady Eugenia accompanied them but went no farther than her father's solar door when he shut it. She still hovered in the passageway when Jacek exited twenty minutes later.

"I am on my way to Biaska today, my lady. The lord is dead," Jacek said flatly.

Her eyes widened beneath her furrowed brows. She quickly cast her gaze down. "Oh." With a quaver, she asked, "When will you return?"

"Perhaps there is somewhere better suited to speaking privately?" he suggested.

His shoulders twitched, and he opened and closed his hands, stretching his fingers as she led him to a deserted salon. He faced her. "I do not know precisely when I will return. I must secure Biaska and the lord's kin."

"Then our wedding day must wait?"

He thought she snuffled, and impatience flared in him. He suppressed it. "I expect to be back in time. We have until after harvest, yet four months away."

"And if you're not? You will uphold your pledge, yes?" Her eyes darted over his face, giving her the appearance of a panicky rabbit.

His brows knotted together. "I am aware of my obligation, Lady Eugenia. I would not have signed the agreement if I did not intend fulfilling it. I have never broken a contract. I am a man of my word," he said testily. Why he felt compelled to defend himself, he had little idea. Perhaps the festering doubt about having signed the damned thing in the first place was jabbing at him. He stuffed that thought away too.

"I …Yes, of course," she stammered. "I did not mean …You will write me, yes? So Mother knows when to arrange the engagement ceremony?"

"Of course."

She looked up at him, her countenance bright, and timidly asked, "And the priest should call the banns even if you are not back?"

He wanted to tell her to do whatever the devil she pleased but bit it back. "Wait until you hear from me," he said instead.

"Of course. You know what is best, my lord."

A pliable wife with good family connections. At least Father and Mama are pleased.

He was about to excuse himself when she reached up and pulled his head down, landing a kiss on his mouth. The bold move caught him off guard, and he pulled back abruptly. She then flung herself against his chest and wrapped her arms around his waist.

"I'm … I'm sorry, my lord. I just thought … I am so very happy," she whimpered.

He disentangled himself and patted her shoulder awkwardly. "I really must go, my lady."

She brought her hand to her mouth, stifling a sob. "Godspeed, my lord."

He strode away.

Cresting the ridge above Biaska, Jacek and Marcin stopped. The men and their steeds were panting, and the horses' necks glistened with sweat. They had been at full flight most of the day as they wound their path homeward through the woods and grasses southeast of the castle. From where the castle perched high above the ground, its limestone battlements and walls shimmered as if lit from within by a lantern. It appeared as it always had. Nothing sinister, nothing out of place.

The sight lifted him unexpectedly. Until that moment, he didn't realize how sorely he had missed it. More than his family's estate, this had been home.

Beside him, Marcin said, "No doubt the castle will be on high alert."

"It had better be," Jacek growled. "Let's go!"

They guided their mounts and spare horses down the slope, exploding into a gallop when they reached the flat stretch of fields. Pounding into the ground, Jacek stood in his stirrups as they flew toward their destination. It seemed an eternity, yet the sun still hung in the sky, countermanding the feeling the distance they now covered was vast. Soon the ramparts sharpened; between cannon, guards stood with arquebuses aimed and bows drawn. The drawbridge was firmly snugged against the outer walls, and Jacek and Marcin slowed to a trot as they approached.

From a side gate, four guards rode out and faced them across the dry moat.

"Ho, guards!" Jacek hailed. He recognized none of them; they were helmed, their features blurred in the slant of the late afternoon sun. The lead soldier seemed unimpressed by Jacek and his retainer.

"What is your business here?" the man called, his voice familiar.

"I am Pan Jacek Krzysztof Dąbrowski, porucznik to Lord Eryk Krezowski and commander of Silnyród's garrison. My man and I are here because your captain, my *namiestik*, Pan Henryk Kalinowski, has called for my return."

The man squinted against the sun. "Pan Jacek?"

"Kasimir!" Jacek cried.

Then came a shout from the battlements. Henryk was waving wildly. He cupped his hands around his mouth and yelled, "Bring them in!"

Jacek's heart thudded wildly, but not from the hard riding. The drawbridge stuttered down in a series of creaks and groans. Impatient, he untied the lead to his spare mounts and handed it to Marcin. He jumped Jarosława onto the giant oak platform, then raced through the open gates, up the rise, and into the courtyard beyond. Before he fully dismounted, Henryk stood before him, holding up a hand in greeting.

"Welcome home!"

Jacek quickly tossed Jarosława's reins to a stable hand, thwarting a small crowd from gathering about him. He politely nodded his head round, calling out quick salutations before grasping Henryk's arm. The two men hugged fiercely, pounding one another on the back, and bussed one another's cheeks in turn. Henryk pulled back and looked him over.

"It is good to see you, old friend. You have not changed at all. You are still as unsightly and feeble as you ever were. A little dusty and hairy too, but these shortcomings we can fix. Come, man. Let's go inside. You must be parched."

"Am I in time?"

Henryk nodded. "Yes. His coffin rests in the *castrum doloris* in the village church. The funeral is two days away, and mourners are just starting to arrive."

As they headed out of the courtyard, Jacek smiled. "It is good to see you as well, though I wish it were under different circumstances."

They briskly climbed the forestairs and entered the great hall. As he stepped through the doors, Jacek's eyes caught on a familiar form, and he froze. Oliwia was seated, facing the hearth, her unbound hair spilling down the back of her sables, her head bent in conversation. It was hard to discern which was a tress and which was a part of her clothing. Jacek began pulling off his gloves, losing sight of everything around him.

Henryk called out something—Jacek knew not what—and Oliwia raised her head. Jacek removed his kolpak and self-consciously smoothed his shaggy hair, full beard, and flowing moustaches. With a small frown, she peered at him, seeming not to recognize him. He took a few steps toward her and stopped. Her eyes widened, and her mouth slackened in a dumbfounded expression. She stood abruptly, fumbling whatever she had been holding in her lap, and wheeled to face him fully.

His mind blanked. Sucking in a quiet breath, he resumed a slow walk toward her, boot heels striking as he crossed the stone floor, the sound seeming to bounce off the pillars. He rummaged through his vacant brain for something to say. *I am sorry for your loss. I've come to uphold my promise to Eryk. I am here to protect you and your son, to fulfill my oath.* With each inhale and exhale, his deliberate pace allowed him to recover the wits he'd not expected to lose. When he reached her, he swept a grand bow. Belatedly, as if remembering herself, she extended her hand, and he raised it, brushing his lips over her soft skin.

"My lady," he rasped as he drew himself up and locked eyes with her.

"'Tis truly you," Oliwia whispered between her fingers. She stared at him without bother of decorum.

Jacek stood stock-still before her as if restrained by invisible shackles. He willed his thundering heart to subside. Expressionless, he took her in, masking another sharp intake of air with a feigned cough. *What had I expected?* If it had been sorrowful, swollen red eyes and a dull complexion, he'd been profoundly mistaken. Her smooth skin still glowed like alabaster, and her exquisite pale blue eyes sparkled like aquamarine gemstones. Gone a year, he was right back where he'd started. Her sins were suspended, and he was hopelessly bewitched and at her mercy. He gave himself a mental shake.

Henryk interrupted the awkward silence when he cleared his throat. "He has come to help, my lady." He added quietly, "and for the funeral, of course."

As if freshly wakened from sleep, Jacek gave her a curt nod and commenced dusting himself off. "I came as soon as I received Henryk's message. We have all lost a great man, my lady, and you have my most heartfelt condolences."

Oliwia stirred, closed her mouth, and fisted her skirts. Her eyes, still enormous, began to pool. "Yes, we have," she said with a quaver. "Thank you, Jacek. I … To say I am surprised at your return greatly understates my astonishment. I never expected you, but I am delighted you are here." She swiped at her cheeks, then gave him a quick dip of her head, her mask of propriety firmly in place.

"Forgive me if we have shocked you, my lady," Henryk said. "I did not tell you of my appeal as I was unsure if or when he would arrive." Curious faces pressed in around them. With a glance at Jacek and Oliwia, Henryk suggested they retire to the solar.

The trio struck out for the short flight of steps, and Oliwia called for a serving maid to bring food and drink. Jacek finally began looking about himself. A large mirror in the great hall was covered. So would all the mirrors be. Before they had made much progress, a shriek pierced the great hall and stopped them short.

"Captain! Sir! Captain! Welcome home, sir!"

Filip threw himself through the doorway and burst toward Jacek. The boy stopped, narrowly avoiding a collision with the group. He came to attention. Jacek grasped his shoulder and embraced him, surprised he needn't bend over quite as far as before. "I will find you later, Filip, and then we will talk," he promised.

Henryk gave Jacek few details of the attack, a sober timbre replacing his typical lighthearted one. Jacek had just finished his second tankard of piwo and was looking absentmindedly at the toe of his boot, deep in thought. He brought his head up.

"Is there a chance this was random?"

Henryk stood up from his seat beside Jacek and walked around the desk, positioning himself next to Oliwia, who occupied the lord's chair. He folded his arms across his chest.

"No." His eyes darted to Oliwia, then back to Jacek.

Jacek gave him a subtle nod. Henryk pivoted to the window, where golden light blazed against the dark silhouette of the horizon. With Henryk's gaze fixed outside, Jacek turned his unfettered attention to Oliwia. She stared dully at the merry flames, seemingly unaware he eyed her. Her small frame showed no sign she'd given birth two months prior. Gray shadows smudged her eyes, but even the fatigue etching her face could not mar her beauty. Unexpectedly, his heart tripped and pulsed, as if awakening. In defense, he called up the raw gouges he'd sustained during their last encounter.

Clenching his jaw, he willed his rising anger to remain within its cage. He lurched upright. Henryk and Oliwia regarded him with bemusement. A knock sounded, and Jacek leapt to the door, opening it to a round-eyed Nadia.

"Welcome home, Captain." Flustered, she flicked her eyes to Jacek's grimy self before continuing. "I beg your pardon, my lady, but the captain's chamber has been prepared, and I wonder if he would like a bath? Anka wishes you to know Adam will soon be abed."

The pronouncements threw Jacek. Had he had any room left in his head to give the matter any due during the hasty journey, he would have presumed to be quartering in the garrison. He now found himself oddly grateful to be treated as a guest; the thought of a bath and a soft bed in which to sprawl was welcome after the long, pounding days on the road.

Nadia's second announcement jarred him into remembering a most important fact he'd somehow shuffled to the back of his consciousness: Eryk and Oliwia's son. The product of their union.

Oliwia's voice and waving hand snapped him back. "Thank you, Nadia. Tell Anka I will be there shortly." Oliwia's eyes traveled from Jacek's head to his boots, and she added, "I am certain the captain would welcome a bath."

After Nadia slipped out, Oliwia rose and looked from Henryk to Jacek. Both men came to attention. All of a sudden, she looked bone-weary, and Jacek resisted the urge to hold her upright.

"I leave you for now. Perhaps you would care to join me for the late meal?" she asked.

"Yes, my lady," Jacek said, Henryk parroting him and adding, "With pleasure."

When Oliwia quit the chamber, Jacek dropped into his chair and scratched his beard. "How is she?"

Henryk shrugged. "Better this past sennight, perhaps because she's been preoccupied by the funeral. I see fewer tears."

"What does she know?"

"Nearly everything I know. She saw the body."

"What?" Jacek spluttered. "How the devil was she permitted to see it?"

"She's his wife, and she insisted on it. I had little choice." Henryk wandered to the desk and picked up a flagon. He jerked his chin at Jacek's cup. "We both need something stronger."

After Henryk poured them each a large measure of wodka, he settled himself in the lord's chair and took a long pull from the cup.

"Tell me everything. Leave out no detail," said Jacek.

"What do you know of the lord's visits to Małylas?" asked Henryk.

"The manor house? Nothing. What drew him there?"

"His mistress."

"I don't understand," Jacek said.

Henryk sighed. "Lord Eryk took a mistress, Pani Zofia, after he wed Oliwia."

Jacek bit back his surprise. *Jesus! How could he do that to her? I could never ...* He blinked, recovering himself. *She chose him. She got what she bargained for.*

"He spent every Thursday night there after he got Oliwia with child," Henryk offered. "Later, he was there Sunday nights too, ofttimes through Tuesday morning."

"Jesus!" Jacek did not check himself this time. "How do you know he was at Małylas with her each time?"

Henryk looked at him evenly. "The guard detail. He always took the same four. I told him to take more, but he refused. I made the arrangements, and I debriefed them after each visit. Other than some six servants, it was just him and her alone."

Jacek leaned forward and placed his elbows on his knees. Henryk topped off his cup and handed Jacek the jug.

Jacek took it. "Why?"

"Why what? Why was he unfaithful? Who the devil knows what goes on behind a bedchamber door? To my knowledge, he never wandered while Katarzyna lived; he was straight and true. But, Jacek, he was not the same man after she died. You found that out yourself."

Jacek nodded, his mind drifting to one of his last meetings with Eryk, when Eryk had turned on him viciously. It still stung.

"Might the mistress be responsible?" posed Jacek.

"I think not, but you're going to pay a visit with me so we can determine for ourselves."

"Does Oliwia know about ...?"

"She has not said, but I suspect she does." After a long pause, Henryk quietly added, "I should have been part of that detail."

"Had you gone, Henryk, you would be food for the ravens, just like them."

"Perhaps," Henryk sighed, rubbing the rim of his cup.

"Any signs of a scuffle?"

"The guards all took arrows. Just enough to incapacitate them until the brigands could cut their throats. Whoever committed this foul act knew what they were doing."

"And Antonin's men found them?" asked Jacek.

"Yes. Radek and a few guards brought the bodies back."

"Coincidence?"

Henryk shrugged. "Appears to be. They say they were at a nearby village on the edge of Antonin's holdings and on their way home when they discovered the bodies. I confirmed it."

"The men Lord Eryk chose for guards were seasoned soldiers, yes?"

Henryk nodded.

"An enemy who had watched him would know his routine." Jacek looked up at Henryk.

Henryk met his stare. "No doubt."

"What else?" Jacek braced himself as Henryk described a horrific scene that included disembowelment and castration.

"And you let Oliwia see that?" Jacek exclaimed, incredulous.

"I tried to stop her."

The fire wavered; Jacek's innards felt greasy. "Who hated him that much? Or do you think it was a mistake, that there was a different target?"

"No mistake. I believe he was the target all along." Henryk paused for a gulp and stared at the corner of the desk. "What I do not understand is the other body we found."

"What body?"

"A tavern maid from a nearby village, over a hundred paces from Lord Eryk and his detail, off the road, in the forest. She'd been horribly defiled. The decay was farther along, as though she'd been left there days before the attack. She was propped against a tree, her shoes missing."

Jacek snapped his head up, agape. "She sounds like one of Bilicki's murder victims."

"I thought so too."

"You think her death was part of the lord's attack?"

Henryk shook his head. "I don't know. 'Tis hard to tell, what with the state of the corpse. But why leave her there and return to kill Lord Eryk and his men days later?"

"Bilicki's culprit was caught, yes? Perhaps this is someone mimicking the previous murders," Jacek ventured, "and it was coincidence he left the body there."

A strange look overtook Henryk's features. "It's an odd thing, Jacek. That killer *was* caught, confessed, and hanged. But the murders didn't stop. Victims are all females from taverns and brothels throughout Sandomierz Voivodeship and are carved up in the same, horrendous way. They're not raped, but their … female parts are mutilated, and their shoes are missing."

Jacek's frown deepened as he sifted through his thoughts. "Either someone else is copying the crimes or they hung the wrong man. Did the murderer confess on his own?"

Henryk shook his head. "I don't know." He then pointed at Jacek's dagger. "Your new one looks just like your old one."

Jacek absently ran his fingers over the handle. "It *is* the old one. Lord Eryk sent it to me with a note saying Bilicki gave it back after the other man was caught."

Henryk pierced him with a hard stare. "Maybe our killer has naught to do with the Sandomierz demon but is someone decidedly disciplined who sought revenge. As you point out, whoever did this hated Lord Eryk."

Stifling silence enveloped the room. Dust motes caught in the late afternoon sun floated languidly while the rays gilded the lines of the polished desk in golden light.

At last, Jacek broke the spell. "Just who is it you suspect?"

Chapter 8

Paradox

Oliwia hurried from the nursery, her insides still knotted from Jacek's startling arrival hours before. Returning to her unrelentingly bustling quarters would not do. She needed a haven, somewhere tranquil where she could bring her turbulent emotions to heel. She dashed into her old bedchamber and bolted the door. The room smelled of must and comfort, and she was suffused with serenity. She plopped onto the mattress, a puff of dust bursting from the coverlet.

As she looked around the room, her mind rushed back to a less complicated time, a time full of promise, when she was young and hopelessly in love. Though she'd aged less than two years since then, those years had multiplied fivefold on the inside.

As for being hopelessly in love?

Oliwia glimpsed the cold hearth where she'd often sat before a bright fire and painted. In a corner stood the desk where she'd painstakingly written letters to Jacek. As she traced her fingers over periwinkle flowers embroidered on the coverlet, she recalled lying atop it one heady night in his strong arms. She pulled in a breath through her nose, recalling his scent, masculine and woodsy. Closing her eyes, she saw his twinkling eyes, so mischievous in the dark as he had tried to explain away his presence in her bedchamber that same exhilarating night. His warm, sweet breath on her cheek, her neck, and his calloused, gentle hands on her body were whispered echoes on her skin. As she'd done so often since that night, she imagined his mouth—full, soft, moist—on her lips, her skin. The memory rippled through her limbs and along her spine. He had driven her to the edge of abandon, where she'd longed to plunge and never return. She'd never been there before him. Or since. And now he was back.

Had he forgiven her? Did he still hate her?

She let out a wry laugh. All the defenses and denials she'd so carefully built to shelter her heart had toppled and washed away like a fortress of sand swept out with the tide. Merely laying eyes on him had completely undone her, leaving her a quivering bundle of nerves. A guilt-ridden quivering bundle of nerves with a dead husband to bury.

With a sigh, Oliwia picked herself up and softly barricaded her memories behind the door. Her mind leapt to why Jacek had returned: Eryk's death. She'd been searching for solace, trying to reconcile his senseless, untimely death. Though she had not relished resuming her place in Eryk's bed, she had been fond of him—despite the harsh words between them—and had prepared to make their marriage a closer union forged by more children. Escape from childbirth released a swell of relief in her and was quickly followed by another stab of guilt.

Notwithstanding his infidelity, Eryk had loved her. And now she mourned him and missed the power of his presence.

She drifted along the passageway like a wandering spirit, then paused to brush moisture from her cheeks. "I pray you are in Katarzyna's arms, my lord, where you spent your happiest days," she whispered, staring with unseeing eyes at the ceiling, "You are no doubt proudly telling her about the beautiful son you left behind."

Crossing herself, she slumped against the hewn stone.

"Oh dear Mary, Mother of God, what's to become of us?" She choked out a sob and covered her mouth.

Jacek's eyes were riveted on Henryk, his breathing accelerating. Henryk's face remained unflappable.

"What makes you think I suspect anyone?" Henryk at last replied.

"Your demeanor, for one thing. You try to act your old easy self, but clearly you are on edge."

"I have good reason to be on edge. Our lord was murdered—no, brutally slaughtered—*on my watch*, and we have little clue who is responsible or why." Henryk crossed his arms.

"But you suspect me, yes?"

Henryk's unreadable expression transformed with a thoughtful half smile. "It has crossed my mind."

"Why me?"

"Why *not* you? Jealousy is a strong motivator for murder. Whoever did this to him *knew* him and *hated* him—that much is clear. Moreover, there was the business with Bilicki and your dagger—not that I ever believed you murdered that girl, but you must admit it is a rather strange coincidence. When I pondered who might be driven to such brutality, my mind leapt to you."

"Are you saying this is what I do to someone I serve? I resort to murder and butchery? I geld my lord-brothers?" Jacek's voice remained calm, his face expressionless.

"No. I'm saying if a man has taken the woman I love for himself, if he is lying with her, I would want to do him violence. Jacek, you're my friend, but I cannot ignore facts, and when it comes to her, I've witnessed you transform from a rational leader of men to a witless loon far too many times to discount the possibility."

"Do you think me so daft I would slaughter a tavern maid while I am exacting my revenge?"

"No. Though you'd lost your fondness for the fairer sex last I saw you, I cannot picture you carrying your dislike to such extremes. Besides," Henryk said as he picked up a letter, "Lesław confirmed your whereabouts."

Jacek humphed.

Henryk scrutinized him. "You're not angry?"

Jacek shook his head. "I'm not angry. You did what you were supposed to do. I would have suspected me too, for all the same reasons."

The remnants of the day crept over the horizon. After a comfortable stretch of silence, Jacek cast his eyes to the window. "I always admired him, you know. In spite of her. You say he changed after Katarzyna's death, and that may be, but I still believed him a good lord, a just leader. I wanted to be like him. Still do."

"What will you do? About her?"

"Make sure she and the boy are safe."

"How?"

Jacek pulled in a long breath. "I will see her married."

"But she cannot take a husband until her year of mourning is up."

"Doubtless an exception will be made in her case, considering the holdings at stake."

Henryk's eyes sharpened. "And will you present yourself as the bridegroom?"

Jacek let out a wry laugh. "No. That foolishness ended the day I learned she was to wed Lord Eryk."

Henryk rubbed his finger over his chin and arched his eyebrow. "And what of you? Have you found someone to take her place?"

"No."

Jacek trailed Nadia to his quarters on the second floor, one floor below the family's apartments. She walked with a prim, shuffling gait, and he had to slow himself for fear of running her over.

Her darting brown eyes followed him into the chamber, where he spotted a steaming tub before a blaze and his clothes unpacked, brushed, and hung on a neat row of pegs. "Please let me know if there is anything else you require, my lord." Her eyes cast down, she curtsied and pivoted, poised to hurry out the door.

"Wait, Nadia."

She froze.

He tugged on his moustache. "Fetch the barber and tell him to bring his sharpest blades, yes?" She scurried away.

Jacek stripped off his dusty clothes and sank into the tub, submerging his head. The water soothed as it enveloped his body and lapped around him. He shifted and contorted his frame until his head rested on the vessel's edge and closed his eyes with an extended sigh. Though weary, his mind was not, and it whirred incessantly, turning over the same questions: Who wanted Eryk dead and loathed him enough to murder him so viciously? Was the attack in any way related to the unsolved ambush four years ago?

Same enemy, different opportunity? Of one thing Jacek was certain. Henryk was right—this was no random act. It had been deliberate, and it had been hatched from pure hatred.

Jacek descended into the great hall the next morning, his trimmed hair skimming the collar of his cardinal silk żupan. He repeatedly ran his fingers over his smooth face, his cheeks chilled from his missing whiskers. He glimpsed Oliwia, harried as she flitted between servants, priests, and guests. Their eyes met for a breathless instant, but he tore his gaze away and rounded on his heel for the stables. There he found Henryk, and the two set off for the site of the carnage. The weather was fine for riding—not hot, not bitterly cold, with frozen planks of clouds suspended high in a dove-gray vault and the ground so dry that their horses' hooves didn't suck mud as they trod. For hours, they tromped over the road and through wooded undergrowth, seeking overlooked clues in dirt, grasses, bushes. The blood had long since washed away, and the only bit they uncovered was the remnant of a broken eating knife, which told them nothing.

They traveled to the village where the tavern maid had lived. She had plied her trade as a whore in the tavern's loft with anonymous travelers and a local clientele who were all accounted for. No one saw her leave the night she disappeared. She was well liked, and folk who knew her could offer no explanation for the appalling nature of her death.

From there, they rode to Małylas Manor, where the grief-stricken Pani Zofia invited them to share a meal. As Jacek observed her over a plate of mushroom pierogis, he was struck by her plainness. A soft-spoken woman, Zofia's unremarkable features were crowned by a head of light brown hair shot with gray and severely pulled back from her face, giving her pasty cheeks the look of dumplings.

The meal over and their questions exhausted, they left for Biaska under a lowering ceiling of iron clouds.

"You look troubled, my friend," Henryk said as he rode beside him.

Jacek shifted in his saddle, making the leather creak. "Pani Zofia. I could not help wonder why …"

"Does it matter why? I do not know what passed between Lord Eryk and Oliwia. He did not spend that Thursday night away and told me Friday morning he would return by midday. I believe he planned to end the affair with Pani Zofia that very day."

Jacek's eyebrows shot to his kolpak. "What of my earlier question? Let us suppose he did end it. Might she have had him killed?"

Henryk shook his head. "You saw how she was. Besides, she would have had scant time to prepare such a meticulous attack. No garrison, no guards. Only a small staff of servants, three of them women. I would wager my favorite horse she had nothing to do with it."

"We should not dismiss the possibility, though I agree with you. The likelihood is more distant than the moon in the sky."

They rode in silence, a biting wind tugging at their cloaks and caps. As they neared Biaska, Jacek pulled up on his reins.

"I wish to stop at the village church and pay my respects."

"I will accompany you."

They dismounted just as plops of rain struck dirt and gravel. Jacek strode into the chapel, its familiar, musty smell enveloping him. He paused, pulling it in, letting his eyes adjust before dipping his fingers in the font. Genuflecting, his knee upon the cold tile floor, he crossed himself. As he rose, he looked upon an enormous structure dominating the church's interior. The castrum doloris—the castle of mourning—soared above Eryk's coffin, dwarfing it. It looked for all the world like an ornate pavilion, its gaudy embellishments verging on garishness. Around the structure burned candles, and amid them stood several beggars. Some cried while others sang "To You, Oh Lord."

Jacek could not recall seeing beggars in Biaska before, and he bent to Henryk's ear. "Where did they come from?"

"Antonin sent them from his estate."

"Is he coming?" Jacek hissed.

"He may have already arrived. All Lord Eryk's kin is expected—his sisters, their husbands and children."

Jacek slowly approached the coffin. Against the castrum doloris, it was a plain affair with a black cross painted upon it, shields representing the Krezowski clan's heraldry along its sides, and an epitaph painted on tin. Above hung a coffin portrait depicting Eryk in his hussar armor. Though the face looking down at him did not resemble the Eryk Jacek remembered, seeing it nevertheless lodged an unexpected lump in his throat.

Laying his kolpak lightly upon the coffin, he murmured, "I say good-bye to you now, my lord-brother." From the corner of his eye, he spotted

Father Augustyn watching him, his hands held as though in prayer, a rosary wrapped around them. He gave Jacek a slight dip of his head.

Later that evening, the hall burgeoned with kin and guests, along with their din, and Jacek sequestered himself behind the solar's oak-planked doors with Henryk. Outside, the rain peppered glass and stone. A long silence hung between them as Jacek twirled a cup in his hands.

"So what's he like? The baby?" he asked nonchalantly.

"Adam? Meet him and see for yourself. He is very much like … a baby." He shrugged.

"That tells me nothing," Jacek grumbled.

"He cries and waves his hands about, making wet sorts of noises. He stays in the nursery much of the time, where he's fussed over by many women, including his mama. If I am to judge by all the female attention he gets, he already has a way with the ladies. You could learn from him, my friend."

Jacek chuckled. "No, thank you. I don't want that many women clucking about, swiping my ass the day long."

Henryk snorted.

"Eryk must have been overjoyed when he discovered Oliwia had given him a son," continued Jacek.

"Naturally, yes. I understand he let out a war cry the first time he saw his boy. He was a very proud papa who spoke endlessly about everything the child did. He was worse than a woman." In a sober tone, Henryk added, "He was good to Adam *and* Oliwia, Jacek."

"Did he ever mention a letter to the king on my behalf?"

Henryk shook his head. "Not to me. You don't think he wrote it before he died?"

Jacek sighed. "Probably not, but there is always the chance. If he didn't, well, I cannot say where I may end up."

"Oliwia will doubtless tell you you've a place here. Perhaps you should ask her about the letter—she may know of it."

Jacek stared into his half-empty tankard. "I'll not trouble her."

When Oliwia rose next morning, she felt wearier than when she'd lain down. The sweet release of sleep had eluded her, hounded as she'd been by her thoughts. Here she was, a new mother, with a son to protect, in the chaos of a vast, masterless estate. How ever would she keep Biaska viable, keep her son safe, direct so many folk? Would they heed her or dismiss her as an unworthy interloper? She was overwhelmed. Lost. Adrift.

"I must look as dark as this gown," she mumbled as Nadia helped her into her overskirt.

"Oh no, m'lady. You've not lost your bloom," she exclaimed in all earnestness.

Oliwia gave her a little squeeze. "Bless you, Nadia."

There came a knock, and Filip peered into her chamber. "Ready, Liwi?"

"Coming." She slid into the white mourning cloak Nadia held up for her. Her feet—all her limbs—felt as though they were bound with lead cords. Yet she somehow held her head rigid and placed one foot before the other without stumbling.

Family surrounded her in the church as she endured one sermon after another. She had been enduring sermons since Eryk's death, for it seemed every turn required another ceremony from another holy man. Besides Father Augustyn, a bishop, four canons, and five priests took part in the funeral.

Covertly, she watched Jacek; he seemed unaware of her. He stood straight, tall, unflinching. If only she had his steel. She certainly had need of it. Amid her fear and sadness lurked guilt—guilt over her heart's telling flutter in his presence. With a stab of regret, she put away the errant thought.

The service at last ended, and the coffin was carried from the church by Eryk's brothers-in-law, Filip, Antonin, Jacek, and Henryk, and placed upon straw lining a wagon. The wagon advanced slowly, rolling the mile to the castle cemetery, urged on by drivers using long willow sticks on oxen. A line of folk snaked after it, led by weeping beggars.

At the gravesite came more songs and prayers. Oliwia, her mind numb, shifted her weight from foot to foot. Not until the coffin was lowered did finality thump her. Rooted in place, tears rimmed and spilled down her cheeks as the great Lord of Biaska, the father of her child, her husband, thudded softly into the earth, where he would remain. A strong hand grasped her arm, and gratitude flushed through her until she realized it was Antonin.

He drew her away from the grave. "Let me help you, my dear. You do not bear your burden alone. We are family, you and I."

She tried to free herself, but he gripped tighter. A figure loomed, and she looked up. Jacek's deep blue eyes were fixed on Antonin, and a spectacular scowl etched his face. Antonin shrank back as Jacek placed his hand on her. Two gripped her arm now.

"I will see her back, Lord Antonin." Jacek's voice was flinty.

"You're not family," Antonin scoffed.

Jacek seemed to growl. Antonin swallowed a protest and released his hold.

"How do you fare?" Jacek asked her in the same hard tone as he led her to the keep.

How she longed to lean against him, absorb his warmth, but he kept his body apart from hers, rigid.

She swiped at her nose. "I am … I'll do. Thank you."

He gave her a curt nod and called Filip over. "Escort your sister to the great hall." And with that, he strode away.

Oliwia saw little of Jacek during the lengthy wake and the next day as visitors dwindled. Antonin, mercifully, departed with them. If Jacek did speak to her, he was terse, his demeanor cold, his eyes darting everywhere but at hers. She was more bereft than when he'd first arrived.

Jacek inspected the armory for what must have been the fifth time. As he strode the yard, he considered where to go next. Perhaps visit the garrison or check the stables again? With the castle nearly emptied of guests, he had run out of excuses for avoiding Oliwia. The prospect left him agitated, though he could not fathom the reason for his mercurial deportment.

Vexed, he climbed the forestairs and crossed the great hall, relieved when Henryk waved him into the solar. As Jacek settled himself, a knock sounded, bringing him to his feet. The knock was followed by Oliwia's head poking through the gap when Jacek opened the door.

"Messages for you, gentlemen." She swept into the room and handed them each a thin bundle. She swept out again as if she were a twirling dancer who had paused mid-step to accept a cup of something refreshing, and his mind leapt to dancing with her countless times before—and the last excruciating dance they'd shared at her wedding.

Jacek glanced at two letters in his hand. He stuffed one away and opened the other, scanning it quickly. "Lesław writes of unrest—the fort's repelled two strikes since the Ottomans declared war in retaliation for the Cossack attacks on the Black Sea ports. Damned Turks. Damned Cossacks."

"But the Cossacks always raid them. Why declare war now?"

"The Ottomans are angry we're supporting the revolts in Moldavia and Wallachia. And they know our border is vulnerable since we continue fighting Muscovy."

"Will we never wipe the infidels from the earth?" Henryk lamented. He lifted his cup and took a deep drink. "So tell me, Jacek. The ladies of Silnyród …"

Jacek snorted. "There are no ladies in Silnyród."

"Surely there's someone appealing enough for a bit of sport? An alewife, a tavern wench, a seamstress?"

Jacek shook his head. "I am sorry to disappoint you. The maids are all spoken for, and the few whores are overworked. Of them, only one still has all her teeth." His mind wandered to Milda's death mask and Adriana's battered body, and fresh sorrow washed over him.

"Well, then, what about Matejko Manor? It sounds a very lively place. Are there no attractive ladies there? A daughter? A sister? A wife?" Henryk smirked.

A knot tightened in the pit of Jacek's gut. Absentmindedly, he patted the letter he'd tucked away. "Henryk, you must attend court at Żółkiew Castle," he deflected. "Not only is there a park filled with exotic animals, but there is an abundance of exotic women too. You will grow dizzy from swiveling your head every time one passes by, and they are diverting to dance with. They have an overwhelming fascination and fondness for hussars. Your bed will never be empty."

As if he hadn't heard him, Henryk said from beneath a dark brow, "Have you spoken to Oliwia of your plan yet?"

"There's been no time," Jacek protested, masking his disquiet.

Henryk shrugged. "There's time enough now. You can ask about Lord Eryk's letter and meet their son."

Jacek said nothing. Finally, Henryk stood and slapped the top of the desk with his palm, exclaiming, "Well, we have exhausted our more stimulating subjects, yes? We have determined Cossacks and Turks are rascals, Silnyród is inhabited by men and toothless whores, and I must visit Żółkiew. Let's eat—I'm famished."

Later that evening, Jacek headed for Oliwia's quarters with determination. When he arrived, he was thrust into a hive of activity. Maids came and went with linens, servants balanced platters and jugs, and a cluster of women cooed together as if they were doves. He could have been attending court for all the noise.

Seeing a familiar face, he grabbed her attention. "Nadia? Where is your mistress?"

"I am here," came Oliwia's voice from within the flock of doves.

As if puppets on one master string, the women parted and revealed Oliwia in their midst. Her gaze rose to his, and for a moment all he saw was shimmering pale blue. A small motion caught his eye, yanking his attention to her arms, where she cradled a swathed bundle. The bundle had a head covered in a white cap with the finest fringe of dark, downy hair peeking out. It emitted a piercing wail, and she rocked it, soothing it. She smiled in a way he had never seen before. The lady was clearly smitten with her son.

She came toward Jacek. "Look, Adam. Our valiant captain has come to call. Don't cry now. It would be frightfully discourteous."

She stood beside him, the top of her head well below his chin, and turned so he could see the babe. "He's just begun to smile." She brushed her fingertip over one corner of Adam's tiny pink mouth. "Will you smile for the captain?" Her voice was melodic, lovely. Adam scrunched his face in what promised to become another howl.

"May I?" Jacek extended his arms.

Oliwia peeped up at him. "You are accustomed to handling infants." Her remark was just that—a remark, not a question.

"I've nephews and nieces aplenty. I can be trusted with a babe."

She seemed to ease, then handed him Adam. Jacek held him along the length of his forearm, tucked against his midsection. Adam's miniscule head nestled easily in Jacek's capacious palm. The threat of a howl

95

disappeared as Adam gazed up at him in blue-eyed wonder, and the tears from the last outburst slid away. The women who'd surrounded Oliwia tittered softly. When Jacek glanced up at them, to a woman, they smiled broadly.

"He's a fine lad, strong like his papa," Jacek said. "He may have your eyes."

Oliwia peered at Adam and touched his cheek. "I am told they may yet change."

He studied the child's face. Though he had distinct features—pudgy cheeks, a bump for a nose, a gooey, wet mouth—they would be a long time refining. Still, Jacek thought he recognized something of Eryk in the boy.

"He seems quite fascinated by you," Oliwia said.

Jacek chuckled. "Yes, well, because I am quite fascinating to fledglings."

She looked up at him and gave him a small but sweet smile—a rarity since his return.

"Uh, before he cries …" He began handing Adam to Oliwia. A young servant stepped forward and took Adam from him.

"'Tis time for his feeding, mistress," she said.

"Yes, of course. Thank you, Anka." As the woman retreated, Oliwia faced Jacek expectantly. "You wished to see me?"

His hand shot to the back of his neck and began rubbing. "I wished to meet his little lordship. I would also speak with you about Biaska's future."

"Biaska's future?" She sounded altogether baffled.

"Yes. My plan for securing the estate. Tomorrow morning?"

She frowned. "I must see my guests off, then I've a few matters to see to. Might we meet here after breakfast?"

"That is acceptable."

"Shall I ask Henryk and Tomasz to attend?"

"Not at the outset."

With no further reason to linger, he gave her a formal bow and withdrew, hastily retreating to the privacy of his chamber. He stripped to his breeches, smoothed his clothes, performed his ablutions, pulled on a cloak, oiled his sabre, checked his pistols—several times—and paced about the space. Unable to think of another task with which to distract himself, he finally picked up the unopened letter from the table.

After reading it, he blew out a great breath and raked a hand through his hair. Eugenia missed him. Eugenia looked forward to his return.

Eugenia was embroidering pillow cases for their wedding bed. *Why didn't I tell Henryk?* Hell, he hadn't even told Lesław; he'd left him to find out on his own.

Jacek lay back on the bed and drummed his fingers on his chest. *I must write Lady Eugenia. But not tonight. Tomorrow perhaps. Or the next day.*

His mind unexpectedly wandered to Pani Zofia and a recurring question spinning in his head: Why had Eryk been unfaithful? The memory of Oliwia's kisses suddenly flooded Jacek's mind, all life and fire. He stopped his restless drumming and relived every detail. The recollection nearly took his breath away, as if he'd kissed her only moments before. He resumed drumming as he sought anchoring thoughts of Lady Eugenia, but they did nothing to warm him, to buffer him against the tempest building at his very center. When he recalled her thin-lipped kiss, his heart sank under the weight of his pledge.

He drew in and exhaled three long breaths, trying to calm himself. The effort helped little. Instead, he found himself swinging from his normal state of anger and bitterness toward Oliwia to something altogether opposite, which irritated him further. Had he been a fortress—even one as buttressed as Kamieniec-Podolski—she had leveled all his walls long ago. He had no wish to let her claw into his heart again and stomp it to bits.

It was time to rebuild his fortifications.

Chapter 9

Turning Point

Jacek had not slept but a few hours for the cacophony of thoughts wheeling through his mind. Oliwia would put up a fight, he thought sullenly. He didn't know how he knew, but he knew, and he did not relish the quarrel. As a servant fastened his żupan here and straightened his sleeve there, he practiced the words in his head once more.

No different than preparing for battle.

The bent, wizened man brushed his clothing, and Jacek pushed back a stubborn hank of hair, all the while reminding himself Oliwia's and Adam's safety was the paramount priority. He would see them safeguarded, no matter what, and fulfill his promise to Eryk. Then he'd leave.

"Here, sir, be seated, and I'll see to that." The old man grabbed up a comb and a rancid concoction in a small pot.

Jacek glanced from the smelly pot to the man's face. "Use water instead." He dropped into a chair beside the window. As the servant fussed over his mop, tutting that the waxy mixture would do much better, Jacek returned to his preoccupation. He had a *duty*—to Eryk, to Oliwia—and there was no other way.

"Are we done here?" he barked at the servant and stood abruptly, smoothing the żupan as he glanced at his reflection. He was freshly scrubbed and impeccably dressed, and the reflection gave him some relief, for he looked every bit the noble officer—whether he felt it or not. The servant stepped back and nodded.

Now for breakfast ... if I can eat.

A quarter hour later, Jacek determinedly willed his boots to carry him down the dim passageway to Oliwia's sitting room. His stomach was so tightly clenched that he'd done little else but push food around his plate. He might be early yet, but she was awake, for the last of Eryk's kin had left. Whatever other matters faced her could wait; he was anxious to get this over with.

He pulled in a deep breath and rapped on the door. Nadia answered in a nervous rush, looked up at him, and grew more anxious still.

"Is your lady here, Nadia? I wish to speak with her," he said in the gentlest voice he could muster so as to not fluster the girl further. Nadia stared at him, and her mouth dropped open. *Has something suddenly sprouted from my head?* Recovering herself, she curtsied.

He opened his mouth to say he would come back, but then Nadia did the unthinkable and invited him into the sitting room as the bedchamber door stood wide. She pivoted from him and announced his arrival to her mistress. He raised his eyes, and before he could look away, Jacek glimpsed Oliwia's creamy shoulders and neck above the rim of a tub resting before the fire. Her glossy wet hair trailed below the water.

She jerked her head toward him, her crystal-blue eyes wide in astonishment.

He quickly dropped his gaze and took several steps backward, grabbing the edge of the door as he squeezed it shut.

Oliwia yelped on the other side. "Nadia!"

He stood in the shadowed hallway as servants and maids scurried by and kept his head down, acting as though a cinder smudge on the floor had caught his devoted attention. While he suppressed a smile and his racing pulse, amplified female voices oscillated behind the heavy wooden door.

A thought smacked him like a cold, wet carp across his clean-shaven jaw.

He was to wed Lady Eugenia.

The door cracked open once again, and Nadia squeezed her body through an impossibly small gap between door and frame. Her eyes darted everywhere but to his face, and she wrung her hands in her apron. Her long pink nose and flitting mannerisms brought to mind a tiny, terrified mouse.

"I am very sorry, m'lord. I … I forgot myself. I … M'lady will soon be dressed and asked you wait, if you can spare the time." She looked up at him. "What shall I tell m'lady, m'lord?"

In her small, round brown eyes was a combination of horror and remorse, and Jacek was tempted to chuck her under her pointed chin to calm her. The gesture would likely have scared her far worse, so he kept his hands firmly clasped behind him.

"I've time to spare for your lady, Nadia. I will wait here until she's ready to receive me."

Nadia looked crestfallen. "Oh no, m'lord. Not in the passageway! You must wait in her sitting room."

He arched his eyebrows at her. "Are you sure, Nadia?"

She stammered. "Yes, my lord. I, um, the door is secured."

Jacek stepped into the sitting room, and Nadia disappeared—perhaps through a mousehole in the wall. He wasn't sure. He surveyed the lavish, feminine room, though not for long, for the same skittish mouse darted out, squeaking instructions to someone to remove the tub at once, before she darted back in and banged the door closed behind her. Oliwia appeared in the doorway and invited him to sit in one of a pair of cushioned armchairs before the sitting room hearth, her hair loose and damp. When she sat, she flipped it over the back of the chair. It resembled the waves of a dark, undulating sea, and he tamped down an impulse to twine his fingers in it.

Nadia materialized with a wide silver comb, which she began dragging through the thick tresses.

"Shall I braid it for you now, my lady?"

"No, it will dry while I sit beside the fire. Would you pour the captain a cup of wine, Nadia?"

Oliwia asked Jacek if he would like any food—she would have a tray brought up—and no, thank you, he did not. Nadia handed him a full cup and flitted out the door, leaving Jacek and Oliwia to sit before the marble fireplace, staring into the blaze.

What thoughts played through her mind?

It was just the two of them. When had that last happened? *That night in her bedchamber.* He steeled himself and cleared his dry throat. *Best get on with it.*

"My lady, I worry for your welfare and that of your son." He paused to sip, but she said nothing. She simply stared ahead. "I have a solution to keep you both safe."

She gave him a sidelong glance, but he fixed his eyes on the fire.

100

"The best way to keep you out of danger is for you to marry a lord at least as powerful as Lord Eryk. As soon as possible. I've several in mind."

From the corner of his eye, he saw her stiffen.

She began to protest. "But—"

He held up his hand, now meeting her gaze squarely. "No, hear me out. Many covet these rich lands. For now, as a temporary measure, Biaska's people acknowledge you are their mistress and leader, but they expect another strong nobleman to step into their lord's place and look after them. Clearly, Adam cannot yet rule, and they will grow restless wondering who their new lord will be. For generations, it has been a Krezowski, but now everything changes.

"There are those who pose a threat, and they see you as neither a leader nor a strong defender of Biaska. Whether they are right or wrong matters not. They will mobilize because they perceive a weakness they can exploit for their own ambitions, and this castle will be vulnerable. If you remarry, they are less likely to attack." Jacek paused, gathering his words around him like a shield. "Therefore, before a husband is chosen *for* you, is there one you would consent to wed? I will negotiate the contract on your behalf."

Oliwia's dark brows drew together, her face altogether like a brewing storm.

"One chosen *for* me?" she exclaimed. "You'll *negotiate a contract*? Am I a barrel of wheat to be haggled over? What of my widow's rights?"

He snorted.

She stood and began pacing. "Tell me, Jacek, why is this garrison incapable of holding the fortress for me, for my son? Is that not *your* duty?"

Jacek gripped his armrests. "The garrison is perfectly capable, Lady Oliwia, but it is not fully manned. Many have left since Lord Eryk's death, and I cannot say how soon we will be able to reinforce—"

"Merciful God! I have just buried a husband, and now you wish to bind me to another!"

A burst of heat overtook him. "Have a care and use the intelligence God saw fit to give you, woman!"

His breathing had grown rapid, shallow. Oliwia turned on him, her lips pressed in a hard line. Her crystal eyes blazed, shooting daggers. Had they been real blades, he would have been pierced a hundred times over.

"I *have* used it, and look where it's gotten me," she said in a tight voice.

He stood and faced her, looking her over from head to toe as the toxic mix that had been brewing inside him overflowed. "I *am* looking where it has gotten you. You did very well for yourself the first time. With your cunning, I've no doubt you'll do even better now."

He regretted the coarse words as soon as they leapt from his mouth. She jerked as though she'd been slapped. He cringed inside and rolled his shoulders to hide it. In a conciliatory tone, he said, "Have you considered Lord Jankowski? His father spoke to me at the funeral about a match. The son favored you once and has yet to marry. With his wealth—"

"If you will excuse me, Captain, I've much to attend." Her eyes had turned glacial; the tone of her voice matched them. She turned her back on him, hands fisted at her sides.

Her venom took him aback. As he watched her pace to her bedchamber, his anger flamed. Ever the soldier, he fell back and issued an order.

"Stop. I'm not done speaking yet."

"But you *are* done speaking to *me*," she replied without a backward glance.

Irked, he posed in what he thought a most logical manner, "I stand here because Lord Eryk, *your* late husband, swore me to protect you should anything happen to him."

She halted and glanced over her shoulder, the look a familiar and haunting one. Fighting the conjuring of his deity, he struggled to preserve what remained of his fractured, thin veneer of control.

"I've no doubt my husband would relinquish you from your oath, Captain." Her voice was laced with contempt. "Consider your obligation fulfilled. You are quite free to leave."

Before he could argue his obligation was nowhere near fulfilled, she slipped through the door and shut it resoundingly behind her. Heat burned his cheeks. He followed and pounded on the wood.

"Lady Oliwia? We are not yet done here. Oliwia? *Liwi!*"

The bar scraped as it fell into place. From behind the door came her muffled voice. "A man I once trusted told me to keep the door barred against scoundrels. I am heeding his counsel."

Staring at one small spot on the door, he puffed his cheeks and expelled one enormous breath after another as if he were a smith's bellows. Then he swung his gaze to the fire and stood for long minutes scratching his neck. His anger sputtered as quickly as it had ignited.

Stupid mare's ass! What in blazes is wrong with me? Why do I let this trifle of a girl bedevil me so?

Seeing her married would take more than he'd prepared for. He rejected the thought of giving up and returning to Silnyród in less time than it took to consider it. Sighing, he thumped out of the room.

Jacek barely glimpsed Oliwia the rest of that day and the next. She seemed to know his movements and vanished like a forest sprite when he appeared in her line of sight. He kept himself busy, if not wholly distracted, evaluating a half-dozen new horses, including one magnificent stallion that was dark, beautiful, and temperamental. He laughed at himself; apparently, he was lured to such creatures, doomed to tangle with them.

When another night passed and he spotted Henryk traipsing down the steps from her apartments next morning, he lamely asked after her health.

"Oliwia's well. She smiled at my jokes, even the poor ones. What leads you to believe she's taken ill?" Henryk replied.

"I have not been able to speak with her, and I thought—"

Henryk grabbed him by the nape. "Come. You and I will go the guard tower, where I have a special bottle of wodka hidden away. And don't argue."

After securing the guard room door and filling their cups, Henryk took a swig and narrowed his eyes. "What the hell is the matter with you?"

Oliwia picked up her sewing only to throw it back down again. Should she visit the nursery? No, Adam was sleeping. She glanced over her shoulder at a book, then at a piece of blank paper awaiting her hand. Breath escaped her in slow flight. Finally, she gathered up a report on the state of the garrison. Soldiers *had* left, at an alarming rate, though she was loath to admit Jacek had been right to be concerned. Most of the attrition came from the foreign ranks, but several towarzysze had also departed. Their reasons all seemed to narrow to one: with Lord Eryk gone, so went the attraction to pledge to Biaska. Worse, rumors swirled of an army gathering outside Sandomierz. What if some of those soldiers had fled Biaska's ranks? Were they to join an attack against her, they had intimate knowledge of the castle's defenses.

Oliwia plucked the cross from its resting place inside her bodice, sliding it back and forth along its silver chain. Hours after their row, she had stopped seeing Jacek's smug face in every pillow she battered. His prickly tone, his entire demeanor, had vexed her no end. Today, her diffused anger allowed that he was right, though it didn't lessen the sting of his vicious words—or make the prospect of taking a husband any less disturbing. One yoke had just been removed, and she was ill-disposed to replace it with another. The irony that *he,* of all people, offered to negotiate the match was not lost on her.

She let out a wry, bitter laugh, then crossed herself and sent a quick prayer to be forgiven her evil thoughts. *But even so, Jankowski!* Did Jacek really think the puny, snively courtier the right match for her? What, then, must he think of *her?* The answer was all too clear: he thought her moved by wealth and power, making Jankowski the perfect candidate in his eyes.

Jacek had cared for her once, and though she'd annihilated his tender feelings, perhaps enough of a shred remained that he would understand and not judge her unkindly if she could explain. No matter the outcome, the time had arrived to tell him what had really happened. Besides pride, what more had she to lose? Looking in her glass, she ran her fingers through her tresses, vainly trying to tame them. Discomfited, she replaced her necklace, smoothed her gown, and headed for the solar.

Jacek gulped his drink. "She would have none of my reasonable counsel to remarry. Then I asked if she'd considered Jankowski, and … well, I'm grateful she had no weapon to hand. Now she refuses to speak to me. Of *anything*! I cannot even entice her to talk to me about Filip."

"Filip? How does he figure in this?" Henryk frowned.

"I recruited him to help me wheedle her. He seemed willing enough," Jacek replied defensively—though in truth, Filip's enthusiasm, at best, had been lukewarm.

Jacek told how he'd encountered Filip shortly after leaving Oliwia's parlor and, finding an ally, had dragged the boy back to beg an audience based on a different pretext.

Henryk raised an eyebrow. "Such as?"

"I, uh, said I needed to discuss his progress with the sabre ... and the horses."

Henryk guffawed. "You could invent no better excuse?"

Jacek glowered at him, uncomfortably recalling how even timid Nadia had become a fierce gatekeeper. When he'd used the same justification on her, he'd nodded involuntarily—as if agreeing with himself that his limp reason was strong enough, and believable enough, for Oliwia to admit him—only to receive the maid's incredulous look in response. Neither woman had been swayed, and he'd been soundly rejected. Even Filip had deserted him.

Henryk crossed his arms and leaned his hip against the desk. "Did you begin your conversation two days ago by asking Oliwia if there was anything she had need of? Or did you just plow ahead, both pistols firing at once?"

Jacek hardened the glare.

Henryk continued. "And just how did you 'ask' her? If you used the same scorn you've been wont to use since your return, I have no doubt she took offense. You still begrudge her—I understand—but you've been treating her as if she's a bit of mud stuck to your boot heel. She just lost her husband, for God's sake! If you cannot have empathy for the woman, at least refrain from using your foul temper on her."

"I do not begrudge the woman, for that would mean I care what she thinks or does, which I do not. *And*, mind, I have treated her with the utmost respect."

Henryk scoffed. "I've watched you. You've behaved with little courtesy or consideration. In short, you've been a brute and a loggerhead. When you returned with Filip, did you bother first extending an apology? Have you tried since then, in any manner, apologizing to her?"

Ignoring him, Jacek threw up his hands and yelled at the ceiling. "By all the saints, women are so ... so *infuriating!*"

"No, Jacek. They really aren't. It is only this one that vexes you," Henryk drawled, topping off their cups. "And I wager you protest merely to cover the deep affection you still harbor. You are so besotted you cannot think clearly when it comes to her. You never could."

"You could not be more wrong!" Jacek stabbed his finger in the air. After a short pause, he grumbled, "But I've no time to argue the matter." Tempted though he was to knock the smirk from Henryk's face, he said instead, "This is a serious business. Tell me how to get through to her. Better yet, *you* tell her."

Henryk's eyebrows shot to his forehead. *"Me?* No, no, my friend. She is fond of me yet, and I'll give her no reason to change her mind."

Jacek waved his hand at him in disgust. "The devil piss on you, then."

Henryk studied him, riling him further.

"What? Are you going to continue castigating me?" Jacek spat.

"Possibly. You've certainly earned it." After a beat, he said, "Have you considered proposing to her yourself?"

"You are daft!"

"Am I? I am not the one picking fights with young widows."

Humphing, Jacek folded his arms across his chest. "Even if I had lost my mind so completely that I could entertain that ridiculous notion, I am not the right one for her. She needs a lord who wields power, and that sort of power requires wealth."

"Are you so certain? I think one formidable *hussar* commanding a wealthy estate and its garrison made up of others like him would give any adversary pause. And do not overlook that one such commander attracts more troops ready to swear to his banner."

Jacek walked to the window, where he gazed beyond castle walls to nowhere in particular. Another *humph* escaped him.

"I don't know what goes on in Oliwia's head," Henryk offered. "She does not confide in me. And even if she did, I could not claim to understand her, or any other woman for that matter. I am at their mercy, compelled to chase them unendingly. They are God's mysteries, put here to enchant and bedevil us, and the most nettlesome are those we have the misfortune of falling in love with."

Jacek gave him a sidelong glance. "Are you saying you've been in love?"

Henryk chuckled. "Of course! With every woman I have ever met. I am in love with them all, for at least one hour."

Jacek shook his head and looked back out the window. Verdant fields came into focus—the fields that, with God on their side, would offer a good yield at harvest. They would need all of it. He turned over Henryk's words, annoyed he could not logically discount them. Nettlesome, Oliwia was! Other women preoccupied him little—like Lady Eugenia, whom he'd barely given a thought. But this one, *this* one! Oliwia had gotten under his skin and taken up residence, where she irritated him like a swarm of fleas, chewing away at him and never letting him forget her presence. Not for lack of trying, he had been unable to purge her from his blood.

Henryk interrupted his ruminations. "You want to know how to get through to her. I cannot help you, my friend, for I'm no good at it. She's a woman, after all, and at times a rather stubborn one. You're better off praying to God for help—or Mary."

"Well, I'm glad you know you're no good at it because you confuse me more than she does," Jacek retorted. "This is getting us nowhere, and it's too early for more wodka. I'm going back to the keep."

Replete with tetchiness, he entered the great hall in the wake of a messenger. When he hailed him, the lad gave him two letters, both addressed to him. One was written in a familiar hand and added to his ill humor. He tucked it away with a scowl. *I've yet to reply to her first letter.* The other letter hailed from Silnyród, but he did not recognize the script. He refrained from opening it until he reached the solar. As he climbed the stone steps to the tune of his scuffing soles, he looked up—and stopped in his tracks. Oliwia blocked the doorway, her small form silhouetted by the watery light beyond. Raking a hand through his hair, he led her into the chamber.

Christ!

Oliwia's heart beat so furiously she thought it might seize. "Captain, I regret the interruption. I know you are busy."

She peered over her shoulder at him as he closed the door. Wordlessly, he strode to the desk and took up a standing position behind it. Today, he wore a żupan of rich indigo brocade that matched his eyes. Lined in emerald linen, it topped dark blue breeches and yellow boots. He stood tall and erect, and she was struck by the force of his stature as he faced her—

he called to mind a reinforced fortification wall. Then he clasped his hands behind him and rocked on the balls of his feet.

He is not going to make this easy.

"No need of regret, my lady. Please," he said stiffly as he indicated a seat.

She'd once thought she could read his moods as the color of his eyes shifted and transformed according to his temperament; but right now, they seemed to bore into her, through her, as if all she kept locked away in her soul was exposed to him. Her legs wobbled under his dark scrutiny.

Oliwia braced herself against a chair but did not sit. She felt like a cat, trapped, her body quivering as her eyes darted from Jacek to imaginary aspects of fascination around the room. She quashed the urge to pull the cross out once more. Jacek's brow wrinkled in his trademark scowl, and his pinpoint focus on her made her twitch. She prayed he did not notice.

The scowl shifted to a look of concern. "Is there anything I can get you, Lady Oliwia?"

Oliwia shook her head, then took a large breath of courage and stilled her body, lifting her head in a regal set she did not feel. She careened onward in a strong, steady voice before her audacity had a chance to deflate and abandon her.

"My lord, two days ago, you said I must wed. You asked if there was anyone I would consent to marry. I still owe you an answer."

A look of surprise, and something else she didn't recognize, flitted across his chiseled face. He recovered himself, his features inscrutable. His eyes softened to a lighter blue, as if a cloud had passed over the sun. Before she could blaze on, he raised his hand.

"It can wait," he said, throwing her.

She swallowed. "I do not believe it can."

He pulled in a deep breath. "If you insist, lady, then I have little choice but to hear you." He paused to scratch the back of his neck. "Before you begin, I wish to apologize for my ... my unkind words when last we spoke," he muttered.

She barely heard the feeble apology. Instead, nausea waved through her belly, and she momentarily lost her bearings. Righting herself, she forged on. "I would like to begin by saying I do not disagree with your counsel; however, I am fervidly opposed to having a husband selected for me, nor do I wish a match based on duty or alliance. I seek a love match."

"Such as your marriage to Lord Eryk?"

A familiar pang of regret rose within her. "No, not exactly. I would explain if you will permit me."

He nodded curtly.

Suddenly, she felt like an unruly subordinate to his superior captain self. She did not care for the feeling. Her nails dug into the backs of her hands from clasping them together so tightly. When she returned his gaze, his face was utterly blank. Anger kindled as the words tumbled from her.

Jacek flinched. It was subtle, and he was sure she hadn't noticed, but an unsettling ripped through him nonetheless. As he prepared to deflect, she pressed her lips in a tight line, her eyes still fixed on his, and swallowed. The ripple ran along her smooth ivory throat. Though her eyes sparked, she wore an incongruous expression of sorrow.

"I know what you must think of me," she began, "but I've something I must first tell you—something I've concealed since that day in the buttery." She paused. "I lied to you."

Confusion must have shown on his face, for she rushed on. "I told you I loved Eryk, that I wanted to marry him." She inhaled a deep breath. "Forgive me, but I did not." Her eyes suddenly filled with tears and spilled down her face unchecked—as if she'd summoned them on command.

He gave a quick shake of his head. His ire, at a constant simmer since he'd returned, rose up and was just as quickly overcome by wretchedness, as if she'd spurned him all over again. But in the mix was one razor-thin ribbon of joy. He stood mute, glued in place as if caught in a web, while his emotions spun wildly.

Finding his voice, he replied, "I do not understand." And he didn't, nor was he inclined to try at the moment. "If you didn't wish to marry him, why the devil did you go through with it?" His voice rose. "By all the saints, how could you stand there and tell me how damned *eager* you were?"

She looked away and curled her fingers together as she twisted her hands.

"I … There was no choice." Her breath hitched. She swiped at her cheeks and tossed her head, as if trying to toss away the unrelenting tears.

Suddenly, he understood, and the realization hit him full force, nearly driving the air from his lungs. He had miscalculated, misjudged so abominably.

"That day, you said it wasn't about the riches, but that was a lie too, was it not? How diverting it must have been, playing one foolish, wretched suitor against the other, keeping them both in the shadows of your manipulations. Did you use me against him so he would lavish you with more expensive gifts? Perhaps your wedding ring was one such piece of plunder. In the end, the wealth won out, but no doubt that was the outcome you'd planned all along."

"You have it all wrong! Let me explain!"

He raised his hand. "I've heard explanations enough, and I care to hear no more."

"He would have *killed* you!" she wailed.

He looked at her, a sham of a smile on his face, and scoffed.

"He was not the man you remember, Jacek."

Picking up the unopened letter, he swatted it against the desk, making a sharp smacking noise. "What a fanciful tale is yours to tell in the ladies' salon when the customary vapid prattle goes round the room."

She squared her shoulders and pulled a long breath through her nose, flaring her nostrils. Now her brows knotted together fiercely above her flushed face, and her hands clenched at her sides. Jacek's heart galloped like a stallion outrunning a pack of wolves, and his insides reeled as though that same stallion had kicked him in the gut. Bile lodged in his throat from his sour stomach, and he knuckled his hands on the desk to support his weight. Transfixed, he braced himself for her to continue, not wanting her to continue.

"'Tis no surprise your mind immediately climbs into the vilest of places when you level accusations. You've been spiteful and boorish since you arrived and only grow more disagreeable with each passing day. I *cannot* speak to you, you imperious, womanizing, villainous, detestable, dung-eating cham!"

Womanizing?
Eugenia!
But how could she know? I burned that letter …

Oliwia turned for the door.

He couldn't let her leave just yet. "A *cham?* Did you call me a dung-eating cham?"

She pivoted, her fury so impressive she appeared to have grown several inches taller.

"Yes, and furthermore, you are not welcome here," she said hotly, stabbing a finger at him. "Go back to your whores, your mistresses, your bastard children, and get the hell out of my solar, my castle, and stay away from me and mine, you ruttish libertine! When I return, you had best be gone from here!"

What ... the ... hell?

"What the devil are you talking about?" he called after her, confusion tamping his bluster.

As she tore through the door, she collided with Henryk.

"Oliwia, are you all right?" Astounded, he set her upright.

"No!" she barked, jabbing a thumb over her shoulder. "Your job as captain of the guard is to remove *his* pompous person from my home. Now!"

Jacek put his pompous person into motion and briskly loomed behind her, only to be slammed back with the full force of Henryk's forearm across his chest.

"Jacek! Hold!"

"I want to know what in blazes she means by that!"

"She means you're arrogant and you need to leave!"

"I understand *that!* But why does she call me a ruttish libertine? And when the devil did I acquire bastard children?" He narrowed his eyes at Henryk.

"Don't look at me, you clodpole. This is your own doing, and you'd best solve it quickly or I will be obliged to escort you from here." Henryk shoved him roughly. He shoved back. Henryk shoved him once more and stepped out of his reach, straightening his żupan.

"Why the devil is she so angry?" Jacek looked into the now empty passageway, expecting her to materialize and explain herself.

"Truly? You've *no* idea? Do you suppose your yelling might have something do with it? Your charm—and perception—are in full sway, as usual."

Jacek seethed. "She brings out the worst in me."

Henryk drew him into the chamber and closed the door. He faced Jacek, his scorn palpable. "*You* trot out the worst in yourself and demand *she* bear witness. You seem to delight in it. For a man who professes unendingly how little he cares for a woman, you spend an enormous amount of time thinking up ways to show her just how little she matters to you."

Jacek glared at him and pivoted on his heel.

"Where in blazes are you going?" Henryk barked.

"I'm going to track her down. She cannot drive me from here, and she cannot disparage me without explaining herself."

Henryk grabbed his upper arm in an iron grip. "Jacek, cool your head! And allow her to cool hers, for Christ's sake!"

Jacek shrugged off Henryk's hold and began stomping to and fro. He stopped abruptly.

"Whores? Ruttish libertine?" His bewilderment bloomed, crowding out his deflating wrath. Distractedly, he picked up the letter from Silnyród, broke the seal, and read the letter's contents.

"Merciful God!"

Chapter 10

A Seed of Redemption

Oliwia charged to her quarters. "The sheer arrogance of the man! He's made a fool of me again!"

As she stalked, she found a sliver of gratefulness that his condescension had stoppered any more of her silly revelations.

"He scoffed! Scoffed when I told him what Eryk would have done to him! Next time …"

No, there would be no next time.

She burst through the door of her salon. Nadia and another maid jumped. "Nadia! Get my cloak and boots. You! What's your name?" Oliwia pointed to the maid.

"This is Wanda, m'lady," Nadia said with a quaver. "The new chambermaid?"

The maid, a pretty girl with strawberry-blond hair and mossy green eyes, dropped her head and curtsied.

"Wanda," Oliwia ordered, "hurry to the guard tower and tell them I need an escort of six guards, no more, ready to leave as soon as I'm dressed. Then tell Feliks to prepare my horse." The maid's body, frozen like her expression, mimicked a statue. Oliwia snapped her fingers under her nose. "Now!" This seemed to enliven Wanda's limbs, for the girl hastened from the room.

When Oliwia strode into the courtyard, a detail of six armed soldiers awaited her. One stood beside her mare with its reins, and he helped her into her saddle.

"Gentlemen, I am off for a gallop to the lake. I wish to ride full-out, so do not crowd me. When I get there, you will take up station at a distance. Understood?"

The lead guard nodded. "Understood, my lady."

"Good. Then let's be off."

"Lesław was struck in the leg by an arrow." Jacek handed the letter to a stunned Henryk.

"Is it bad?" Henryk scanned the note.

Jacek shrugged, then rapped his knuckles against the desk. "The priest who penned the letter says not, but for the time being Lesław is hobbled. Someone else must take command."

"Will you return?"

Jacek's mind whirled. "I must." He crossed to the window and cracked it open, drawing damp air into his lungs, expelling his frustration on each exhale.

"'Tis probably best you go now anyway."

Something caught Jacek's eye, and he stiffened.

Henryk joined him. "What is it?"

Jacek pointed. "Is that ...? What devilment is she up to *now*?"

A sleek chestnut horse carried a woman's form, a brilliant blue cloak fluttering behind her. Racing across a flat meadow toward a dense wall of trees, it threw up clods of earth like spattering rain as its hooves dug into soft ground. The woman leaned over the animal's neck as she galloped for the wood.

"I think it is, and she appears to be headed for the lake." Stalking across the chamber, Henrky bellowed, "Where are her guards?"

"They're there, coming up behind her," Jacek replied. "Six. That's not enough!"

Jacek spun on his heel and barked at Henryk, who had already reached the door and thrown it wide. Two guards met him to report Lady Oliwia had left the castle walls.

"You're late!" Jacek shouted at them even as Henryk snapped commands.

"Tell Feliks, anyone in the stables, to get the stallion—the new one, the black one—tell them to get him ready for me *now!*" Jacek ordered one guard. "And have my retainer bring my weapons and spurs." The guard nodded and tossed out a quick "yes, my lord" before turning and falling in behind his brother-in-arms.

Jacek clutched at his hair as if to yank it out, then locked gazes with Henryk. In a tight voice, he said, "I will go after her alone, and I will bring her back. When I catch her, I will give her a tongue-lashing such as she has never heard, and then I am going to wring her pretty neck! *You never should have taught her to ride!*"

Henryk shot him a glower.

Grabbing up his gloves, Jacek bounded down the steps to the hall, vaulted through the oaken doors, and raced down the forestairs, boot heels clicking *tap-tap-tap* on the stone. He strode so swiftly as to be just short of a run, heading toward the stables, where Marcin was bringing out the stallion—or trying to. The animal was not pleased, cocking one big brown eye at his escort. Marcin jumped back in time to avoid a crushing hoof-stamping.

"Are you *sure* you wish to ride him, my lord?"

As Jacek fitted his spurs, he said, "Too late now. My horses are in the far pasture."

"I could saddle one of the stable horses for you." Marcin clenched the reins, his arm jerking with the horse's pitching head.

Jacek pulled on his gloves and took the reins from his *pacholik*. "I need a fast mount."

"I will be right back with your weapons, Captain." Marcin was already in a sprint.

A small audience had gathered. Jacek tugged the reins down, pulling the great beast's head next to his as he stroked him and crooned.

"What's his name?" Jacek addressed one of the stable boys who gawped at him.

"His name, sir?" The lad was ashen. Between the frothing horse and Jacek's temper, he looked as though he might spin and bolt.

"Yes! What do you call him?"

"Uh, well, they've been calling him 'Smok,' sir."

Dragon. Jesus!

Jacek continued stroking the big horse's neck. "All right, Smok, my handsome lad. I will take care of you, and you will do the same for me. I will give you your head and you can ride as hard as you like, but you're going to mind me. If you behave, I promise to go easy on you."

With that, Jacek put one boot in the stirrup and smartly swung his other leg over the saddle while the beast pranced in place. He pulled on the reins gently, and the stallion settled. Jacek quickly seated the primed pistols Marcin handed him. Leaning over the stallion's neck, Jacek spoke to him while he ruffled his black mane. He walked the animal around the stableyard several times, then into the inner ward and through the gate.

Once they crossed the drawbridge, Jacek released the patience he'd bottled up and let urgency retake him. Patting the horse's neck one last time, he nudged its flanks. The animal grunted and stayed where he was; Jacek nudged him harder. The stallion turned his huge head and eyed Jacek. Then he faced forward again and suddenly surged, setting a pair of cranes flapping into the sky. Jacek and Smok were off, streaking across the field in tune, racing to the wood where the other riders had disappeared.

Oliwia dismounted and yanked off her hood. Then she unfastened her cloak and whipped it over a wet patch of grass. The dappled ground was damp where the sun hadn't touched it yet, and the spot she'd unconsciously chosen was under a large canopy of lacy green shade. She began pacing around the blue velvet.

Clear your mind!

The ride hadn't uncluttered her thoughts as she'd hoped, but maybe the calming vista would do it. The lake, its glassy surface dotted with languid circles made by drifting dragonflies, always soothed her. Perhaps here she could muster her thoughts and sort through her next moves. She couldn't think coherently back at the castle, with everyone watching her, following her, the prospect of Jacek at every turn.

Jacek. His blatant contempt showed like a medallion emblazoned with his hatred for her, and he wore it proudly—doubtless fortified by the scores of women at his disposal to, from, and in Podolia. Biaska too. He would have laughed himself sick once he divined where her confession had been leading.

Swine! Rake! Rogue!

Along with her mounting tally of Jacek's imagined lovers, she had convinced herself he had as many children. The number was blossoming into the population of an entire village.

She cast a rock into the lake, sending ripples across its shimmering surface.

Shameless scoundrel! Libertine!

As she trod back and forth, she picked up more rocks, pausing now and again to hurl one into the water with a choice insult. A nuthatch lit on the low limb of a leaning alder and trilled, seemed to look at her, and quickly flapped away. She plunked one more rock, then straightened herself. Why the devil did she need Jacek anyway? Or any man for that matter? She could fill the garrison and run the damned estate herself! Now all she need do was wait for Jacek to clear out of her home, her sight, and her life.

Oliwia jerked her head up. Overwhelmed by her own tumultuous thoughts, she'd paid little attention to anything else—she had guards, after all. But she'd held them back in a separate copse, and they couldn't see her. Now she cocked her head and held her breath. Thumping, rhythmic and steady, insistent, coming toward her hard and fast.

Oliwia dashed to her mare, but she hadn't secured her, and the horse shied just beyond her reach. She tried again, but it bolted and stopped, again out of her reach, as though taunting her. It moved when she did. She lunged and slipped on damp grass, landing hard on her back. The air fled from her lungs in a *whoosh!* Dazed, she sat up and tried to call out, but she had no voice.

This is all Jacek's fault! Damn his conceit, his harems, and his illegitimate children anyway! The devil take them all!

Oliwia's rational mind had taken full flight in rather spectacular fashion, leaving her at the mercy of her own ludicrous imagination. The pounding paused but then resumed, coming closer, growing louder, shaking the ground now. Where were the guards?

She searched frantically for something else, anything, to defend herself with. Naught but the stones were within her reach, so she snatched them while the thundering reverberated about her. Her hands shook, and she dropped several before she could stow them.

Hurry! Hurry! Hurry!

The rumbling bore down on her.

A few more sharp rocks …

The pounding halted with a juddering *whomp!* She whirled to see a large mounted man restraining a huge horse as he guided it down the slope to the lakeshore. She took a step back and squinted at the rider still ten paces away, though his build left no doubt of his identity.

Mary, Mother of God, the last person on this earth I wish to see!

Jacek leapt down; the stallion snorted and highstepped in place, fighting his hold. She knew how it felt. Jacek quickly tied off the reins to a sturdy trunk, secured her mare, then came straight for her, his strides chewing up the ground.

Taking in a sharp breath, she held herself steady. She had seen his most menacing glower countless times, but she had never seen *this* homicidal look—and it was directed at *her.* This ferocity must have been what his enemies saw as he thrust his kopia through them or cut them down with his nadziak. She shrank back, bumping into an elm, each hand in her pocket closed about a rock.

"Oliwia! *Oliwia!*" he roared. "What the devil is wrong with you? You have put yourself, your guards, and me in grave danger by leaving the castle walls!"

Oh, this is too much!

"I didn't ask you to follow me, Jacek!" she screamed. "I distinctly remember telling you to leave!"

The quaking she'd felt when he first launched off the spirited horse was engulfed by a flame of fury. Squaring her shoulders, she stood her ground as he drew up toe to toe with her and towered over her, his eyes a massive, churning storm boring into her. For an instant, they were locked in each other's stares, each breathing hard. His face was so close she saw his nostrils flare with each breath, saw the divot above his right eyebrow, and the deep creases between his dark brows.

He abruptly stepped back, his gloved fists at his sides. As he inhaled deeply, repeatedly, his hands clenched and unclenched. He blew out huge breaths and swung his enormous arms in circles, lending him an absurd appearance akin to a double water wheel being moved by a giant bellows. Fisting his hands, he shoved them on his hips as he looked her over.

Fire pulsed through her, making her hands tremble, so she kept them deep in her pockets. She stuck out her chin and continued glaring at him, praying he couldn't see her body quiver and mistake her anger for fear. Jacek looked toward the treed canopy and mumbled under his breath, then scrubbed a hand across his face. He leveled his eyes at her and half coughed, half barked.

"It is true, Lady Oliwia," he rumbled. "You did not ask me to follow you. But if I hadn't, Henryk would have, or Marcin, or perhaps ten more guards, and you would now have the pleasure of yelling at them about doing their duty to protect you from your own foolishness." His voice had been steadily rising, and now he stabbed a finger in the air. "In light of everything Biaska and its people have suffered, yours was a poor decision."

"A poor decision? Something you're quite familiar with, Captain!"

"My decisions may not always be the correct ones, *my lady*, but at least I give them due consideration." Now his voice was low, tight, as if he struggled to keep it even.

"What a shame we cannot all be as perfect as you. Never a garment askew, an enemy you cannot best, or a woman you cannot bed."

"Oliwia, you've taken leave of your senses. Stop this childish nonsense and return to the castle *now*."

"I am entitled to ride where and how I please, for as long as I please. *You* are not my master." She crossed her arms and lifted her chin a little higher.

Glaring, he pressed his lips together in a firm line.

And then he yelled.

"Surely you could have had your jaunt *within castle walls!*"

She yelled right back. "No, I could not! I cannot think in there. Everyone nags at me. Especially you!" She pointed an accusing finger.

He folded his long arms across his sizeable chest, his expression inscrutable. His breathing slowed, and he seemed to root himself to the ground. Oddly, this calmer pose made her even angrier. She stuffed her hands back in her pockets.

"Well, you need not worry yourself about that, my lady. When I get you safely back, I will not trouble you again. Then you can think all you like," he said coldly.

He held out a gloved hand to her, much as he'd done so many years ago in Vyatov, and something inside of her let loose like a metal band that had been cinched too tight.

"No!" She stamped her foot.

He eyed her curiously and withdrew the hand, refolding his arms. "No, you will not go back to the castle? Or no, you *do* want me to trouble you again? Or no, you do not wish to think? Which is it?"

Oliwia yanked a hand out of her pocket and loosed a stone at him. She had aimed at his infuriatingly unreadable face, but he dodged and swiveled his head, watching as it flew past and thumped harmlessly on the ground behind him. He jerked back and avoided the next projectile she threw at him. And then he coolly resumed his pose.

"I can play at this all day, Oliwia. But it's hot, and I'm hungry. Can we return now? Have you finished with your games?"

She launched several more stones, and he neatly avoided most of those too. A few thunked against his żupan or bounced off his glove when he raised a hand to deflect them. One landed squarely on the crown of his head, and he flinched but said nothing. He began a slow, deliberate walk toward her.

"If you're so hot and hungry, then turn around and go! Leave me be! You're not wanted here!" She flailed a dismissive hand at him. With her pronouncement, she backed away, stumbled over a root, and plunked her bottom onto her outspread cloak.

Damn the arrogant blackguard!

Jacek rubbed his head and rolled his eyes. "I must disappoint you once again, for I am not leaving." Then he took two long strides and loomed over her.

Ow! Jacek ran his fingers over his head. He needed to put an end to this, and he began walking toward the spitting cat with no idea what to do when he reached her—he only knew what he would *not* do, which was surrender to his powerful inclination to shake some sense into her. He concentrated on slowing his steps and his rapid breathing.

Deep breath in, deep breath out.

She screamed at him to leave her alone. *You're not getting off so easily, Oliwia.* He kept his eyes pinned on her and tracked her as she tripped and dropped onto her cloak. There was no mistaking her lethal look; she was angrier than he had ever seen her. If she could have, she would have impaled him with those fiery crystal eyes. Her cheeks and nose were a deep shade of purple-pink. It was not a becoming color on her. Her whole demeanor, in fact, was unbecoming.

She brings this on herself. It's her own damned, pigheaded fault.

Arms firmly crossed, he stood over her, tapping his toe rapidly. She would not look up at him, would not acknowledge him. Fatigue suddenly seeped into his shoulders. Time had come for a new strategy—that, of course, presumed he'd had one to begin with. He dropped beside her, sitting as close as he dared without sitting on her, leaving her little room to maneuver. She leapt up, still ignoring him.

"If you choose to remain here, then so shall I. I must see you safely back. Let me know when you are ready to go, Liwi. And if I happen to fall asleep, do me the courtesy of waking me when it's time." He let out a long sigh as he lay back on the soft folds and closed his eyes, tucking his sidearms close to his body lest she thought to use them on him.

"Do not call me Liwi!" she snapped.

Well, at least he'd gotten a response from her. Gloved hands folded across his stomach and booted feet crossed, he grew still. Then he heard her rustle, so he cracked one eye open and found her staring at the lake, her profile in sharp contrast.

This isn't working either.

His weight on one elbow, he rolled to his side and looked at her. Sweet Jesus, but she was beautiful! Utterly unreasonable, exasperating, but *so beautiful.* It almost hurt to look at her. It brought to mind a too-sweet treat that ends in a toothache. And those kisses that haunted him still—the taste of her soft lips, the feel of her soft ...

He sat up. "Li—Lady Oliwia, I must return to Silnyród. I wish to dispel this rancor between us before I go."

She turned toward him, her arms firmly cinched over her chest. "So you return to your soldiering once more, and the others. Nothing changes," she said tartly.

"The others? What others?"

121

She rolled her eyes. "Jacek, since I have known you, you have attracted countless women like bees to honeysuckle blooms in summer."

This surprising remark completely blindsided him. "What has that to do with what we're arguing about? What *are* we arguing about anyway?" The notion popped into his head that he might soon learn the reason for her earlier tirade, though he could not say he was eager for the discovery.

"We're arguing about your foul temper, and about the true reason you are forever gone."

"I admit I have been a bit … a bit cross, but I confess I do not understand what my being gone has to do with any of this."

"You leave in order to return to your lovers, your mistresses, in villages, other estates, throughout the realm, and the children you have fathered." Without looking at him, she waved a careless hand in the air with a dramatic flourish.

Jacek bolted to his feet. *"What?"*

"I know you … you keep … you have many lovers. 'Tis no secret," she sniffed.

"'Tis a secret to me!" His jaw muscles tightened and bunched. *Has she lost all her senses?* "You say you know," he spat. "How?"

"I've heard the talk for years. I, well, I just know. That's all," she countered defiantly.

He gaped at her, sure she would turn at any moment with a smile and declare her jest. But she moved not at all, save her chin, which inched even higher. The composure he'd clung to was dissolving in the face of this allegation, his bearing giving way to something most unpleasant.

"Oliwia. Who has filled your head with this rubbish? Surely you did not come to this on your own."

"It does not matter where I heard it. I know it to be true." Her voice had lost some of its conviction, but her jaw remained set.

His mind whirred like an irretrievable, careening top. As his outrage blossomed, he dismissed the voice in his head telling him to maintain control—just as he conveniently dismissed all thought of Lady Eugenia and the duplicity wrought by his pledge to her.

"First of all," he ground out, "I leave because Lesław, my loyal friend and lord-brother, is wounded." She gasped, but he ignored her and plowed on. "Second of all, my romantic associations have been so scarce I could doubtless claim a monastic cell with the good brothers at St. Francis! But you have always thought me no better than a promiscuous dog, so you of course have this all decided, regardless of the truth." His voice dripped with sarcasm, his innards flaring.

Oliwia began to fidget, and her haughty look vanished. "What of Lesław? Is he all right?"

"For now. But he is not part of this discussion, and you will not escape justifying your shameful accusations so easily. Of all people, you—who exhibited no fidelity whatever when you were presented with a more favorable opportunity—dishonor me greatly by indulging in such idle gossip. We were speaking of truth, which appears nowhere in your charges. Tell me, since you know everything, do I do aught but spend my nights lolling about in brothels?"

"I was not speaking of you keeping company with … with …"

"Whores? Is that the word you search for? You can say it, my lady, just as you did so eloquently before. Well, I am gratified I've *that* sliver of your good opinion."

He began pacing a short line beside the outspread cloak, to and fro, with hands clasped behind him. "You've clearly no idea what I do in a day, so I will enlighten you. When I'm not battling an accursed enemy, I am ensuring our security, worrying if we can withstand an attack, whose mother I will need to tell she has lost a beloved son, whose father will weep because I could not rescue his child from the Tatar curs—and the list grows. Amid these worries, I have little time to indulge myself with whores." He paused. "No, I must correct that remark. I have neither time *nor* desire."

She said nothing; he went on seethingly. "So if we both agree I am not whoring, tell me what woman, or women, or mistresses, or concubines, or whatever the devil you think these imaginary creatures are, what sort you *know* me to keep?" His pacing widened, now encompassing the entire perimeter of her cloak.

"The towns …" she stuttered. "What of the ladies in the estates you visit? You are not warring then." Incredibly, she thrust that stubborn chin higher still.

"Nor am I doing what you're accusing me of doing!" He spun and flung his hands to the skies. "Ah! Of course!"

She began to speak, but he stopped her with a glower and a wag of his finger. He focused on the ground as he stalked, crushing clumps of grass beneath his boots. Oliwia stood mutely; Jacek had only begun. Years of frustration—of falling in love with her, failing to declare himself, readying their future only to lose her to Eryk—were finding a release, a channel where all his agitated emotions aligned to tumble out of him. He forged on heatedly.

"So you have discovered my secret," he mocked. "My harems are vast and wide and not limited to towns. No, no, no. As we travel, I recruit a company of ladies for my sole companions, but I must make them draw twigs to be selected. It can be rather tedious, but I endure it. And I do it all while trying to keep myself and my men safe, sane, and fit on meager rations. And because there are so *many* women, and I am so diverted in my debauchery, I find it hard to keep track of them all. I can scarcely be blamed for the oversight." He gave a little shrug. "When one trades females like horses, as I do, they are all alike. Except those I get with child. Them I simply abandon, with no regard for the babe, for I'm no better than a Swede or any other enemy soldier."

His pace had accelerated, punctuating the angry words he tossed at her. He gave her just enough due to notice her blush deepen, and she seemed to shrink into herself.

At least she has that much decency!

"Let us not overlook the battlefield camp. After we have picked up our wounded and buried our dead, with the sweet smells that make us all heave what little food we have in our bellies, well, then I dance, of course, to the incessant lively music played at the end of each wretched day before bedding at least two to five women in my tent at once. And our muddy marches are nothing short of riotous merriment! You should try it sometime. Oh, but you have, have you not? *So you should know better!*" he stormed, pausing to dart daggers at her. "My depravity is not without its risks, however. I wear countless scars because my back has been flayed by these creatures clawing my flesh in the throes of passion. They fight over me! It's a wonder I ever leave such pleasures behind!" Jacek bellowed the last bit. His strident voice matched the generous arm gestures accompanying it.

She had craned her head round when he began his outburst, and now she gawked at him with owl eyes. Her expression seemed to be one of astonishment and contrition, but it did little to assuage him. He narrowed his eyes at her. "It's time to go."

Jacek stalked away. The horses had been foraging, and he stripped off his gloves as he neared them. Keeping his back to Oliwia, he unbuckled, rebuckled, and unbuckled again. As his hands flew over the trappings, his mind turned over her words.

She brings out the worst in me because she thinks *the worst of me!*

Oliwia was the only woman he'd dreamt of for as long as he could remember, the only one he'd wanted. She had consumed him, cursed him, left him too hollow for anyone else. And now she had the cheek, the gall, to accuse him of keeping not just one, but a multitude of lovers—*and* fathering their children!

Sweet Jesus Christ, Oliwia!

Is this what she thought of him? An indiscriminate, licentious scoundrel? Based on what? Not his actions, surely. *The audacity of the woman!*

He cinched the buckles more tightly on the animals. They grunted and shifted, and he loosened the fastenings. He ran his hand over each flank before readjusting everything yet again.

He turned to call her over, but she was nowhere in sight. *Now where has she gone?*

"Oliwia!" he hollered. "Time to go!" No answer.

Cursing under his breath, he walked back to the cloak and heard rustling in a nearby stand of shrubs. His blood froze, and his hand gripped the hilt of his sabre. As he began to slide it from its sheath, she emerged from the bushes.

"I had to, um, well, um …"

She shrugged and fluttered her big eyes, peeping at him innocently. Slamming the sabre back into its scabbard, he jerked his thumb toward the horses. As annoying as she was, as irritating as she was, she still lit a blazing torch of desire in him, which only added to his aggravation. He was struggling not to be mollified by the petite, perfectly formed beauty gazing at him with her luminous, remorseful aquamarine eyes. He was losing the battle.

"What?" he shouted belligerently, stupidly. "Why do you look at me like that?"

"I am sorry, Jacek. I did not mean to … to …"

He exhaled and clasped his hands behind his back, feet apart, in his usual soldier's stance. The uncharacteristic, explosive counterblast had deflated him, and though he willed himself to remain outraged, the effort was melting away more quickly than a fragment of ice under a scorching summer sun. Maybe he shouldn't be looking at her.

Instead, he asked the question that riled him the most. "Oliwia, how can you think me guilty of these appalling accusations you have thrown at my doorstep? If I truly were such a man, then I would indeed merit your scorn and the title of womanizing libertine—and then some."

She said nothing, just kept wide eyes fixed on him. Exasperated, he said, "For pity's sake, whatever else you think of me, say you do not believe me guilty of such heedless behavior."

His earnest tone had lost its harsh edge, regaining most of its usual composed, deep timbre. Though his face was still firmly screwed in a frown, the anger had fled. Had she accused him unfairly? Had she gotten it wrong? The words she'd heard over the years had become linked with the pictures they'd conjured until she'd believed they were real: him in a cozy cottage with a beautiful woman and a child upon his knee, more at his feet; him lying beside a flawless noblewoman he held in his powerful arms, their naked bodies intertwined. She hadn't *wanted* to believe any of it was real, but it was difficult to dislodge what she'd accepted for so long.

More images and words whirred through her head. The images, what she had witnessed with her own eyes, were of him staying dutifully in camp; avoiding myriad ladies who sought him out, scowling at them; seeking *her* out whenever he returned from a mission. Offering *her* his smile. No one else.

It struck her in that moment that these were the truths she should have heeded.

Oh, dear God. What an imbecile I've been!

"I think … I am beginning to better understand the schemes of people who … who have told me things about you to their own purpose, people I foolishly believed for years," she said forlornly.

He stood tall, a perplexed look replacing the scowl on his striking features. She had nothing left; nothing remained to forfeit. So she continued before he could interrupt.

"What I know of their designs I will relay, if you will hear me as I have listened to you. It is immaterial what you think of me, but you must know the entire tale. Let me begin with Lady Katarzyna, who, on her deathbed, made Eryk and I swear an abominable oath to marry."

Jacek's confused expression deepened, knotting his eyebrows. "What?"

"I did not know, and Eryk only told me after we wed, but she'd prepared me to take her place since the beginning, when Filip and I first arrived. I would not have been allowed to wed anyone else unless Eryk permitted it, and for a while after Katarzyna died, I thought myself safe, for his grief consumed him. I prayed he would never call upon me to uphold the oath. But eventually he grew to … to accept the idea. He learned how I felt about you, and he …" She bit her lip. "He promised if I did not submit, he would destroy you. At the very least, he would have stopped you ever getting your land. Worse, I believed he would kill you. And he would have sent Filip far away." Her breath hitched. "I saw no other way, Jacek, so God forgive me, I refused you. But never because I wished to."

He shifted his weight. "Why did you not tell me? What you tried to say earlier … You truly did not wish to marry Eryk? You did *not* love him?"

She shook her head vigorously. "Never like that."

He crossed his arms. "For someone who did not want someone else, you were very convincing. I believed you." His tone was even. No contempt, no condemnation. *Yet.*

"It was the only way I knew to prevent you going to him, challenging him. I could not have lived with myself knowing I had been the reason you would never get your land, or, far worse, if I had precipitated your death. As it was, I could barely live with myself knowing the pain I brought you." Tears suddenly clogged her throat. She tried to swallow but couldn't.

"You said you were eager to wed him," he said softly, as if to himself.

Now the tears fell in earnest, and she let them come. "Oh, dear God," she wailed. "It tore me apart to say those awful words. But I had to. Can you not see?"

He raked a hand through his hair, his expression unreadable. She pulled in a deep breath and stepped closer, where she could clearly see his eyes. They drilled into hers.

"I know it's unforgiveable," she said. "I suppose 'tis impossible to understand, but I did not want him. I admired him as one would an uncle, and the thought of ..." She suppressed a shudder. "I tell you this truth, my truth, so you might understand why I did what I did."

Jacek's broad shoulders seemed to ease. He swung his head up, looking at the canopy as if taking in the pleasures of a warm, carefree day. Swiping at her cheeks, Oliwia sank to the cloak in a miserable heap.

Chapter 11

Grace Before Salvation

A lacy green ceiling wavered overhead. Between playful, twitching leaves peeked brilliant blue sky. Wisps of crisp white cloudstuff moved at a leisurely pace, and the horses nickered softly in the background. The smell of sweet, plump grasses filled Jacek's nose. A perfect late-spring day.

He swung his eyes to Oliwia. She wiped tears from her cheeks, and her slight shoulders dropped as her breath fled. Her glistening eyes stared somewhere far distant. Stepping toward her, he unbuckled his sword belt and dropped it on a corner of her cloak, then settled himself beside her. Lifting her chin, he tilted her head so her eyes met his. She did not resist. Her dark lashes were clumped in starpoints, framing her pale blue eyes.

"What do you mean, Lady Katarzyna prepared you?"

She blinked, her eyes rimming again.

"Tell me," he gently urged. "I want to understand. Please."

She began speaking. As the story spilled from her, he listened quietly beside her on the cloak, their bodies so close he could feel warmth radiating from her. His face masked the clenching in his stomach with each revelation. She had thrown herself away for him, then grappled with all of it alone. He had failed to safeguard her. Instead, he had blamed her for his wretchedness. He'd cursed her. Been angry with her. Despised her.

With another lurch in his gut, he recalled the words he'd spewed at her—mere hours ago. The enormity of her sacrifice leveled him. Why hadn't he seen it? Suddenly, it was as though a heavy, dusty curtain had been pulled back and the sun's rays washed everything clean in its dazzling light, uncovering what had been in front of him all along.

"In the buttery that day, had you already decided?" He stared at his boot toe.

"When you asked me to go away with you, for an instant I held hope I could run and all would end well. But when you said he could never stop you, I realized what I must do. I held on to you because I could not bear to let you go." She sniffled. "I was fond of Eryk, but I never wanted him or his wealth."

In a small voice, she said, "I only wanted you."

Her eyes shimmered with indelible sorrow. In stark contrast, a glimmer of hopefulness—something he'd long despaired of—flooded him. He picked up one of her hands, marveling at its pearly delicacy in his own tanned one. It felt good resting there. So feminine, like her. So fragile, unlike her. *If only I'd known* ...

A joyful laugh escaped him. He cleared his throat, recovering himself. "Oliwia, from whom did you hear stories about my supposed scandalous ways?"

She glanced away.

"I would know my accusers to better understand why you placed faith in their words."

She squirmed. "I heard it first from a garrison soldier. He ... he said you had, um, companions, and children, awaiting you wherever you—"

"Is this a soldier who took part in campaigns with me?" He rummaged through his brain for the identity of this deceitful brother-in-arms.

"I do not believe so, no." She gave him a contrite look and picked at her cloak.

A memory flashed in his head. "Was the soldier George MacMillan?"

She drew in a breath and nodded.

"Did it occur to you he might have a motive to besmirch me?"

Her porcelain skin pinked. "Why?"

He shrugged. "If he believed our friendship made me his rival for your affections, he might say such things to turn you against me."

Her eyes grew round, like twin moons. "What do you know of him?"

Calmly, he replied, "I know he kissed you and Kasimir stopped him doing more."

Her mouth dropped open.

Jacek swallowed a smirk. "And it's good Kasimir did. MacMillan left the garrison shortly after when one of the miller's daughters accused him of getting her with child."

"I thought Kasimir made him go."

Jacek shook his head.

"He would not marry her?" She appeared astounded.

"She would not marry *him*. He'd forced himself on her, and several other maids—including her young sister. She married her sweetheart instead and was grateful he would still have her and raise the babe as his own."

Oliwia stared at him slack-jawed. She blinked, then opened and closed her mouth several times. Were she not so lovely, he might have likened her to a fish.

"So a scoundrel accused me, behind my back, of his own heinous deeds. Who else poisoned you against me?"

She tried pulling her hand away, but he kept it trapped between both of his. It fluttered, like a songbird attempting to escape.

She bit her lower lip, her expression crestfallen. "Two I trusted to speak the truth. Lady Katarzyna told me you would never look my way because … because you had so many … and Eryk said the same. I believed the wrong people."

He arched an eyebrow at her. "One wanted you to fulfill her schemes, and the other simply wanted you. You could not know they deceived you. But why did you never ask me? Why did you not trust *me*?" The question wedged in his heart even as it escaped his lips.

"How could I? I was nothing, a girl, and you were this … this tower of intimidation. Besides, I forever witnessed maids and elegant ladies pursuing you." She pressed a finger to the side of her mouth. "Should I have come to you and said, 'Pan Jacek, satisfy my curiosity. I have heard tales of your romantic conquests and would very much like you to explain yourself.'"

He chuckled wryly. "I suppose not." Then he stood, brushing the back of his żupan. "I must speak to the guards."

Oliwia leaned back on her hands, tracking Jacek as his broad back disappeared over the rise. She gathered her legs to her and laid her cheek on her knees. He had listened quietly to the awful truth of it all while it tumbled from her in fits and starts. He'd squeezed her hand during the hardest bits, and she'd drawn courage from his touch, strong and warm, as her hand had nestled in his. She had wrung it all out with no detail unsaid. When she'd finished and searched his deep blue eyes, she hadn't discerned what thoughts lingered there. The confession likely did nothing to nudge his regard, but he had deserved to know. Though his spiteful words still stung, what he thought mattered to her more than she could have ever known. It always had, since they'd first become friends. Time had changed nothing.

She looked up. The sun was well beyond its zenith; evening was on its way. Staring out over the lake, she watched bubbles rise and pop on its surface between tall, reedy grasses. Behind her, the guards' laughter carried on the breeze like gentle murmurs.

Jacek ran back down the slope, startling her. "Henryk sent more guards."

He plopped beside her and handed her a hunk of cheese, a fistful of almonds, and two dried plums. "And they brought food." He unstoppered a wineskin, tilted his head back, and squeezed a generous stream into his mouth. He held it out to her.

She took it. "Did Henryk send a large party?"

"At least double what you rode out with, which is as it should be—what you *should* have started out with."

She felt a small twinge of remorse flare with a flicker of anger.

"Is it time to go?" She looked over the morsels he'd deposited in her hand.

"I fear it is." He offered her a small smile, one that brightened his eyes. "All those bustling women in your quarters will have want of someone to fuss over and will wonder where you've gone. If others have not yet noticed you are missing, they soon will, and they will sound an alarm. There will be no help for it; we'll be swarmed. Besides, it would not do to fuel gossip."

He flicked a few almonds into his mouth and chewed. "Liwi, I've some things to say to you yet. Will you walk with me on the ramparts after supper?"

132

The food suddenly looked unappetizing, the thought of wine no better. "Yes, of course." She drew in a breath. "Jacek, I have never blamed you for hating me. I just hope we can be … friends again."

Without taking his eyes from hers, he scooted closer, scooped up her hand, and kissed each knuckle softly, sweetly, sending a delightful shiver up her arm. Rather than judgment, consternation, or pity, she recognized warmth, affection, devotion, deep and enveloping.

In a tender tone, he said, "I've never hated you, Liwi. In fact, I've never stopped loving you."

The words surprised him as they left his mouth, flowing easily, as if they'd been hovering on his tongue all along. The hint of a smile lifted her cheeks, reaching her eyes. He brushed his thumb over her mouth, then tipped her face up and brought her lips to his. Christ, he'd longed for this! The taste was so much sweeter than he remembered.

She came to life, returning his fire flame for flame. Her hand slid to his neck; the kiss deepened. His mind spun riotously, joy threatening to burst his heart. The guards were forgotten. He pulled her into his lap, enfolding her in his arms as he set about kissing her into oblivion. Something rattled and dug into his hip. Breathless, Oliwia pulled away and began to giggle.

His own breathing was ragged. "What is that?"

She reached into her pockets and produced several sharp stones.

"You were prepared to chuck all those at me?"

"When I heard you coming, I wasn't sure if you were beast or enemy, so I filled my pockets as fully as I could." She proceeded to empty said pockets of their ammunition.

He shook his head, half smiling. "Surely you did not ride out unarmed, Oliwia."

She glanced away.

"How would you have protected yourself if I had been an enemy? A beast?" he chided.

"But you turned out not to be an enemy. A beast, perhaps, but not an enemy." Her eyes, like quicksilver, seemed to dance.

"You need a true weapon on your person at all times. Had you perfect aim, rocks would still not have helped you much. You have a strong arm, but we need to improve your timing and mark. When was the last time you knocked a pheasant out of a bush?"

She laughed, a laugh that shook her whole body. It was lovely, melodic, and it caught him up. When was the last time he'd let merriment take him? For so long, he'd been submerged in misery that he could scarcely believe how quickly his fortune had turned on its head—for the better this time. It felt good.

Chuckles still bubbled in him when Oliwia took him by surprise, capturing his jaw in her hands, planting her mouth squarely on his. He tipped over with her atop him, wrapping his arms around her. She ran her hands over his shoulders and tunneled her fingers in his hair, sending chills over his scalp and down his back. Her touch ignited a burgeoning passion, and he kissed her back, pulling her against him. His mind emptied, refilling with the feel of her soft curves; the taste of her mouth, berries and honey; and the fragrance engulfing him—lemon, a trace of mint, the sweet scent of her skin.

Jacek lost one hand in her thick waves and splayed the other against the small of her back as he shifted her body alongside his. Oliwia soughed and pressed herself against him. As unquenchable fire coursed through him, his memories and fantasies were supplanted by the real flesh-and-blood woman. He kissed her long and deep, his tongue exploring her succulent mouth while he roamed his hands over her, rediscovering her. The lyrical moans rising in her throat sent him closer to an irretrievable edge.

One of the horses shook its head, jingling its bridle, and snuffled loudly, bringing Jacek's virtuous voice to the fore before his overpowering want could carry him off completely.

Gasping, he pulled back and peered at her. "The guards stand by. We must stop or risk their discovering exactly what I have in mind at this moment."

She brought his head back to hers and breathed, "Just a few minutes longer, Jacek. *I* would discover what you have in mind at this moment."

With barely a rational thought in his quiver, he quickly abandoned the idea of denying her. Instead, he pressed her onto her back, keeping the bulk of his weight to the side. She spread her hands over his shoulders, tugging him closer, urging him more fully on her.

"This is no soft mattress, Liwi, sweet. I will crush you," he mumbled against her neck.

She whispered back, "No, you will not."

He kissed his way up her throat and nibbled her earlobe. "If I put my full weight on you, I *will* crush you."

She began laughing. "Oh dear! How ever will this work?"

He rolled off and propped himself on an elbow, grinning, and ran his fingertips along her cheek. "We will find a way."

A gentle breeze had picked up, and it ruffled the grasses surrounding them, bringing the sounds of horses and men drifting along its invisible waves. Oliwia expelled an extended sigh. She pushed a lock of hair from his eye before drawing herself up to a seated position. Reluctantly, he followed and led her and the horses to the awaiting guards.

Jacek rode beside Oliwia as they made their way back to the castle, oblivious to the fight the spirited stallion gave him with every step. Stealing glances at her, he suppressed the silly grin quirking his lips. In turn, she caught his eye and gave him demure smiles that lit him up. Any guard paying attention to their silent exchanges might guess the why of them, but they seemed diverted by their trek. He turned his mind to more urgent matters: securing Oliwia's hand for himself, even as he reconciled his guilt over Lady Eugenia. He would break his word for the first time in his life. To a man he held in great esteem.

Chapter 12

Familiar Strangers

It was late afternoon when they entered Biaska's outer gates, the guards peeling off to the garrison while Jacek and Oliwia continued into the courtyard. As they approached the keep, a clamor arose in a cloud of dust before them. Jacek trotted ahead. Two villagers, each restrained by a Biaska guard, shouted at one other, their anger rendering their words unintelligible.

"What the devil is going on?" Jacek bellowed.

Oliwia reined in beside him, and he extended his arm to warn her back. But she urged her mount ahead of his, halting between the arguing men. Alarmed, Jacek followed, hand on his hilt, but she held up her hand while looking down upon the fellows embroiled in the fracas.

"Why do you quarrel on my doorstep?" she demanded.

One villager, an elder, began to speak, but his adversary protested, drowning him out.

Oliwia spun. "Quiet, or I will have you removed!"

"You!" she called to the village elder. "State the quarrel."

An audience gathered while the elder complained of being insulted, not shown proper reverence, when the villager refused to drink with him.

Oliwia swiveled to the villager. "Now you may speak." After a meandering series of disparaging remarks against the elder, she cut him off.

Jacek sat back, fascinated, as she berated them both. "You come here and disturb my peace over petty squabbles. Is this not a matter for the tribunal?"

The elder piped up. "Begging your pardon, m'lady, but your husband *was* the tribunal. Since his death, no dispute has been deliberated nigh on two months."

Oliwia stilled, calculations flitting over her face. "Tell everyone with a complaint to submit it in writing within two days. I will hear them in Biaska's great hall three days hence."

The elder's surprise mirrored Jacek's—and every other man's present. Jacek's, however, was tinged with amused admiration. Judging by their incredulous expressions, none shared his attitude.

Oliwia must have detected their reluctance too. "Would you prefer to be heard in a *different* court?"

The men gawped at her. "They don't understand our way, lady," the elder protested.

"The choice is yours," she said.

The elder darted his eyes to Jacek. Jacek shrugged. *Not my fight, old man.* The elder twitched his gray caterpillar moustache and puffed. "Yes, m'lady."

"I look forward to it." She turned her back on them all.

Jacek caught her up and helped her dismount. "Brilliant." He swallowed the laugh caught in his throat.

Oliwia's hand flew to her forehead. "Merciful God, I should have appointed Tomasz in Eryk's stead, not myself. You will help me, yes?"

Now he let the laugh escape. "Liwi, I do not see that you need my help. You've come a long way since the days you could barely ask Feliks for a count of caparisons on your own." He grinned. She looked at him with a plea in her eyes, and a compulsion to help her surged in him. "What little experience I have settling affairs between civilians comes from governing Silnyród, and folk there fear I am as likely to use a weapon as a decree, so I hear few complaints. But I will ensure everyone conducts themselves in an orderly manner. You have doubtless caused an uproar. I wager many will come just to watch a woman preside."

"And to judge *her*," she muttered.

Privacy was a rarity, and the garden that night was no exception, so they strolled in the obscurity of the upper ramparts on the castle's far side. Built between two limestone formations that resembled knobby-headed, long-faced giants, the walkway spanned nearly two furlongs. At its farthest point from the keep, it rose along a rock ridge to a set of steps carved into the crag's slope. A guard tower stood at the top of the stairs, though few sentries patrolled here.

"When do you return to Silnyród?" Oliwia asked as they ambled.

Disquiet unsettled him. "After I've gathered what I need. Not before the hearings."

She plucked at her sleeve and nodded. "Is Lesław in grave danger?"

"Not grave, though he is hobbled at present."

"Must you return? Is there no other there capable of command?"

"No one experienced. My duty lies there as well as here, and as 'tis only a small garrison, I've no choice." His own words rang bleak and hollow in his ears.

He ignored a pang of guilt and pulled in a deep breath. "Liwi, there are things I must say to you. I pray God you will find it in your heart to forgive me." As they strolled side by side, he kept his hands firmly fastened behind him to prevent them wandering to some part of her—the wisps framing one side of her face, for instance, that he longed to brush behind her ear.

"For the scolding?"

He shook his head. "Not for scolding you, no. Well, yes, for that too, and for behaving like a churlish lout. But mostly for misjudging you. When I learned of your betrothal, I felt … betrayed. Anger blinded me. I should have considered more carefully before losing my head. I always fancied myself your protector, but I did not safeguard you this time. *You* in fact safeguarded *me*. I find the twist rather difficult to stomach."

"If you fancied yourself my protector, why did you never declare yourself?"

Jacek hesitated revealing himself and began his narrative reluctantly, but Oliwia listened with a quiet empathy that nudged him to forge on. Leaves quivered and swayed in the night breeze, and torchlight threw lacy patterns to dance upon the stones.

As he talked, bits of crust that had for so long contained his yearning fell away. Much as the meat was exposed when a lobster's shell was peeled back, Jacek laid himself bare. Oddly, it dispelled the anguish he had abided.

"Liwi, I never declared myself because I wanted the land first, to prove my worth. By the time I recognized my vanity, I was too late." He paused. "Are you still angry with me?"

A wave of Oliwia's hair tumbled forward, and she pushed it off her face. "No, I am not angry with you. Are you not angry with me?"

He took her hand and squeezed it. "No."

"Despite my accusations and calling you a—merciful God, the rocks!"

"You should not remind me," he chuckled. Warmth spread through him.

A serious frown scrunched her features. "You do think me in danger?"

"Yes, you and Adam."

"Eryk left a will. As his widow, I may use his income, his holdings, and personal belongings as I see fit for the duration of my life. Is that not enough?"

"Not to protect your widow's rights or to protect Adam's inheritance. If a blackguard takes them, it leaves you both with nothing."

"But if I remarry, my husband gets the estate."

"Then choose the *right* husband. One with no designs on the estate." Suddenly, he was careening toward uncharted depths.

"Like the sort of candidate you proposed? With his own fortune?"

"Yes, that is one sort of candidate, if he is not greedy." He paused a beat. "Another is a man for whom your wealth is not what drives him, even though he possesses few riches of his own. Everything to do with *you*, your safety, is his overarching purpose."

"Such a man exists?"

"He does."

"And you will negotiate the contract?" Did her voice betray a smirk?

Jacek stopped and faced her. The shrill cry of a nighthawk tore through the gloom, pulling his attention to the sky, where he saw no stars—the canopy was shrouded by ominous clouds. Dampness clung to his hair but not his dry throat. He swallowed, trying to coat it.

"Earlier today I asked, ah, if there was any man of your acquaintance you would wed—"

"And you stopped me answering."

"Another instance of my boorish behavior. Will you answer me now?"

"There *was* one. But ..."

Her words undid him, threatening to cleave him. His heart leapt to his throat, cutting off his speech. Her luminous gaze fixed on his, unwavering.

"Henryk?" he croaked at last.

She rolled her eyes.

"I knew I should have thrashed him long ago," he muttered.

"Certainly not Henryk!" she retorted. "Some women are immune to his charms, you know, and I am one of them. He is an adult Filip to me. No, not an adult at all—just Filip on a larger scale and much more dangerous."

"Who, then?" He held his breath.

Oliwia's heart rattled inside her rib cage as she eyed the very handsome man whose hopeful gaze rested on her. She'd dreamt of this moment, and yet ... And yet, would attaching herself to him feel like another yoke was cinched about her neck? Is that what she was preparing to do right now, bind herself, like a starry-eyed girl in the seductive, black-velvet night? This was a man whose truculence was frequently on display. A man who would more often be away than beside her. A man who drew women to him, women she would forever wonder about, be jealous of. Would he treat his oath of fidelity as lightly as Eryk had?

Torchlight capered on Jacek's hair, streaked in gold, and reflected the bottomless depth of his eyes. She checked herself reaching up and running her fingers through his strands. Shadows played over his powerful jaw, highlighting muscles that bunched and twitched.

"Oliwia? Not Henryk, then, but might that one be a friend to him? And is there aught that man can do to dispel your doubts?" His hand tightened on hers. "Liwi, please tell me I'm not too late yet again."

She might have to marry, but this time she had a say about whom she would marry. The only one she'd ever considered now stood beside her.

"You are not too late," she murmured.

Jacek's shoulders seemed to drop several inches, and his features eased.

It took her a beat to find more words. She tried not to stare at his mouth. "What of your estate, your command in Podolia?"

His eyes shifted, as if calculating, then pierced hers anew. "When Lesław recovers, I will place him in charge. Unless Eryk penned a letter to the king before his death, there is no estate." He leaned his forehead against hers. "Nor do I care. All I care about stands before me now."

He cradled her face in his hands. "Lady Oliwia Krezowska, I beg you, consent to be my wife, my Aphrodite, and bless me with heaven on earth."

Her breath flew from her lungs, and a moment passed before she recovered. "If I am to agree, Jacek, I must first hear a promise from you."

He brushed his thumb over her bottom lip. "Anything. What is it you wish of me? I will grant you anything within my power."

"Swear to me, on your honor as a hussar and everything holy, that you will love and care for Adam as if he were your own—*our* own. You must raise him as you have raised my brother. If you agree, then you have my promise."

"I would never suppose to win you without him—or Filip—in the bargain. Your son needs a father, and I would be honored to raise him as my own. Adam will be Biaska's lord, and I will pledge him my fealty and steward his holdings until he comes of age. This is a promise I swear before you and before God. Yes, Liwi, I give you my oath—gladly."

Oliwia's eyes brimmed.

"So, my sweet Liwi, I have made my promise to you. Will you now make yours to me? Will you do me the great honor of becoming my wife?"

She nodded the "yes" wedged in her chest.

He looked around, then crushed her to him and kissed her thoroughly. When the kiss ended, she threw her arms about his neck. "Oh yes. A thousand times, yes," she whispered.

Jacek couldn't recall a time when he'd been happier. Everything he wanted he held in his arms; he would not risk losing it.

When they disentangled themselves from the embrace and he saw her frowning, he placed his finger on the tip of her nose. "I see your mind grinding other thoughts."

She ran her hands up his arms. "I was wondering if Tomasz should prepare a marriage contract before you leave."

Still holding her, Jacek flinched and darted his eyes to the ground. "What is there to put to paper? When I return, you will marry me, and I will marry you." He shrugged with a nonchalance he didn't feel.

"Yes, but should there not be a formal arrangement? Especially where Biaska is concerned?"

"Liwi, there is something you should know."

Reluctantly, he set her apart from him. "When I first returned, I discovered Henryk suspected me of killing Eryk."

Her eyes flew wide. "*What?* Why?"

Jacek smiled at her reaction. "Henryk knew how I felt about you, and he had to consider anyone with a motive. He felt I had a strong reason, and he was right. But I did not kill Eryk."

Her voice rose. "Henryk knows this, yes?"

"He knows. But it does not mean others do not suspect the same. So I think it would be wise not to divulge our plans until I return. I shall not even tell Henryk. But I will be back before summer's end, and I will get Father Augustyn's blessing, and we can announce it then, when the grieving has subsided a bit. We will wed right after the banns are called. I promise it won't be long—a few months at most."

Oliwia stared at him for a few beats, then nodded. "Yes, I suppose that makes sense."

She began tugging at the silver chain beneath her bodice, where her mother's cross was ever suspended. Freeing it, she pulled it over her head and placed it in Jacek's hand, folding it closed with both of hers.

"What are you doing, Liwi?"

She pressed his hand. "It is a token from me to you, Jacek. It is my heart. I wish you to wear it and keep it close. For me. It will keep you safe and bring you back to me."

Astonished, Jacek opened his palm, revealing the necklace gleaming within. "But this is all you have left of your mother, Liwi. It is too precious to give away."

She shook her head and pushed his hand when he tried to return it. "Take it. Please. Consider it a wedding gift."

Relenting, he pulled it over his head, kissing the cross before tucking it beneath his żupan, close to the lock of her hair he always carried.

"I will bring it back to you," he vowed, "and I will place it around your neck. In the meantime, I wear it with honor."

A wet morning wind ruffled clouds and rattled leaded windows as Jacek sat beside Oliwia and Filip in the packed village church, his eyes wandering over the partially dismantled castrum doloris. Before Eryk's burial, work had been postponed—even the simple grinding of grain or spinning of wool had stopped—and folk had leapt to their labors after the funeral. But today was Sunday, and work was once again suspended, replaced by devotion. So too was the castle of mourning suspended, its pillars resembling a leering skeleton.

Now as Eryk's coffin portrait looked down upon them all, Father Augustyn bid the congregation pray, and pray Jacek did. Locking out the feel of Oliwia's leg brushing his while he knelt, he begged for forgiveness for his deception. When Oliwia had spoken of the contract, the specter of the one he'd signed—and the woman who came with it—had loomed, threatening to destroy what he most cherished. So Jacek had quickly worked it all out in his head, even as he'd held Oliwia in his arms.

Upon his return to Silnyród, he would immediately visit Matejko Manor, for such delicate matters needed to be settled in person. If everything went according to plan, Jacek's friendship with Klemens would be forfeit, along with his reputation as a man of his word. Though these losses and their consequences would doubtless prove thorny, they paled in comparison to the alternative—an alternative he would not accept as long as he drew breath.

Only when Oliwia was his wife, after they'd exchanged vows and consummated their union, would he confess to her his broken betrothal. Until then, he would not risk inviting the ghosts of non-existent lovers to linger between them and give her reason to bolt. As her husband, he might be subjected to her formidable wrath, but he reckoned she would eventually forgive him. Not honorable, but logical.

He had other practical reasons. One did not enter into the same agreement with two different people, nor should a widow announce her betrothal to a new husband a month after burying the last. It was unseemly—especially when said new husband's name had been bandied about in connection with the death of the first.

So Jacek set his scheme and was anxious to execute it even as he asked God to absolve him of it. He should have been steeped in guilt, but he couldn't muster it; his joy vanquished it.

As his mind churned, his body went through the motions of Mass. He sang, prayed, chanted, knelt, sat, and stood as he solidified his strategy. Now, how best to help her in the short time he remained?

During the Gospel, he, like other knights, raised his sabre. He looked about, surprised at their numbers. Some were familiar, others not. As he made his way to receive Communion, he glanced up and down the benches and made note.

After walking Oliwia out of the church, he told her he would join her at the castle later.

"I've some business to attend."

She raised one eyebrow. "On God's day?"

"Enemies plot, even on Sunday, and so must I. I will tell you more later."

"You will sup with Filip and me this evening, yes?"

"Only if you promise to join me on the ramparts afterward," he replied.

"What, again?" she countered with mock surprise.

"The sky appears to be clearing. I wager it will be a warm night under a bright moon. Perfect for strolling the ramparts." He grinned.

Henryk, who stood beside a comely young woman, had been darting inquisitive eyes between Jacek and Oliwia. Jacek returned the looks blankly, masking his impatience. After Oliwia and Filip left, he called him over.

"What is it?" Henryk swiveled his head to the woman who gave him a little wave.

"Have you time to visit the brothel now?" asked Jacek.

Henryk quickly turned back to Jacek, a question mark screwed on his face. "What?"

"The brothel." Jacek jerked his chin toward Henryk's companion. "She's a distraction to be sure, but certainly you've not utterly forgotten your favorite place in—"

Henryk laughed. "Are you inviting me to accompany *you* to a brothel, Jacek?"

"No. I make for the tavern."

"What the devil are you saying?" Henryk seemed to have forgotten the woman.

"We've an abundance of lords about. I suspect some came for the funeral and remain. I wish to speak to as many as I can. They might be keen to soldier. I expect I'll find them either in the tavern or the brothel. You're better known at the brothel, so …"

Henryk glanced back at the woman. "I like this one, Jacek."

"You don't even *know* this one," Jacek countered.

"My point exactly."

"Arrange a time to meet her later and come with me now. Two in one day."

"She's a townsman's daughter, only here for the night." Henryk paused and glanced at her again. She smiled back sweetly. "She may take some convincing."

Jacek raised an eyebrow. "Doesn't appear so. I wager she'll wait."

Henryk smirked. "You'd better be right, my friend. I may like her, but not enough to venture into a wretched town after her. Time spent in her company must be here, before she leaves."

"Come. I'll buy the first drink."

"Forget the drink. Buy the first whore."

When Oliwia climbed to the ramparts, her eyes immediately found Jacek along the limestone crenellations, illuminated by the setting sun. Her heart leapt at the sight of him. With his side to her, he stood tall and straight-backed, his hands clasped behind him. He turned his head toward her and smiled, his eyes shining in the amber light. He held out his hand, and she checked the urge to rush to him. She peeked over her shoulder at the guards before hugging his arm; he covered her hand with his. As she leaned her head against him, his warmth seeped under her skin. Thusly entwined, they sauntered along the narrow path.

"Will you tell me now about your important business today?" she asked.

He looked down his straight nose at her, his warm breath ruffling her hair.

"I spent the day in the tavern," he said evenly.

"Drinking was your business?"

"Liwi, do you know how much business is done in a tavern?"

She let out a snort.

He picked up her hand and kissed it, then tucked it back in the crook of his arm. "I sought soldiers for the garrison. You may not know this, Liwi sweet, but the best place to find an idle soldier is either in a tavern or a brothel. I went to the tavern and sent Hen—" Jacek made a sort of choking noise.

"Naturally," she said dryly. "Were you successful?"

"We did not do as well as I had hoped." He blew out a breath. "It seems these men are either long past warring, have never warred, are on their way to a conflict, or still begrudge Biaska for not siding with them in the Sandomierz Rebellion."

Oliwia frowned. "The one led by Pan Mikołaj Zebrzydowski?"

"Yes, the Zebrzydowski Rebellion. They are one and the same."

"But that was seven years ago!"

"Nevertheless, some will never fogive Biaska for marching with Hetman Żółkiewski to fight on the king's side. I was at the battle in Guzów, where the rebellion was put down. It was swift and brutal."

"You were there?" she yelped.

"I was a nineteen-year-old serving Eryk's company. We were there to reinforce Żółkiewski, but he didn't engage. Didn't have to. The grand hetman of Lithuania, Chodkiewicz, led the royal troops to defeat the rebels. Our force remained idle."

"So you were an idle soldier. If I had looked for you, would I have found you in a tavern or a brothel?" She bit back a smile.

"Neither," he replied smoothly, "for you wouldn't have looked for me. The battle was in July. You were what, twelve?"

A clever dodge. "I was twelve."

"And no doubt just as cheeky then as you are now." He smirked.

"So no new soldiers, then?"

"Perhaps a few. Time will tell. But truly, we don't need a large force to defend this fortress, so do not fret overmuch. Men enough will come."

They strolled a few moments in silence, she lost in her thoughts.

"There is much I have yet to learn about you," she finally said.

"For instance?"

"For instance, we have not spoken of children. How many do you wish for?" She felt a blush creep over her cheeks. The familiar fear of childbirth bubbled, then receded.

"As many as you and God are willing to give me. A manor full," he declared. "And at least one girl who has her mother's beautiful eyes."

The last remark shot straight to her heart, but she scoffed and arched her eyebrows at him nonetheless. "Would you have me forever heavy with child, then?"

He considered momentarily. "Yes. Especially if it means forever *trying* to get you with child. *That* is a very pleasurable prospect." He waggled his eyebrows.

Oliwia's mouth dropped open. *"Jacek!"*

"What? Is something wrong?" His tone was overly innocent.

"You are rather forward." Propriety stifled her smile.

"I merely speak the truth." He stopped, raised her hand to his lips, and planted a chaste kiss, giving her a sly look. "We've established I'm no womanizer—at least I pray we are past all that. But have no doubt, Liwi— thoughts of, ah …" he raised his eyes skyward as if searching, then resumed, "spending time with you in the bedchamber often distract me in a wholly enjoyable fashion."

A small gasp escaped her. She should have been outraged but failed utterly in the conjuring. His dark eyes twinkled; he seemed to be deriving a great deal of amusement from her discomfort. The night air suddenly grew heavy, stifling, and Oliwia fought the urge to fan herself. She let out a nervous laugh.

"I thought I knew your nature, but I see I was mistaken. These many years, I've observed your terribly, um, grave character, even at a grand celebration. You were even serious in the matter of a dance."

"Well, I have a high standard, you see. Rarely does anyone measure up." He caressed her hand, still tucked in the crook of his elbow.

"Yet I do remember one lady …"

"Only one now. That's a relief. Who is this mysterious creature?"

"The Lady Izabela," she said triumphantly, "from the tournament four years ago. You danced with her all night and laughed every time she whispered in your ear—which was quite often, I would add. You even took her outside. For an hour! Now that I am bit wiser, I better understand the lure of a dead garden at night."

Jacek swallowed, and the small knot of his Adam's apple bobbed.

"Oh. Have I said something wrong?" A sliver of remorse stabbed her.

"No. I just had not thought of her in a long while," he replied quietly. Then he stammered, "I, uh, had known her many years and was sotted with drink at the time. She was to wed within the month and asked me to … to … escort her through the garden."

Oliwia slid him a sidelong glance. "Is that what you call it?"

"I confess I do not recollect much of that night, though I do recall being annoyed with Henryk for taking *you* outside."

"Were she not betrothed, would you have married her? Were you in love with her?"

He took her by surprise when he hotly replied, "Most assuredly not!"

"Oh, I thought … Well, I always envied her." He looked at her in puzzlement, so she explained, "Katarzyna told me she was a highborn noblewoman from a well-regarded family, that she sewed beautifully, played piano like none other, and her voice put songbirds to shame." Oliwia fluttered her hand in the air.

Jacek stopped. "Liwi, I've never heard you sing. Do you play an instrument?"

Bewildered, she replied wistfully, "I cannot sing, nor can I play any instrument well. Lady Katarzyna used to say I rather reminded her of a screeching cat."

"And sewing?"

Her heart began sinking. "Tolerably, if of the practical sort. But elegant embroidery or lace? No."

"So you cannot sing, you are mistress of no instrument, and you do not sew well. Yet you paint, and there is another thing you can do, which of itself is so extraordinary it outweighs all other gifts combined. Shall I tell you what that is?"

"Yes," she said with trepidation.

"You, my wild beauty, can knock a pheasant out of a bush with one well-placed rock. I shall never go hungry." One corner of his mouth twitched.

She pushed him, then swatted at his arm as he burst into laughter. He pulled her against his chest and stroked her hair, rumbling, "I do not care if you cannot stab at a bit of fabric, or sing, or pluck away at an instrument. What matters is how good you feel, how sweet your kisses taste, and how being near you makes my pulse race. What else is there?"

"Oh." She melted into him, her own pulse racing feverishly.

Remembering herself, she wriggled out of the embrace, and they resumed walking. Overhead, brilliant stars had emerged and freckled the indigo vault. A full moon would rise and obscure the pinpoints of light, but for now the display dazzled. Oliwia's stomach had been fluttering for quite some time and, rather than still itself, only grew more ticklish. The unexpected whimsical side of Jacek delighted her, and she was a giddy young girl the longer she remained in his company, tempted to skip beside him rather than walk. She hauled her mind back on track.

"In spite of your quest for land, I believed you would have taken a wife by now. When I came to this grand castle, I saw the lovely ladies swarm the noble, handsome, self-assured officer and knew you had your pick. Nothing has changed since. And the stories you've told me of your mother's procession of would-be brides—"

"You think me handsome?" he interrupted. A gleam lit his eyes.

She shot him a quick look, shaking her head.

"Well, I did distinctly hear you say noble, self-assured, *and* handsome."

"I'm not certain I should tell you. You seem quite pleased with yourself as it is." She smirked at him, and he tilted his head and grinned at her. The endearing look crushed her defenses.

She rolled her eyes. "All right, then, yes, I admit I do find you somewhat attractive."

"Then it's agreed. You are exceptionally beautiful, and I may be somewhat attractive. We will no doubt make very appealing children together." He paused, scratching his chin, and glanced at her with a concerned look. "Might we discuss how we are to go about it? We have a dilemma to solve, after all, and while I have no wish to squash you, I very much look forward to getting started." He looked her up and down. "Perhaps if we practiced—"

"*Jacek!*"

"What?"

She peeped up at him. "You are flirting with me, lord, and rather boldly at that."

"That I may be, but I am nonetheless earnest—and practical."

149

The sound of clanking rose from the courtyard below, followed by a few friendly voices drifting on the bracing night breeze. A bat on the wing flashed in and out of the darkness. As they sauntered past a sputtering torch, Oliwia turned her head to hide the fierce blush creeping up her neck. Her face would be on fire shortly, but not from any torch flame.

"Have I embarrassed you?" he asked.

"Yes!" she hissed. Bees fairly buzzed in her head.

He looked amused. "Liwi, one thing I've always enjoyed about you is that I can speak to you easily of so many things. And I made this happy discovery early on, on the journey from Vyatov. Since that time, you have been as dear a friend to me as any I've ever had. When I'm not with you, I miss you dreadfully, for I am left alone with naught but my miserable self for company."

"And you are *my* dearest friend, Jacek. I owe you my life, and Filip's, several times over."

"You owe me naught—but your hand, that is." He squeezed said hand and drew in a breath. "Liwi, I am humbled that despite my ill-mannered behavior, you have consented to bestow me with your generous affection. I will spend the rest of our days proving myself worthy of you."

He had once more stolen her breath away, and she knew not what to say. They walked a few more minutes in silence. She looked up at him when she felt her blush finally fade. Her stomach was still somersaulting; perhaps it would calm once she was not so close to him, breathing in his very appealing, very masculine scent.

"It is late, and tomorrow will be here soon. Though I am loath to part from you, I believe it is time we returned the ramparts to the guards and the owls," she said regretfully.

"I would be only too happy to walk beside you until dawn, but I will escort you to your chamber now, as long as I have your promise I will see you first thing tomorrow."

"Of course."

They dragged out their steps to their separate quarters.

After Jacek delivered Oliwia to her door, she entered her now quiet chamber. Gone was the bustling that had been ever-present during the waking hours, and peace imbued the tapestried walls. Nadia lay on her pallet in an alcove, her back to Oliwia. The little maid slept soundly, and naught would disturb her. Oliwia sank into the mattress and sighed, only to rise and prepare herself for bed.

One floor below, Jacek stripped to his breeches and paced the room in bare feet. It was a cavernous chamber dominated by little more than a canopied four-post bed, and it afforded him space to walk about as he pressed his thoughts through the sieve of his mind. Those that dominated were of Oliwia and of his impending departure. When had he faced such a powerful unwillingness to leave before? Never.

He performed his ablutions, pulled off his trousers, and settled himself beneath the counterpane. The evening was warm and sticky, and the window stood open, bringing the smells of lush, damp fields inside. The moon had risen and now washed the chamber in silvery light. Not one normally troubled by sleeplessness, Jacek could not keep his thoughts at bay and rolled about fitfully, devising ways he might steal into Oliwia's bedchamber. He'd gotten away with it once a long time ago, but she'd not had a maid sleeping with her then.

Punching his bolster, he replayed the words and embraces they had exchanged, which did naught to relax him. Much later, he sank into the mattress with a long exhale. On his back, his arm under his head, he shut his eyes. He drifted and dreamed.

"Jacek." Oliwia's voice floated under the hood of sleep.

"Jacek." Her call was soft, distant, musical. It pulled him from slumber much as a net was pulled from the water by a fisherman searching for his catch.

"Jacek."

He broke the surface of sleep. He was not dreaming.

Chapter 13

Moonlight and Magic

Jacek's eyes flew open. He lay in the same position, his head resting on his bicep. Dazzling moonglow illuminated everything in his line of sight. Propping himself up on his elbows, he looked toward the voice.

And there she was.

Oliwia stood at the foot of the bed, shadows and silver playing off her loose, dark curls, her lapis wrap iridescent. One arm hugged the bedpost, and her head rested against the turned wood of the pillar as she looked at him. Panic swept over him and tore away the cobwebs of his reverie. His heart thudded.

"Liwi! What is it? Are you well?" Jacek pulled himself up, ready to spring from beneath the counterpane. But the stirring from hearing her voice was still evident, and he'd lain down with nothing on, so he sat straight-backed against the wooden wall panel and secured the covers about his waist, his foot twitching.

"Everything is fine, Jacek," she hummed. "I could not sleep. I have tried without success and wondered if you were also awake. I am sorry I woke you."

He scrubbed a hand over his face. "Do not be sorry, Liwi. I was merely dozing."

She was all right; his heart decelerated. He patted the bed cover next to him, and she slid onto the proffered seat, perching at the edge of the bed. She turned to him. He reached up and tucked her hair behind her ear, then cupped her soft cheek. She leaned her face into his palm and sighed. Her eyebrows bunched above her moist eyes.

"What troubles you?" he asked gently.

She took his hand and held it in both of hers, keeping her eyes fixed on him.

"Knowing you will soon leave ... after only just discovering ..." Sadness clouded her eyes.

"I will be back," he said lamely, his thumb brushing her palm. "How can I comfort you?"

She cast her eyes to their coupled hands. "Would you ... would you hold me close, just for a little while?"

A tussle broke out inside him. The part that honored her wrestled with the part that wanted her desperately, wanted her now. Masking his inner roiling, he raised her chin so her gaze met his.

"Liwi, I would like to grant your wish. You must know that. But if I do, it will not be like last time. I will not stop at holding you."

Oliwia did not break the gaze. "I understand."

She stood, sliding her hands from his. The desirous part of him slumped in regret, and the nobler part was not nearly as elated as it should have been in its triumph. But then she did something utterly unexpected. She pulled her silk cloak from her shoulders. It slipped the length of her white nightdress to the floor, where it folded onto itself around her bare feet. It made a soft swishing sound, like the whisper of the summer breeze through birch leaves.

Jacek's heart flared and sped up again. Oliwia stood before him, backlit by the moon's otherworldly luminescence. The light radiated through the gossamer fabric draping her body, gilding her in silver.

He swallowed hard. Every nerve in his body twinged and every muscle tensed. He held perfectly still, transfixed as incoherent thoughts careened and collided in his head. Oliwia held his eyes as she slowly, deliberately pulled free the satin ribbon that fastened the nightdress in place about her shoulders. This too slid languidly down the curves of her body, pooling on the wrap. She remained unmoving and silent while he feasted his eyes on her. Moonlight limned her hair and every creamy curvature, and a wildfire that had been smoldering ignited deep inside him, catching fire and setting him ablaze.

"Mother of God, Oliwia, you are the most stunning creature I have ever laid eyes on."

He lifted the bedclothes, and she slid beneath. As she molded her body to him, her smooth, warm skin caressing his, the wrestling match between his integrity and his desire came screeching back to the forefront. He rose above her, cradling her face, and looked into her limpid eyes.

"Are you sure?"

She pushed his hair from his forehead and traced his jaw. "More sure than I have ever been of anything."

He lightly stroked her hand and interlaced his fingers with hers.

"I adore you, Liwi."

As he took her mouth, he shoved his conflicted selves to the outer rim of his consciousness. His last mindful thought was a prayer that, if he were dreaming, he never wake.

Oliwia suffered no bouts of conscience when she decided to shed her clothes and lie with Jacek. Yearning had overpowered her as she fought wakefulness, and it had emboldened her and sent her tiptoeing to his chamber. She had missed so very much with him. Respectability was pulverized by the overwhelming siren call of her want.

When she'd found him sleeping, his lean body had been exposed above the waist, and for long moments she'd watched his smooth, carved chest rise and fall in tranquil cadence while his head rested on his bulky bicep. Her cross lay against his skin, silver metal capturing silver light and winking it back at her. His was a warrior's body—sculpted, strong, and glorious to behold—and looking at him left her breathless. Desire had washed over her, and she'd let it take her along its crest and guide her into his arms.

Now a tidal wave rolled over her as she pressed herself against him, thrilling to the feel of his skin against hers, breathing in his pine-and-earth scent while she roamed her hands over his broad shoulders and back. He was hard-muscled and long-boned, and where she was soft, he was solid, all sinew and steel. Every place his warm, rough hands touched her, wherever his mouth alit on her, a trail of tiny bumps followed. Chills and heat rippled through her, unleashing a flood of sensations she'd only glimpsed before. They swirled together and carried her to a different plane in a spiral of passion.

Their limbs entwined, they became a torpid mass of motion, rolling across the mattress, first he on top and then she. Cool air skimmed her exposed skin where the coverlet had slipped away. His hands swept the length of her body, then crushed her to him as he poised to roll her on her back, but she stopped him, pulling her lips from his. He looked at her through half-closed eyes.

She slid down his body languidly, tasting the mild saltiness of his skin as she explored him with fingers, mouth, and tongue. He surrendered to her touch with a drawn-out, throaty "Jesus!"

It made her feel *powerful*.

The sweet smell of night-scented stock wafted into the chamber, fragrant and heavy in the air. An owl hooted from the ramparts beyond the window, echoed by a call moments later. It all sounded so far away.

Suddenly, he sat up, hooked his strong hands under her arms, and hauled her to him. Tangling his hand in her hair, rasping her name, he urgently brought her lips back to his. Engaging the whole of her mouth, he kissed her ravenously, his need overpowering. She was no longer in control. He flipped her on her back and braced himself above her, locking on her eyes, his sapphire gaze burning into her. She shifted her body beneath his, and he stroked the length of her inner thigh, sending shivers along her fractured senses. His eyes still riveted on hers, he lowered himself between her legs and entered her with a long, slow thrust. Gasping in a sharp breath, she arched into him, then let the breath out in a high-pitched moan.

He froze, his ragged exhales falling warm on her cheek. "Liwi, am I hurting you?"

"No. *Don't stop!*"

He hesitated. She raised her hips and spread her hands over his backside, drawing him deep inside her, the slick banked coals of her core enveloping all of him.

His eyes sparked, and though words tumbled from his lips, she had no idea what he said.

"Now!" she demanded breathlessly.

He resumed and joined with her, and they rocked fiercely into a wild oblivion.

They lay on their backs, arms and fingers interlaced. Oliwia's pounding heart and breathing had returned to their even rhythms, though her skin still tingled. Jacek rolled onto his side, pulling her against him, wrapping her up in his arms and planting warm, sweet kisses on her eyelids and cheeks. She nestled against him, throwing a lazy leg over his.

"Are you cold?" he asked.

"No, I am perfect," she purred, nuzzling a little closer.

He sifted his fingers through her hair, cupped the back of her head, and kissed her forehead. "That you are."

Resting her head against his chest, she felt the vibration of his thumping heart. She stroked his smooth back, then abruptly pulled back and peered at him.

"What is it?" he asked.

"You did not crush me."

"So I didn't." He grinned. "Good that we practiced."

She chuckled, then ran her fingers along his eyebrow, lingering just above, on the divot where his brother had shot him with an arrow as a child. She kissed it, then frowned. "I do not feel the other scars."

"Other scars?"

"Yes. The scars on your back."

His expression grew puzzled. "I'm not sure I know what you mean."

"The scars from all the women you've had in your wagon, in your cot, in your stirrups. At least twelve at a time, you said, and they tore your back in the 'throes of passion' while screaming out what a wonderful lover you are." She suppressed a giggle.

He burst into laughter. "In my stirrups? Twelve? Did *I* say that? I could not have said anything so outrageous."

She smirked. "Nearly so. But I'm beginning to believe it must have been all lies because truly I feel only the one on your shoulder and this one, right here." She feathered her fingers lightly over a raised six-inch line on one side of his waist. He spasmed, and the skin under her touch erupted in gooseflesh.

"Are you ticklish?" She brightened, still stroking the site of the scar.

He grabbed her hand. "Yes. Are you pleased with yourself? Now stop it!"

"But what of the scars?"

"They have all healed over."

She wrestled her hand, caught lightly in his grip, and ran it over his ribs, making him twitch again. "I think you are lying. I don't believe there are any scars, and I don't believe there were any women," she whispered against his lips.

"You certainly did believe it before," he whispered back.

"Yes, well …"

"You were wrong?" He gave her a cockeyed grin.

Without answering, she drew her fingertips down, over a firm buttock, running them along the back of his thigh with a playful touch. His knee jerked.

"Stop!" he laughed.

"Not until you confess the truth of it." Her hand returned to his waist, but now she also nibbled his earlobe and ran the barest tip of her tongue along his corded neck. He rewarded her with a multitude of tics and twinges.

"Stop! I yield! I was out of my mind to say something so ludicrous. There are no scars."

"And the women?" She kissed his cheek while he gathered her hands in one of his.

"Oh, they're real. All the dozens upon dozens you invented in your beautiful, daft head."

His hand clamped on hers when she tried to extract them, and he trapped her head with his, mushing it into the pillow. *His* leg now draped over *hers*, and she was pinned in spite of her spirited squirming.

"It's no use struggling; you are my captive. Now shall we discover where *you* are ticklish?" he mocked, his free hand caressing and probing her tenderest parts.

"Stop!" she shrieked.

"Ooh, here's an enticing soft spot I have yet to explore."

Uncontrollable peals of laughter rolled from her.

"Stop!" She wriggled in vain. *"Mercy!"*

"A kiss first, then mercy you shall have." He relaxed his grip and kissed her. She hiccupped and snuggled back against him. He massaged the back of her neck, and she began to drift. His voice rumbled through him, through her.

"Liwi? Are you still awake?"

"Yes."

"You will still marry me, yes? You must."

She stirred and gazed at his face, painted in shimmering light. He looked at her tenderly as he pushed strands of hair behind her ear. The look tugged at her heart. She ran the back of her finger over his stubbled jaw. He captured her hand and kissed it before tucking it against his chest.

"Why must I?"

He chuckled, his warm breath ruffling her hair. "You have compromised my virtue. You must marry me and set everything right."

"I? Compromised *you?*"

"Yes, *you.* I believe it was *you* who entered *my* chamber and seduced *me.*"

"I could not hear your protests over your moans. Do you now regret what happened and wish it undone?" She kissed his neck.

"Spirit of God, no! Never! If I roast an eternity in hell, I will do so without regret."

"So your precious virtue, is it the only reason I am to become your wife? Or is it that you're to become my husband? Is it reversed when one accuses the other of seduction?" she posed in feigned seriousness.

"No. You must marry me because I am likely to charge off a cliff if you deny me." The grin faded, and he grew solemn. "I can scarcely breathe for thinking of losing you, Liwi."

Tears pricked her eyes. "I love you, Jacek," she murmured.

She pulled his face to hers and kissed him, holding nothing back. The heat from the press of lips and skin sent her into a renewed state of arousal, and he matched her, transforming the nature of the kiss into another show of once-buried, now unrestrained desire. But their lovemaking this time was more leisurely, less frenetic. Her body moved with his in a slower, deeper rhythm until she dissolved with him. Spent at last, she fell asleep in the warm cradle of his arms.

Chapter 14

By Dawn's Early Light

Unable to return to slumber after Oliwia had stolen back to her chamber, Jacek's thoughts remained fixed on her and their night together. His mind repeatedly revisited what it had felt like to hold her close, whisper with her in the dark, be joined deep inside her. All his flimsy fantasies about making love to Oliwia had been erased, faded in a colorless wash. Reality's vibrancy outshone anything he could have imagined.

Pulling on his linen undershirt, he smiled to himself. He'd had little idea what fires were banked in her. For that matter, he had discovered a few surprises simmering inside him—things she had pulled from him and shown him he was capable of when she'd transformed him into a raging inferno. He'd never felt like that—as though fire burned in his blood. With her, he was powerful, unstoppable, in a different sort of way than his warrior self, and he liked it. He craved it. This morning, he should have been sated, but now that he'd had her, it had only whetted his appetite. He wanted her more than he ever had, if that were even possible.

He traipsed down the steps to the hall, where he helped himself to several heaping trenchers of food, constantly scanning for any sign of Oliwia. When at last she sailed down the stairs, his heart lifted, his pulse quickened, his appetite vanished. She was beautiful.

"Good morning," she said with a shy smile.

"It most definitely is." He beamed and pushed his platter away.

Her cheeks pinked. "You've eaten?"

"Yes. You?"

She nodded.

"Good. I have something to show you. Are you wearing your boots?"

She gave him a puzzled look. "Yes, but—"

"Come. You'll see."

Filip raced after them. "Join us," Jacek said. He guided them to the stables.

He leapt to the first rung of a fence enclosing a large corral abutting the stables and surveyed some dozen horses penned within. He held his hand out, pulling Oliwia beside him. Filip clambered up.

Her brows scrunched together. "What—"

"Look at them. What do you see?" Jacek asked with a sweep of his hand.

She shrugged. "Is that the stallion you were riding?"

"These are the new warhorses, Pan Jacek, yes?" Filip sputtered excitedly.

"Correct, Pan Filip."

Filip's curls bobbed, a flush and a grin spreading wide over his face.

"I sought a few horses among the regular stock for my upcoming trip to Silnyród," Jacek continued. "Then I was drawn back to these beauties. Eryk bought warhorses nearly every year, and these were the latest to arrive. They always come from the same breeder in central Podolia. Eryk would have only the best." He dropped his voice. "Just like all else in his life."

Oliwia shot him a sidelong glance, and he winked at her. Quickly, she looked back to the horses, shading her eyes with her hand. "Why do you show us? Will you take them with you?"

He shook his head. "I questioned Tomasz, who told me how much Eryk paid for them, and I began to wonder, why not raise fine specimens such as these here at Biaska?"

Oliwia swiveled her head toward him. "Do you mean breed warhorses? To sell?"

"Breed, train, and sell to towarzysze. They will pay handsomely."

Oliwia's eyes traveled over the horses. "They do seem different. Bigger, grander."

"They're the best of old Polish and Arabian lines bred specially for heavy cavalry. They're average size, but they're fast, strong, withstand the cold, and can stop *and* recover quickly—just what a heavy lancer needs. Jarosława is such a breed."

"How long does it take to train one?"

Before he could answer, Jacek caught Smok coming fast for Filip, head down. "Watch yourself! He bit Marcin."

Filip leapt down just in time, and Smok angled toward Oliwia. Jacek hauled her down and spewed several choice oaths at the dragon.

"Some are easier to train than others," he snickered. "This one is especially belligerent, but he's a handsome beast. And can he fly!"

"Is he trainable?" Oliwia tracked the stallion with her eyes.

"With a heavier hand and more patience, yes, but I wager he's worth it."

She smirked. "He brings to mind someone I know."

Jacek flashed her a grin. "To your question, it takes at least seven years before a charger is ready. And more training follows that. In the end, he still may not prove suitable."

"And you think it wise to raise these here? Wherever will I find men to train them? And how much will I need to pay them for the next seven years?"

"I can train men to train the horses, and I cost nothing. Well, you need not pay me in *złote*, at any rate." She mouthed the word "scoundrel" at him. "We will work it out, Liwi swee—uh, look at that one there, the one the color of Malmsey. He'd be a good one for Filip."

Filip whooped. Oliwia shot Jacek a glare.

"When he's a little older, of course. He will need a horse, Oliwia. 'A Pole without a horse is like a body without a soul.'"

"He's not Polish. He's English."

"No, I'm not. I am Polish, just like Pan Jacek," Filip squawked.

Oliwia rolled her eyes. Jacek shrugged and turned them all toward the keep. "Filip, like any good Pole, you'll complete your chores." When Filip gave him an "I wish to stay with you" look, Jacek lowered his brows at him. Filip exhaled noisily, relented, and scampered away.

Jacek grasped Oliwia's arm. "Come. I've one more thing to show you."

She picked up her skirts, dodging a soupy mud puddle. The castle yard had come to life, smoke and noise belching from the blacksmith's forge, maids chattering around steaming laundry vats, and the fowl clucking and crowing.

"To the ramparts we go." He guided her to the front this time, where the walls overlooked the guard tower and fields beyond.

"See those woods there?" He pointed; she nodded. "They need to cleared, thinned in order to see an approaching enemy. The western border has been peaceful so long that people forget such precautions, but 'tis best to be prepared. And Liwi ..."

He looked down at her light eyes fixed on him and nearly lost his train of thought. "Ah, take the timber and sell what you don't need. Put the money in your coffers. The tenants will owe you labor, so have them do the felling, but wait until after harvest. And consult the hunt master first. Now. Do you see those two redoubts?"

She frowned. "The humps?"

"Those are, or were, redoubts. They had guard towers, but they rotted away long ago. When more soldiers come, post sentries. The thick brush will need to be cleared first. We've kept up with clearing silt and debris from the dry moat, but make sure it continues to be done. I will also tell Henryk."

"I had little idea, Lord Dąbrowski, that you knew so much about managing an estate."

He chuckled. "I know little beyond defending one. Any trained soldier can do the same. You, on the other hand, *really* manage it. The livestock and gardens, kitchens, distillery, brewery, castle staff. The most crucial functions: food, drink, and people to prepare and serve them."

"Always food and drink with you," she laughed.

"Not always." He wiggled an eyebrow at her.

Oliwia's early morning giddiness had receded as the day's duties piled atop one another. Now she sat behind the desk in the solar, reviewing complaints with Tomasz and the village marshal. On the other side of the desk, Jacek licked his fingers after clearing an eye-popping platter. Her mind veered to a different sort of hunger. She inadvertently let out a shuddering breath, and six eyes turned to her. Picking up a piece of parchment, she rattled it overmuch before dropping her head to hide the flush creeping its way to her scalp.

"Um, this complaint from one woman states her neighbor 'did raise her skirts and expose to light her inferior face.' What exactly did she do?"

Jacek coughed; Tomasz tugged his collar; Oliwia's blush deepened, though she was unsure why.

"She, ah, bared her backside, m'lady," the marshal explained.

Oliwia blinked.

"'Tis not uncommon, my lady." Tomasz, flustered, dipped his head in an altogether pigeon-necked manner.

"Not uncommon for a woman to expose herself? Or for another to complain about it?"

"Both," Tomasz replied.

Jacek was hiding his mouth behind his hand, but a smile reached his eyes.

"Never mind," Oliwia huffed.

She shuffled through more papers. "Ah. Here is the elder's complaint against the villager he claims would not drink with him. What sorts of punishment did Lord Eryk dispense?"

"Well," the marshal began, "I knew him to have persons fined for showing irreverence to a village official. The fine was more serious if the offender abused the official in public. Once, he exiled a man for threatening to, uh, soil an alderman's shoe."

"And for insulting another villager?"

"He made the offender carry a tongue-shaped stone through the village. For showing their backsides, he fined them, and if they couldn't pay, he sometimes had them flogged."

Barely a muscle twitched in Jacek's body. Oliwia darted her eyes to him.

"This is why I am a soldier, my lady," he offered.

Her lips quirked. "I am sure soldiers have had, on occasion, their own foibles."

Tomasz cleared his throat. "True, my lady. And Biaska's soldiers sometimes find themselves on the wrong side of a complaint."

Oliwia gave him a puzzled look, and he handed her a paper, which she perused. "A member of our garrison owes a debt to one Regina Kawecka. Who is she?" she asked.

"Kawecka is a moneylender, and she advanced him a sum so he could pay gambling debts. Kawecka alleges he has made no repayment, but he claims he has."

"I didn't know we had a woman moneylender in Biaska Village."

"Oh yes, my lady. We've several. Cities and towns, like Gdańsk, for instance, have many. Women take their pocket money and save it until they have large enough sums to loan out with interest. Most of their clients are men of industry. Manufacturers, shippers, and so forth."

Jacek had sat up a little straighter. "Who's the soldier?"

Tomasz mopped his brow. "Ah …"

"Kasimir," Oliwia replied.

"Kasimir?" Jacek scoffed. "Everyone knows he's a terrible gambler, but in all the time I've known him, I've never known him to not pay a debt."

"Perhaps she's mistaken, then," Oliwia offered.

"Here are her records." Tomasz pushed more papers at Oliwia, then pinched his glasses from his nose and began polishing them.

"These appear in order," Oliwia mumbled, then passed them to Jacek.

"My lord," Tomasz directed at Jacek. "How soon do you leave for Silnyród?"

Jacek shifted his weight, and his leather seat creaked. "Four days." He shot Oliwia a quick look.

Her eyes widened. "So soon!"

"I just received word Silnyród suffered another onslaught. I must go and see what can be done to turn back this Tatar horde that spreads across the steppe like a canker."

Oliwia bounced inwardly between tears and curses. She'd known he was leaving, but this, this was so … final. Four days. Four nights. All she had left with this man she loved. And then would come months of waiting, wondering, hoping for the day he would crest the ridge and fly back to her. Until that day, she would not be whole.

"M'lady?" The marshal interrupted her wretched thoughts. "As I was saying, I believe we are ready for tomorrow's deliberations. With your permission, I will take my leave."

"Yes, of course. You as well, Tomasz. Thank you both for your help."

When the door was latched, her eyes flew to Jacek's. He seemed ready for it. "Liwi, I'm sorry. I intended telling you tonight."

"Is there no way I can convince you to stay here with me?" Blast it, but she could not keep the quaver from her voice.

He rose and came to her and, sinking on one knee beside her, took her hand in his. "Sweetest Liwi, I want nothing more than to stay here with you. I want to make you my wife and spend every hour of every day loving you. But I have no choice right now. Lesław, the outpost, they need me, and I am not at liberty to do what I most desire. I promise that once I fulfill my duty, I shall return as quickly as I can."

"Jacek, *I* need you. *We* need you. Here. Can you not send someone else? Henryk?"

He gazed at her, regret etching his face, then let out a long exhale. "Would that I could."

Oliwia stared at him, her thoughts turning to the two different men who occupied Jacek's body simultaneously—the warmhearted one alongside the warrior. A puckish one lived there too, but of him she still had much to learn. He could easily become her favorite. Whatever else he was, he was honor, nobility, justice, duty. These traits were tightly woven into the fabric of the man beside her and would never be divided from him while he breathed.

Defeated, she growled, "I hate Tatars."

He kissed her palm; his sapphire eyes took on a playful glint. "Another sentiment we share. Although not all are bad."

She gaped at him. He rose and leaned against the desk, crossing his arms. "There are the Lipka Tatars who settled in Lithuania. Though they are Muslims, they are citizens of the Commonwealth, aligned with Christians."

"Do they fight against the *other* Tatars?"

He nodded. "Since the Battle of Grunwald, when they helped defeat the Teutonic Knights, they've had light cavalry in every major Commonwealth battle."

"I had no id—"

Henryk stepped in. "There you are."

Jacek wheeled. "Looking for me?"

"Not really." He shrugged.

"So tell me of the raiders *you* chase, Captain Dąbrowski," Oliwia said. "We were always warned about them in our village, but beyond the terror of enslavement, I know little of them."

165

"I was just telling Lady Oliwia about Tatars," Jacek told Henryk.

"Ah. The scourge of the earth." Henryk settled himself into an armchair.

"Those of the horde, the ones we endlessly fight, trade in nothing but horses and people," Jacek began. "Horses, they raise; people, they steal. It's been that way for centuries."

"What do they do with them all?" asked Oliwia.

"They march them along the Black Way to the Black Sea and sell them in slave markets, such as Kaffa, which is one of the most notorious in Crimea. Merchants sail in with goods and leave with slaves."

"And from there?"

"They're taken to Constantinople and beyond, to the Mediterranean. There is an unquenchable demand throughout the Ottoman Empire for light-skinned folk."

"You," Henryk said as he pointed at Oliwia, "with your fair skin and eyes, would no doubt be bought for a high-ranking man's harem."

"That," Jacek added, "does not mean straight passage to a favorite's station. You would be taught, have to fight your way above the other wives, to gain favor."

"Taught what?" Nausea percolated in her stomach.

"Taught to embrace their faith, taught the ways of a gentle lady— playing an instrument, singing, all those same pursuits as a *szlachcianka*." Jacek poured himself a goblet of wine.

"You'd also be taught in the ways of pleasing a man," Henryk interjected.

Jacek gave him a mean glare. "Do you know of Roxelana?" he asked Oliwia. She shook her head.

"She was a fifteen-year-old Ukrainian girl captured in the early 1500s by the Tatars. She entered Sultan Suleyman's harem as a slave and quickly rose above all the other women to become his favorite *and* his wife. It's said he loved her so much he would bed no other." He paused to sip. "It's also said no other woman wielded as much power. She even convinced him to put his firstborn son, delivered by another wife, to death. Few enslaved women's fates are so charmed, however—if one can call being ripped away from one's home, marched to a foreign land, sold into captivity, and then despoiled a charmed existence."

"You could have been she, Oliwia," Henryk added. "You were fifteen when that blackguard tried to take you from Vyatov. He might have sold you to the Tatars, and there you'd be, queen of a harem."

"I shudder every time I think how different things would have been had you not taken Filip and me with you." She smiled warmly at Jacek.

The head table had been placed at the very edge of the dais, a tapestry draping it so it presented a wall of woven richness to those standing before it. Behind it perched Oliwia in a high-backed carved armchair, Tomasz an arm's length to her right. Their slight figures were dwarfed by the heavy assembly. In one back corner sat Jacek, the marshal opposite him. Both guarded the Lady of Biaska, today's court adjudicator. As Jacek had expected, the great hall was packed with the curious and the critics; only a smattering gathered to present legitimate cases they wished settled.

Oliwia had wobbled during her first hearing, garbling a complainant's name, stammering over a few statements, but as the morning wore on, she gained a calm resolve and handed out decisions with poise and authority. Complaints ranged from a stolen prized pig to a drunken exchange of fisticuffs to a jilted lover's theft of his former sweetheart's necklace. Then came the case of the moneylender Kawecka and Kasimir.

Oliwia first heard the plaintiff Kawecka, then invited Kasimir to defend himself. His brow pulled together in one long dark line. Beneath it, his black eyes smoldered as he turned them on Kawecka.

"I have made my payments."

Oliwia held up papers. "Here is her ledger, Kasimir. It shows your signature beside the loan figure, but the columns recording payments are empty. She has shown us her ledgers for other loans, where each payment is clearly initialed by her hand and the borrower's. Have you any sort of written proof of your payments?"

Kasimir turned a frustrated gaze on Oliwia. "My word is my proof! You know me, my lady. Are you going to disregard that and take the word of this … this useless—"

"I would caution you, Kasimir. Disparaging this woman will gain you naught but a lighter money pouch. If you've proof, I would review it. I welcome it, in fact."

Kasimir sneered. "You women doubtless put your heads together and decided the outcome already."

"Your proof?" Oliwia sat up a little taller.

There's my Liwi! Don't let this goat turd intimidate you.

Kasimir muttered something. Jacek caught a word or two, and he sat forward. Kasimir seemed to register the movement. Scowling, he swept his gaze from Kawecka to Oliwia to Jacek and back to Kawecka. The moneylender's head was high, but her worry was unmistakable. The spectators' burble had quieted, and tension, like heavy fog, settled over the hall.

Oliwia's voice cut through. "This woman did you a service, Kasimir. Like you, her money is hard-earned, and she has every right to not be cheated."

Kasimir scoffed. "Are you accusing me of cheating her?"

"Kasimir, what I am saying is that she has proof she's not been paid. So far, I've seen naught to refute her claim. Help me help you resolve this dispute by providing some evidence of your recompense."

Kasimir stared at Oliwia for long moments. Jacek checked himself barking at the fool and stood to his full height, his fingers dancing over his hilt; he matched Kasimir's glower eyebrow for eyebrow.

The lines on Kasimir's face eased. "I have none. It would appear my poor record-keeping will cost me double." Kasimir dipped his head to Oliwia, then Kawecka. The crowd seemed to exhale as one.

"Then I have no choice but to order you to repay the woman in full," declared Oliwia.

"But I don't have the money!" he protested.

"Have you some portion?"

"Maybe a third, but—"

"Then pay her a fourth now. Until you can make regular installments, Biaska will pay on your behalf and deduct the sums from your wages. Is this agreeable?"

Regina Kawecka nodded her head. "Yes, m'lady."

Kasimir groused his acceptance.

"Good. Tomasz, draw up the agreement for the parties' signatures."

Folk seemed disappointed when the hearings concluded, as though their entertainment had come to an end, and they dispersed reluctantly.

Jacek swept Oliwia a grand bow. "I deem your first tribunal a success, my lady. Each side to every dispute was left equally unhappy. Justice, therefore, was served. And I was compelled to stand only once—more to get blood flowing to my backside than anything else."

Oliwia's shoulders seemed to lower several inches as she blew out a great breath.

He drew her away. "Truly, Liwi, I am proud of you. You listened, but you suffered no fools. You were swift, direct, just. And your solution for Kasimir's debt? Brilliant."

A smile formed, spread, and lifted her lovely face. "I enjoyed it, Jacek."

"Then don't appoint Tomasz to the task. Keep doing what you did today. They will grow used to you. In fact," he said as he grasped her hand covertly, "ride with me tomorrow and see your estate, meet villagers and yeomen in the fields. Let them see who you are."

She bit her lower lip and frowned, as if calculating. "Eryk told me meeting them at the *dożynki* was enough and to have no closer contact."

"Seeing faces at a harvest festival is not the same. See them where they live, where they work. Think back to when you were a village girl."

Her eyes lit, as if understanding had just dawned. "Yes, I would like that."

"I will arrange it. On the way back, you can fetch more rocks for your armory."

She elbowed him.

When he left her, he found Henryk and ordered an escort for the next day.

"I'm glad you and Oliwia have reached an accord," Henryk said.

"What makes you think we've reached an accord?"

Henryk chortled. "Because you no longer resemble a snorting bull in her presence. I've even seen you smile at her once or twice. And then there's her cross hiding beneath your żupan." He pointed at Jacek's neck.

"What makes you think it's hers?"

"I recognize it. She has a habit of sliding it along the chain."

Jacek unintentionally patted his chest.

"What can one conclude from you wearing the lady's jewelry?" Henryk smirked.

Jacek glared at him. "It is a token, and you need know nothing more about it."

Oliwia reined in her mare and shaded her eyes.

"What is it?" Jacek pulled up beside her. He was astride Smok, who danced in place, causing Oliwia's horse to shy away. Oliwia pointed, seeming not to notice the horses maneuvering. When Jacek settled the stallion, he looked to where she pointed.

"Why are those fields so narrow?" she asked.

What he looked at were a series of undulations, striped in different shades of green, that rolled over the countryside. Some strips were long and narrow and might abut one five times their width. Not only did the bands vary in breadth and color, but in texture, height, and density. Some were lush with grasses so thick it was hard to imagine navigating them, while others were so sparse it was hard to believe whatever grew was worth cultivating. Bushes and trees huddled in sporadic clumps. The entire spread resembled a patchwork assembled with long quilt strips that followed the rounded contours of the land.

A man and woman had just finished working one narrow field.

"What are those spiky plants there?" Oliwia asked. "They are different from the grasses."

The sun was high and brilliant, and Jacek shaded his eyes against the glare.

"Hemp," he replied.

The man and woman had traversed three fields and begun working a fourth one.

"Why do they not work the fields in order?"

"The fields in between are not theirs. They belong to different freeholders. And those people there," he pointed to a group of five in a larger field, "are working your demesne. That bit lies among theirs."

"So each of these strips is owned by different families?"

"Yes. Over the years, pieces are divided, sold off, acquired by other freeholders, and they end up with disjointed parcels."

"That seems most inefficient."

He shrugged. "It's been this way since the feudal system of old."

"And what's this if not the feudal system of old?" She swept her gloved hand before her.

"Well, these people are tenants, yeomen. Not serfs."

"Yet the law forbids them moving away. I do not understand how that's any different from the old way. They are tied to the land, regardless of whether they wish it. And their children are bound as well, yes?"

He scratched the back of his neck. "You have been studying. The laws were passed to ensure labor for the manors. Tenants are needed to work their own land and their lord's."

"But what if a farmer decides he wishes to move to town and become a tradesman? Is that path open to him? Or to his son?"

"Not really. How could you harvest your lands if the laborers abandoned you? As it is now, there are not enough people to go round."

"The 'free' in 'freeholder' is deceptive." Her eyes scanned the fields once more. "If a freeholder has a grievance with his lord, he cannot even bring it before a judge."

"Because their lord *is* their law."

"Seems he is stuck upon a wheel that goes endlessly round and round and from which there is no escape. If *you* so chose, you could stop soldiering and become a magistrate or an official in the king's court. A merchant, if that's your pleasure."

"Not a merchant, no. A nobleman has many paths to choose from, but becoming a merchant or a tradesman is not among them. As for freeholders, the Crown would need to pass a law to release them from service, and it is the szlachta who write those laws. They who make the laws are not likely to enact a system that is to their detriment."

"I suppose not."

"Come. Enough politics. 'Tis time for the midday meal and—"

"Yes, I know. You are famished." She smirked.

"Is this what I am to look forward to?" he said with feigned indignation.

"If a timid, pliable wife is what you seek, I am not the one for you. I can be won, but I will not be conquered. You've time enough to retract your offer." Her eyes narrowed mockingly.

Jacek let out a snort, and his horse jerked. As he stroked Smok's neck, he looked Oliwia over. "You may be a slip of a girl and sweet beyond measure, but I have *never* thought you timid or pliable. You are far more difficult to conquer than any enemy army I've ever encountered, and the times I was fool enough to underestimate you, you made me painfully aware of my flawed thinking." He absentmindedly rubbed the top of his head.

Oliwia's cheeks pinked. "I simply remind you of what you bargain for. I give you fair warning, I will be trouble. I am not a meek mouse, and I am not obedient."

"You're telling me nothing I do not know, for you *already* cause me trouble—and have since I've known you." He paused a beat. "But I welcome the challenge, and I give *you* fair warning, my lady. I will not relent. I can be just as pigheaded as you."

She flashed him an impish, provocative smile, stirring him quite noticeably. The resilient girl he'd met four years ago had grown into a strong, sensual, vibrant young woman. He liked the transformation. Very much. While the pull was powerful to care for her, to protect her, to bring her joy, he didn't want someone he could cow, who would await his command, trudging after him like so much livestock.

He shifted in his saddle. "Come. There's an inn nearby that serves decent stew. I can smell it already."

The afternoon had grown late when they returned to Biaska. Oliwia clung to Jacek as he lowered her from her mare, relishing the feel of hardened muscle beneath his clothing. *One more full day. Two more nights. I must make the most of them.*

Unfortunately, Adam took ill that evening, and while he'd recovered by morning, she'd been unable to go to Jacek.

After washing up and changing her garments, she went to the great hall, where she found Jacek waiting for her. Concern etched his chiseled features.

"Is all well with Adam now?"

"Yes. I'm not sure what ailed him the night long, but he is sleeping peacefully now."

Relief softened Jacek's features. "I missed you last night."

"I missed you too. But with Adam ill, I could not—"

"No, of course not. I am glad he's better. I must warn you, however, you may have ruined me. I do not believe I can sleep without you."

"Nor do you sleep *with* me," she chuckled softly.

"Either way, I am tired. But *with* you, I am blissfully tired." He grinned. "Come. Let's get you some food."

"Have you eaten?"

"Yes, and now I must tend to final preparations for tomorrow's journey."

Her heart, which had lightened with Adam's recovery, tightened anew. *One night now.*

Oliwia did not see Jacek the rest of that morning nor at the midday meal. She had just checked on Adam and returned to the solar, where all manner of documents awaited her. Unable to muster enthusiasm for the task, she stood beside the window and leaned against the wall. The door rattled behind her, and when she turned, Jacek's large form filled the frame.

"I came to see how you and Adam fare."

"We are fine, thank you."

He closed the door behind him and dropped the bar in place. Two quick strides, and he swept her up in his arms even as his mouth descended on hers. Her feet nearly left the floor; she would have gasped had she any breath. When he released her, she wobbled. Her body tingled. She ran her hands over her hair, bodice, and skirts, smoothing her rumpled self. The warmth from Jacek's touch lingered. Gazing out the window, seeing nothing, she tried to steady the percussion of her heart. His heat radiated as he closed in behind her and wrapped his corded arms around her middle. He swept her hair aside and feathered kisses along her neck. She turned in his arms, and he pressed her hand to his heart and trained his eyes on her, intense but tender.

"We've only a day, Liwi, and I need you to promise me something."

In that moment, she would have promised him anything. "Promise you what?"

He pressed the tip of her nose. "Promise me you will do what Henryk tells you while I am gone. You cannot behave foolishly, as you did when you rode off without a proper escort."

"Only a day." "While I am gone." Sadness spiked, threatening to undo her joy. She tipped her head to one side and frowned at him.

"You admitted it yourself," he said good-naturedly. "You are naught but trouble. An outright menace."

"You're the one who flew off his horse and frightened me half to death with your withering look." She jabbed her finger into his chest—or tried to. The motion was more akin to bending her finger backward against a stone breastplate.

"Withering look? Me? Liwi, I was being gentle with you." He paused, looking amused. "Did I really frighten you?"

"Yes! I'm not used to … to … an enormous, red-faced warrior hollering at me, looking as though he wants to break my neck."

"I was red-faced? I didn't know I *ever* became red-faced. Well, good, then. I meant to scare you. And I was thinking more of wringing your neck, not breaking it. It's far too lovely to break." As if to prove the point, he kissed said neck, sending fresh shivers through her.

Resting her hands on his chest, she gazed into the depths of his sapphire eyes.

"Oliwia, what troubles you? You know I would never actually wring your neck, yes? I will not harm you. Ever. Now if anyone thinks to mistreat you—*anyone*—they will regret the day they left the womb, but I will never lay a hand on you in anger."

Oliwia studied him as she considered his declaration, and warmth flooded her. He *would* kill for her, *had* killed for her.

Jacek arched his eyebrows at her, one side of his mouth twitching.

"Yes, Jacek, I know."

"Liwi, I would tell you something."

"What is it?"

He inhaled. "You say you're not timid, and so it is. I see a torch blazing within you, a spirit like none I have ever known, and it draws me like a moth to light. You are courageous. You are fiercely loyal. You've the heart of a lion. In your own way, you are an unstoppable warrior. But you also possess beauty and a power to bewitch that surpass any goddess of the ancient myths. You're not only the loveliest woman I have ever seen, but you are the canniest. I think you cannier than most men I know, including me. These are a scarce few reasons among countless that I want you beside me as my consort. Not because I think you docile. You are my match, Liwi. I know full well what I bargain for, and you are what I want."

She pulled his head to hers, and, hovering her lips near his, whispered, "You steal the breath from my lungs."

Chapter 15

I Cross my Heart and I Hope to Die

Oliwia awoke nestled against Jacek's side as he slept on his back. His arm curled under and around her, his hand warm and heavy where it rested on her waist. Their feet were tangled together, and the bedclothes were bunched in disarray where they swaddled the foot of the bed. The strident chirping of crickets was fading along with the black night. She peered over her shoulder at the window, where dawn's faint light would soon glow.

Gone was the moon's radiance, but she was still here with him, really here. She yearned to stay like this forever, breathing him in and feeling the heat from his chiseled body beside hers, holding him close as his breath moved through him.

Shifting to better watch him, she took in every part of the man next to her. Her hand rested like a feather on his chest. As she looked at him, felt him beneath her touch, an overwhelming tenderness welled inside her, overflowing her heart. She softly stroked the side of his face with the back of her finger, tracing his strong jaw. A songbird chirped an early tune somewhere distant. She sighed. They had taken too many chances already. It would not do for the Lady of Biaska to be discovered in her captain's bed. Not until he was her husband.

Reluctantly, stealthily, she disentangled herself and swung her legs over the edge of the frame. She would let herself out of his chamber before he woke. Gingerly, she picked up her nightdress from the floor and pulled it on. The garment hung off her shoulder, and she began to gather up the ribbon when a large hand wrapped around her arm and pulled her back down on the mattress.

"Where are you going in the middle of the night?" Jacek asked in a voice thick with sleep.

"It is no longer the middle of the night. Do you hear the birds? I must get back before we are discovered," she whispered urgently.

He had encircled her in his strong arms, and as he hauled her back to him, he nuzzled her neck and fondled her breasts through the thin fabric.

"The devil take anyone who dares say anything. This is where you belong. With me. In my bed."

He slid the nightdress from her shoulder and softly kissed her bare skin. Quivering, Oliwia let him pull her against him, the heat of his body seeping into her back. It felt so good—*so safe*—to be in his arms. It was where she should be; it was where she wanted to be. But she could not stay.

"Jacek, I must *go!*" She tried not to giggle at his determined advances.

"Not yet. Come here, my wild beauty," he mumbled from somewhere behind her.

He snugged himself against her bottom, hard and insistent, and she nestled into him with a drawn-out sigh.

"See what you do to me?" he murmured in her ear before nibbling said ear. Then he worked his way across her neck, sending all manner of shivers through her.

He sat up, placing his feet on the floor, and hoisted her onto his lap so she straddled him. He looked her over, his drowsy eyes partly covered by his ruffled brown hair. She pushed a thick lock off his face, and he gave her a sleepy, boyish smile. Her insides turned to jelly, and her resolve evaporated. *Maybe just a little while longer.* She kissed him.

He broke the kiss and lifted the nightdress over her head, letting it drift to the floor without taking his eyes from her. He ran his calloused palms along her thighs, over her arms, across her shoulders, down her chest, where he cupped her breasts. Bending his head, his soft hair caressing her sensitive skin, he drew each one into his moist mouth, tasting, nipping, suckling in turn. Embers ignited within her. She burrowed her fingers in his hair and rocked against him. Her breathing came in gasps. He raised his head, locking his gaze on hers as his hands lowered to her hips.

"My God, but you're beautiful," he whispered.

With a stutter of breath, he buried himself deep inside her. She let out a guttural cry, then began moving with him. Her hands slid to his shoulders, and she bent to kiss his mouth, but he grasped her wrists and held her away while he studied her. "I want to look at you. I want to memorize everything about you."

Her breathing quickened.

With his now fully open eyes traveling over her, she rode him at a pace he controlled. As she gave herself over to him, she dropped her head back. Moans rolled from her throat. He went faster. Her ragged breaths sharpened until her entire body seized. She shuddered, calling out his name on a long exhale. He slowed. When she opened her eyes, his were still fixed on her. Then he tugged her hips, and the motion of their joined bodies resumed, its rhythm intensifying.

"I want you to tell me you're mine, Oliwia," he murmured.

Barely capable of a thought, much less a word, she looked at him through half-lidded eyes, and he met her gaze with fire.

"Tell me you're mine. Say it, Oliwia. Say it!" His tone grew fervent, insistent.

"Tell me!" His hands stayed locked on her hips, moving her faster, faster against him as he drove deeper and deeper.

Oliwia's last coherent thought was that she would shatter, and then she did. She threw her head back again as tremors rocked her, crying out what he longed to hear.

"I am yours, Jacek! *I am yours!*"

He let go with a roar. Chest heaving against hers, he clutched her to him. He kissed the side of her head, murmuring "my sweet Liwi" over and over, then buried his face in her hair.

They remained in the embrace for long minutes, Oliwia's sense of time adrift. Jacek at last lay back, pulling her alongside him. Her finger twirled circles on his chest while he stroked her hair.

Then he regarded her with an achingly tender look. "As you are mine, Liwi, so am I yours. I always have been and always will be."

Chatter rose from the floor below, sending Jacek into the murky shadows beside a flight of stairs. Soon he would be gone, and he needed to hold Oliwia one last time. Was this how a starving man felt? Hunger so powerful it hollowed him, leaving him with a desperate craving to fill himself over and over? That hunger drove him to where he now stood, concealed, waiting for her to descend from her quarters. His heart thudded against his ribs.

Light footsteps ran along an upper corridor, then scurried down the steps and hit the landing beside him. He caught a glimpse of a blue gown and glossy sable hair. Pitching forward, he grasped Oliwia's arm and hauled her into the dimness.

"In here!" he hissed.

Into a dark chamber they tumbled. He closed and barred the door just as two servants rounded a corner. He pivoted and reached for her. Her startled expression turned to one of euphoria, and she threw herself into his open arms and pressed her cheek against his chest.

"Praise God, I captured the right girl," he chuckled softly. "It would not do to abduct the wrong one." He leaned down to kiss her. "You are the only one I want," he whispered. She sighed against him.

He released her, putting several strides between them. She watched him with a puzzled look. Most of his self-control had drained away like a tapped barrel of piwo discovered by thirsty soldiers, and he needed distance. If he kept doing what he was doing, he would be incapable of quelling the want gnawing at him. Again.

To distract himself, he looked around the gloomy chamber, taking in bits of dusty furniture and random ornaments. No bed was there to tempt him.

"What is this place?" he asked, his voice a little thick.

Taking her eyes from him, she glided to the opposite end of the chamber and pulled aside a tapestry. Diffused light lit a cloud of dust as it streamed through a window. "It was a guest chamber but has become a place to collect the odd piece."

His composure regained, he walked toward her. "Liwi, I wished for a private farewell between us. The public parting we are to have will be watched by many and must remain one between the lady of the estate and her officer."

The plea in her gaze tore at him. *What if I stay?* Hadn't he sacrificed enough of himself already? He dismissed the thought as quickly as he'd taken it up. His heart squeezed as he drew her close and grasped her elbows, placing his forearms under hers. Her fingers dug in.

For a split second, he feared his voice would fail him. He swallowed. "Liwi, I hope you know … I want you to know that I love you with all that I am. You hold my heart in your hands, and it will always be yours. The words I offer are inadequate, but they are all I have to give you for now. When I return, I will lay the world at your feet, and I will slay it first if I must. I will scatter rose petals upon every path you walk so your feet never touch the ground, if that is what you wish. Whatever you desire, I will get it for you."

She threw her arms around him and held fast; her body trembled.

"I don't want the world, and I don't want rose petals. I just want you." She sobbed softly. "Come back to me, Jacek. That is what I most desire."

She pulled back, teardrops like dew upon her dark lashes. He cupped the back of her head and kissed her forehead gently, then fumbled in his pocket.

"I have something for you." He picked up her hand and pressed his wood-beaded rosary in her palm—the one his mother had given him when he was a small boy. "It's not a fat ruby or a thick amber pendant, but it's very special to me. Like you."

"I've never seen this." She examined the necklace in her open palm. "It's beautiful."

"I pray over it on the eve of a battle."

She shoved it back at him. "Then you must take it with you. It's guarded you well for so long. You may have need of it."

Wrapping his hand about hers, he closed it in a fist. "And now it will guard you. This one has served me well, and I want you to keep it so I know you are in God's hands. As you have given me your mother's cross, I give you my rosary and ask that you keep it in your care until I am safely back in your arms. Use it to pray for my swift return," he urged softly. Putting a knuckle under her chin, he raised her head to meet his gaze.

"Yes," she whispered so quietly he barely heard her. Her eyes were filled with sorrow. "I love you, Jacek—so much."

He pulled her to him once again and rested his head against hers. "I promise I will return for you, Oliwia. And when I do, I will claim thousands upon thousands of your sweet kisses, so you'd best be ready."

She slid her arms around his shoulders, pulling him close as she stood on tiptoe. "Then here is the first, so you do not forget." Her soft mouth was on his, and she kissed him with a depth and longing that stirred him to a precipitous edge. Upon that edge, his thoughts shattered, becoming shards amid primal sensation. Her kiss was to him as a spark was to dry kindling.

One hand cupping her head while the other cupped her bottom, his lips descended greedily on hers. As he plundered her mouth, he walked her backward until her back pressed against a wall. She clutched and molded herself against him, riding the thundering wave of his formidable fervor with him, fueling the conflagration inside him.

Something savage possessed him and propelled him to join with her. Yanking the hem of her skirts, he shoved them up around her waist. She held them fast while he loosened his breeches and lifted her; she wrapped her legs around him. With a fevered thrust, he entered her. Her throaty gasps echoed in his ears as she took all of him in.

Out of his mind, out of his body, he took her hard, driving into her over and over while she held on and clawed his back. She moaned his name, he groaned between breathless mutterings, but it was far away, muffled. The connection between his body and hers was all there was, the only place that existed in his world. Everything else around him fell away.

Wailing something incoherent, she jolted to a trembling stop. With a guttural cry, he emptied his seed and his soul inside her.

Their heavy breaths rose and fell together in the same rapid rhythm, and as lucidity returned, they slowed. At last, he let her down gently and gathered her back to him.

"Dear God, Liwi. What you do to me," he rasped. *You drive me out of my mind.*

Her cheek lay against his chest, and she laughed softly. "I marvel no walls collapsed."

He held her tighter and chuckled into her soft hair. Pulling back, he trailed his fingertips along her flushed cheek.

She smiled. "If each of those thousands upon thousands of kisses are going to end the same way, my love, it will take more than a lifetime to get through them all."

"And I will die a very happy man." He could die a very happy man right now.

The small group—Jacek, Marcin, Stefan, Dawid, a few servants—rode out of the gates soon after the sun had begun its daily arc from the eastern horizon. Oliwia stood with Filip and Henryk on the ramparts and watched the men climb the ridge. She rested a hand on Filip's drooping shoulder and held herself erect. Inside, she crumbled. Tears caught in her throat, and she cleared it repeatedly to keep them in check. No latitude would she give the emotions churning away inside.

The column headed away with Jacek leading the men as he always did. Today, he rode the headstrong, majestic stallion Smok. Jarosława and his other horses trundled in the line of mounts pulled behind the group alongside two wagons.

As Jacek's silhouette slipped over the ridge and was swallowed up by the woods, her heart shrank right along with his form. She sought to comprehend, to put order to the events of one head-spinning week. Had it really happened? Reaching into her pocket, she ran her fingers over the smooth wooden beads of Jacek's rosary. It had happened. Saturday last, he'd awoken as her surly captain, but within a day he had transformed into her lover and her intended.

As she sent a prayer heavenward for his safe return, she crossed herself and looked around furtively. Did folk know what had passed between them? She had spent heretofore inconceivable nights of passion in his arms, where she learned sharing a bed with *this* man offered a wildly different, delirious set of sensations from those she had known. She'd behaved like a brazen, unabashed wanton. And she'd liked it.

A blush crept up her chest, threatening to spread over her face.

But as fulfilled as she'd been, his leaving left her equally bereft. Could she fill the hollowness within without his presence? Foreboding crept over her and seeped into her heart.

Chapter 16

The Long and Winding Road

The party headed south, bypassing Kraków, then trudged north of the salt mines at Bochnia, pointing eastward, traveling through Tarnów until they reached the village of Krasiczyn days after they'd left Biaska. Soon the squad was billeted in an inn that stood in the shadow of Krasiczyn Castle. As they guided their horses toward the stables, Dawid kept his gaze on the square structure anchored at each corner by a different tower.

"Who owns the castle?" the young hussar asked no one in particular, pointing at the multi-storied edifice. "And why aren't we sleeping there tonight?" he added with a laugh.

"Pan Marcin Krasicki inherited it from his father, who began rebuilding it decades ago," Jacek said. "The son continues his father's endeavor, but 'tis not complete. It used to be a wooden fort, I believe. We might not be staying there," he added with a jerk of his chin, "but we're staying in Krasicki's village. It's probably his inn too."

"Isn't Silnyród a wooden fort, Captain?" asked Stefan.

"It is." Jacek dismounted and swiveled his head in search of a stable hand.

"Well, then, perhaps someday it too will be transformed into something as magnificent as this." Stefan waved his hand.

Jacek snorted. "Not by me." His mind unexpectedly jumped to the luxury of Matejko Manor, and then naturally to the people within. "Where the devil is the ostler?" he huffed impatiently.

As if in answer, a man sprinted from the stables, panting and puffing. "Begging your pardon, m'lord, but a number of towarzysze and their retinues just arrived, and we are a bit shorthanded."

"Are they inside?" Jacek shot a sidelong glance at the inn, a cream-plastered, two-storied affair with dark wood-framed windows under a steep thatched roof.

"Yes, sir. They are come from Rohatyn." The man gathered up the reins.

"I hope there's room enough for us all," Jacek muttered, then added, "Watch the stallion. He has a bad temper."

He strode toward the building, calling to his fellows, "Let's go and meet our lord-brothers." Behind him, he thought he heard the ostler mumble, "God's teeth, I hope the wodka and the women are locked up."

As Jacek stepped through the inn's arched entrance, he was enveloped in fusty dimness. The smoky air gave the space an umber haze from the low, beamed ceiling to the wood-planked floor. Voices buzzed around him, metal tankards clanked, and moving shadows began to sharpen as his eyes adjusted to the gloom.

"My lord-brother!" someone called.

Jacek squinted at a large table packed with soldiers dressed in garb not unlike his own. A tall, bony man with a walrus moustache striped ivory and gray stood up and came toward him, his arms wide in greeting.

"Welcome, welcome! I am Pawel Liskoski of Lelów. Won't you join us in our celebration?" the man said. Then with a flick of his gray eyes over Jacek's shoulder, he added, "And your companions too. The Malmsey here is excellent."

Soon Jacek and his squad were introduced to a dozen hussars, all of them draining their drinks and ordering another round for themselves. They included a round for Jacek and his men. Standing beside Pawel, Jacek scanned the group of towarzysze growing more boisterous as tavern maids topped off their drinks.

"What do you celebrate, Pan Liskoski?"

"Our success at Rohatyn."

A cheer rose up. "Rohatyn! *Na zdrowie!*"

Puzzled, Jacek asked what had taken place in Rohatyn, to which Pawel replied, "We defeated our rebel Commonwealth troops. Their commander,

Jan Karwarcki, was taken in chains to Hetman Żółkiewski. Those bastards won't plunder their own countrymen anymore."

Jacek arched an eyebrow. "When did this happen?"

"A fortnight or so ago. We were led by a stripling named Koniecpolski," he laughed.

"Stanisław Koniecpolski?" asked Jacek.

Pawel nodded. "The same. He's an apprentice to Żółkiewski. The hetman grew tired of the rebels roaming the countryside, terrorizing their own, and decided to put an end to it. So he entrusted Koniecpolski with stopping them once and for all. And we did!"

Another hearty *"na zdrowie"* boomed.

Jacek scratched his stubbly chin. "Koniecpolski served at Kłuszyn with us. As I recall, he's a bit younger than I."

"Seems about right. Though he's young, he's distinguished himself well. So well, Żółkiewski might see his daughter Katarzyna married to him. Not a bad match. Two powerful families united." Pawel nudged Jacek with his elbow.

Jacek flashed to his time at Żółkiew Castle where he had idled, waiting for recognition among the powerful nobles who held sway with King Zygmunt III, nobles who could lead him to the estate he'd coveted. He'd reluctantly spent time in Katarzyna Żółkiewska's company, whom he'd been told was taken with him. But even had he found her the least bit attractive, fourth-born sons did not wed daughters of such elevated families. Any favorable impression he'd hoped to leave was done for his land, nothing more. In the end, his entire stay had been wasted. Worse, his ambition had kept him from Oliwia's side, and Eryk had laid his claim.

"So, Pan Dąbrowski, tell me. Where are you and your men headed?" Pawel asked over the rim of his metal cup, jolting Jacek back to present.

"To Silnyród. I command the garrison there."

Pawel's dark caterpillar eyebrows climbed to his receding hairline. "I have heard of it. You have been recruiting there, yes?"

"Yes. Are any of your men interested?" Jacek took his first sip. It *was* good wine.

Pawel let out a rumbling laugh. "These are not my men. We have merely fallen in with one another. But who knows? A bitter hatred of Tatars and a love of adventure might convince a few. Eh, Janusz?" Pawel lifted his cup to a young, dark-haired hussar. Janusz nodded.

The men drank and talked—of politics, battles, the border, family—growing more raucous as the night wore on. At last, the innkeeper begged Jacek and Pawel to remove their party to the tavern and went so far as to escort them there—whether out of courtesy or necessity, Jacek knew not.

The tavern was a grubbier, bawdier version of the inn, as much brothel as pub, but the drinks flowed strong and his men found entertainments.

Much later, after convincing Pawel and a half-dozen hussars to accompany them in the morning, Jacek congratulated himself and decided to snatch some well-earned sleep. Surveying the group riotously enjoying the drink, music, and wenches, Jacek debated whether to order his men to retire to their quarters. Marcin caught his eye, then jerked his head at Stefan, who fondled a maid on each knee. His lips seemed to be traveling indiscriminately between their chests. Jacek stifled a laugh. Marcin shook his head and grinned.

In a departure from his usual disciplines, Jacek left them to their carousing and whoring. *We've a dull ride before us tomorrow. They can sleep it off in their saddles.*

In the morning, Jacek rode amidst a grumbling, reeking contingent. The air was still, and summer's heat shimmered through the grasses to the sounds of droning insects. The prospect of arriving at Silnyród buoyed him, for only scant weeks would pass before he was back at Biaska. He whistled loudly, garnering a spate of curses.

By midday, the men had quieted. Some snored in their saddles. They moved through the torpor single-file along a narrow, shallow creek flanked by dense trees and shrubs. Leafy canopies offered a shady respite; all was still. In the lead, Jacek was lulled by warmth and the drudgery of the unremarkable journey. He'd traveled this way before, and he let his mind wander back to Biaska to climb into bed with Oliwia. If only his body could follow.

Loud cracking startled him. Men on horseback swarmed from either side of the creek, blocking the path forward. Smok pulled up hard, and Jacek unsheathed his sabre.

What the hell?

Someone bellowed in a foreign tongue—Wallachian? Moldavian? *Are they friendly?* Firearms popped, horses screamed. *Not friendly.* Far too late, he hollered and jerked his head to the back of the line. Men—his men—went down, and more brigands blocked escape behind them. Blood, dust, commotion, chaos.

Christ, Christ, Christ!

Smok poised to break through the front line, and Jacek spurred him. More shots fired, the noise echoing in his ears, gunpowder smoke filling the creek trough. They were trapped. Smok reared up, turned, struck out. Shouting, screaming, men's cries everywhere. Smok's hooves thundered to the earth. The impact jolted up Jacek's back.

Men surrounded them. Jacek swung his sabre. It hit something, and he swung again, catching naught but air. His arm was wrenched from behind. The sabre flew from his grasp. Then he was tumbling to the ground. Smok reared again, and Jacek scrambled to avoid the stallion's flailing hooves. Those hooves caught one of the attackers and sent him sprawling sideways, howling and grasping his side.

Jacek lumbered to his feet, pulled his dagger, lurched forward. The blade bit into hard muscle. An agonized cry followed. Jacek yanked, but before he could free the handle, he was caught from behind. Hands clamped onto his limbs, grabbing him, grabbing Smok. *So many!*

More gunfire. Smok shrieked, thrashed, collapsed on his side, his big eyes on Jacek. The barrel of a firearm pointed at the horse's forehead.

"No!" Jacek roared, twisting his arms, straining to break free. Cords along his neck tautened, near to tearing.

Smok's legs scrabbled as he fought to stand. Flash, percussion, more smoke. The majestic stallion's head rolled slowly backward, blood leaking down his muzzle. Something crashed down hard on Jacek's head.

His world went dark.

As Oliwia's pining grew, so did her busy work. Jacek had told her it would take two Sundays to reach Silnyród, so she knew better than to expect a letter just yet. In a cellar storeroom, as she counted barrels of flour by candlelight, another calculation played through her mind: Jacek and his men were halfway there. What would he find when he arrived? Lesław's injuries had not been grave, but what if they had worsened? How long would it take for Jacek to do what must be done and come back to her? Seven days? A fortnight? More? At the very least, two more Sundays would pass before she laid eyes on him again. Those weeks would prove long indeed. But dreaming of what lay beyond that time, when she could hold him again and he was truly hers, her giddy heart fluttered.

These last days had been tolerable enough during her waking hours—the estate and Adam distracted her—but at night, time slowed to a morbid crawl. She slept fitfully and was often at the window staring at the heavens. Did Jacek look at the same canopy of stars and think of her? She had surreptitiously brought his pillow to her bed and fretted she would smell the scent right out of it. *Well, he will just have to come home and replace it.*

Several Sundays later, a hot spell settled over Biaska, wrapping it in a wet blanket of heat. Leaden clouds hung full-bellied in the sky, clinging stubbornly to their posts and moving not at all. One was tempted to reach up and wring the cool moisture from them, allowing them to then scamper off.

Late one stifling, sticky afternoon, Oliwia sat in the solar with Henryk and Tomasz, reviewing a new list of desertions. The sentries called an alert, and Henryk's eyebrows rose. She followed in his wake as he made his way to the ramparts. A lone rider plunged down the ridge and galloped directly for Biaska's drawbridge. Barely upright, he flopped in the saddle as though he were a rag doll. Oliwia held her breath and waited alongside Henryk for the man to come into view. When he did, Henryk let out a string of curses, followed quickly by a spate of orders. Oliwia's heart began thundering.

Henryk wheeled and grasped her arms. "Stay here." Then he took off at a run. Oliwia picked up her skirts and followed him to the courtyard just as a horse carrying Marcin trotted laboriously through the upper gates. Henryk flicked his eyes at her and frowned; she frowned back. Then he grabbed the animal's reins and brought it to a standstill. The pacholik weaved atop the saddle as though in a drunken stupor before toppling sideways. Had Henryk not broken his fall, he would have thudded to the ground. He was in a pitiful state as he lay across Henryk's lap. Filthy, reeking, his clothing in tattered disarray.

Someone handed Henryk a waterskin, and he dribbled liquid on Marcin's cracked lips.

"Marcin," Henryk murmured, holding the lad's head. "Marcin," he repeated. Marcin's eyes flew wide and fixed on Henryk's.

"Dead, all dead ... Stefan ... help him." Marcin looked terrified. He reached up a bloodied hand and seized Henryk's żupan.

Squelching her rising panic, Oliwia followed woodenly as guards moved Marcin into the garrison and laid him down in a cool, dark room that smelled of earth. Bruises and weeping lesions covered his face and neck. She ordered a mixture of piwo and water, sent for the physician and healers, and sank beside Henryk at the young man's side. Taking Marcin's hand in hers, she glanced up at Henryk, whose agitation showed in every line on his face.

When the drink appeared, Oliwia removed her linen collar and dipped it in the liquid, then wrung drops into Marcin's mouth. Her calm movements belied the agony twisting her gut and firing every nerve. Marcin at last settled back and drifted.

"Send word if he stirs," Henryk instructed after the healers appeared.

He took the bowl from Oliwia's hands. "Come. I will see him moved to the keep. For now, he is in God's and the healers' hands." He gently grasped her elbow and lifted her up.

"What do you make of it?" she ventured warily as they stepped from the coolness of the garrison into the humid afternoon.

"I don't know. I will check the horse. I do not recognize it—'tis old and worn and resembles a beast of burden one would find among peasant stock." Henryk shaded his eyes, looking toward the stables.

Oliwia's voice rose, trembling. "Where are his mount, his trappings, his weapons? How did he come here, in this state?" She kept her questions about Jacek's state penned up, for Marcin had quite possibly lost much more than his belongings. He might have lost his master.

Henryk opened his mouth to speak when another alert sounded from the ramparts. Oliwia froze beside him in the courtyard as they awaited another rider: a scruffy, stout peasant with a large sack dangling from his back. The sack appeared to have limbs. As the peasant drew closer, she realized it was not a sack at all, but another man seated upright and bound to the peasant with a length of rope. The sack man's head lolled on the peasant's shoulder, and his arms and legs flopped in rhythm to the horse's steps. Oliwia recognized Stefan, and she bit back a cry.

"What the devil happened?" yelled Henryk.

Stefan was lowered into a cot alongside Marcin, his shallow breathing the only indication he lived. His eyes swollen shut, he was covered in cuts, scabs, and bruises visible through rents in the grubby, tattered rags that were once clothing. He had no footwear, and his feet were carpeted in oozing sores.

Oliwia countermanded Henryk's wish to question the peasant in the guard room alone.

"Oliwia," Henryk protested, "let me talk to him first. He may say things you should not hear."

She shook her head vigorously. "I am the lady, and I will hear what he has to say at the same time as you. I will not hear his words coated with honey."

With an exasperated sigh, he nodded. Soon she was seated, Henryk at attention beside her and the man facing them across a desk, a plate of cheese and bread and a tankard of piwo before him. The man looked from her to Henryk with conspicuous curiosity.

Henryk cleared his throat. "This is Lady Oliwia Krezowska of Biaska, and I am Pan Henryk Kalinowski, her captain of the guard. The man you delivered is one of ours. He is called Pan Stefan Pakulski. Might I know who I am addressing so that you may be properly thanked?"

The man grunted and swallowed another gulp of piwo. He wiped a grimy sleeve across his mouth and regarded Henryk with a glint in his eye. Oliwia felt as though she were a ghost in the room.

"My name is Denis, my lord, and you are welcome."

"Denis," Henryk continued, "another of our men, Marcin Jakimowski, arrived shortly before you and Pan Pakulski. Do you know him?"

"Yes, sire, I do. Both men stumbled into our village yesterday in a very bad way. My wife tended them as best she could. She bid them rest, but they insisted on coming here. Pan Marcin grew impatient and outran us."

"We are indebted to you and your good wife," Oliwia said as a guard refilled Denis's tankard. "Where is your village?"

Still looking at Henryk, he replied, "I am from Brenna."

"Brenna? And they came to you there?" Henryk's tone was filled with surprise. And no wonder. Brenna was a two-day ride south-by-southwest of Biaska, whereas Silnyród lay to the southeast.

"Yes, sire. They said they had escaped a band of thugs. They climbed into a wagon, and it brought them to Brenna."

Oliwia's blood froze. Beside her, Henryk stiffened. Her pulse quickened. "What became of the rest of the party?"

"What little I heard was told to me by my wife after she tended their wounds." Denis, still looking at Henryk, swallowed a chunk of cheese. "Pan Marcin ranted the duration about their party making their way to the border when they were beset by highwaymen. I suppose it was highwaymen. He never did say. But the brigands surprised the thirty of them, killing more than half at the first. He said he and the other man, Stefan, managed to escape."

"Was there an officer? Did he mention names?" Oliwia held her breath.

"No names, but he spoke of a captain. Over and over."

"So the captain was alive when he last saw him?" asked Henryk.

"No, sir." Denis shook his head gravely. "Pan Marcin was distraught, you see, because the other man, Pan Stefan, saw this captain executed."

Oliwia had been teetering, but now blind fury exploded in her gut, and she jumped up, fists balled.

"No!" she shrieked. "No, that's impossible! You're lying!"

Denis pulled back, big-eyed and open-mouthed. Henryk grasped her arm, but she shook it off.

Denis swallowed. "Maybe … maybe I heard him wrong, m'lady," he stuttered.

Oliwia's chest constricted. She couldn't breathe, as though she'd been slammed against a boulder and the air stolen from her. Dizzying waves rolled through her body. She trembled and thought she would be sick. Her vision clouded, and she fell hard into her seat. She breathed rapidly, her heart galloping. Her hands turned clammy, and sweat broke out on her forehead; the room spun around her.

Someone—Henryk—leaned down to her ear, and she jumped. "Oliwia?" he said.

She remembered nothing else.

By the time Denis left with his spare mount, a bundle of provisions and a reward, Marcin and Stefan had been moved to the keep and Oliwia had convinced herself Denis had it wrong. Jacek still lived. After all, the peasant was mistaken about the number in their party. They had been no more than ten, not thirty.

As she sealed a letter to Lesław, Henryk entered the solar. "Marcin is conscious, my lady."

She stood, straightened her shoulders, and set her chin in a steely pose far removed from her state of mind. As she walked beside Henryk, she calmed her barreling breaths. When they entered the dim chamber, she was bolstered by the sight of an upright Marcin clad in a fresh shirt. He watched them blearily as they approached. Stefan lay prone in a separate cot on the opposite wall of their makeshift infirmary.

"My Lady Oliwia. Captain Kalinowski," Marcin rasped, looking from Henryk to Oliwia and back again.

"Marcin," Oliwia sat beside him and reached for his hand, "I am glad to see you awake. How do you fare? Do you need anything?" Beside him was a half-filled tankard of the piwo-water mixture. His lesions glistened with uncture; other parts of him were swathed in bandages.

"I'll do, my lady. Weary, sore, but I'll do."

Henryk stood behind her, his hand on the back of her chair, his presence steady. "We heard a little from Denis of Brenna."

Marcin inhaled a big breath, and his limp brown eyes wandered to the hearth, where they remained fixed as he unwound his tale. When he reached the point of the attack, she relinquished his hand and clenched her own together, her nails digging into her palms.

Henryk bent to her ear. "Are you sure you wish to hear this, my lady?" She nodded, suddenly unable to stop her bobbing head.

Marcin took another sip. Oliwia held herself still, feeling altogether like brittle leather.

"They shot that beautiful stallion. Just killed him outright. The captain went out of his mind, and they cracked him over the head. Only way to subdue him. Then they pulled the trappings off Smok and slung them over

Jarosława. She'd been tied with the spare horses, and I can't figure how she came to be right there. Strange, isn't it? They could have had no idea she was his, but they threw his saddle on her. Damn, but he loved that horse." Marcin snuffled before continuing.

"A few of our party fled to the trees during the fight. I was one of those. They murdered the injured outright, along with servants. A few brigands lit out after any who escaped. They gathered horses and weapons, and the towarzysze—there couldn't have been more than six or seven left—were bound and marched off. I followed for a bit, staying out of sight, until I nearly stumbled over Stefan. We ran like blazes for help, but there was none to be found," he said dismally.

Oliwia shook her head, as if shaking off Marcin's words.

Stefan had stirred during Marcin's narrative and now stared at the ceiling where he lay. Henryk moved to his side and propped him up, giving him a drink. He sipped, shut his eyes, and began to speak, seemingly unaware of Oliwia's presence. She was numb as she stared at him.

"They trussed us all up. One of the devils tied the captain's ankles to his saddle and dragged him. Miserable son of a bitch kept looking back at him, laughing. I'm not sure how far we went."

Stefan pulled in a shallow breath. He took another gulp from the tankard and rested the bottom of the vessel on his thigh. Henryk stood stiffly at his side.

"They walked us back to their camp," Stefan continued, "and they loosened our bindings and told us to take off everything but our shirts and breeches. They made us sit and started retying us. They had cut the captain loose. He didn't move, and we thought he was out, but he surprised us all when he got up, screaming some war cry, and bashed the ones closest to him.

"He caused such a commotion that they all turned away from us. It was then he ordered us in Latin to run. I was the only one who got away. One of the men—I think his name was Andrzej—ran toward the captain. The brave idiot was … Christ, I don't know *what* he was thinking. It was chaotic. Lots of shouting and confusion. They must have knocked the captain out again because I glanced back and saw him on the ground. One of the bastards raised his sword and thrust the point down." Stefan stifled a sob. "He couldn't even defend himself."

Jacek's not dead. Jacek's not dead. Jacek's not dead.

The warrior looked up at the dark-timbered ceiling hovering not far above their heads, tears spilling freely down his cheeks. He swiped at his face, and, all at once, choked out, "There was nothing he wouldn't do for his men. He was a fierce brother. He saved me—sacrificed himself to save us all. The man had the heart of a lion."

Jacek's not dead. Jacek's not dead. Jacek's not dead.

Stefan dropped his head and squeezed his eyes shut, and his body convulsed with silent weeping.

Oliwia cupped her mouth, clamping down on a wail erupting from deep within her. She had built battlements in her mind, had persuaded herself—and believed—that Denis was wrong.

But for an instant, desolation swamped her, and the truth lay bare before her. In that instant, her world shattered into slivers as numerous as the stars. Irretrievable. Beyond repair.

Jacek is dead.

Chapter 17

Broken Promises

A s quickly as Oliwia's defenses had ripped apart, she began gathering them once more, marshaling her fragile fallacies around herself like a cloak of feathers.

Jacek's not dead. Everyone is wrong.

But her mind leapt to new horrors.

Jacek's injured. He needs help. He's all alone. We must find him.

When Filip sought her out, his blue-gray eyes wide and wet, she was ready.

"Liwi, is it true? Is … is Jacek dead?"

She drew him close, and he hugged her tight. "I've seen no proof, Filip, and until I do, he's not."

Jacek's not dead. She would have *felt* it. It would have rattled through her heart, shaken her soul. But she had felt no wrinkle, no stab when he had supposedly been slain.

Pulling back, she pushed a curl off Filip's forehead and brushed a tear from his cheek. "Pan Henryk is taking a detail to find Jacek. He might be hurt."

Before the sun lit the horizon the next morning, Henryk's squad, along with Father Augustyn, rode out. They would travel light and hard, trading out horses along the way. It would take days to reach the site of the attack, days to return. Oliwia struggled to contain the serpents slithering in her gut, to lock out images of Jacek in agony. As she fingered the pocketed wooden rosary beads, she prayed. And prayed. *Please, Holy Mother, I beg you. Keep Jacek safe.*

After Henryk's departure, she drifted, pale and wraithlike, from the nursery to the infirmary to the chapel to the solar, only to repeat the cycle again. At night, her miasma lifted, and her bed became a hell on earth where she found no respite from the horrible images unendingly bounding through her head.

In the face of it all, Marcin and Stefan recovered. One morning, as she helped the healer change Marcin's bandages, she asked him, "What are your plans?"

He seemed not to hear her, frowning at what lay beneath his dressings. Beyond him, Stefan, who had shed his pallor and more closely resembled the man rather than the near-corpse he had been, stared blankly out the window as though oblivious or disinterested in anything taking place around him.

Kasimir poked his head through the door, and Oliwia invited him in.

He bowed to her and smiled, asking after her. If he'd harbored any ill will after her decree, he hid it well. Her heart climbed a few rungs when Stefan spotted his friend, and his cheeks lifted in a near-smile.

Marcin at last raised his eyes to hers. "Plans? I had not given it much thought, my lady. I suppose I shall return to Pan Jacek's home. His family knows, yes?"

Oliwia's words unexpectedly caught in her throat; she cleared it. "Yes. Pan Henryk wrote them. I am sure they would welcome you."

"Then I shall go as soon as I'm recovered. I wish I had something of his I could bring them." He cast his eyes from hers.

She reached into her pocket and drew out Jacek's rosary. Prying Marcin's hand open, she gently nestled the smooth beads in his palm. He looked up at her, confusion on his features.

"When he left this with me for safekeeping, he said his mother gave it to him many years ago," she said. "Please see she gets it."

Laughter rose from the other bed, startling her and interrupting her melancholy. Stefan and Kasimir exchanged what, she had no idea, but she warmed to the glad noise.

She rose to her feet. "Let me know if you need anything, Marcin. Anything at all."

He reached for her hand and squeezed it. "I shall, my lady. Thank you."

Days later, when the guards heralded Henryk's party's return, Oliwia watched them trot into the yard, her breath wedged in her chest. As many rode in as had ridden out. Her chary oblivion was about to end. The afternoon sun lit the crenellations in a blinding display. Shading her eyes, she blinked. And blinked again. *The light must be deceiving me.* She flew down the stairs. When she reached the yard, her side cramped with a stitch.

"Henryk!" she gasped, her eyes glued to something behind him.

He had dismounted and was handing his horse's reins to a stable hand. But it was another set of reins that drew her eye, for they were attached to a familiar mount who carried familiar armor devoid of the warrior who once wore it.

"Jarosława!" a voice behind her croaked.

Oliwia whirled. Marcin hobbled toward Jacek's beloved mare, and the horse threw her head up. When Marcin reached her, his fingers skimmed the armor. He pulled the horse's head to his and rubbed her muzzle. She snuffled his hair, as if breathing him in. Tears ran unchecked down his face.

Covered in road grime, Henryk looked down at Oliwia blearily. *Does he suffer from fatigue? Despair? Both?* All around her, stable hands kicked up dust as they ran to tend the party's mounts, sending it swirling in the air amid men's subdued voices. Somewhere distant, children squealed, chickens clucked, and dogs barked. It was a lovely summer day, and everything went on as it always had. The world had not changed. But hers had.

"Come to my sitting room, Henryk. I will have food and drink brought up for you." She clutched his arm as though it were the only thing holding her up; likely it was.

Henryk covered her hand with his own. "Are you well, Oliwia?"

"Of course," she lied.

He gave her a curt nod, and she reluctantly released her hold on him, fearful she might topple over. She made her way to the forestairs as though she walked on legs of melting butter.

Henryk joined her soon after. He dropped into a chair across from hers, separated by a table holding a tray with a pitcher, goblets, and food. He propped an elbow on the armrest and stared at the remnants of the fire, grim-faced. She barely noticed he'd freshened up.

"Are you hungry?" She poured out two cups of wine.

"No, thank you, my lady."

The social niceties were absurd. She scanned the cheese, bread, and fruit, and though she'd not eaten this day, her stomach was heavy, as though lined with ingots of lead. Even the few sips of wine sat sour in her belly.

She drew in a breath. "So, Henryk. What have you to tell me?"

Without looking at her, he began his narrative as though he recited a list of wagons and their contents. Just as described, they'd found the site of the attack and a horse's carcass sprawled alongside a creek. Henryk recognized the once majestic stallion, Smok, despite its sorry state of decay. They followed a trail to a small clearing screened by saplings and shrubberies, pulled there by a dreadful smell. Here they discovered the devils' camp.

Oliwia kept her unwavering gaze on Henryk. He sat rigid, his eyes riveted as though he watched one sliver of hypnotic flame. "I was in the lead," he continued in a flat tone, "so I was the first to reach the ... scene."

She reached over and gripped his forearm, and he flinched. He gave her a sidelong glance. "Oliwia, you don't want to know."

She gusted out a breath. "Everyone dictates what I should and should not know. *I* will decide."

He sipped his wine. "At first, I saw naught but the wrecked camp. But I pushed through dense thickets and came upon another clearing." He paused. "I couldn't place what I saw at first. A black pile that seemed to be moving. As I walked toward it, I realized ..."

She braced herself. "Go on."

"I saw bodies. Burned bodies in a heap, covered in flies and insects. We knew they were our men by their dress, their armor, their pennons. It fell to me to identify each one." He looked at her then, a look of utter despair. "Jacek's gone, Oliwia."

"You saw his face?"

"The fire, animals, the decay ... Features were obliterated. It was impossible to identify anyone that way."

"Then how?" she cried. "If you could not see his face, how do you know it was Jacek?"

Henryk pulled in a huge breath, then seemed to sag in his chair. "I buried him myself. Few men are so big as Jacek. The body I put in the ground, one wearing his armor and the żupan Jacek always wore on the road, was big. Just like Jacek."

"What color was his hair?" She was desperate to contain her welling panic.

"Oliwia," he said quietly. "There was no hair. It all burned. And then there is Jarosława. Jacek would never leave her."

Oliwia gripped her armrests, her knuckles white. "How did you find her?"

"She found me. We were praying beside the graves with Father Augustyn when I heard a horse nicker. At first, I paid it no heed. But it whinnied again, and I realized it came from the woods, just beyond where I'd placed Jacek. Just then, Jarosława crashed through the underbrush. I recognized the bridle—the one with the turquoise medallions. She was still saddled, and Jacek's *pałasz* hung from the straps. When I reached out, she rubbed my hand." He hung his head.

"The saddle was askew, but otherwise all looked to be in order. She was unharmed. I have no idea why she was there. She should have been taken, or she should have tried to find her way to Silnyród. All I can think is she was waiting for him to return." He swallowed more wine.

They sat for long minutes, unmoving. Suddenly, Oliwia shot to her feet and began pacing. The composure she'd held so tightly unwound around her. Henryk tracked her with his eyes.

"This proves nothing, Henryk. I would feel it. I would know, in here!" She slammed her fist against her chest. "He cannot be gone! If the corpses were as unrecognizable as you say, if the flies and the animals … You might have been mistaken."

Henryk sighed and stood, walking toward her. "There is one more thing." Reaching into his sash, he extracted a length of chain. He picked up her hand and turned it palm up, depositing the chain there. "I found this on that same body."

Oliwia peered into her cupped hand at a glinting object attached to the chain, and her world ruptured. She let out a wail that seemed to come from somewhere unearthly, from a thousand wretched souls crying out from a pit yawning in hell. She crumpled. Henryk caught her before she sank to the floor and helped her into her chair.

"Come," he gently urged.

The object fell from her hand and clinked with a metallic ring on the stone hearth. It lay at Oliwia's feet in a pile of silver chain. Her mother's silver cross, still attached, was now crusted in soot and blood.

She hugged herself and sobbed, rocking back and forth. Time was suspended in that chamber, and after what could have been hours or minutes, she reached a trembling hand to the necklace at her feet.

"Here." Henryk snatched it up and dropped it into her palm.

After another long silence, Oliwia looked back at Henryk, surprised to see moistness on his cheeks. "I'm sorry. I should have realized … I am not the only one who grieves."

He shook his head, staring at his lap.

Oliwia swallowed. "How did you know about the cross?"

He sniffed, cuffed his nose, and cleared his throat. "I recognized it before he left. He meant to keep it secret. That was his way. When I found it on the body, I knew it belonged to him. He would never have given it up."

Oliwia turned it over, staring at it as if seeing it for the first time. "I gave him this before he left and told him it would bring him back to me. He asked me to wed him, and I agreed. I was so happy. He promised to return …" she murmured, her eyes pooling anew.

With all the force of a gale, reality rocked her. Jacek was no longer on this earth. Her world was gone, leveled. Again.

Filip appeared in the doorway, his face ashen. "Liwi? Pan Henryk?"

Oliwia shook off the urge to drop her head in her hands and weep. Instead, she clawed her armrests, girding herself as she plummeted into a well of strength that was utterly drained.

"Come, Filip. I have news about Pan Jacek."

He crept into the room as though he were a deer readying to run away at any moment. When at last he stood before her, she grasped his hands and looked into his glistening eyes.

"Filip, Jacek is not coming back."

He blinked, and his eyes rimmed. His lower lip quivered.

"But you said he was hurt, Liwi." His voice began rising. "You said he wasn't dead!"

"I was hoping, Filip, praying it was so. But Henryk discovered otherwise."

Filip dashed his eyes—now spilling tears down his cheeks—to Henryk. Yanking his hands away, Filip scrubbed angrily at his face.

"You were wrong, Liwi. You were wrong!" he yelled.

Henryk stood and placed a hand on his shoulder. "Listen to me, Filip. There was naught to be done. Your sister is not to blame here. God must have decided He needed a valiant soldier in His army of angels, and He chose Jacek."

Filip looked at him, fury twisting his face. "The devil with God!"

When Romek stole into Antonin's solar, he found him reclining in his chair, his bootheels on his desk and his hands laced over his belly. It was dark in the chamber, for blackness absorbed light in the cool, damp night, and Antonin's hearth held only meager flames of a stingy fire. Two tallow candles stood on the desk, casting tight amber circles on the dark wood desktop.

"No one saw you, did they?" asked Antonin.

"Only your … Only the maid Krystiana, when she admitted me below."

Antonin broke out in a malevolent grin and raised a battered metal cup. "Have some wodka and raise your cup."

Romek pulled off his gloves and swept the hood from his head. Moving in measured steps, he poured himself a cupful from the jug. "What are we toasting?"

Antonin's cup was still aloft. "Tonight, we drink to the death of one of Biaska's hussars!"

Romek's brows shot to his forehead. "Which one?"

"That bastard Dąbrowski! Someone took care of the cocksucker for us!"

Romek raised his own cup. *"Na zdrowie."* He gulped a quick sip, the harsh liquid burning its way to his stomach. "How do you know?"

Antonin threw back the rest of his drink and reached for the jug, chuckling. "My spy at Biaska tells me everything."

"Who killed him? How?"

Antonin stared at him from beneath one long, furrowed brow. "He was killed on his way to Podolia. Imagine! Some witless band of thieves took him out." One side of Antonin's mouth curled crookedly. "I must go and see my cousin's poor little widow. Offer her aid. I expect she needs——"

Romek set his cup on the battered desktop a little harder than he'd intended, bringing Antonin upright.

"I thought we agreed I would dispatch her," Romek said in a tight voice.

Antonin fisted his hands on the desk and growled, "Patience, Romek. You will have your chance, but first she shall have a period of mourning, and then I am going to marry the little morsel. As planned." Antonin's tone turned icy. "Your job is to see no harm comes to her in the meantime. After everything is under my control, *then* you can see to her tragic demise. A little more time is warranted to hold your eagerness in check."

Romek spun and stalked from the room without awaiting Antonin's dismissal. Moments later, reason surfaced. Sweet revenge was worth the wait.

Oliwia stared at a carved leaf upon her bedpost as she cradled Adam in her arms. He slept in bliss. She yearned to close her swollen eyes and join him, to lose herself in sleep again and escape the unbearable ache. Though it had been weeks since she'd learned of Jacek's death, her anguish hadn't diminished. A heart could truly break, and loss manifested itself in physical pain, as though one was struck by an arrow. Dear God, but it hurt so!

Fatigue weighed her down, though she'd spent the previous day abed. *What if my heart simply stops? Would that I could lie down and never wake up again.* The thought shook her as she looked at Adam's angelic face.

Nadia entered the chamber, her arms laden with a tray. Oliwia cared not a whit what it held. Her scant stomach contents rose up, and she looked away.

"Beata has sent some of your favorite foods, m'lady," the little maid said.

She set the tray on the bedside table and began pouring mead. Oliwia waved her off. "No, Nadia, not now. I'm neither thirsty nor hungry."

Nadia's pebble eyes blinked. "But you have not eaten in days, m'lady. Please. You must have something. A tart, perhaps?"

Oliwia shook her head. "I will be sick if I eat."

Nadia bit her lower lip. "Forgive me, m'ady, but Beata was wondering … That is, will you be giving her some direction soon? And the brewmaster was asking—"

Oliwia sighed. "Tell them I will see them tomorrow."

Nadia studied her, a rare frown on her face.

"What is it?" Oliwia looked at her dully.

"I, um … am that concerned, m'lady, you not eating and being tired all the time."

Fatigue. Nausea. *Spirit of God!* Oliwia had held a dim awareness her courses were late, but just how late?

"I am fine, Nadia." Oliwia's voice held a betraying quaver.

Adam stirred and began to fuss. Nadia clucked and took him. Alone, Oliwia calculated, her uneasiness blooming, her mind rapidly running through consequences. A fresh round of tears stung her eyes. She flung herself onto Jacek's pillow; only a trace of his scent remained.

What if Jacek left something else behind that now grows in me?

She stilled and flashed to holding a new babe in her arms—one with beautiful sapphire eyes she could get lost in. Jacek might yet endure. Elation twined with her despair.

Oliwia perched at the edge of her chair in the solar, chewing on a jagged nail she then tried to smooth against her wool skirt. She shoved a hank of hair behind her ear. Straightening her back, she brought her attention to bear on was happening and tracked Henryk as he paced from hearth to window. His mood reminded her of the tempest raging outside, his movements like the wind lashing rain against the glass.

"You are going to wear a trough in the floor," she said.

"What?" He seemed to waken. "I beg your pardon." He dropped into a chair with a huff and looked at Tomasz in the seat beside him.

"As I was saying," Tomasz began, "once we've delivered this year's rye crop and collected payment, we'll have more funds for soldiers' wages."

"And this year's crop is decent, Henryk, despite the wet weather," Oliwia added. "It will bring an ample sum."

Henryk nodded. "Which we sorely need. Thank the saints the harvest will soon be done."

Tomasz adjusted the glasses astride his nose. "The Amsterdam merchant we've always dealt with contracted for this year's crop, so payment is assured. Barge space has been reserved, so 'tis only a matter of getting the grain to the Vistula. From there, I will sail with it to Gdańsk."

"Getting it to the river is simple enough," said Henryk.

"And we've enough in the treasury to pay the river tolls?" Oliwia asked Tomasz.

"Oh yes, my lady. Lord Eryk … That is, 'tis our custom to set aside those sums when the merchant sends his advance payment, and this year is no different."

"We are in no danger of forfeiting that advance?" she asked.

"None, my lady, as long as the grain is delivered as planned. We've never failed."

Oliwia clapped her hands. "Then we've naught to do but wait for the end of harvest. Thank you, Tomasz."

Tomasz gathered his ledgers and gave them a head bob as he headed out the door, looking altogether like a quail with glasses.

"You see there, Henryk?" she said when they were alone. "A bit of welcome news is ours at last. Once the harvest is over, we will hold a dożynki such as Biaska has never seen. 'Twill be a merry festival, and the tenants can rejoice in their success instead of mourning their lord."

The thought of revelers capering appeared in her head and was crowded out by a memory of dancing with Jacek. She pressed her thumb in her eye.

A guard appeared in the open doorway. "Letter for Captain Kalinowski."

Henryk rose and accepted the folded paper, then closed the door in the guard's wake. "From Lesław, my lady. I pray 'tis more good news."

She stood. "Well, open it and let us hear what he has to say."

Breaking the seal, Henryk unfolded the letter. He began scanning but stopped abruptly and looked at Oliwia with wide eyes.

"What is it?"

"N-nothing important."

Oliwia could not recall hearing Henryk stutter before. "What does he say?" she prodded.

205

Henryk shrugged and darted his eyes out the window, casually refolding the letter. "Ah, he is much better, and ah ..."

Oliwia snatched it from him.

"There's naught to read, Oliwia," Henryk protested, reaching for the letter. She stretched, keeping it from him.

"Like it or not, Henryk, I am in charge, and I will know what is taking place in my holdings. Besides, you are a terrible liar. How ever do you win at cards?"

Henryk dragged a hand over his chin and stood back, watching, as Oliwia began to read.

Silnyród, 26 June, in the Year of our Lord 1614

My dear Henryk,

God's blessings upon you and the Lady Oliwia. I thank you for your kind words of concern after my health. I am in no danger, having recovered completely. My heart, however, is broken beyond repair over the death of my commander and friend, for surely such a man was deserving of a better fate.

I will continue to see to Silnyród's defenses until such time as the lady decides otherwise. In addition, I took it upon myself to deliver the terrible tidings to Jacek's betrothed, the Lady Eugenia of Matejko Manor. As you likely know, they planned to wed upon his return to Silnyród. In light of their promise and affection for one another, she was, naturally, inconsolable with the news of her beloved's death.

Please do not hesitate to call upon me for any other service I might render.

Your loyal servant and friend,

Lesław Bieczski

Oliwia's head shot up as her mouth swung open. She stared at Henryk, who stared back at her. She dropped the letter to the floor and let out a high-pitched, mad laugh.

"Did you know?" she asked sharply.

He shook his head. "No. I'm as astonished as you. Perhaps Lesław has it wrong."

"I doubt this Lady Eugenia creature *invented* a betrothal, Henryk."

He eyed her sympathetically. "Oliwia, *if* Jacek agreed to marry this woman, he had some mysterious motive only he understood."

She barely heard him, insteading recalling Jacek's uncharacteristic flinch at the mention of a marriage contract.

"Oliwia," Henryk's voice pierced her thoughts. "Jacek loved you beyond measure and had for a very long time. In truth, you drove him to distraction, made him daft, and I goaded him mercilessly for it. Did he ever tell you we came to Biaska at the same time, when we were boys? Well, we did, and we became brothers. We fought like brothers, defended one another like brothers, loved like brothers. I knew him better than anyone, and I know he never felt for any woman what he felt for you."

Oliwia's shoulders drooped with a sigh. She picked up the letter and set it upon the desktop, its stubborn creases causing it to fold on itself. She glanced back at Henryk, who watched her quietly. "Thank you, Henryk. You are a good friend."

Henryk gave her a head dip.

Who, and what, the devil is Lady Eugenia?

For days after it arrived, Lesław's message set a string of questions careening through Oliwia's brain. Her curiosity drove her to find someone who might know aught of Lady Eugenia—which was why she faced Marcin across the polished desk one afternoon in the solar.

"Marcin, I am glad to see you doing so well."

He fidgeted, shifting his weight from foot to foot.

"Please sit," she offered.

His eyebrows rose slowly to his hairline, but he did sit. At the farthest edge of the chair. "How may I be of service, my lady?"

"What would you say to remaining and serving Biaska as a towarzysz husaria?"

Marcin opened his mouth, but nothing came out for several beats. "I … I haven't the armor or wings, my lady, nor the horses."

"But you do, Marcin. You have Jarosława and Pan Jacek's armor. I will see you get the wings. We need good fighting men here, loyal men of integrity, and I wish you to stay."

He gawped at her. "But Jarosława is *not* mine, my lady. And the armor … It's too big."

"Who does Jarosława belong to, then? Pan Jacek bought her with money he earned, trained her himself, and loved her dearly. I've been thinking whom *he* would choose to be her master. As for the armor, the smithy can cut it down."

"Both should be returned to Pan Jacek's family," he insisted. "Or given to Master Filip."

"Both would be wasted on Master Filip." Oliwia held up a folded square of ivory paper. "I've been given Pan Jacek's family's blessing to award you all his possessions—even the rosary, if you choose."

Marcin's eyes darted about the desktop, and his expression shifted from elation to confusion in rapid succession.

"Perhaps you'd rather *not* serve Biaska?" she asked sweetly.

He nearly shot out of his seat. "Oh no, my lady. I ... I ..." He swallowed. "I can think of nowhere else I would rather serve."

Oliwia smacked her hands on the shiny wood. "Good! Then you shall." With a wave of her hand, she bid him sit once more. "On occasion, I may have need for you to travel to Silnyród. Will you be amenable?"

"Of course, my lady. Whatever you wish."

"The fortress is familiar to you. Did you enjoy your time there?"

Marcin's brows drew together again. "I could not really say, my lady. The people there are good, hardworking folk, but it is a rougher place than here, and the countryside is unremarkable, not so beautiful as Biaska."

"I understand there was an impressive estate close by, owned by a well-placed family. Have you met Lord Matejko, or perhaps Lady Eugenia? She is quite lovely, I hear." Her tone was light, belying the roiling in her belly.

"I've *seen* Lord Matejko, my lady, on campaign or from his stables, but I was never a guest inside his home. As for Lady Eugenia, she is Pan Matejko's youngest daughter, I believe. I saw her once and found her rather plain." His expression quickly became one of contrition. "I beg your pardon, my lady. That was unkind of me to say. I know little of her. While I accompanied Pan Jacek each time he traveled there, 'twas only a few times, and I never spent time in her company."

The roiling slowed. "Not even when she paid a visit to Silnyród?"

Marcin frowned. "Only her father visited." He began looking at Oliwia quizzically.

"I, ah, heard Pan Jacek fancied her, and I thought, well, I thought to send my condolences."

Marcin looked as though an eagle had lifted off behind him, so surprised was he by this remark.

"I take it you knew nothing of this," Oliwia said. He shook his head. "Perhaps I heard wrong, then. Welcome to the garrison, Pan Marcin."

After he left, she looked about the chamber without seeing anything. Had the union with Lady Eugenia been arranged *for* Jacek? He must have agreed to marry her before he learned of Eryk's death, before Oliwia was free. Had Jacek loved the lady? He could not have loved her more than he loved Oliwia. Could he? This was Jacek, after all. He would never have said the things he'd said or looked at Oliwia the way he did had his heart belonged to another. His plans must have changed after his return to Biaska. That *must* have been it.

Pulling in a tremulous breath, she closed her eyes and conjured her many images of Jacek: his smiles, his scowls, and the fierce face he'd presented the day they'd argued by the lake. But mostly she recalled the tender looks he'd bestowed upon her during their secret nights together and the words of love he'd spoken.

"I adore you. Make my life heaven on earth."

He could not have loved another.

Misery flooded her. She brushed a tear from her cheek. As she contemplated crawling back into her bed and losing herself in sleep, a rap startled her. Filip's curly head poked in.

"There you are, Liwi."

"You needed me?" She stood.

"Yes, well, no. I just saw Jarosława and wondered what will become of her?"

Oliwia leaned against the desk. "Marcin is to become a winged hussar, and I thought to award her to him." She held her breath.

To her surprise, Filip offered no protest, no pleas. In a quiet, thoughtful tone, he said, "I think Pan Jacek would've liked that."

Her heart clenched for the little boy suddenly a man. Filip's pluck seemed to have shriveled and died along with his mentor. When had he last smiled? She stepped to him and gathered him in her arms. His slight frame shuddered against hers.

"I miss him too," she whispered, her tears falling along with his.

Chapter 18

The Enemy of My Enemy is My Friend, Unless He's Not

He descended down, down, drifting into a warm black bog. Oliwia appeared before him, her smile and the light behind her dazzling. She spread her arms wide, beckoning him, and white wings twice her height unfurled languidly behind her. Though her lips moved, he couldn't hear her for an incessant buzzing in his ears. He slumped against her, gratefully giving himself over to oblivion and to her.

How I love you, Liwi.

Take me home.

Something tugged at him, pulling him from the abyss. He fought it. He wanted to stay where he was. But he came to nonetheless, his head pounding like a piece of metal being beaten relentlessly by a smith's hammer.

I'm so thirsty.

Seering pain shot down his left side, its intensity second only to that in his head. His mind began whirring in panic, but his thoughts went round and round in a hazy stew.

I'm so cold.

He tried to open his eyes, but they were glued together. His tongue stuck to the roof of his mouth; he tried to swallow to ease his arid throat, but he couldn't.

I'm still dreaming.

With that thought, he eased until he realized his hands were fixed behind him at an awkward angle, and he couldn't feel his fingers or shoulders. Something clawed and bit his wrists and neck, and he tried to wrench himself away from the beast sinking its fangs into his flesh.

A grunt. He froze.

Why can't I free my hands?

Another ache registered—a dull gnawing in his gut. He was hollow.

I'm so hungry.

Was he trapped in that strange twilight between sleep and wakefulness when dreams are vivid and one cannot move one's body except in small twitches and tics? Warm breath fell on his neck, its sour stench inescapable. Something warm rested in his groin, but it didn't feel right and he tried to pull away.

"Captain!" a voice hissed.

Who is that? Where the hell am I?

And then he remembered.

Don't leave me, Liwi.

You promised you would stay with me forever.

Consciousness flooded back, bringing dark dread with it. Jacek knew where he was. He cracked a crusty lid and peeked through the oozy, razor-thin slit. All was dark, but he saw the silhouette of a head a hand's breadth from his. Then he made out voices and laughter. The sounds were muffled, as if his pulsing head was packed with linen.

Thirsty. Cold. Hungry.

He shifted, and the voice hissed again. "Stop moving." It came from the head.

"Janusz?" he croaked.

He heard furtive voices. They reminded him of rats scurrying and scratching across a stone floor. Finally came one he could understand.

"Christ, you woke me up." This was a heated whisper behind him. Close behind him.

"Who is that?" Jacek whispered back.

"Now you ask? You've been holding my rod all night. I thought at least you'd remember my name."

Jacek jerked his hands, and the voice chuckled softly.

211

"Wiesław. Your dance partner tonight. That must have been quite the dream. Janusz is in front of you, remember? Doubtless he's holding *your* rod." Janusz grunted and shifted his hands. Jacek flinched.

"Scoot your hands down. My wife might get jealous," Wiesław continued. "Now stay quiet, or we'll all feel the lash."

The lash. Jacek flinched again.

Wiesław. Janusz. Pawel's hussars. Pawel and Dawid were among them too, but the five were all that remained of the thirty that had left Krasiczyn. Jacek yearned to flee his bright lucidity, to return to Oliwia hiding behind the mists in his mind. But he would find no such salvation the rest of this night.

He lay very still, staring through the sliver of his lidded eye. They were in a Tatar camp—it was their captors' voices he heard—snatching what little rest was afforded them. They'd been marching for days. Or had it been weeks? He'd lost count. He was so hungry. So thirsty.

Why his group of five lived, he hadn't a clue. Nor was he sure he was grateful. But God had His reasons—if He was even paying attention—and lived they did, if one could call it that. Bound with lengths of rope and braided leather around their necks, feet, and hands, they dozed, marched, pissed, and breathed together. They starved, stumbled, were beaten, and prayed together. Which explained why he was pressed between two men as he lay prone on the ground, dampness seeping into his ragged clothes. When one twitched or shuffled, his fellows felt it too.

But the Tatars had not been their attackers; they'd been the scavengers.

He flashed to the first enemy camp, where they'd been herded after the ambush. When they'd cut him loose, he'd fought them, buying time so men could flee before they'd bashed his head and knocked him out again. Had any escaped? A familiar pang stabbed him hard, and he fervently prayed at least one had gotten away. One of the men—his name had been Andrzej—ran at the devils in a courageous, senseless, desperate attempt. For his trouble, he'd been sliced open from groin to throat and had died in a river of his own blood.

After that had come a riot of men pulling on the hussars' gear, strutting in cardinal żupans, cockeyed armor, and red and yellow boots. The devil who'd dragged him from his saddle had spun, flashing crimson and shiny metal with a nasty grin. About his waist had sat Jacek's belt, replete with his szabla and dagger. His nadziak, other odd blades, and a Silnyród pennon had been tucked in the belt haphazardly. Saddle Dragger had glanced down at himself, immensely pleased.

"Szlachta has nice clothes! Not big man now, eh?" he'd chortled and grabbed a fistful of Jacek's hair. That's when Jacek had seen Oliwia's cross about the man's neck.

"Untie me, you rancid piece of batshit, and let's have a go," Jacek had spat.

"Still want fight?" the man had hooted. He'd shoved Jacek backward and pressed a yellow boot on his chest, flinging his arms wide. "Good! We fight!"

Still laughing, Saddle Dragger had stumbled to Andrzej's corpse and relieved himself, the stream wavering along with his laughter, then shouted something at his men. One squeezed drink from a skin, and another lunged for it. They began shoving and cursing, and a fight broke out.

Jacek had counted ten brigands in all, ten drunken fools, and he'd raged at himself. *Spirit of God, how could I have let these halfwits best us?*

Saddle Dragger had tried to stop the fight, and as he'd stepped between them, he'd shrieked and dropped. That's when Jacek had heard telltale whizzing, followed by *thwacks* and *thunks* and men's screams and groans. He'd thrown himself to the ground, flattening belly-first in the dirt, hands still bound behind him. The arrows stopped almost as soon as they'd flown, and when he looked up, a dozen squat forms had materialized from the woods like specters. And his heart dropped.

Rather than rescuers, they were a new enemy. Tatars. Brandishing a lance, one man among them stepped to Saddle Dragger, who writhed and cried hoarsely, arrows protruding from knee, shoulder, and chest. And that's when Jacek recognized the man looming over him—the man who'd raped Milda's girl, who'd overseen her brutal death.

His sallow, pocked face held a cruel slash for a mouth. Above it was a black, wispy moustache that twisted into an equally wispy beard and hung to his chest. His most prominent, unforgettable feature was his nose. From a bony knob, it waved along his thick, pitted skin to a broad, flattened tip. On the right side was a horrific scar puckering its length.

Scar Nose looked at the squirming Saddle Dragger indifferently, then reached to his belt—Jacek's belt—and whipped out a pennon, turning it over in his hands. And quick as a snake, he rammed the tip of the lance into Saddle Dragger's groin. There was blood, so much blood, and screaming so loud and shrill Jacek thought surely it would rent the heavens.

As the man's squeals filled the air, Scar Nose strolled to Jacek and motioned for him to be hauled upright. Jacek knew his time was over, and he loosed a fleeting prayer. But then Scar Nose thrust the butt end of his lance into his gut. The tender spot was still there. The blow doubled him over, and he landed on his knees. A leather band was quickly dropped over his head and cinched around his neck. Scar Nose yanked him back up by the restraint, choking him. Jacek sputtered and wheezed, every gasp sending a shockwave through him. The man watched him with eyes as black and dead as coke, and he chuckled before releasing him.

After the Tatars finished slaughtering the highwaymen, they ransacked the camp but left the bodies clothed. Jacek and his four companions were thrown the brigands' battered boots, then they were tied together and secured to horses.

The Tatars—fifteen in all—stacked the hussar-garbed bodies on makeshift pyres, which they flamed. And Jacek understood. Silnyród and Klemens' hussars had devastated Scar Nose's war band, and here was his revenge—and his warning to other Commonwealth troops. Jacek also understood he and his companions could never let these bastards know who they really were, and so they marched, ever southeast, leaving the Carpathians and Poland far behind. At times, he'd been delirious, even euphoric, and though he welcomed his mind's escape, he'd lost track of time and space as days tumbled over one another.

But as he lay this night, he had no such extravagance. He knew what awaited him. Morning would bring another grueling march—with scant food or water—and he'd feel the reverberation of each footfall of their human train in each weary bone, every twisted muscle, every piece of shredded skin. If they were lucky, their captors would tire of whipping them through field and wood for not keeping up with the horses—or for whatever reason moved them. If they were lucky, the sun wouldn't beat on their heads. Instead, the heavens would open, and drenching rain would run in rivulets over their faces and into their mouths and soothe their parched throats and dry, cracked lips. If they were lucky, the Tatars would throw them an extra strip of horse meat.

The abuse had weakened them, had kept them from fighting for freedom. An effective strategy, Jacek admitted bitterly.

For now, he shut it all out and concentrated on Wiesław's rhythmic snores against his back. He also shut out the itches he couldn't reach and the crawlers on his body that caused the itching. Instead, he prayed as he'd done countless times since their capture. Was God listening? He prayed on as if He were. When he reckoned God was sick of hearing from him, he catalogued everything he'd observed and searched for the inevitable flaw that would allow escape. He'd seen none to exploit. Yet.

He drew in a lungful of foul air, and as he closed his eyes, he let it out slowly.

Come to me, Oliwia.

Come take me away from this hell.

Chapter 19

We Are Family

Surprised by his unexpected knock, Oliwia bid Tomasz enter her sitting room. Henryk followed close on his heels.

"Tomasz, you are back already? Did you choose not to sail with the grain, after all?"

Uncustomarily disheveled, Tomasz cast his eyes to the kolpak gripped in his hands. His white sausage fingers clenched and unclenched the sable cuff. He brought his head up.

"My lady, I am so, so very sorry." He dropped his head.

"The grain never made it to the barge," Henryk said, his face grim.

"*What?* Why not?"

Henryk's hazel eyes smoldered. "The wagons burned up on their way to the Vistula. The entire crop was lost."

"Merciful God! Was anyone hurt?"

"No," Tomasz replied.

"A few burns and scrapes, too much smoke," Henryk added, "but nothing serious."

"Who was in charge? How did it happen?" Oliwia's belly began cramping.

Henryk shook his head. "Kasimir was in charge. He was at sentry, watching a lightning storm. He thinks a bolt hit one of the wagons. Flames began in one wagon and spread quickly. By the time he rousted the men, it was too far gone."

"And now we must repay the sum advanced by the Amsterdam merchant," Tomasz added, seeming to droop farther.

Oliwia's knees were watery. She dropped into a chair and looked up at two sets of eyes fixed on her.

"Whatever will we do now?" she whispered.

She listened while Tomasz haltingly recounted the impact of the lost shipment on Biaska's treasury, on its tenants and others relying on the estate. When she asked for solutions, she heard few, and those either man proposed were quickly discarded by the other. So she proposed her own solutions, but each flaw was exposed and debated. In the end, little was left but asking the freeholders to contribute a larger share, searching out any swaths of under-harvested grain … and praying.

Exhausted, Oliwia called for Nadia to loosen her undergown after the men had left.

"It appears my lady has begun her courses," the little maid said as she untied the skirt.

"So it does." A tendril of sadness hooked around Oliwia's heart.

Romek stood before Antonin in dim twilight, twitching with excitement.

"The plan went better than we dreamed, my lord. It is done," he said evenly.

"The entire shipment?"

"Every last wagon, every last grain." Romek snapped his fingers. "Gone. 'Twas a beautiful bonfire."

Antonin's weathered face split in a wolfish grin. "Such a pity. I expect Lady Oliwia will have rather a time of it, trying to entice more soldiers to her garrison."

"Or paying the ones already in her employ," Romek added with a wicked laugh.

"Yes. Has our friend been compensated?"

"Handsomely. I took care of it personally," Romek said.

"Excellent."

"We need more men for the garrison, Oliwia."

She bristled at Henryk's all-too-familiar refrain, then inwardly admonished herself for her petulance. Henryk had been a stalwart at her side. Whatever would she have done without him?

"What of the tenants and the service they owe the estate?" she suggested.

"And leave us more shorthanded? They are still working from dawn to dusk gathering and threshing what grain remains. For their service, we must wait."

Wanda rushed in, hefting a tray. "Food and drink, m'lady."

"But we already have food and wine." Oliwia waved at another tray upon the desk.

"Oh! How silly of me," Wanda giggled. She stole a glance at Henryk, but he seemed not to notice. "Excuse me, m'lady, Lord Henryk." She left the solar in a swirl of skirts.

"Back to the business at hand, Henryk," Oliwia said. "What about enlisting more Scots? A warm place to bunk this winter might entice them. And I speak their language."

Henryk shook his head. "I tried. Many in the Kraków settlement have found posts elsewhere."

"We've exhausted most other choices. What of our allies?"

Henryk gave her a wry smile. "Lord Eryk did not build alliances, and our neighbors think Biaska is too rich."

"Should we look to the men of Silnyród?"

"Most are Lithuanian and will be reluctant to leave their homes. But perhaps Lesław knows border mercenaries who would come. I will send a missive."

She let out a heavy sigh. "I received a letter from Pan Antonin. He plans to visit before the Feast of St. Hedwig."

Henryk's eyebrows shot to his hairline. "Why?"

"He says he is concerned for me, that we are family, and he wishes to present an offer of help. Wąskadroga enjoyed a bountiful harvest, and he is 'moved' to share that bounty."

Henryk let out a snort. "He is 'moved' to flaunt all he has in the face of Biaska's difficulty."

"While he is here, perhaps I should speak to him about pledging some of his troops?" She suppressed the shiver slithering up her spine. *At what cost?*

"I would rather embrace a viper. He's not to be trusted, Oliwia."

"Then what of Jankowski?"

Henryk frowned. "What *of* Jankowski?"

Oliwia held up a piece of paper covered in an elegant scrawl. "He has asked to court me."

"What? You're not twenty Sundays a widow! Has he no propriety?" Henryk swiped at the letter. "Let me see that. Ha! His father wrote this. Or his father's secretary." Henryk paused and puffed. "Jacek was right. You must marry. But not Jankowski. Jacek was also right to want to break his skinny neck."

"Jacek wanted to break his neck? I suspected he wasn't fond of him, but—"

Henryk flapped a hand at her. "It was years ago, when Jankowski and his sister were guests here. Jacek was … well, he found Jankowski too attentive toward you. Regardless, Jankowski's a feckless toad. I take that back. A toad has a backbone."

"Well, here's another letter you might care to read. It's from Pan Zebrzydowski, and he states King Zygmunt has 'politely' asked what's to become of Biaska, and should he perhaps suggest some suitors?"

"What?"

"Read for yourself." She passed him the letter.

He did read. His eyes grew round, then they stormed. "Spirit of God, the jackals are on the hunt."

"I want none of them."

"Then they will not bother you." He tugged his cuffs. "But you must consider some sort of match, Oliwia. Meanwhile, we are back to the problem of hiring and paying men-at-arms."

She ignored his remark about a match. "I've an idea to hire help. We've treasures we can sell, like this one." Oliwia extracted a velvet pouch from her jacket pocket and handed it to him.

He fumbled with the drawstring, shooting her a puzzled look. "What is this?"

"A gift from Eryk. I think it could be put to better use."

Henryk spilled the brilliant sapphire necklace from the pouch into his hand and studied it. She slipped her wedding ring from her finger and placed it atop the necklace. He gaped at her.

"You can't sell these, Oliwia."

"Why not? Will no one buy them?"

"Of course someone will buy them." He folded the necklace into the pouch. "But these are gifts from your late husband." He held her ring out to her; she shook her head.

Henryk looked about the chamber as if gathering his thoughts. "Are you sure you wish this?"

"I have all the memories of Eryk I need when I look at Adam, so yes, I am sure. Moreover, I believe Eryk would agree with my decision."

Henryk dropped the ring into the soft pouch and carefully cinched the drawstrings. "This will be helpful, my lady. Thank you."

Oliwia possessed other treasures she could not bring herself to part with—a jeweled dagger and a pearl-and-aquamarine comb from Jacek, secreted in the floorboards alongside his letters. She would sell every possession in Biaska before selling those, for they were all that remained of him.

Pain hitched in her chest, taking her by surprise. She looked away before Henryk noticed the tears welling in her eyes.

Oliwia's spirits lifted at the sight of Father Augustyn's cherubic face. She couldn't help herself. Perhaps it was because the priest had always been kind to her, long before she became a Catholic, when she was a scared fifteen-year-old among people she'd always counted as enemies. Or perhaps it was because he was a great dumpling of a man. Whatever it was, it bathed her in warmth as she entered the village church, Adam asleep in her arms, Filip beside her.

"And how is my lady this beautiful Lord's day, and my lord Filip?" Father Augustyn grasped her elbow and tilted his head sideways. Then his eyes lit on Adam, and they seemed to brighten all the more. "Oh! And my Lord Adam. We are so blessed to have you all here."

Oliwia smiled. "As we are blessed to have you, Father."

He reddened and swept his hand toward the nave. "Please. Welcome. 'Tis a wonderful thing you do, Lady Oliwia, choosing to attend Mass among us when you could remain in your private chapel. None would blame you. But here, we may all worship God's grace with you and your family."

After she settled in the manorial pew, her mind wandered, yanked back occasionally by Filip squirming or a word uttered by Father Augustyn. Though her thoughts did not remain on the rites, the liturgy, any of it, they did remain on the folk around her, and those thoughts became her prayers. *Please, Lord, let the food stores last. Don't let these people suffer.* What would happen to them all? If only they hadn't lost the rye!

A question had been niggling at her, and she let it float to the fore. How could lightning ignite a wagonful of grain so quickly? She hadn't recalled lightning strikes in all the time the grain was being toted to the river. For that matter, how could the fire have jumped from cart to cart so swiftly that *none* of it could be salvaged?

She let out a little sigh, trying to focus on the homily. But her mind rebelled and meandered. Should she ask Antonin for help? Dread rose in her like tree sap in spring. He *had* been flaunting his riches, judging by his fine trappings and the Tokaj wine he'd sent along with news of his upcoming visit. Pity he'd had no bad luck with *his* grain shipments. *That's unkind. What of his people?* How ironic that the estate accustomed to abundant harvests might be beholden to one that, until this year, was unaccustomed. Had fate erred?

Oliwia sharpened her ears as Father Augustyn prepared Communion. "… behold him who takes away …" The last words caught and bounced about her brain. Was God punishing them by taking away their crop? Another thought struck her like the thunderbolt that had supposedly leveled their shipment. *What if neither God nor fate took it away, but human mischief is at play?*

Who gains from Biaska's misfortune?

Chapter 20

Step Lightly When You Walk a Razor's Edge

O how much better to lie on one's bier, than to be a captive on the way to Tatary ~Polish proverb

The Tatars had split up, Scar Nose taking eight warriors with him and leaving six to continue driving Jacek and his companions to their destination. Wherever that was. Jacek reckoned they traveled within territory wholly controlled by the Ottoman Empire. Poland seemed as distant as the stars. Never allowed to wash or groom, Jacek and his men reeked and itched with lice, mites, and insects he never saw—only felt as they squirmed over him. Water and food were given more liberally— though scarcely enough to keep a running man alive—but Jacek could not say their lot was improving. This smaller force made up for their reduced numbers with their exuberant whips. The lashes flew indiscriminately on the men's scourged bodies, as if they were horses' tails given to habitual swishing and flicking, and it didn't matter the reason—or if there was one. And when they tired of whipping, they turned to pummeling and caning.

As they lay trussed together one night, Wiesław dared a whisper.

"Jacek, do you know where we're going?"

Hearing his own name was strange to him. When the Tatars called them anything, they used "Dog" and "Slav" interchangeably; their favored way to communicate was with the whip or the butt end of a lance.

"The Black Sea. Probably Kaffa. Have you heard of it?"

"Yes," Wiesław said flatly. After a few beats, he asked, "Have you a wife? Children?"

"Not yet."

A horse nickered, and the wind waved over the ground.

"I miss my daughters' sweet little faces," he said so quietly Jacek nearly didn't catch it.

Lashes came raining down, out of the dark, accompanied by a Tatar guard's growls. Jacek hunched his shoulders and drew up his knees, curling his body as much as his bindings allowed. Along with his brothers, he endured the whips until the devil turned and trundled back to the campfire. The five breathed out at once. No one spoke.

Survive first.

Escape second.

As Jacek nestled into the shallow depression that served as his bed, ignoring the silt that formed a scratchy layer over his skin, he listened for the guard, but only night sounds filled the air: chirping crickets, wind ruffling the grass, the odd rustling creature. His mind meandered to Oliwia, and a question came on, crowding out other thoughts. Had their lovemaking produced a seed now growing in her? If she did give birth to their babe, would he ever see that child?

The questions tore at him, and he pushed them down a hole, out of his consciousness. Instead, he turned to thoughts of escape. Calculating, stewing, thinking of a way out *before* they reached Kaffa. Once they were brought into that wretched fortress city, there would be no escape. Ever. And it wasn't just his escape. If he fled, then so would his brothers—he would leave no one behind. But how? Grit they had, but without weapons, in their pathetic state, how would they overcome their well-fed, well-armed captors? And how much grit did each man possess? How much did *he* possess? He knew not, but he did know where it came from: it burned deep within, a flicker of fury he coddled and nursed, ready to let it burst from him when the time came.

At last, he drifted off, his dreams blooming with babies, wedding nights, and wedding feasts—a crucial respite from hunger, thirst, cruelty, guilt, and his growing rage.

223

Countless days of rain driven by chill gusts forced the five to huddle together at night, pummeled without shelter by wind and water, while their captors ducked into cozy tents. Jacek's spirit plunged into its deepest despair. When the rain at last moved out, the sun hung like a pallid yellow ball in gray gauze. But he found no solace in it. His brothers dragged him upright, pushed, and pleaded until at last he shuffled his part-numb, part-agonizingly festered feet. He had done the same for them in turn.

They trod under sullen skies, and Jacek looked about to prevent himself wallowing in misery. *Harvest is finished at Biaska.* He imagined golden stacks of grain overloading creaky wagons; stubbled fields; and the raucous dożynki, the festival where peasants and nobles came together and rejoiced at harvest's end. He'd not partaken of a harvest celebration in many years for all his soldiering. But he remembered early ones during a more carefree time. The music, the color, the laughter, and the pretty peasant maids all converged into one delirious daydream, shielding him from the folds of brown land stretching endlessly about him and the straps biting into his flesh. But his reverie evaporated at the tail end of a lash.

With a series of sharp barks, their captors drove them over a rise and into a camp beside a stream with shallow banks and sparse, bushy trees. A collection of logs, staked in the ground and snugged together, formed a curved palisade similar to a corral. Into that corral they were herded, then tied to the posts. The men looked across the empty space at one another after their captors secured the gate. Something had changed.

That night, Jacek dreamed he sat at a long banquet table that creaked from the weight of food upon it. Savory meat platters steamed beside tureens of mushroom soup while fresh-picked sweet peas swam in creamy butter. Jugs brimmed with piwo and mead, and he searched for a cup amid the crammed plates. The fragrance of baking bread and pastries filled his nose. He reached for a plum, and when he bit into it, the juice ran down his chin onto his crisp linen shirt. His mother appeared and admonished him for staining it before handing him a warm pear tart. Just as he put the tart to his lips, whips cracked, and he was running furiously.

He opened his grainy eyes and found himself seated upright; stiff, cramped muscles reported their insults. He groaned. The mouthwatering smells from his dream evaporated, replaced by his body's stench.

When I finally escape these devils, I will throw myself into the nearest river and scrub every part of my body. Then I shall eat … and eat … and eat … and sleep, every limb stretched out, in the sweet summer grass.

They spent the better part of the day in the pen with little idea what came next. Squeezing his eyes shut, Jacek willed himself anywhere but where he sat under the sun's relentless rays. But his parched throat, oozing sores, and aching arms would not let him retreat into the dark cavities of his mind.

At last, a buzzing swept through their captors.

"What's happening?" Jacek asked Dawid and Janusz, who had a view to where the commotion grew louder.

They craned their necks, and Dawid's eyes widened. "The others are returning."

"And it appears we will soon have more company," Janusz hissed. "They are marching more people our way."

Jacek twisted and glimpsed the Tatar soldiers, whips flying. Lines—made up of people of varying heights and girths linked together by their necks—snaked toward them, followed by horses and livestock.

"Now we know why they split up," Jacek said morosely. "It's going to get crowded."

As folk were shoved into the corral, a rising cackle nearly liquefied his spine. He spotted Scar Nose showering the new captives with lashes from atop his mount. The assaults were unprovoked, but he slashed cruelly into clothing and skin already torn, as though he were in a competition that would earn him a heavy purse. One boy—he could not have been more than twelve—fell when the whip hit his knees, and for this offense, he was kicked by the guards.

Men, women, children, filed into the makeshift prison, stumbling miserably over one another; the space began to bulge. Once they had been packed in and gated off, the captors casually tossed orts into their pen as though feeding scraps to hogs.

In the descending dusk, Jacek chewed his tidbits while he studied the newcomers. All Slavic, he reckoned they were Muscovites and Ruthenians. None were very old nor very young, and men made up a proportionally small number. People lay or sat on each other for lack of space, and there was a great rustling and the constant sounds of children whimpering and women sobbing. From outside the corral came prisoners' shrieks amid men's laughter.

Several arm's-lengths away, a fair-skinned, blue-eyed girl caught his eye. Her long, caramel-brown hair was matted as it fell down her back. She was clad in a dirty, tattered gray dress and brown apron, and he guessed her to be fifteen. Though she did not resemble Oliwia, he saw the Oliwia he had rescued in Vyatov when he looked at her, and it pulled at his carefully confined heart. She turned and buried her face against a woman with similar features, more lines and streaks of gray in her otherwise brown tresses. The woman gathered the girl to her; a younger girl rested against the woman's other side. Farther away sat a man who looked at the woman with a weak smile, and she smiled back feebly. A sable-haired boy—he looked to be nine or ten—slumped against the man's chest.

They were clearly a family—but not for long, Jacek thought miserably. When they spoke, they did so in hushed tones between bent heads. At times, they appeared to pray, with the father speaking over them as they squeezed their eyes shut.

Have you abandoned your children, God?

Weariness and sorrow settled into Jacek's every bone. He was so tired. He ceased studying the poignant display—the thought of what would befall them ripped through him, and he didn't want to feel. Settling between two of his companions, he closed his eyes.

He stirred at first light, knees drawn up for lack of space. His head and body leaned against Wiesław as Paweł lay against him. Waste and vomit clung to the fetid mass in the corral, and he nearly retched.

Coming fully awake, he shook his head to rid himself of harassing flies. His companions shifted and grunted. He itched to dig at his eyes but could only swipe the side of his face against his shoulder. It helped not at all. He felt eyes on him, and he looked up. The blue-eyed girl darted her gaze away, and it occurred to him she was pretty; he hadn't noticed yesterday.

A commotion waved through the crowd. Jacek turned and saw Tatars shoving tattered women into the corral. Some looked about furtively; others sobbed, their tears cutting tracks through the grime on their faces; still others collapsed, seemingly in a stupor, their expressions vacant. Then the soldiers began moving through the masses in the pen, pulling up a woman here and dragging off another there, unaffected by their screams and cries. The herd of humanity stirred and buzzed, and whips were unfurled and put to work.

A Tatar appeared before the girl and yanked her up. Her blue eyes went round with fear, and she shook her head vehemently.

"No! No! No!" she cried, echoed by her mother, who pitched herself on the girl.

The Tatar slammed the mother with the butt end of his whip, knocking her sideways. Without conscious thought, Jacek got his feet under him and lunged with a growl, only to be jerked back by his restraints before he could bring himself fully upright. The Tatar spun and stared at him. Then he pointed at Jacek and barked to his comrades who still moved about the pen. After a heated exchange and animated gesturing, three more Tatars appeared. Two sliced the line tethering Jacek's neck band to his companions and hauled him to his feet, their iron hands like vises holding him in place.

The third Tatar stepped in front of him and grinned.

Christ!

Scar Nose kicked him in the gut thrice and the groin once. Jacek's knees buckled, and he would have doubled over but for the guards holding him up. He bit back his groans and the burning bile in his throat. Scar Nose grasped Jacek's face in his blocky brown hand. From the corner of his eye, Jacek caught a flash. Before comprehension sank in, Scar Nose began carving the side of his face. Jacek fought for air while the soldiers held him firm. He squeezed his eyes shut and fired off a prayer. Scar Nose did not hurry, seeming to take an extraordinary amount of care—and delight—in his work. It felt as though a bolt of lightning slowly seared its jagged way along Jacek's left temple, over his cheek, to his jaw. His flesh gave way, pulled apart. Gasps rose all around him.

The pressure was gone, and Jacek's eyes flew open.

"Very pretty," Scar Nose said with a self-congratulating nod.

He released Jacek's face, and Jacek cried out. As he sucked air into his lungs in errant gasps, blood ran warm and sticky over his skin, landed on his shoulder, and soaked into his shirt. The Tatars shoved him on his backside. Jacek's neck band was tightened and relinked to the others, and Scar Nose ordered the mother dragged upright and pulled behind him. Her family's terrified screams rose together.

"Jesus, Jacek!" hissed Wiesław. Blood obscured Jacek's left eye. The girl kneeled before him, crying and babbling, before she was wrenched backward and bound. He fell back against someone and let himself descend into a whirlpool of unconsciousness.

Once more, Jacek lost all sense of time. Throbbing pain flamed the left side of his face and rib cage. They were marching again, and his midsection creaked. At times, his breath flew from him in a sharp gasp. Someone sobbed. He recognized the sound came from him. When at last they stopped for the night, shivers ran through him.

"Captain, have mine," came Dawid's voice. Jacek couldn't make out what he meant until he felt a ration of horsemeat fall in his lap. He tried to pick it up in his teeth, tried to chew, but he was too tired. The movement re-opened the wound, causing fresh blood to flow.

He drifted that night, as though bobbing on the sea, at once conscious yet dreaming. At one point, he thought he was in a hussar camp and had rolled out of his bedding into a fire. He tried jerking his face out of the flames, but he couldn't move. Someone muttered behind him, and he remembered where he was. Chills danced up his spine, through his limbs, and his teeth clacked together. A body, hard but warm, pressed closer to his back while another snugged his front.

In Jacek's delirious, fevered dreams, Scar Nose's face floated before him, taunting him. Jacek was forced down a gauntlet, whips snaking on one side and blades slicing on the other.

There's no escape.

As he trod in a haze of pain, driven relentlessly between strings of prisoners, Jacek willed himself not to succumb even as he stood on the very brink of surrender. He slipped from dream to nightmare to reality and back again.

During a short rest midday, lucidity was momentarily with him, and he recognized something was different. He could smell it and feel it in the air. A sharp tang in his nose, a sticky dampness on his skin, a mounting velocity in the wind, and gulls crying overhead. He swiveled his head and noticed a prisoner watching him. The man gave him a nod and the hint of a smile. Fair-skinned, he had eyes of palest green. His light brown hair was tipped in gold, not unlike Jacek's when it was clean. He wasn't big, but a strong frame and tough hands showed he was accustomed to labor.

The man began speaking to Jacek quietly and rapidly. Jacek picked out familiar bits but didn't understand. When he replied in Latin, the man cocked his head, then shook it.

Dawid, who sat beside Jacek, leaned into him. "Don't know French?"

"No. You?"

Dawid nodded. "He says that was a brave thing you did."

Jacek thought to snort, but the stitch in his ribs and the flame along his cheek stopped him. He was suddenly overcome by fatigue and shivered. "Not brave. Foolish," he replied.

Jacek vaguely heard Dawid's voice. "He says you stopped them using the girl. The commotion drew their commander's attention, and he ordered them not to take her because she'll fetch more if she's unspoiled."

"So instead I got her mother killed and only delayed what's going to happen to her." Jacek's words came out in a slur.

"He says the mother wasn't killed. She was only ... Well, she's alive."

Jacek curbed a sudden stab of sorrow. "How does he know?"

After more undecipherable words, Dawid turned to Jacek with a grim look. "He understands their language—he's an escaped galley slave—and he thinks they are taking us to Khadjibey."

"What's Khadjibey?"

"Nothing much. This lot's been arguing about bringing all of us to Kaffa or splitting us, taking the men to Khadjibey to sell for galley slaves. Apparently, they didn't capture as many as they'd hoped."

Jacek was confused. "Is there a slave market there?"

"Nothing formal. He says it's a makeshift port where commanders pick up slaves from time to time on the sly. They avoid taxes and pay less than in other ports. Some are merchant ships, others warships. He says last time he was caught, he went straight to the bench, on the oars. He also says some of our captors rode toward Khadjibey this morning—seeking buyers, he reckons," Dawid replied.

"How many times has he been captured?"

Dawid shrugged. "At least twice. He was first sent to a French galley on a false charge. His real crime was being a Huguenot. You know—Protestant."

Jacek grunted. "Ask how he escaped. Not that I've any wish to follow a man who gets himself recaptured."

They had been marching in two columns separated by gender when their human train came to a stumbling stop. Whips unfurled, and commands were shouted out. A slight boy was roughly cut away from the ropes and hauled aside. The lad collapsed on his side and lay motionless. A howl rose from Wiesław's line, and a man began twisting and pulling against his bindings, yanking other prisoners with him. He strained toward the boy, shrieking at him.

The next movements were so swift that Jacek wasn't sure he'd truly witnessed them. The man was disentangled from the other captives. With hands still bound behind him, he was shoved to his knees beside the boy and beheaded with one stroke of a scimitar. In the blink of an eyelid, as he was unleashing a wail, the boy's throat was slashed, even as the man's body was still slumping on its side. The boy twitched and choked, and then he was still. The jackals rechecked ropes and yokes as though the carnage had never taken place, and the lines of captives resumed trudging under the bite of the whips.

Jacek stumbled by the child, where a macabre halo of blood was blooming around his head. He sent a prayer heavenward—he'd already sent so many. His fevered thoughts were overcome by the loathing he nurtured. Each stroke, each inhumanity visited was another piece of kindling Jacek put on the slow burn inside him. He stoked the fire in silence—a warrior's fire—and continued tempering his iron will. For a moment, his inflamed, oozing wound was forgotten.

They halted after the sun had descended. The ground had become marshy and boggy in spots, slowing the horses. Jacek thought he saw shimmering silver in the distance. *Water?* Cattails shivered with the wind. The sky was streaked in brilliant oranges, purples, and pinks. Bats darted and swooped in fitful flight. Another time, Jacek would have sat back and marveled at it all.

A rough camp was set up on a dry strip of ground stubbled in spiky grasses. Jacek's face throbbed, but he forgot it when Dawid announced the horsemen were back. Craning his head, Jacek saw several Tatars dismount briskly and head toward a cluster of raiders beside a campfire. Voices rose and fell, and Jacek gave the Frenchman a questioning look. The man let out a soft litany of words. Dawid nodded.

"What's he say?" Jacek asked.

"The men go to Khadjibey tomorrow. We will be on a galley by the end of the day."

Jacek looked around, finding each hussar. All were in tatters—their clothes, their skin, their spirits. He kept his thoughts and feelings tightly wrapped under a stony countenance, tamping down the fear rising in his belly. And the fear was not just for himself, for the men on this hellish passage with him had become his brothers in every measure of the word. He would give his life for each and every one. But first, he would do everything in his power to free them.

Exhausted, chills rippling through his body, Jacek sagged against the hard, cold ground and sought oblivion.

After another night spent in feverish sleep, Jacek awoke and looked eastward. What he'd seen in the dim twilight appeared to be a large interior body of water—perhaps a lake or estuary—fed by ribbons of river. Before him, the land stretched in flat planes broken up by rises covered in grasses and shrubs. The going looked easy if the contours remained the same. What would happen at their destination, however, was cause for more dread surging in him, and his hollow stomach clenched. The path to escape had eluded him. In his condition, though, he wouldn't last anyway.

He glanced at Wiesław and Pawel. Worry etched their faces. Jacek shoved his own fears back where they belonged, deep inside. Instead, he let himself feel the agonizing slice down his face and the anger it germinated. The gash throbbed hot, and it reeked.

"Where are Dawid and Janusz?" he asked.

"Over there," Wiesław replied with a head jerk. "How do you fare, Jacek?"

"I expect the same as you," Jacek rasped, easing a bit when he caught sight of Janusz's and Dawid's backs.

"So you've had your fill of breakfast and are looking forward to a day of hunting, followed by feasting and dancing with beautiful ladies?"

"Just so."

"I expect we'll see our destination shortly," Pawel said in a gravelly voice.

Wiesław began scuffing lines in the dirt with his heel. "The Frenchman said each Tatar gets his share of the captives. After they divide them up, they brand them with a red-hot rod so they can identify which captives belong to which Tatar."

"We're a small group. We may escape branding," Jacek said dully, knowing his words were hollow. His mind slithered to all manner of dark places he tried to stave off. His bowels were loose; he shuddered. At slave markets he'd heard of, like Kaffa's or Constantinople's, they might be held in dungeons and succumb to starvation, beatings, or disease. *If I last that long.* If chosen for sale, they would be stripped and put on display before a crowd. Buyers could inspect any part of them. He thought of the girls, the women, and his heart ached.

"What will they do with us, Jacek?" Wiesław's voice cracked.

"We're big, we're strong. It's hard labor for us—fields, mines, quarries, galleys. If a wealthy khan finds you pleasing, maybe some type of domestic service in his palace—or his male harem."

Wiesław coughed.

"That leaves all of us out," Pawel said grimly as he flicked his eyes to the left side of Jacek's face. "Hopefully, they leave our cullions intact."

"What will become of that family?" Wiesław jerked his chin toward a group of women prisoners that included the girls and their now-vacuous mother.

"They will be pulled apart," Jacek replied. *And never see one another again.*

"The father looks like a strong farmer. Maybe he'll go to the fields and do what he's done his whole life," Pawel added. "Women and children with their coloring are always desirable."

Wiesław nodded dejectedly.

Jacek glanced back at the girls and their mother. If she survived, the mother would work as a domestic. Though he had no doubt she was used to hard work, thus far it had all been for home and family. Not as a slave. As for her son? If he was lucky, he might be turned into a janissary. If not, well, Jacek didn't want to think about it.

As if reading his mind, Pawel continued. "Pray the girls are bought by decent men who don't abuse them." He swiped his cheek against his shoulder. "Their mother has the same color eyes as my late wife. I wonder if my first grandchild has been born yet."

"Jesus, I wish we could do *something* to help them," Wiesław said miserably.

"As do I," Jacek said, "for that would mean we could help ourselves."

"Brace up, lads. Here come our hosts." Pawel fixed his gaze on Jacek. "God be with you."

Jacek gave him a small head dip, then stumbled to his feet and looked overhead. Somber clouds crowded in, threatening to soak them all, while bright white gulls wheeled and drifted on the air currents. He watched Scar Nose trotting toward them, Tatars in his wake like athletes taking the field for the next contest—but this was no game.

Jacek glanced over at the family. Fat tears spilled down the youngest girl's cheeks like water being poured from a jug; she sobbed uncontrollably, her narrow shoulders jerking. The oldest girl's lips quivered as she fought the terror she no doubt felt. She stood bravely as her mother wept against her and moaned. Jacek saw no sign of the boy.

"Papa," the oldest girl whimpered as her father was shoved toward Jacek's line.

Despite the fear and devastation that must have been rending him in two, the father replied in a strong, steady voice, his head on a pivot as he strained to look at his family. Jacek heard fragments of his last words to them.

While the father was secured, the mother's shrieks flew to the sky, echoed by the girls' wails. Jacek watched helplessly as the women were pulled apart by their captors. The mother screamed out names Jacek guessed were her children's while the girls keened for their parents. Each was removed to a different cluster of captives. Though he could not see him, Jacek heard a child howl and saw a ripple go through a huddle of children.

"Papa! Mama!" the boy bawled pitifully.

The father dug his heels in and shouted to them all. "God will protect you! Stay alive!"

Scar Nose swiftly struck him with a well-placed hilt to the gut, staggering him to his knees. Amid the cacophony of cries, the father pulled himself up, recovered his breath, and yelled, "Do not give up hope! I will come for you! I love you all!"

Something was shoved in his mouth, and he was yanked hard by the neck restraint. The only sounds Jacek could hear from him were his desperate pulls for air—more desperate than his impossible promise of coming for his wife and children.

Their line lurched to life once again. A wave of motion undulated through the line, and people jostled one another. Urgency seemed to take hold. Numb, Jacek reeled but remained upright, and the train found its cadence as feet marched together in time. Locking out the family's wretched cries, he reflected on the miracle that had kept him and the other hussars together. It was unthinkable to lose even one of their number. Yet the likelihood of another miracle, like the father's promise, was as distant as Biaska. He quelled his growing disquiet.

The flame in Jacek's cheek and the chills in his body rose and fell as the men made their way south. On their left, the estuary snaked in and out of sight. Before them, an enormous expanse of water grew more visible, and the paths they trod were now sandy patches dotted with grassy clumps. The smell of the sea, borne by the ever-stiffening wind, assaulted his senses and clung to him.

It was midday when they reached Khadjibey. An overwhelming, inescapable reek struck him, a dreadful mixture of decaying fish and the stench of malodorous ships anchored close together. They'd stopped atop a crest, and from his vantage point he glimpsed a collection of randomly moored longboats on shore. Sparse ramshackle buildings rose beside the water, and rickety wooden piers jutted over its scummy surface. Beyond, in a deep blue bowl-shaped harbor, were the ships, five galleys in all, their perfectly spaced oars resembling neatly rowed porcupine quills hovering above the water. Sleek and shallow, the craft might have evoked awe had their green banners and populated oar benches not weighed him down with foreboding.

Down a slope they trundled, urged by the whips. He spotted all manner of people swarming over the piers, many light-skinned, like he. His group stopped on the shore, where Scar Nose argued with a spriggy man who carried an air of authority atop his narrow, sumptuously attired shoulders. Jacek scanned the ships, guns, soldiers, rowers, and anything else he could see.

Dawid pressed against him. "Frenchman says four are merchant ships owned by the admiral there." Dawid nodded toward the spriggy man, whose arms were folded across his chest as he listened to Scar Nose's heated words.

"What's the quarrel?"

"The admiral refused to pay the Tatars' price, so they threaten to take us to Kaffa instead," Dawid replied. "Frenchman says to pray the admiral takes us."

"Why? We're galley slaves either way."

"The admiral might treat us better."

Jacek grunted.

One of the Tatar guards barked at them, and they quieted. The admiral began surveying them, grabbing a bicep here, a shoulder there. When he reached Jacek, he pinched his chin and turned his face, inspecting the wound. Jacek fought the stars behind his eyes and the wave of nausea. What a savage fright he must look, if his fellows were any measure. Wild-haired, bushy-bearded, sickeningly smelly, wretchedly filthy, clothed in rags—and now a purulent gash the length of his face.

The admiral let out an explosive litany directed at Scar Nose. Muttering, Scar Nose cut Jacek away from the rest of the line and gave him a rough shove. He barely stayed upright. The others were urged toward the longboats. Dawid stole a backward glance at him. Jacek now stood apart, alone. Panic tore through him. *Oh Jesus, you're all I have left! Don't leave me behind!* He pitched toward his companions while Scar Nose and the admiral continued their heated haggling; a slaver yanked him back.

The admiral suddenly faced him and ordered his shirt cut away. Then he walked around him, prodding his ribs, chest, and back with the butt end of a leather crop. Jacek winced. The admiral called to a soldier. The man approached, cocked his fist, and landed a blow to Jacek's belly, rocking him back on his heels. Jacek groaned and, somehow, didn't fall over. Scar Nose nodded at the admiral, his face split in a ghoulish grin.

Jacek darted his eyes to his departing fellows, staring at them numbly as they clambered aboard the longboats awkwardly, still hobbled together. Pawel and Wiesław gave him bleak nods. *What will become of my friends? Of me? I'll never see them again!* The longboats hit the water. In that moment, he was consumed by incalculable sorrow. Tears jammed his throat and pricked his eyes. One last line of prisoners stayed behind; he stood among them, strangers all.

He had only vaguely noticed Scar Nose approach. Jacek gave him his full attention when Scar Nose wrenched his hair; the gash split apart once more. The beast chuckled, so close Jacek could smell his rank breath. Jacek planted both feet and brought himself to his full height, causing Scar Nose to loose his grasp. Then Jacek leaned over and drilled his fevered eyes into him, one side of his mouth curled up in a feral grimace.

Finish this!

With a snarl, Scar Nose yanked Jacek's beard and poised the tip of a dagger in front of Jacek's right eye. A Turkish soldier loomed, shouting.

Scar Nose dropped his hand, then shrugged and headed away, tossing one last cackle over his shoulder at Jacek.

Dear Lord, if I live, please let me meet him again one day when I am unshackled. Amen.

Jacek was prodded toward a longboat and sagged into its hull. Though utterly spent, he forced himself to take notice, to give a damn what was happening around him. As he did, he fed his tiny prayer to the smoldering ember of his rage, the rage that, if he lived long enough, would alight when he blew on it. But he would control the breath to keep from dousing it completely. It was the elusive ring he would ram his imaginary kopia through in order to capture the prize: freedom.

The longboat, powered by sinewy, gaunt oarsmen in garments of rough cloth, rode over choppy, dark waters to a cluster of vessels. Each rower wore an iron cuff from which a heavy ring dangled. They stared vacantly and did not speak as they pulled. Their faces, necks, and arms were covered in raw sores, as though something ate at their skin, and Jacek had little idea how old they were. One final longboat trailed behind, filled with the last of the men. It held the Frenchman and the father, the former with a look of abject terror and the latter abject despair. That boat veered toward a solitary galley anchored apart. This galley was sleeker than the larger, wider one Jacek was headed for, and it bristled with cannon.

The war galley.

God help them. God help us all.

Through a mournful, fevered haze, Jacek watched as a two-masted vessel loomed and blotted out all else. The oars—twenty a side—so like porcupine quills when seen from shore, now grew immense, as long as three men lying head to foot. This behemoth was nothing like the ferries he'd ridden, or the boats of his boyhood. And now it would be his home, the full breadth of his world. The thought was unfathomable.

Once aboard, uniformed Turkish soldiers swarmed them, unfastening them, yanking this one from here and shoving another roughly over there. Their chatter grew voluble while they sorted the prisoners. Jacek was pulled about as they pleased, feeling altogether like an onion being arranged in a basket for market.

Slaves were organized into four groups, one for each merchant galley. The admiral appeared and, using his crop, pointed at four Turks. These, apparently, were the shipmasters. Each drew a straw and, in turn, selected one row of roughly ten prisoners each. Soon the captives fell in behind this officer or that and left the ship. Orderly, submissive.

Jacek followed a burly Turk who took his group aft along a wooden causeway flanked on either side by rows of benches to which myriad skeletal wretches were manacled. These men sat, their backs to the prow, five to a bench, their heads level with the walkways and gangway, as though they sat in a hollowed-out husk beneath the water line. None looked up at the newcomers. Whether their vacant stares hid their fears or their disregard, Jacek did not know, but he reckoned the men-at-arms lording over them with whips and cudgels might be the reason.

He was pushed onto an aft deck, where he, like every other newcomer, was shaved from chin to crown, stripped, and given a set of rough garments like those worn by the longboat rowers—a tunic, breeches, and a cap for his bald head. A wiry brown man approached and motioned for Jacek to sit on a wooden stool. He was helped to it by two soldiers who pinned him on either side. The wiry man brought his face in close and inspected Jacek's wound, prodding, squeezing, and tsking between Jacek's sharp intakes of breaths. The man drew back and shook his head, then motioned to someone behind Jacek. That someone seized his head. The wiry man cleansed his wound with seawater. It so burned and stung it brought tears to Jacek's rapidly blinking eyes. Then the man picked up a small blade and began scraping his flesh, each stroke feeling as though a white-hot metal sliver were being inserted in the pus-filled, inflamed tissue.

Despite his most valiant efforts, Jacek jerked, yelled, and gasped, though his head remained trapped in the viselike grip. Chains clanked dully, and strange voices mumbled and muttered around him. The sharp stink of unwashed bodies together with human waste and fermenting, decaying food grew unbearable. He began to heave, and the soldiers released him. Nothing came up. At last the wiry man—the barber-surgeon—troweled an unctuous salve, smelling vaguely of honey, vinegar, and wine, into the wound and left him alone. It was only then that the waves of pain and nausea subsided and Jacek caught his breath.

An iron ring was clamped about his ankle and a length of weighty chain attached. The cuff was heavy and sharp, and it pressed on his ankle bone. Already, it chafed. He was led to a bench and fastened between two other galley slaves who looked him up and down. He sat in the second space from the gangway, close to the butt end of the loom on a foul, stained hide.

Surveying each man beside him, wondering if they would become the brothers he would live and die with, he rasped, "Jacek."

"Polska?" the man to his right grunted. He was deeply tanned and gnarled. He reminded Jacek of an ancient, stunted tree that had spent its life struggling to grow from a crack in a rock while being harassed by unrelenting wind. His face held a black beard speckled with white and was etched in lines that looked as if they held every sorrow he had ever endured. Shaggy, dark hair was streaked with gray, and his dull brown eyes reflected little life within.

"Yes," Jacek replied.

The man looked away, as if bored.

Jacek rested his hands on the oar and glanced to the man on his left. This man was also deeply tanned, but he sat straight, as if at attention. Matted, curly, dark hair clung to his scalp, and coal whiskers held neither silver nor white. Scars adorned the man's thin, corded body. As Jacek looked him over, the man did the same, and Jacek recognized an unmistakable fierceness in his obsidian eyes. The man's fire still burned inside him; it had not yet been extinguished.

"Gian," the man said, then nodded to the oarsman on Jacek's right. "Titas." Titas nodded so slightly Jacek might have easily missed the motion.

Don't expend any more energy than necessary.

Jacek checked for guards, then turned to Gian and in Latin asked him how long he'd been aboard.

"Duo annis." Two years.

"Titas?" asked Jacek.

With a hint of a grin, Gian replied, *"Vita sua. Quinque annis."* A lifetime. Five years.

Titas turned his head and spat.

Reality throttling him, Jacek suppressed a tremor.

Christ Jesus!

He looked down at filthy scraps awash in murky brown water beneath his feet. Then he looked about at his new tribe, noting deep brands on cheeks and foreheads or scarred-over slits on nose or ear. He vaguely wondered what other marks they bore as testament to their enslavement. They were all barefoot, scrawny, stooped, and covered in peeling skin and lesions. Some slept and slumped on the oars.

Trying to block out his throbbing cheek, Jacek continued observing. He knew little of seafaring vessels, so he catalogued the animate and inanimate features of the galley ship. *Who are the keepers of the keys?* He noted the positions of the guards and their weapons. Dual drums fastened to the narrow deck between the pits were an oddity, though he suspected he knew their purpose. His calculations told him the contingent of enemy aboard ship was large, though smaller than the body of slaves they controlled.

Now he assessed his immediate environs. Glancing down at his manacled ankle, he raised his foot and tested the chain. The iron bracelet bit into his skin. He would not break it. The seats were little more than the width of a man's body, leaving barely a gap between a rower and his bench mates. Each was covered in what appeared to be a worn sheep's skin and smelled of feces and urine. This small, disgusting stamp on a hard wooden bench, smoothed over the years by the myriad galley slaves' sitting bones, was now his enduring home. From here, he was sentenced to work, eat, sleep, relieve himself, and live out the rest of his life. However long it lasted.

The ship prepared to sail soon after Jacek and the others were settled. Though woozy, Jacek tensed and listened, learning the new sounds and motions. Shouts rose all around him, and the ship juddered as men ran up and about the decks. Slaves scurried from the walkways into open seats on the benches, fairly hurling themselves into the depths of the rowing pits. Once in their places, other slaves—including the longboat oarsmen—reattached their chains to the benches and waited dutifully as guards in turn fastened them.

"Why were they unfettered?" Jacek asked Gian.

"They are trusted men who work aboard ship or on the piers."

Jacek grunted, thoughts awhirl. As if reading his mind, Gian added, "You will likely not live long enough to become so trusted."

Then he glanced at Jacek's hands and nodded to his own. "Do what I do when I do it." They began by pulling the oars hovering above their laps, feeding their shafts through oarlocks in the galley's side, and levering them to the water's surface. Jacek could not see the last bit, though Gian explained under his breath as they went.

Anchors and ropes were hoisted aboard. Jacek gripped the loom when his bench mates did. The beating of the drums began in a tempo that vibrated through them. They sounded slowly at first, but the pace soon increased.

Boom! Boom! Boom!

The ship creaked and shuddered and began to drift slowly as it turned toward the open sea. In time with his bench mates, Jacek stroked the oar away, then rose as they pushed it above their heads in time to the drumming. The oars bit into the water before he crashed back down to his seat and yanked the mighty loom into their laps. Off balance, Jacek bounced off Titas's shoulder and took an elbow to his sore ribs. Together, they pushed, stood, heaved, sat. Tightly packed, they rotated shoulders and arms with little room to maneuver. Pushed, stood, heaved, sat. Over and over and over again.

With the tattoo of the drums came the sound of long leather whips idly cracking, and Jacek flinched involuntarily. He soon felt stinging bites on his back and shoulders. One struck the gash on his face, and shock waves rippled through him, darkening everything for an instant. Though he didn't recall it, he reckoned he must have cried out, for Gian growled through the side of his mouth.

"You are new, and you will feel the lashes until the bastards are convinced you understand. And don't let them see you slack."

Just then, a length of leather cracked on them both.

Boom! Boom! Boom!

The ship glided away from Khadjibey, powered by oar strokes. Shadows grew long, but the weather was fair, and the shipmasters drove them until dark. Jacek was a strong man—at least he had been when he was well nourished—but the muscles in his shoulders, forearms, and thighs bunched and burned mercilessly. Blisters covered his calloused hands, and splinters jabbed into his fingers and palms. His ankle ached from the too-tight cuff where his skin was rubbed raw. Sweat ran from under his cap, along his face, seeping under the salve where sea spray had stung and eaten at the throbbing tissue.

At last, the ship came to a stop and oars were shipped while it anchored. Jacek could not remember the last time he had eaten, so when a meager meal of beans and stale, wormy biscuits stinking of rat urine was distributed, he savored it as if it were a meal laid out at a lord's table on All Saints' Day. This was accompanied by a ration of watered wine, which he relished as he would a goblet of the finest Hungarian wine.

A canvas tent was pulled over the rowers, signaling sleep. Jacek took in the sounds and rhythms of the ship. In the dark, he heard susurrations sweep up and down the benches and saw heads bent as they murmured together. Beside him, Gian took to prayer. Jacek joined him before folding himself over the hard wood and closing his eyes.

In his fitful sleep, he dreamed of home, but it brought no solace. Henryk appeared before him, and Jacek was overjoyed. When he asked Henryk to free him, he shook his head, saying, "I have wed Oliwia." Henryk became Scar Nose, and he cackled, "And now she's mine."

Jacek awoke in the dark. Men sprawled, scratched, jerked, and snored on the benches, where they rested in contorted poses. The ship moved with the wind and the tussling waves that lapped at its hull, but otherwise all was still. He brushed away tears coursing down his chapped cheeks.

Chapter 21

Alliances

"Take off your hood and join me, Romek, and let's have your report," Antonin said over the rim of his wodka cup.

Romek pulled the cowl down, poured himself a measure, and dropped into a chair. Then he grinned. "It's as our spy said, my lord. The lady will call upon farmhands and boys, then provide their livery. They will stand in for soldiers and make Biaska's garrison appear fully manned. With wooden sabres, no doubt."

Antonin laughed wickedly. "This was her idea?" When Romek shrugged, Antonin added, "She has a brain, I will admit, and would make a diverting ally. 'Tis a pity we will be at odds."

"She's a woman and cannot be trusted, no matter what," Romek snarled.

"Not all women are untrustworthy, Romek," Antonin said flippantly. "*This* one, however, is too clever by half."

Romek snorted. "Yet you wish to keep her after you marry this ... this ..."

"She will not best me, Romek. When I am done with her, I will own her—and everything else my cousin ever had."

"When Antonin arrives, he will see strength in our numbers. Is the livery ready? Are the banners repaired?" Oliwia had been pacing the solar and stopped to chew a nail.

"We will be ready." Henryk leaned against the windowsill, his arms folded across his chest. Light coming through the rippled glass sat on his head like a bright, wavy headdress.

"I've been thinking about what you said—that you'd rather embrace a viper," Oliwia continued. "Long ago, Lady Katarzyna told me she didn't trust Antonin. She suspected he coveted Eryk's lands." She paused to pull in a breath. "What if Antonin ordered the grain burned?" It was the first time she'd uttered her suspicions aloud.

Henryk's brow furrowed.

"And," Oliwia hurried on, "what if Antonin is behind Eryk's murder?"

Henryk blinked. In a lowered voice, he said, "These are serious accusations."

"Perhaps, but I've been turning it over in my head. Who gains if Biaska is weak?"

Henryk pointed to her desk. "Many do, judging by the lords writing to pay court."

"But who has the strongest claim?"

"Antonin." He drew the name out.

"Henryk, we must appear formidable."

He eyed her skeptically. "If he doesn't look closely, then so we shall."

Oliwia took in a few rapid breaths and blew them out. Rather than smoothing her skirts and hair as she might have on other occasions, she clenched her fists, digging her nails into her palms as she repeated under her breath, "Show your strength, Oliwia." *No one need know your legs tremble.*

She plunged down the stairs before she could give it another thought, before she could turn back, flee to her chamber, and feign illness. Steps above the great hall landing, she surveyed the gathered crowd. Standing conspicuously in the center was Antonin, his clothes rich and impeccable, but they couldn't hide the greasy smile that matched his greasy hair. Off to one side, Filip grinned at her, lifting her spirits. As she reached the foot of the steps, she was taken by surprise when Henryk appeared, hand out to her. She felt it close around hers, warm and strong, as he guided her across the floor. Antonin gave her an elegant leg, and she returned the greeting with a deep curtsy, all while Henryk held her fast. She drew power from his grip and felt as though no one, not even Antonin, could cause the butterflies in her stomach to take flight.

As fitting a guest of his stature, she had Antonin sit beside her but girded herself to feel his hand snaking toward her under the table. It never came. What came instead was his mouth close to her ear.

"I would speak with you, my dear, of an alliance between our two estates. Tomorrow?"

"What sort of alliance?" she threw back.

He looked about, chuckling. "You are very direct. It is of a private nature."

"No one can hear us," she prodded.

He leaned in closer, his sour onion-and-wine breath wafting over her; she willed herself not to recoil. "I planned to offer a proposal, my dear."

"Your letter said as much. What sort of proposal?"

A malevolent look clouded his features but was instantly replaced by his slippery smile. "Really, my dear, this is neither the time nor the place."

His condescension fired her belly. "I disagree. If I am to grant you a private audience, I must know the nature of the offer."

Antonin's eyes darkened and glittered. "It is an offer of marriage," he said evenly.

Oliwia clamped her jaw to keep it from swinging open. She cleared her throat. "You would be wasting your time, my lord."

The malevolent look returned. "Why is that? Are you entertaining another offer?"

Just then, Henryk leaned in and asked if there was aught she needed. Antonin's eyes jumped from her to Henryk and back again. "I see." Antonin smirked.

On the verge of correcting Antonin's thinking, she held back, instead touching Henryk's hand lightly and thanking him for his attentiveness.

It was long after midnight when Nadia helped Oliwia out of her brocade gown. "Tired, my lady?"

As if in answer, Oliwia yawned. Wanda burst through the door with a tray, both it and her appearance askew. "I beg your pardon, m'lady. I was … detained." Her cheeks aflame, she nearly ran to the table, rattling the contents of the tray.

"At this hour?" Oliwia asked casually. "Detained by whom, pray?"

Wanda's cheeks stained a deeper shape of red. She twitched. "The, ah, well, I …"

Containing her amusement, Oliwia dismissed her. After a bobbed curtsy, Wanda fled.

Later, as Oliwia lay in her bed, her eyes were drawn to the window silvered in moonlight. How long had it been since she'd lain with Jacek? *An eternity.* Her thoughts danced from that thought to the giddiness Wanda surely felt in her lover's arms. Sorrow seized Oliwia. She'd kept it secured, but tonight she let it take her, weeping for the love she would never again know.

The next day, Oliwia sat before her glass, pressing cold cloths on her puffy eyes. "The devil with this!" she exclaimed to no one and thumped the cloths onto the vanity. She went in search of Henryk and found him awaiting her in the solar.

"Are you all right?" he asked, a serious expression etching his handsome features.

She smiled wanly. "As bad as that? You're looking a bit rumpled yourself, Henryk. Up late enjoying feminine company?"

He darted his eyes to her and cleared his throat. "I thought to take Lord Antonin's guards to Łac last night for some … to see if I could shake anything loose and to keep them from looking closely at our garrison."

"And were you successful?"

He poured a cup of wine and offered it to her. When she shook her head, he took a sip. "With the garrison, yes. But I learned nothing of value, though Stefan and I plied them most of the night. Hence, my appearance."

She frowned. "You were not with Wanda?"

Now *he* frowned. "Your maid?"

"Yes, the very one. I thought you and she …"

"Not I, I assure you," he said mildly. "Antonin appeared to chew your ear throughout the meal. Did *you* learn anything helpful?"

She filled her lungs with a deep breath and let it all out at once. "Nothing, though he would make me a proposal … of marriage."

Henryk made a derisive noise.

"I told him he was wasting his time," Oliwia offered.

"He will not stop."

"I know," she sighed. "Any of them would be better." She swept her hand over the myriad courtship proposals upon the desk, then chuckled. "He gave the distinct impression, however, that he believes you and I fancy one another. Perhaps *that* will stop him."

Oliwia sought the amused glint in Henryk's eyes but didn't see it. She saw something altogether different—and unexpected.

Chapter 22

Blessed are the Weak

Each morning, the cover was rolled back and the oars taken up. Exhausted, Jacek barely noticed the sky. Had it rained that day, or had the sun's rays beat down on him unmercifully? He didn't know. He recalled little of the first nightmarish days of rowing except his stinking wound and the pain that racked his body. It was all that had filled his mind, and somehow he'd kept going, kept rowing through it all.

Vaguely, he remembered men puking around him and was thankful he held down the scant food and water in his shriveled body. The barber-surgeon had checked him, tsking, prodding, slathering. Whether it was the barber's care, the stinging sea spray, or Jacek's obstinance, his fever at last receded and his skin seemed to stitch itself closed.

One particular morning, as guards rousted the rowers, Jacek noticed a man two benches ahead still flopped over the loom. He recognized him. The man, a youngster really, had come aboard with Jacek. He couldn't have been more than fifteen.

"Is he dead?" Jacek hissed to Gian.

"Not yet," Gian whispered back.

When the lad didn't move, a slavemaster unfurled his long whip and sent it licking along his shoulders. He twitched, but little else. Another lashing, and nothing. After striping his back several more times, the slavemaster shouted, and another guard began beating the lad with his cudgel. The boy lifted his head, only to slump again. Swiftly, the guard unfastened him and hauled his limp body from the bench. His head lolled, and he looked at Jacek with glazed eyes. Guards dragged him to the gunwale, removed his shackle, and stripped him. He seemed to awaken then and began a pitiful struggle, wailing "Noooo!" as they heaved him up and over the side. Jacek thought he heard a splash, then nothing more. The slavemaster barked his orders, flicking his whip, and the rowers fell into rhythm as they began the day's tortuous drudgery.

Perhaps Neptune was unhappy with the scrawny sacrifice he'd received, for they rowed all the day through tumultuous seas. Jacek fought the loom hour after hour and folded as soon as they'd shipped the oars. Titas surprised him when he croaked in Polish, "Good effort, Pole."

Gian nodded. "You're strong like an ox."

Jacek didn't feel strong. Just rickety, spent. "My superior officer once said the same thing, but he meant my head," he mumbled.

Gian turned quickly and looked Jacek over. "You are a soldier?"

"Yes, a commander of knights." Then Jacek's heart tripped. Had he revealed too much?

Gian nodded, and the hint of a smile tugged his lips. After a beat, he said, "I am also a soldier. In the Republic of Genoa, I am a lord. Here, I'm less than a goat dropping."

Under the threat of the whip, they quieted. Until they received their rations.

"Look. They've given us six extra beans for battling Neptune's temper today," Gian said sarcastically. He carefully laid half his biscuit on his tongue, licking every crumb off his fingers.

"Has anyone tried to ransom you?" Jacek asked.

Gian looked him over. "When I first came here, I wrote three letters begging my wife, yet here I remain. Did the admiral send my letters, or did he throw them in the sea? I don't know. Did my wife receive them and send money that was stolen? I will never know until I get off this godforsaken floating cesspit."

Jacek savored a bean.

Gian glanced to the sky. "You are a noble son, and perhaps, if you send a letter, you will have better success than I. If Admiral Rifat allows you paper and pen. If he sends the letter. If it reaches them. If an offer arrives before you die. If he entertains that offer."

Jacek deflated, then tilted his head toward Titas. "Him?" Titas stared at the rail as if he had no idea they spoke.

"A Zaporozhian Cossack from Ukraine. He sailed a pirate ship that ravaged Turkish cities and ships, like this one, on the Black Sea. Now he is a prisoner of war. No ransom."

Jacek turned to Titas. The man said nothing; not even a muscle twitched.

"He does not talk much." Gian shrugged.

What is there to say?

Jacek jerked awake to the tent cover being rolled up, the same routine he'd grown as used to as one could, sleeping on a hard bench, leaned against a harder loom, amid hundreds of smelly, cadaverous men. He'd lost track of the weeks, the months he'd been aboard the admiral's most prized ship, the *Cesaret*.

The fleet, led by the *Cesaret*, hugged the western shoreline as it headed south. Fatigue and hunger were Jacek's mainstays. At times, he was too spent for anything but the rowing required of him. Like the pitiful lad, two more slaves had been tossed overboard like so much rubbish, too weak to resist. Their lives meant naught to those who ruled them, for they were easily replaced in any port where the *Cesaret* docked along her journey. Jacek reckoned the price of a slave must have amounted to a paltry sum.

As Jacek stretched his arms in the crisp air, his breath steamed, and he noted frost on the gangways and rails. The lightening milky-blue sky arced above. Wisps of clouds hovered low in the east, their edges gilded in brilliant pink that turned them purple. He inventoried his sore muscles, numb legs, and aching backside. Crusted in dry seawater, he removed his cap and scratched his scalp, trying to dislodge the salt from his short, matted hair. Nothing seemed to help; the brine forever drenched all the slaves, eating skin and clothes while plastering them in grit.

"Cold," Gian said, looking enthralled with the wispy puffs he blew out.

Jacek gave him a quick nod. It was routine, this brief exchange, and there would be no more talk today. Maybe tonight, if they had the strength and the guards didn't pay attention. Jacek likened his abysmal existence to dying a protracted, painful death only to reawaken and die the same way all over again every day. His worst fear, the fear that visited him in the night, was that he would endure like this for decades, part-living, part-corpse, haunted, undead. That fear led him to fantasize about escape, just as he did this morning when he'd finished his prayers.

They hadn't been underway very long before he was reminded his dream was pure folly. The reminder came when a commotion broke out on the bench before him. Two slaves began tussling with each other, jostling the others in their row. It was a short-manned bench, so when a third slave joined the fight, the last rower lost his grip and the oar began falling back, threatening the balanced rise and fall on the starboard side. All Jacek saw was the falling shaft about to crash onto one or four heads, so he plunged under his own loom and grasped the loose one, holding it up, keeping it from dipping into the water out of rhythm.

While the slaves remained bitterly entwined in their struggle, Jacek held the oar aloft, ducking and twisting as his nearly slammed him. The guards advanced quickly, snapping their whips, shouting, swarming with their cudgels. Jacek was caught up in it and suffered blows of his own, but he held fast to the loom. The drumming slowed and eventually stopped. So did the oars. Admiral Rifat ran along the gangway to benches already crowded with guards and slaves. The commander screamed and waved his arms about furiously, and Turks began untangling the brawling men. Jacek gingerly lowered the oar into the hands of the bench's lone rower and maneuvered into his own seat. Before he could settle himself, two guards seized him. He jerked his arms involuntarily and heard Gian muttering, "Mary, Mother of God," as Jacek was unchained and hauled to the gangway to stand beside the instigators. They were subdued now, shoulders bowed, blood trickling from mouths, cheeks, and ears.

One of the men who held Jacek was the admiral's slavemaster, Cenk— a short, squat Turk with dull black beads for eyes. Expressionless, he looked Jacek over, but he had to crane his neck to do it. It might have been comical. But not today.

Breathe in, breathe out. Don't let them see fear. Or anger.
Survive first.

The admiral yelled gibberish and gesticulated, and his officers yelled back, pointing at each slave in turn. Jacek had learned some Turkish, but when they spoke quickly, as they were doing now, he understood little. Soon only Cenk spoke, and he did so rapidly, jerking on Jacek's arm.

Admiral Rifat narrowed his small eyes and gave Jacek a hard stare. Jacek's heart hadn't stopped hammering. His head spun when, five minutes later, he was shoved back in his seat and shackled while the three agitators were dragged toward the admiral's fighting position, a small platform that held a seat from which officers supervised the rowing.

Titas leaned into him. "God must be on your side today, Pole," he said in a low growl. "Cenk told Rifat what you did. Rifat didn't believe him at first."

"What happens to the others?" hissed Jacek.

From the side of his mouth, Gian answered, "You'll see."

The first man, who had been the last man into the fight, was stripped to the waist and laid facedown on a bench placed on the gangway where all could see. Slaves held each of his limbs fast, stretching him like a canvas sail. Standing above him was a Turkish guard, also stripped to the waist, who wielded a whip. When he slashed the first blow across his bare back, the prone man jerked and gasped. Cenk barked at the lasher, and another guard, also holding a whip, stepped up behind the whipping guard.

"What are they doing?" Jacek asked.

"If the guard doesn't strike his victim hard enough, he too will be flogged. That's his only warning," Gian replied quietly.

When the next blow landed, it made a terrible slapping noise but was lost in the slave's howling. Another blow fell, and another. Jacek counted twenty before the man stilled. But his punishment did not stop, for his back was struck ten more times. When he at last heard whimpering, Jacek knew the wretch had regained consciousness. The barber-surgeon began slathering a mixture on his back, and the slave commenced howling again.

"Salt and vinegar," Gian said before Jacek could ask.

The two remaining offenders had been restrained close by, and now each man's face held a sickly pale cast of fear. When the first man was peeled from the bench, the next was shoved in his place. A new guard wielded the whip, and he showed no qualms about applying savagery to each awful lash. The victim passed out after twenty-three strikes. Jacek counted seventy in the end, meted out by different guards.

"Poor bastard," Gian mumbled.

"Will he live?" Jacek asked.

Gian shrugged.

The last man quaked and keened pitifully when his turn came; he too was flogged seventy times. Incredibly, all three men were placed back on the bench and ordered to row when the time came. Their tunics were soaked with blood, and they shivered uncontrollably. One man never recovered, and by morning he was fed to the hungry sea.

Thoughts of the slaves' treatment plagued Jacek. It wasn't their suffering that ate at him—there was so much suffering he'd hardened himself to it. Instead, he wondered at his own integrity, for he had been joyful he'd been spared a merciless flogging of his own. Had he become a man devoid of morality, no better than his captors? He fed his doubts to the tiny flame, the one he nurtured with every thought, every picture of his previous life. It was the flicker that drove him, the spark that kept him alive, waiting to be kindled into a conflagration that would explode from him when the time came.

That time was not today.

The routine of incessant rowing in time with unendingly reverberating drumming had been broken these last days, for they were anchored in a harbor before a stone fortress. The admiral, his wife, and their sizeable entourage had gone ashore and stayed. Some of the prisoners had worked off-ship digging stone, fortifying walls, repairing wharves—and as Jacek bent his head in prayer this particular morning, he added a silent one that he might be so freed, if even for a few minutes. Of late, he had escaped the whips that drew welts and slashes and had twice been unfastened along with his fellows to bail water. Standing upright, stretching his wobbly legs, simple things Jacek had always taken for granted, were now luxuries he craved, and he hoped God would forgive being bothered with such a trifle.

God must not have minded, for Jacek's section was released to work aboard ship. He trod the walkways, relishing the feel of standing, of being out of the excrement, of his bare soles slapping sodden wood. Standing atop a narrow walkway running along the ship's side, he rested his hands on a starboard rail adorned with circular painted discs that reminded him of colorful shields. As he scanned the sullen sea, he saw the three merchant ships anchored nearby, along with the warship. Did his companions still live?

His thoughts turned from them to the openness of the deep blue water, the marvel of the stone that made up the fortress, the vegetation clinging to hillsides, and the bright clothing of people moving freely about on land. His world had compressed to benches, oars, Turks with booted feet and whips, and, sometimes, the sky overhead. Now the world was spread before him, and he drank it in.

Today, he scrubbed decking, surveying the ship while he worked. It would have been a marvel if not for the wretched slaves powering it. It was slung beamy and low, with a ramming beak painted red, blue, and black. Below the rails were holes through which the oar blades jutted. Two solid masts rose from the gangway, lashed with white furled lateen sails.

Jacek's eye was drawn to the raised fighting platform at the bow, below which was the gun deck that housed cannon. He'd noticed soldiers coming and going from the gun deck, disappearing beyond his line of sight, sometimes returning with armaments they'd not had previously.

Aft, a brilliant green standard of the Ottoman Empire with its white crescent fluttered pompously atop the starboard side of the blue-and-gold-awninged stern deck, which held the admiral's quarters beneath. The fighting position straddled the stern deck and the rowing benches. Today, Cenk sat there, engrossed in a chessboard while his opponent looked on blankly.

Jacek stole a few glances their way and was hailed by a guard. His heart caught in his throat but lowered itself back to his chest when the guard indicated he wanted two barrels moved. As Jacek passed by the chessboard empty-handed, he craned his head. Pointing, he indicated a move to the absorbed Cenk. The man seemed to enliven. He moved the chess piece and smiled broadly while his opponent let out a derisive sound. As Jacek hefted the second barrel, Cenk gave him a quick nod.

Just then, something shrieked and darted from the admiral's quarters. It flew to the quarter deck, followed by a screaming woman who stopped at the foot of the ladder, jabbering and pointing upward. Jacek averted his eyes, for Gian had told him never to look at any of Rifat's women. He didn't know if this one belonged to Rifat but saw no reason to find out. Instead, he put down the barrel and ran for the ladder on the opposite side, his eyes riveted to a small form shinnying up the rail. He and the form seemed to be the only things moving on that ship, and he felt as though he moved leadenly while it darted quick as a cat.

The thing—a boy child—laughed as he gripped a piece of rigging and threw his little leg atop the rail. The woman screamed—whether for the child or for Jacek touching the child, he knew not—but he lunged for the boy and pulled him against his chest just as the boy's second foot skidded along the rail. Jacek fell, landing on his back, cradling the child on his chest. The boy patted Jacek's good cheek and laughed riotously. Guards had finally found their legs, and two sprang to Jacek's side just as he sat up. He quickly handed the boy into a pair of arms and stayed down, his hands atop his head. The move didn't save him from cudgel blows about said head. More guards arrived now, as did Cenk. Soon Jacek was yanked to his feet and shoved down the gangway. At Cenk's direction, his wrists were fastened to the mast and hauled above his head. Dread seized him. He wondered how much flogging he could take before he lost consciousness.

Consolation during those desperate moments came as his gaze wandered over the shackled oarsmen in the *Cesaret*'s pits, and something snagged his attention. He narrowed his eyes, not believing what they saw. A familiar head bob. His breath caught, and he was nearly overcome when he spotted Dawid seated on a bench, Pawel nearby. *They're here! They live!*

Good fortune multiplied, for the whipping never came. His deed, it seemed, led instead to his removal to a bench that enjoyed scraps from the section commander's table.

Days later, as the cold fingers of an autumn night stole over the sea, he knew what a whore must feel like when she landed a wealthy regular, and it didn't trouble him as it should have. His guilt lasted only as long as his meal, for the usual biscuit and beans were augmented by a half slice of fresh bread, a bite of fish, and one fig. He savored them all.

They remained in the harbor for weeks, it turned out, as a show of strength to prevent attacks on the fortress while its fortifications were repaired. Jacek enjoyed more unfettered time as he moved about the ship, throwing himself at anything any watch asked of him. He drained bilgewater and seawater, scrubbed surfaces, moved sails, tarred longboats, caulked planking. He even helped chain and unchain other slaves, which was when he discovered Janusz and Wiesław among them. He could have leapt for joy. As he could, he snuck all his friends the occasional scrap.

He also continued to help Cenk defeat his chess opponents. Once, while Admiral Rifat was still ashore, he even played Cenk. Though it nearly undid him, he let the mate win.

Reality roared back harshly when the *Cesaret* picked up anchor and headed south, and his world shrank back to the oar and that one slab of wood little wider than his backside. After unrelenting hours rowing, the pain, the cramping, the tearing of muscle, and the monotony grew unbearable, and Jacek allowed himself to succumb to the unthinkable: he was forever and hopelessly trapped on this ship. No more would he tear across a lush meadow on a fine horse, wind ruffling his hair; no more would he lounge before a fire sipping mead in sumptuous brocade and fur; no more would his hand touch a woman's soft skin, nor would his lips brush hers.

Utter despair flooded him.

Chapter 23

Worlds Apart

Oliwia looked out the solar window, deep in thought after her meeting with Tomasz. She barely noted winter's frigid bluster or the icicles dangling from parapets and roofs. Instead, she thought of the depleted granaries and the provisions she'd cut back, rationed, distributed. Despite her efforts, their stores were diminishing more rapidly than she and Tomasz had anticipated—even game was scarce. And though the number of soldiers had shrunk to little more than a score, they still needed to be fed and paid.

When someone cleared his throat behind her, she wheeled. With a gasp of relief, she said, "Oh, Henryk, 'tis only you."

His eyebrows crawled up his forehead. "*Only* me? I venture I've become too familiar to you, my lady, like one of the hounds in the hall."

She gave him a contrite smile. "I didn't mean …"

He grinned back. "I'm sure you didn't. Now tell me, what has you so vexed?"

"The report from Tomasz is worse than I thought, and though the hunt master has been busy, luck has not been with us. Game is meager this year."

"No doubt your tenants are helping themselves," Henryk snorted.

She stared at him slack-jawed. "No."

He raised his eyebrows even higher, then handed her a letter. "This arrived as I was making my way here."

Looking at the seal, she sighed. "Lord Antonin. Merciful God, say he is not returning."

She read it and let out a mirthless laugh before handing it to Henryk. "He's giving me one last chance to accept him before he appeals to the king. Can he do that?"

Henryk frowned. "Possibly. Have you reconsidered the other offers?"

Oliwia shook her head.

He let the paper flutter to the table and puffed out a great breath, seeming to haul himself up to his full height. Squaring his shoulders, he smoothed his brown hair and his deep blue velvet żupan.

"Oliwia, you must make a choice, and soon." He gestured to the chairs before the fire. "Please. Let us sit for a moment. May I pour you some wine?"

His normally easy smile was suddenly tight. Oliwia perched at the edge of the chair. "Do I have need of it?"

He let out a nervous laugh. "I believe we both do, my lady."

With that, he poured two generous shares from a glass pitcher, passing her a full goblet as he took the seat beside her. He gulped down the amber liquid. Oliwia watched him with a sidelong glance and several sips of her own. Henryk drained his goblet and stood abruptly to refill it, offering her more at the same time.

She covered her cup. "No, thank you."

He sat back down as brusquely as he'd stood and took another big pull; his eyes wandered to the blaze. Normally a man of elegant movements, his lurching behavior unsettled her. She waited, suddenly uncomfortable in his company. She scanned the room. *The shelves need dusting; the credenza needs polishing; that worn corner of the carpet needs mending; is that chicken broth I smell?*

Henryk turned his head to her in another quick movement. Slowly, she raised her gaze over the rim of her goblet. He leveled his hazel eyes at her—a mesmerizing mix of muddy brown and moss green—and cleared his throat.

"My lady," he began in a crisp, stern manner very unlike him. "Oliwia, we have known one another a long time now—ever since you came here as a girl."

"Yes, and we have been good friends," she replied, bemused.

"And I value your friendship greatly."

"As I do yours."

"Oliwia, it has been over six months since Jacek was lost to us both."

Her breath hitched inadvertently, and Henryk paused, then raced on. "He always meant to safeguard you. No man living could have done so better than he. His devotion to you was unwavering."

"And to Lady Eugenia?" She cringed at the bitterness in her own voice and darted her eyes to the flames.

"You will never convince me love drove him to it. Jacek greatly admired Klemens Matejko—almost as much as he admired Hetman Żółkiewski. I believe he agreed to marry the daughter to please her father."

Oliwia felt the familiar stab in her heart and its accompanying ache. She had managed to cover it, hide it, but here it was before her again, reminding her how much she had lost. She took a deep, steadying breath and nodded.

"Nonetheless, just as Jacek swore to Eryk to keep you and Adam from harm, so did I pledge to Jacek when he left. I did it gladly, never imagining fate would call me to it. But fate has, and here we sit, you more in danger than ever and me sworn to keep you from it."

He continued softly. "I wish to offer you another solution, an alternative to Antonin and these other men you do not want."

Oliwia turned back to Henryk, her eyes wide. He deliberately set his cup down, then took hers and put that aside too. Leaning toward her, he gathered her hands in his. His touch was solid, and it was warm. A man's touch. It felt good. A thoughtful, grave expression overtook his features. He glanced at their joined hands, then back to her.

"Oliwia, I know I cannot replace Jacek in your heart. No man alive could do that. But I ... I wish to try, if you will allow me. I have little to offer in the way of wealth, but I offer you my family's name, a noble name with a proud legacy, and my friendship, which you already have."

Spirit of God!

He cleared his throat, breaking his gaze for an instant. "Would you do me the honor of becoming my wife?" His words were so hushed as to resemble a whisper, but they were no less earnest.

Oliwia stifled a burst of laughter. Marry Henryk? It was unthinkable.

His Adam's apple bobbed as he swallowed. "Obviously, I have shocked you. Take your time before giving me your answer."

"This is not a jest?" she blurted.

A smile tugged one corner of his mouth. "I never jest where betrothals and marriage are concerned. Not that I am in the habit of proposing either, mind."

Her head nodded of its own accord. She remembered to close her mouth. He rose, bringing her with him, then leaned down and kissed her cheek chastely. "You will think on it?"

"Why are you doing this, Henryk?" The words rushed out of her.

He sighed. "You are my friend, and I do not wish to see others take advantage of you. And what better way to safeguard you than to marry you? Besides, this is what Jacek would have wanted."

A small laugh escaped her. "You realize, do you not, that he was wont to show a jealous side when it came to you?"

He grinned. "I am painfully aware. He showed me that side on more than one occasion, as he did everyone else who dared look at you. But he is there," he pointed upward, "and at worst can hurl silent curses at me."

After a beat, his expression grew solemn again. "We can begin as dear friends, which is more than most do, and in time our affection will grow stronger."

She freed a hand and lightly cupped his cheek. "Yours is a very generous gesture, Henryk, but—"

He placed a finger on her lips, startling her. "You must marry, Oliwia. Think on it."

She made her way back to her apartments, her heavy heart twisted. Henryk had thought to help her, but his proposal only added to her quandary, for she would now be forced to reject him. Her thoughts were interrupted by Filip wending his way through the passage.

"There you are," he said, sounding altogether grown-up. He stood straight, his hands clasped behind him.

Her heart lifted. "You were searching for me?"

"Yes. I wondered if you might like to watch my swordplay."

"Of course. Is everything all right?"

He looked up at her, and his blue-gray eyes suddenly misted. Shaking his head, he dug his thumbs into them.

She placed a light hand on his shoulder. "You are missing him today, yes?"

But she already knew the answer.

"I will become a warrior just like him."

"I see how hard you work at what he taught you," she replied with a quaver. "You rise each morning and reflect, and you practice on the backs of the horses and in the lists for countless hours. He would have been so proud of your diligence."

Filip gave her a quick nod. As he stood at attention, she saw Jacek in his firm stance and the scowl on his young face, and her heart splintered. How could she think of life with a different man when thoughts of the only one she'd loved crowded out everyone else?

Chapter 24

Aeolus

J acek reckoned they were deep into the winter season and Christmas had come and gone long ago like any other miserable, monotonous day. Was Ash Wednesday close? The weather had warmed as they headed south, sailing the Bosphorous into Constantinople, where they anchored just long enough to take on supplies, a dignitary, his wife, their attendants, and a few sorry slaves. Jacek remained shackled to the bench, and his view of the city was scant more than hills, fortresses, vast walls, bastions, and the flocks of screeching gulls that wheeled overhead. It seemed Admiral Rifat was anxious to move on and outrun the shifting weather, so the *Cesaret*'s oarsmen were pressed to an altogether more urgent tempo beat out by the drums. As they rowed over the Sea of Marmara toward the Dardanelles, they left the warship behind. The Black Sea was also left behind, though Jacek felt no relief. Not only was he a world away from home, but the slave markets of Alexandria and Tripoli—and perhaps a worse existence than this one—awaited.

So did the storms of the Mediterranean.

As the ships headed into the Aegean several mornings later, they turned south under lulling skies. But to the west, clouds were gathering, building themselves into towering columns that were every sailor's nightmare. For the remainder of that day, without rest, the sails and galley slaves powered the ship under the unrelenting boom of the drums, the rhythmic chants of the Turks, and the bite of their whips. The leaden western sky sent sword-steel clouds racing at them and wrapped darkness over the day, ushering in an early, blustery twilight.

The tillerman guided the ship to the island of Lesbos, and they dropped anchor in Mytilene's sheltering harbor. The cacophony of the drums and chants stopped at last, and the sails were furled and oars pulled out of the water. Rowers folded over in exhaustion. Jacek sensed waves slapping the wooden hull in a noisy, irregular pattern, as though they boiled. At first, he thought fatigue or unease thrummed through him, making his taut muscles jittery. But now he felt a juddering in everything, everywhere, and the oarsmen ate rapidly to avoid losing their meager meals in the fetid *zupa rybna* sloshing below their feet.

As night wore on, he *smelled* something different. The wind was stirring up a chaotic frenzy, pushing cool moisture at them. The air was heavy, juicy, as massive clouds came at them, bright bolts illuminating thunderheads with pulsing brilliance. He'd endured countless rainstorms and squalls aboard the *Cesaret*, but this was different. More ominous, more menacing, as if an enraged colossus stormed across sea and sky.

Jacek curled up on his seat and tried to shut out images of being pulled down with a drowning ship, of his lungs filling with dark water, unable to kick free. The rising storm tore all other noise away, scattering it to the boiling clouds. He covered his ears against the furious whistling and the sound of rain pelting the tent cover, but he couldn't escape the heaving and rocking of his prison. Water drenched him as he hovered between nightmare and wakefulness, and he shivered and prayed.

He lay thusly for hours until the creaking of the timbers brought him fully alert; they sounded like souls screaming, pressing in all around him. Between inky darkness came searing flashes of lightning. Then the ship pitched violently, straining at its tethers as the roiling sea pushed and pulled it. Wind tore across the decks, driving more cold air into the rowing benches while it tugged and jerked rigging, lanterns, canopies, and flags. And he prayed harder still.

The galley lurched to starboard and bobbed upright, clattering beams against masts. The *Cesaret* swayed wildly before listing to starboard once more, but this time a huge wave captured her and turned her cockeyed. A frothy crest shattered over top of them, straining the cover above. All around him, slaves, fastened to their benches, desperately yanked on unbreakable chains, screaming and wailing as they scrabbled about, some climbing atop one another in their panic. He jerked his own chain, though he knew it was hopeless. The few soldiers and sailors he saw fought for footing as water licked the sides of the ship and sent sheets of water skittering across walkways. Cannon lurched against their restraints, rumbling and rolling precariously across the decking.

He wondered if drowning hurt. How long would he gasp for air before everything went black? He always imagined that were he to die a violent death, it would be as a warrior in battle, not as a rat chained to a dying ship. His thoughts turned to Oliwia, to his family, his brothers-in-arms. In his mind, he said good-bye to them all and asked for their absolution. He shook in the dark and the wet and the cold, and someone grabbed his hand, and he held on fiercely. He wept. Wept and ached for all he'd lost.

The hand he held slipped away, and he was alone. He clutched his arms to his chest. It was in this maelstrom of nature and his desolation that he lifted his head and saw Ruta before him, shimmering like a veil of pearls. Swallowing hard, he stared, transfixed by the apparition of his long-dead twin sister.

"Have you come for me?" he said aloud, though none could hear him in the howling gale.

She smiled serenely and shook her head. "No, Jacuś. It is not yet your time. God has other plans for you."

He should have been terrified, but the sound of his diminutive, uttered in Ruta's sweet voice, wrapped him up in an unseen, warm cocoon. The sounds wrought by the storm dulled. He took in a great breath, and his clenched muscles unwound.

Will you help me get home?

As if the vision had read his thoughts, she said, "Watch for your chance, dearest brother. It is not this night, but it will come soon. Do not hesitate. Believe in Him, and all will be well."

She reached out her hand. Just as he thought he felt it brush his cheek, she dissolved and the terrible noises rose about him once more.

Following the storm, Jacek and scores of slaves were unchained to clear the *Cesaret* and make repairs. Despite his diminished frame, he felt invigorated, as if his sister had left something of her spirit behind.

Wait for me, Liwi. I am coming home.

As Jacek helped chain and unchain rowers, he pressed whatever scavenged morsels he could into eager hands and spoke to Dawid, Pawel, Janusz, Wiesław, Gian, and Titas of a plan. It fueled him, fed his strength, even as he gave up his own pilfered rations.

At last, the ship was ready, and they rowed out of port into the Aegean. They had turned south when, seemingly from nowhere, a new storm rose up and chased them back to Mytilene. And again. And so it went for another sennight. The ferocity of these squalls did not rival the first until one drove the *Cesaret* to Mytilene and scattered the other three ships between two nearby ports, where they remained that night.

The next morning, Jacek spotted Dawid standing rigid, slack rope in hand, casting his gaze to Lesbos under a somber sky. Once more, they had been unshackled in order to labor about the ship. "What has you so enraptured that you risk the wrath of our captors?" hissed Jacek.

Dawid snapped his head to him, startled. Then a grin spread over his sunken face. "I was thinking of all the beautiful women on that island waiting to pleasure you and me."

"You confuse the present with ancient Greece," Jacek scoffed as he coiled a rope. "Regardless, *we* would not be bestowed with such favors."

"Not even for a full pouch of silver?" posed Dawid.

"Assuming you *had* any silver, that island's in Ottoman territory. You'd pay the devil for touching one of their women. Besides, the desirable ones are locked away in harems." Jacek paused to wipe sweat from his brow. "The gales have made you daft."

"Ah, but one night with a wench ..." Dawid let out a long sigh.

Jacek thumped him in the chest. "Get your mind back on your work, or you'll end up a eunuch. See the tent's pulled over the benches before the rain comes." Dawid glanced at the sky and hurriedly picked up a strap.

Just then, guards barked out, and a group of women emerged on deck and shuffled toward the rail. Jacek and the other slaves turned their gazes and waited while they, Admiral Rifat, his guests, and a snaking line of soldiers bedecked in their finest silks and gold braiding departed the ship.

"What the devil?" Jacek said aloud.

Another slave, an old salt who stood nearby, said Rifat was going ashore for a wedding feast hosted by Lesbos's governor.

"Why all the soldiers? He must be taking over half with him."

The old salt shrugged. "Admiral Rifat enjoys flaunting his wealth."

Jacek grunted.

When he looked around later that afternoon, it struck him the ship looked empty. The drums were silent and unmanned. No one strode the gangway except a cook who trod toward the quarterdeck where the cooking fire was housed. *Where the devil is everyone? Sleeping belowdecks?* He had never seen the ship so quiet.

And then it hit him.

"Make ready," he said urgently.

"What can you be thinking?" whispered Dawid. "We'll all be slaughtered."

Jacek looked into his eyes, conviction coursing through his veins like molten steel. "Trust in God. All will be well."

Then he headed for the quarterdeck.

Chapter 25

The Cesaret

As Jacek closed the distance to the quarterdeck, blood surged through his veins, pumping every taut muscle with fuel. He glanced about furtively, then narrowed his gaze to the housing for the cooking fire. The cook stood beside it, a look of boredom on his face.

I'm just another slave.

Just as Jacek reached the housing, he snatched three metal rods, setting off a clatter. The cook startled from his torpor. Jacek was already in motion and struck him across the temple before he could cry out. The man crumpled. Jacek eased him to the deck and turned him on his back. Then he stomped his heel hard and heard the crunch of a crushing windpipe. He wheeled to see Dawid and Pawel behind him, their expressions fierce, and he shoved a rod into each one's grasp.

"I'll fetch the weapons," Jacek said. "Release the other four first. Then we carry out the rest of the plan." He sprinted down the walkway to the stern, the rod tucked between his body and arm. His eyes strafed the tent cover as he went; it was taut, hiding the rowers beneath.

When he came to the forecastle, he leapt into the hold, taking the guard defending the arms store by surprise. The man managed to crash the hilt of his scimitar into Jacek's shoulder just as Jacek hit him with the rod. The strike landed on the man's forearm, and his sword rattled to the floor. Jacek snatched it, gripped the hilt, and slashed the blade just below the man's ribs. The stunned guard staggered, a look of surprise on his face, blood blooming on his jacket. Jacek brought the point up and thrust it into the man's neck, dropping him before he made a sound.

Jacek pulled in large breaths and rubbed his shoulder. He looked at the scimitar clutched in his hand. Jesus, it felt good to hold a weapon again! He laid it aside and wiped his shaking hands on his pants, then gathered an armload of scimitars and swiftly ran up the ladder to the closest row of slaves.

"Distribute these among yourselves quickly! Quietly! I'm getting more," he hissed. The astonished oarsmen took them as Jacek pivoted on his heel. He could hear their voices buzzing behind him.

Again and again, he carried out blades. He stubbornly locked out all that could go wrong. His chest heaved, and sweat trickled down his face under his shirt, plastering it against his chest. When Dawid appeared beside him and grabbed up a load, Jacek nearly jumped. Then he nearly kissed him.

"Pawel got the keys and set the others loose. They're taking charge of the rowers. So far, we have not been detected," Dawid said.

"Praise God!"

With the next hurried delivery of weapons, Jacek assigned the task to two oarsmen who'd just shed their shackles. Then he and Dawid armed themselves and ran aft in a crouch. Pawel and Wiesław fell in behind, and Janusz and Gian headed the opposite direction. A sentry, who had been looking out to sea from the stern, suddenly swung his gaze. His mouth and eyes went round.

"This is it," Jacek growled. Just as the words left his mouth, the sentry shouted out an alarm and unsheathed his scimitar.

The battle for the *Cesaret* was on.

Jacek reached the sentry first, deflecting a strike from the man's right. Before his foeman could complete another blow, Jacek kicked out, landing a foot on his left hip. The impact spun the man just enough that his blade missed. Jacek's didn't. The man doubled over, clutching at his midsection, where blood brightened torn fabric.

Like ants scrambling from their labyrinths, soldiers emerged from every opening on the ship, releasing scimitars with telltale metallic whines. Freed slaves poured from the benches, and they were a terrifying sight: feral, cadaverous men armed with sharp blades and fury flaming in wild eyes, fearlessly running at their oppressors. They roared beastly, frightening cries as they came, outnumbering their captors three-to-one. Some had no weapons, so they grabbed up whatever they found—chains, hanks of coiled rope, pulley blocks, lanterns—and swung them with savagery. Others used their hands, choking, clawing, heaving this Turk or that over the rails to their deaths.

As captor and captive came together, metal rang against metal, wood splintered and thudded, and iron tools and barrels crashed. Fighting was deadly and fierce. Amid the clashing blades and men's desperate shouts was the continuous sound of clinking as long chains were pulled through iron rings. More slaves swarmed into the mayhem.

Jacek hoisted himself atop the stern deck. Below him, a handful of Turks grasped the ropes tethering the tent cover and tried to enfold the rowers. He bellowed an order, that order was repeated in different tongues, and the slaves trapped beneath began rolling up the tarp, fighting off the Turks.

"Do not forget who you are and what they are!" he boomed. "Give no quarter!"

Then he roared out another command, and slaves burst fore and aft to hack at the lines holding the ship at anchor. Others scrambled up rigging, unfurling sails. Blood, thick and oozing, slicked benches, decking, and walkways. Ragged slaves continued grappling with soldiers while others scrambled to seat the oars. One started a rhythmic rowing chant, and the ship shuddered and began to move. Everything was unfolding as Jacek had planned. His pulse raced ever faster, for soon the enemy ashore would know. The peril was about to erupt a hundredfold.

He steadied himself and pulled in deep breaths, drawing himself up strong and tall as he tightened his grip on the scimitar. He raised it to the sky.

"Go! Go! Row! Row for your lives, you Christians!" he yelled. "Pull! Row! God sails with you!" Again, his words echoed around him in foreign tongues.

He kept at it, kept hollering, straining his voice until he was nearly hoarse.

Survive first.

Escape second.

He heard a telltale whistling and looked up. Arrows flew thick, like a flock of straight, tapered birds against the storming sky. They were swallowed up in the sea. *They've spotted us.* Then he heard the boom of cannon and jerked his gaze to the shore. White puffs hovered in thick clouds about the fortress walls as splashes sounded all around the ship. Up to his waist in the sea, a turbaned man shook his fist and screamed. Rifat.

Jacek started to clamber to the lower deck but was stopped by armed soldiers surging up the ladder. His eyes narrowed on the closest threat; all sound dissolved. A scimitar in his right, a dagger in his left. He planted his bare feet and sliced his scimitar through the first Turk's hand. The man shrieked; his sword clattered on the decking. Blood spurted from his severed wrist as he cradled it against his chest. Jacek shoved him into the next man climbing the ladder, and they crashed to the fighting platform below. A third man roared onto the deck, eyes blazing, snarling ferociously.

Now!

Jacek raised his blade and brought it down hard. His edge bit into a sinewy neck. He never felt the impact, didn't realize he'd connected until warm blood sprayed his face, his hair. The body twitched, reeled, fell backward, and thudded a long second later.

Jacek's heart pounded against his rib cage as if trying to burst free. He should have been utterly spent. But with each enemy he struck, with each one he felled, he grew stronger. A swift current of heat coursed through him like a molten river of fire, and he felt as though towering flames leapt from his center and licked the heavens, catching up everything in their path.

With a thundering roar, he unleashed the warrior.

"Kill them all!"

He leapt to the main deck. Rowers heaved the looms, and the wind pushed the sails as the *Cesaret* turned for the open sea. At the rail, Dawid wrestled with Cenk. Jacek dove for his legs and hoisted him up. Together, they hurled the fat man into the sea, his screams following him down.

Behind them, Pawel yelled something about a woman. Wiesław and Janusz swung with unbridled ferocity at a knot of armed Turks pinned by the admiral's quarters. Jacek and Dawid plunged into the fray. Jacek was bellowing. He rammed his sword through a Turk's gaping mouth, then wrenched the blade free, slashed deep into another's belly. Blood and innards spilled out of the gash, splashing slick on the deck between Jacek's toes. He stepped back.

The *Cesaret* trembled and twitched around him, and shouting rose from the benches. Like cockroaches, more Turks appeared and swarmed the oarsmen.

Christ! So many!

Janusz flattened one man, then leapt over his body and disappeared, leaving Jacek and his brothers to the frenzied brawl. Metal rang amid grunts and thuds, reverberating loudly in the cramped space. Motion blurred around him. They drove the enemy back, battering at them.

Wiesław dropped one man. "That leaves five!" he hollered.

Four skinny hussars against five fat sailors. Now it's more than an even fight!

The four struck, parried, retreated. They kept moving, always moving, small steps in a small space. The Turk in front of Jacek lunged. Jacek shed the strike, then launched his own counterblow. His foeman parried it, thrust his blade forward. Jacek elbowed him, crashed the flat of his blade on his hand. The weapon flew from his enemy's grasp. Jacek buried the dagger in the man's middle, dragged it through soft tissue, yanked it back out again. The man squealed.

The barber-surgeon came at Jacek now, his eyes flaring, a grimace twisting his features. Jacek sidestepped, smashed the hilt of his sword into his face. He heard the *crunch* right before Pawel finished him off. Jacek's joy surged with each devastating slice. The more he fed his bloodlust, the hungrier the beast within him became. Everything seemed to speed up yet slow down at the same time. He was dancing, stabbing, yelling he knew not what.

A soldier swung wildly and missed. Jacek drove his dagger into his thigh. The blade snapped, lost in meat and muscle. A Turk came at Wiesław but slipped in blood, landing on his side. Wiesław dodged the man's whipping legs, and Dawid drove his blade into the Turk's heaving chest. The man groaned, grabbed at the steel. Dawid wrenched the blade out. Wiesław wheeled, stepped into the next foeman, hacked, knocked him to the deck.

Sucking in air, the four hussars looked at each other, Turks dead or dying around them.

Pawel eyed Jacek. "You all right?" Pawel's face was a grimy mask of blood that held two enormous blinking gray eyes.

"Are *you* all right?" Jacek countered between breaths.

Pawel dragged a sleeve across his face. "A few cuts. Nothing serious."

From the corner of his eye, Jacek saw Wiesław lurch. Dawid howled and lunged at a propped Turk. The man fell sideways, shuddering, groaning. Jacek jerked his head toward Wiesław and froze. Wiesław, his mouth open, stared at a knife protruding from his chest. He wobbled, staggered, and fell to his knees just as Dawid caught him.

Dawid cradled him and cried out, his hands glossed with bright blood. "Wiesław! No!"

Jacek stabbed two Turks through the neck when he thought they twitched. He dropped into a crouch beside Dawid and Wiesław. Pawel looked on, his expression dismal, dark. Wiesław, ashen and waxy, stared vacantly somewhere above him. Blood saturated his tunic, Dawid's breeches, and the decking beneath.

Dear God.

Dawid raised red-rimmed eyes to Jacek's. Jacek grasped his shoulder. "There's nothing you can do for him. We still have a ship to secure and an enemy to outrun."

Godspeed, Wiesław.

Janusz emerged from the captain's quarters, panting, streaked with blood.

"Are you injured?" Jacek asked in alarm as he rose.

From behind Janusz stepped a slight blond woman with wide blue eyes. She too was sprayed with blood. She turned and looked at Janusz. "He is fine," she said in Polish. "We are both fine. He saved my life."

Before Jacek could give the strange scene much thought, Gian shouted at him from below. He stood beside Titas, who pounded the rowing beat on the drum. Gian pointed aft. Jacek pivoted and ran to the rail. Closing behind them were three Ottoman war galleys, all lighter and swifter than the *Cesaret*.

Christ!

"Janusz, take Dawid and search the ship for any living Turks," he commanded as he ran down the ladder to the gangway. To Gian, he said, "We need more men at the oars!"

"They're working on it."

Jacek's eyes swept the benches. The Turks in the pits had been subdued. Even as men rowed, more scrambled and hefted the unwieldy oars in place. He reckoned all but seven benches per side were rowing full-out.

"No teams," he shouted at the top of his voice. "*Everyone* rows! Make haste! They're gaining! Go! Go!"

Gian hollered, "Faster!" and Titas increased the tempo.

How long can they hold out?

Everywhere, slaves manned sails, swarmed up and down rigging, and ran along walkways. The old salt was bellowing orders. Jacek drew in a great breath and squeezed his eyes shut. "God, You have not brought us this far for naught," he murmured.

"Amen." Beside him, Gian crossed himself.

Moments later, he yanked on Jacek's sleeve. "Look!" Jacek raised his head to the sky and saw a familiar sight: blackening clouds building into boiling towers. And they were coming at them fast.

"Oh Christ!"

"We can't turn back," Gian said. "Our only chance is the open sea."

"So we stay the course?" Jacek fought the urge to shake his head.

The old salt nodded grimly. "Keep praying. We're in for a devil of a ride."

Despite his dread, Jacek marveled as he moved about the ship, for men dashed in a well-ordered way as though three galleys and a gale did not ride on their tail. The storm hastened night, closing in and plunging the *Cesaret* into a deep blue-black maelstrom that cast a shroud over her and everyone aboard. Below him, men were rolling the cover over the pits and taking turns at the oars. Others ran along the benches, shoving morsels and water into gaping mouths.

"How long before it's too dark to sail?" he asked the old salt.

"Not long. I'd be more worried about keeping her afloat," the man answered.

"If we can't, it might be a better fate," Jacek muttered.

The old salt gave him a curt nod.

As the ship rocked in the surging sea, Jacek looked from the port side aft for what must have been the hundredth time. The lanterns of their pursuers glowed, pitching in the murk. When rain began lashing the *Cesaret*, he looked again—and blinked. The lanterns appeared fainter. *'Tis the rain.*

He called Gian to his side and shouted to be heard above the storm. "Is it the rain, or do their lanterns dim? I can only make out two ships now." He shouted.

Gian pulled up a metal tube, placed it against his eye, and aimed it at the ships.

Jacek frowned. "What is that?"

Gian was silent for long moments as he swept the tube, still held to his eye, back and forth. "See for yourself." He grinned and handed the object to Jacek. "Put it up to your eye—one eye—and look at the ships."

Jacek brought the tube up, the metal cold against his skin. His eyelashes rested against glass. At first, he saw nothing save darkness. Pale light from the sun's dying rays glimmered in a thin band on the horizon, just long enough to illuminate an outline. He stared, trying to puzzle out what he was seeing. It was the side of a ship. He could see its swaying lanterns and men on the rigging and masts.

"Jesus! They're closer than I thought." He brought the tube down, his skin prickling. He still saw the vessel, but it was smaller now. Raising the tube, he spied the ship again. As he moved the cylinder from side to side, the other ships came into focus, but they were farther away. He saw the broad beam of their backs and the aft decks rising on the water's swells.

"What the devil?" he muttered.

Jacek looked at Gian, still grinning beside him, his pearly teeth flashing in his dark, shadowed face. Gian pointed at the instrument in Jacek's hand. "Compliments of the admiral. That's a looker. Somehow the glass makes everything bigger when you look through it so you can see things far away."

Jacek raised it again. "The closest ship is broadside, but if they fire on us, they will only waste shot," he said in disbelief. "And all I see of the others are their sterns. What are they doing?"

"They're not going to fire. They're turning. The bastards are running for port. It's just us battling old Neptune now!" exclaimed Gian.

Jacek's thudding heart nearly climbed into his throat. He studied the scene once more, then handed the object to Gian. In his elation, Jacek had nearly forgotten the storm—until the *Cesaret* lurched. She heaved in choppy waves ruffled with white froth. Steadying himself, he looked up at heavy clouds pressed together so tightly that he couldn't discern where one ended and the other began.

"We're not fighting Neptune," he yelled. "God sent this storm!"

And he loved it. He took in a great lungful of air and turned his face skyward, letting the rain fall on his face. The vessel might go down and pull them all with her, but he would leave the world a free man.

Time seemed suspended as the galley quivered and quaked in the unrelenting, churning sea that lashed her, tore at her, shattered itself white against her. Wind whipped over her like a spectral wave, keening as it went, like a thousand wretched souls speeding from hell. And so it went throughout all that long, dark night and the next day as the fatigued crew bailed her, cajoled her, and nursed her groaning timbers.

Night reigned again, and Jacek had finished his turn at the oar and was braced against a rail, scanning the vessel and its crew like a sentinel. Exhausted, he didn't trust the shift he felt at first. He looked at the rain as it spattered on the wood, then listened for a long while. *The tempest is quieting.* Standing erect, he paced the walkway and peered to the east; a charge ran through him. A ragged, dull dawn was emerging, its feeble glow lightening the horizon and the dim sky. As he looked around, men's silhouetted shadows enlivened. A few hoarse cheers went up.

The *Cesaret* was battered, but she was still afloat.

His legs shook as he headed back to the rail. Cold, chilled to the bone, he willed himself not to shiver.

Gian ambled to him, a smile plastered on his face. "You look as though you could stand some food and a long sleep."

"As do you."

"We made it, by the grace of God—and one crazy Pole," Gian said, leaning beside him.

Jacek shook his head. "I did not do it alone. We were *five* crazy Poles, one mad Italian, and hundreds of Christians fighting for their lives. And their freedom."

We were five Poles. Now we are four.

Gian let out a long breath and glanced up at Jacek. "I am sorry about your friend."

Jacek nodded. His eyes stung. He cleared his throat. "Where are we headed?"

"We go to my home, to the Republic of Genoa," Gian declared. "These men are eager for their own homes, their families, and with regular rations and rest, they will press. If we maintain this pace, our voyage will last twenty-two, twenty-three days."

Jacek gave Gian a sidelong glance. "How long since you have seen home?"

"Nearly three years. My daughter … She was not yet two when I left," Gian replied softly. Then he chuckled. "I pray my wife does not die from fright when she sees me."

Jacek bit back the question on his tongue. *Will she be waiting?* Instead, he looked across the gangway when someone replaced Janusz at sentry. The hussar walked purposefully to the Polish girl, Hedwiga, a slave who had served Rifat's household. Jacek had never noticed her for averting his eyes and wondered fleetingly what other women he'd missed. The couple spoke in the darkness of the quarterdeck, then disappeared below. Anguish, sudden and searing, spiked in Jacek, stealing his breath away. In that moment, he was consumed by an aching for Oliwia such as he'd never felt. It tore at him. He fought a clog in his throat.

It's fatigue.

"What of you?" Gian's question caught Jacek off guard. "Have you a woman who waits for you?"

Jacek swallowed and cast his gaze to the still-brooding sea. "There is … someone … We were to wed before autumn." He coughed. "She likely thinks me dead."

Clapping him on the shoulder, Gian jarred him. "When we reach Genoa, you and your men will be my honored guests. There, you will wait out the winter until you can return to her."

Though Jacek nodded, he had no intention of outwaiting winter.

Men scuttled about the decks and rigging in misting, sullen daylight, removing banners and standards, tossing enemy corpses into the maw of the sea, scrubbing away ghastly reminders, securing this and straightening that. How in blazes did they keep at it?

Jacek glanced to the fighting deck, where his dead brethren were being laid out, carefully wrapped in spare cloth or sacking as the rain pattered softly. A priest—a former slave—stepped among them, his lips moving as he prayed and brushed crosses with his thumb. Soon they would all gather to say good-bye and watch them buried at sea.

The fragrant smell of broth and a cooking fire caught and wafted, making Jacek's stomach groan. He spotted Dawid and Pawel at their posts, haggard and gray. His heart jolted as he caught himself seeking out Wiesław's square frame. He crossed himself yet again and sent another prayer heavenward. For the brave warrior, his brother. For his widow. For his little girls.

When at last he cleaned up and lay himself down, stretching out on his back in the admiral's berth, he relished putting his head on a pillow and not wood; of feeling warm and clean. It didn't matter that the bed was too small; he could place his twisted limbs where he chose. He soon drifted into a dreamless sleep.

Sailing during the following fortnight was mercifully uneventful. No Turks, pirates, or foul weather thwarted them. Like the others, Jacek eased himself back to eating, and though provisions were stale, they were plentiful. Under Titas's command, men rowed in shifts when the wind didn't belly the lateens, and they cut through the waters swiftly. It was as if one hand of God pushed them forward while the other held back the storms He'd unleashed at Lesbos. Now the sea showed her gentle side in a surface of glass, and the wind was like a playful child as it filled their sails. Though still a specter of his former self, Jacek grew stronger. His men grew stronger too, their gaunt faces and frames no longer resembling skeletons.

As he dozed on deck in the sun's warm rays one afternoon, he startled upright to panicked shouting from the crew. Looking from the starboard rail, he saw what they yelled about—a large ship heading their way, its square sails bowing like full bellows sacks. When he found Gian, the soldier already had the looker to his eye. He lowered it, his expression dour.

"Spanish man-of-war. Pray they in fact carry Spaniards who do not sink us before asking questions."

Jacek nodded and barked out an order to Titas; the oars rose up and hovered above the water, and men slackened the lines to douse the sails. Though they displayed no Ottoman symbols, there was little mistaking the origins of the merchant galley. Now two sailors hoisted a flap of canvas up the *Cesare*'s foremast and stood back, watching it snap in the breeze. It bore a cross of tar, and every man aboard raised his eyes and crossed himself. Not taking his eyes from the ship, Jacek willed his nerves not to twitch and jump as he waited.

The ship came at them, slowed, and turned broadside.

"Mary, Mother of God!" someone exclaimed.

"Oars down, Titas," Jacek yelled. "Have the helmsman turn the ship so we're a smaller target, but we stay where we are."

A puff of white smoke rose from the Spanish ship's hull in time with a boom. Jacek braced himself, but the shot splashed harmlessly twenty yards off the bow. Everyone aboard the *Cesaret* gawped then cursed.

Gian trained the looker on the man-of-war. "More gunports opening up," he hollered.

Jacek yanked off his Turkish officer's jacket, exposing an ivory linen shirt.

"Take off your jackets!" he yelled and sprinted to the stern deck. He began jumping up and down, waving both arms.

"What are you doing?" yelled Dawid from the quarterdeck.

"Trying to get their attention."

The *Cesaret*'s crew teemed up ladders and rigging and waved. When Jacek looked down, he was surprised to find Hedwiga stripping to her snowy chemise, jumping beside him as she unbound her hair.

"I am fair, like you," she said as her pale blond strands flew about her. "We are white flags, yes?" She was breathless, though he thought he saw a glimmer of a smile.

I hope they've a looker aboard.

The Spanish ship heaved and advanced toward them, head-on. Jacek stopped jumping and began praying.

Chapter 26

Between Scylla and Charybdis

Oliwia stood at a window in her sitting chamber, staring at the fields frozen wintry white under a pearl-gray sky, imagining the rich soil moist, warm, and fuzzed in green. Sliding her cross along its chain, she said a silent prayer that spring would be here soon and bring a plentiful harvest. The silver metal warmed as she closed her fingers about it. Henryk had had the necklace repaired and buffed to a soft luster soon after he returned it—a thoughtful gesture—though she had only recently brought herself to wear it. She had struggled to look upon it without recalling the dreadful smear of Jacek's blood.

Whether she donned the cross or not, Jacek frequently appeared in her dreams, all steely strength. Passionate. Alive. She would waken bereft, incapable of reconciling he was gone.

In a flurry of skirts, Wanda swept in, startling Oliwia from her reverie. Oliwia flinched and clenched her jaw. The girl was always about, always in constant motion, like a blustery spring wind.

Wanda dropped into an awkward curtsy. "Captain Kalinowski seeks an audience with you." Said captain appeared in the doorway.

"Yes, of course," Oliwia replied. "Come in, Henryk."

He handed her a letter. "From the king."

Oliwia accepted the letter and ran shaky fingers over the seal. The hairs on her neck pricked up. Wanda poured out two cups of wine, handing one to Oliwia and the other to Henryk, looking about nervously before Oliwia dismissed her. As soon as the girl was gone, Oliwia tore open the seal.

She let out a mirthless laugh. "The king says he's had word of a Swedish army gathering in the north that intends attacking the Crown's western border, and that he's tired of Biaska flapping about in the breeze like so much laundry. He has given me until the Octave Day of Easter to choose a husband. If I do not, he will select one for me *or,* if I 'insist' on remaining a widow, he will assign stewardship of Biaska to 'his trusted friend Lord Antonin of Wąskadroga.' In the meantime, the only military help we may count on to defend Biaska and the border is from Lord Antonin, who has pledged his troops to the king for that very purpose. The king goes on to 'encourage' me to consider Lord Antonin as a prospect, 'for the union would make for a strong family alliance and greatly benefit the Crown.' Ha!" She shook the letter at Henryk, her cheeks flaming.

He took it from her with a sidelong glance.

"Have *you* heard of an army gathering in the north, Henryk?"

He shook his head. "No. Only one near Wąskadroga, but they are not Swedes. They are rumored to join Lord Antonin's troops."

Oliwia jerked her head up. "What if they intend Biaska harm?"

Henryk frowned. "I would expect them to bolster its defenses instead."

"But what if I'm right and Antonin has been undermining us, ingratiating himself at court, preparing to strike us?"

Henryk blew out a breath. "Oliwia, the king expects you wed eight Sundays hence. And he's right. Every day you delay is another day that brings more danger to you and to Biaska."

He gathered her hands in his and softly said, "Jacek is not coming back. Have you given my proposal any consideration?"

How can I marry anyone? Oliwia searched his eyes and saw only concern. "I have. I am not yet ready to answer."

He tilted his head and held her gaze. "If you are to have any choice, you *must* decide."

Despairing her betrayal of Jacek's memory, she swallowed the wad in her throat. "You will have my answer by Ash Wednesday."

Releasing her with a nod, he slipped a folded letter out of his sash. "In the meantime, I have some good tidings. Lesław has recruited a contingent of Scots. While they are not many, they are experienced soldiers. Having them may not completely remove the need of Antonin's troops in a full-on attack, but their numbers will otherwise help."

She brightened.

"Ah. There's the look I hoped for," Henryk said with a dimpled smile.

"When does he arrive?" She suddenly felt as though she had bobbed up to the surface of a lake and could draw breath.

"He sets out after Ash Wednesday." Meaning flashed in his eyes.

Her cheerfulness sank. "Why the delay?"

"Well," he said, looking amused, "it seems Pan Lesław has taken a wife."

Oliwia had just downed a large gulp of wine, and she nearly choked. "Lesław? Who has he wed?" She struggled picturing the shy hussar wooing a wife.

Henryk shrugged. "I have little idea, but he is reluctant to leave her side just yet. He says 'tis the weather, but I suspect 'tis an altogether different reason. Hence the delay."

"Well, I am pleased for him." She took another sip and let her eyes drift to the fire.

"'Tis uplifting to hear of a wedding during our troubled times, yes?" Henryk said. She could feel his eyes on her, but she let silence hang like a velvet drape between them.

Chapter 27

Crossroads

Jacek sat at Rifat's desk—former desk—staring at a pristine piece of paper for long minutes. Unsure whether he wrote to his own betrothed or another man's wife, he faltered. Countless times during his ordeal, he'd relived how Oliwia had felt beneath his hands, under his body. How she'd given herself to him with unbridled passion. Picturing another man touching her sent white-hot bolts through him. Yet Jacek had been the one to insist she remarry. Had she heeded him? He sucked in a breath and took up his faith and the quill.

10 February on the Ionian Sea, in the Year of Our Lord 1615

Dearest Oliwia, thou most cherished angel of my heart,

I scant know where to begin, except to say I live. I was captured soon after I left your side and have been an Ottoman galley slave these past seasons. With God as commander, we took the ship and now sail for the Kingdom of Naples under escort of a man-of-war belonging to the Empire of Spain. Our new Spanish friends, good Catholics all, bring us to this port, where we will exchange our Ottoman galley lest we are mistaken for the enemy and destroyed as the Spanish nearly did.

At the earliest opportunity, I will secure passage home. Sailing the Baltic Sea in winter is nigh on impossible and would take far too long in the best of weather. Therefore, I will travel by land to Vienna and Biaska. Though mountain passes may prove difficult, snow and ice will not stop me getting to you. If all goes well, I expect to reach you before Easter, if not soon after this letter.

Dearest Liwi, but for thoughts of being with you again, I would not be alive now. The day I hold you in my arms will not come soon enough. I am keeping my promise to return for you and pray you will keep yours. Do not forsake me, my sweetest heart, for I have let no Tatar, Turk, or sea keep us apart. I love you beyond all measure, all time, and all reason. I long for the day when I see your sweet smile again.

Your ardent betrothed, most humble servant, and dearest friend,

Jacek

He dispatched the letter as soon as they could disencumber themselves from the priests and folk who swarmed them as they disembarked the *Cesaret*, lauding them as heroes. His next mission was to find a way home. Frustration simmered when he discovered his quickest path was aboard the ship carrying Gian to Genoa, for it meant his stay in Naples dragged for days.

Resigned, he joined his companions submerging and scrubbing in the baths. Next came a shave and proper trim—leaving moustache and goatee in the Spanish style—and he traded his Turkish clothing for a Spanish costume that included doublet, breeches, bucket-topped cuffed boots and a wide, feathered hat. He waved off a stiff ruff in favor of a collar with the least amount of lace he could find, feeling altogether foppish nonetheless.

He noticed little of the city for all the commotion. During their stay, they sold and divided the treasure between them and distributed Ottoman flags among churches, holding out the best for the Pope. The men were hosted, celebrated, and honored in a parade where maids tossed flowers—and themselves—at them. The beckoning looks he received from women, the sort of looks he'd been accustomed to most of his adult life, gratified him. It wasn't that he sought them, but they were a measure his horrific scar was not so off-putting; perhaps Oliwia would not recoil at the sight of him.

On the day they left for Genoa, Titas came, arms wide, and Jacek hugged him fiercely. "I cannot convince you to return with us to your own country?"

Titas flicked his new gold earring. It glinted garishly in the Naples sun, and he grinned broadly. "I far prefer Naples's fair seas, fair weather, and even fairer women. I will remain here, where folk are fascinated by Cossacks," he laughed. "After all, 'tis the Paris of the Mediterranean, and I will enjoy all it has to offer. Perhaps when I tire of it, I will travel to Paris and compare for myself. And if I've a desire to fight filthy infidels again, I will go to Venice."

Jacek clasped his shoulder. "If ever you pine for home, you will seek me out?"

With a nod, Titas said, "Never doubt it."

Then, with Gian, Dawid, Pawel, Janusz, and Hedwiga, Jacek set sail. At last.

I am coming, Liwi.

They had been sailing six days, and Jacek's impatience could barely be contained, so he was relieved to see Genoa's hills and the clustered red-roofed buildings climbing them. The sun shone bright, sparkling a path on the water's dark surface. As they closed in on the port city, he spotted a breakwater, soaring fortification walls, and towers guarding the harbor's narrow entry.

Passing what appeared to be the mouth of a river, Gian pointed excitedly. "There is my home!" Squinting, Jacek nodded, though he could not tell one from the next. The closer they got, the more Gian seemed to vibrate. His hands clenched and unclenched the rail, and a nervous smile repeatedly appeared and disappeared from his tanned face.

After the boat bumped softly against a mooring, a sodden gangplank thudded, and they disembarked. Around them, dockworkers shouted, ropes creaked with heavy cargo, gulls shrieked, dogs barked, bells clanged, and vendors sang out invitations to buy their wares. The stench of fish, mollusks, and rotting guts laced with stagnant seawater under a pulsing sun filled Jacek's nostrils. As they were swallowed by the busy burble on the docks, they passed a crowded market bursting with people, fruit, fish, leather, pots, and fabric in a riot of color. They climbed narrow, winding streets between crowded buildings. Wood smoke mixed with the pungent reek of tanneries, sewage, and humans living close together.

Despite his long strides, Jacek was challenged to keep up with Gian. They reached the end of a street that opened onto an emerald garden square, and Gian came to a stop and gazed at a creamy-yellow plastered edifice across the green. The flat-faced building stood three stories high, shoulder to shoulder with its neighbors, its dark rectangular shuttered windows in symmetrical rows. Gian began swiping at his cheeks.

He cleared his throat and rasped, "There it is."

The group followed in Gian's wake as he strode to the front door and let himself in. They stood in a cool, high-ceilinged foyer with whitewashed walls. Jacek removed his hat, and before he could take it all in, a woman appeared and squeaked. She stared at Gian but made no move to embrace him, seemingly rooted to the floor.

"Alina," he said softly.

Her mouth slack, she looked from him to the rest of their number, her eyes landing on Jacek, where they stayed.

"Alina, where is Rachele?" asked Gian.

Alina seemed to remember herself; she looked back at Gian, swallowing.

"Gian, you are back!"

"Yes. It has been quite a journey," he said with a wave toward the group. "I've brought new friends."

Her eyes immediately darted back to Jacek. They were light mossy green and set in a smooth, golden face with high cheekbones. Chestnut hair was pulled back in a net, and a bound braid draped over her shoulder. He gave her a curt nod, shifting his weight from one foot to the other, and resisted the urge to run his fingers over the pink weal on his face.

His attention, like everyone else's, was soon pulled to a doorway when something crashed to the marble-tiled floor, scattering shards in the shape of a fan. A woman dashed to Gian, crying out his name. As she threw herself into his arms, he caught her with a laugh. While the group looked on, the couple clung to one another, weeping, kissing, talking over one another as though no other existed. Jacek stole a sidelong glance at Alina. She was looking back at him.

In a guest chamber, Jacek tossed his hat on the bed and was surveying the room when a knock sounded.

"Come," he called, and a young servant entered carrying a tray heaped with bread, smoked fish, cheeses, grapes, oranges, and wine. Jacek's mouth watered. Behind the servant swept Alina—whom he'd learned was Rachele's widowed sister—seemingly inspecting the room.

She fixed her eyes on Jacek and waved gracefully at the servant. "This is Flavio." Flavio tucked his arms to his sides and bowed from the waist. Alina went on, "He will serve you during your stay, my lord. Have you need of anything?"

"No."

She whispered to Flavio, and he scampered away. Alina glided toward the table that held the tray, swaying as she went, and poured out a goblet of wine, which she brought to Jacek.

"You must be thirsty after your travels."

He accepted the goblet and moved away from her. "Thank you."

"Your comfort is of utmost importance. You will let me know if you need anything?"

He nodded. When she let herself out, he blew out a breath and guzzled the wine.

Jacek dashed off a letter to his family and Klemens; penning these had been easy. He also sent a letter to Lady Eugenia, a far more challenging undertaking, but he reckoned she should hear from him that he'd survived. He promised to come to Matejko Manor but said nothing of the oath he planned to break. Once he'd finished, thoughts of her fled, and he turned back to his mission, passing the first two days acquiring maps and supplies for the journey home.

"Have you completely lost your mind?" laughed Gian. "If you try to cross the mountains now, you will surely freeze to death. If you do survive, it will take you months. Best wait and be comfortable here, my determined friend, until the passes have thawed."

Jacek's exasperation was assuaged, barely, by swordplay practiced in a sun-splashed courtyard with his fellows. Alina seemed to appear whenever his turn came to spar. Her presence among the spectators nudged his brothers to fiercer competition, and he rose to meet that challenge. They were showing off; he was sharpening his skills.

The third day, Janusz found him as he prepared to search out horses.

"Eager for Poland, Jacek?"

"Yes. You?"

A peculiar look overtook Janusz's features, and he shrugged. "Not especially."

Jacek eyed him curiously. Janusz must have recognized his bemusement, for he continued. "I left behind some … unpleasantness in Poland and am not inclined to return. Especially now." He gave Jacek a small smile. "Hedwiga has agreed to marry me."

Jacek clapped him on the shoulder. "Blessings to you both!"

Janusz shuffled his feet. "She's … I've never met anyone like her. She's kind, she's brave, she's … God, she's beautiful!" His face lit. "Why she wants a wretch like me is beyond comprehension, but I am glad of it."

"I'm that pleased for you, Janusz."

Janusz cleared his throat. "We are anxious to wed, and Gian has offered to secure a priest and hold a wedding feast here. I beg a favor of you too."

"Of course. What can I do?"

"I know you're keen for home, but I, ah, wonder if you would honor me and serve as my best man? After all we've been through together, I want you there to celebrate with Hedwiga and I. Would you consider delaying your journey?"

Jacek's heart dropped. Of all the things Janusz could have asked of him, postponing his departure ranked amid the hardest. Janusz was a man of few words and fewer emotions, but right now the plea was written on his face. Jacek swallowed hard. "How long?"

Janusz's features eased. "Two days, no more. It would mean so much to us both."

Jacek resisted the urge to huff. "I would be honored."

Five days later, Jacek stormed into town accompanied by Dawid who, along with Pawel, would return to Poland with Jacek. *If they ever hold the damned wedding!* One thing and another had postponed the nuptials—such as accommodating Genoa's Cardinal Orazio Spínola's wish to preside—and Jacek's patience was in shreds. *Jesus, another day.*

They passed several wenches idling by the entrance of a tavern; Dawid's eyes were trained on them the entire way. One sashayed into their path and looked Jacek over.

"Aren't you a big one! Buy a thirsty maid a drink?" she said in Italian. Jacek ignored her, but Dawid flashed her a smile. Jacek left her and her companions in his wake to cluck after him.

She called out, "I don't bite, handsome—unless you want me to."

He snorted. A whore's idea of handsome had more to do with the coins in a man's pouch than his look. Once more, Jacek dismissed the troubling question of how Oliwia would react to his disfigurement.

"Not interested in company, Captain?" asked a grinning Dawid, who glanced backward, twisted his feet, and stumbled on cobblestones.

"Not today," Jacek replied as he strode past a leather shop, its tang filling his nose.

Dawid recovered himself. "Can't blame you with that beauty of a sister about."

Dodging a cart, Jacek snapped his head to him. "What do you mean?"

"The way Lady Alina looks at you—"

"As if she's sickened by the sight of my face?" Jacek nodded at a passing priest.

Dawid shook his head and laughed. "No, no. As if she might devour you. Doubtless she'd welcome you plowing her field. You hadn't noticed? I've even heard her sister remark on it."

Jacek said nothing.

"She's an exotic beauty, that one," David persisted. "And *mio Dio*, that body! It haunts my dreams!" With his hands, Dawid sketched an hourglass, then held his cupped hands in front of his chest. "I wager she could make you smile."

"I'll smile when I'm back on Polish soil," Jacek grumbled.

They came to a stop at a merchant's door, and Jacek peered in. He stepped into the cool, musty shadows of the shop, Dawid following, and acknowledged the shopkeeper. Dawid pivoted his head round. "On the hunt for a trinket for yourself, Captain? Or your mother?"

When they left the store a long while later, Jacek patted a soft pouch stowed in his doublet, sidestepping a scrawny black dog who watched him sullenly. He smelled garlic cooking somewhere, quashing the foul city smells, and his stomach began to rumble.

"I will miss Janusz when we leave," Dawid remarked.

Jacek rounded the corner of a building. "Do you wish you accompanied them to Rome?

"No, though it would be quite something to present banners to Pope Paul. But I am eager for Poland. Who knows? When I return, perhaps I will find myself a congenial girl and sire a horde of children."

Jacek smirked. "And give up the wenches?"

"I would, yes. I envy Janusz, you know. I do not covet Hedwiga, but I covet the happiness he's found with her."

"I think we all do."

Jacek's prayers were answered when at last Janusz and Hedwiga's wedding day arrived. The cardinal's presence marked Gian's celebrity. That celebrity spilled over to Jacek and his companions in the form of added prayers, blessings, and a lengthy Mass. The service gave way to a jubilant feast made more festive for the miracle of the *Cesare*'s survivors.

In an unguarded moment, Jacek marveled he lived. What a glorious thing it was, a divine miracle that he was here, his feet upon the earth as he rejoiced with his brothers. With a stab of guilt, he locked out haunting, sobering thoughts of the fates suffered by so many others: Wiesław, Marcin, Stefan, the farmer and his family, the Frenchman. Consequently, he indulged as though the chance might never come again, consuming copious amounts of wine to quench the thirst brought on by dancing. And dance he did—with abandon! He danced with Hedwiga; he danced with his fellows; he danced with Rachele and Gian; he danced with Alina and every other willing female, of which there was a seemingly neverending supply.

It felt wonderful to hold a woman in his arms again, to smile down at a pretty face smiling back at him, to unexpectedly brush a supple wrist, to place his hand on the small of a waist, on something soft, even for the brevity of the dance.

Though his lean body was regaining its muscular form, he'd discounted his capacity for drink. Before long, he was in the grip of an alcohol-fueled overabundance of cheerfulness; but his exhilaration was merely one of two powerful emotions seizing him this day. He reveled in gaiety, yes, but he also struggled to batten a tarp over the abyss deep down inside where an ever-present, unfillable pit of remorse dwelled in him, threatening to swallow him whole. Self-control usually kept it tightly covered, but today the wine let the lid slip, let it expose the hollow within, and after much laughter, he despaired.

He stumbled to a quiet garden under the black-velvet canopy of night. Several scant torches cast flickering pools of light, and these he shrank away from, seeking instead the obscurity of the dark. Air, moist and warm, caressed his skin, and a light breeze ruffled leaves, carrying with it mingled fragrances of citrus and honey.

Oliwia.

The only sounds were the shuddering foliage, the crackle of the torches, and the jaunty splash of a stone fountain. Looking up, he took in the moon's nearly full face and the shimmering stars suspended in their constellations like dainty diamond necklaces. *Does she look at the same sky at this moment?* Plopping onto a stone bench under an arched trellis, he dropped his head into his hands.

When he heard a rustle, he realized he was not alone. He glanced over his shoulder to see Alina standing behind him, straight and still as a marble statue, her eyes glittering in the moonlight. Her loose hair, glossy and dark, fell over her shoulders to her waist. It reminded him of Oliwia's, and he nearly reached out to touch it before a sliver of sobriety checked him.

"Why are you here and not enjoying the merriment?" he asked.

Serene and sleek, she shrugged and looked around the garden. "It was a bit too gay."

"How can it be too gay?"

"It reminds me of my own wedding four years ago. I might ask you the same, for here I find you, all alone." Her voice was soft and sad, and his heart tugged.

He mustered kindness. "How long were you wed?"

"One year." With a sigh, she added, "Hardly enough."

"Why have you not remarried?"

One corner of her mouth quirked. "He was a special man."

"Would you care to tell me about him?" he offered, though he had little idea why. His mouth seemed to operate of its own accord.

She shook her head and quickly asked if he would like a cup of wine.

"No, I have already had far too much wine, but I thank you." He scooted over, and she slid beside him. She reminded him of a padding cat—all jewel eyes, long limbs, and liquid movements—and now that she was within scant inches, his mouth stopped working. A charged silence hung between them. The sweet fragrance of star jasmine curled up his nose. Though his mind fogged, he picked out strains of mandolins and pipes drifting from another part of the manor amid muted laughter.

Alina slid her hand into his where it rested on his thigh. "You remind me of him," she said, a hint of a smile in her voice.

He blinked, then stared at where her hand disappeared into his as though he didn't recognize it.

"You are a strange man. Different. In the past, I've had to push Gian's friends away." Her words sank into the murk of his mind, illuminating a corner.

"My heart abides elsewhere," he said at last.

With those words, desolation flooded him, nearly suffocating him as a lump rose in his throat and wedged there. He craved Oliwia so. It had been far too long. The gulf dividing them spanned wider than the mountains and forests between Genoa and Biaska. Rather, the distance was as that between the earth and the moon and, in that moment, felt just as impossible to conquer.

They sat quietly for long moments. Despite a voice niggling at him, Jacek relished Alina's thigh resting against his, her heat reminding him he was not alone. He brushed his thumb over the back of her hand. Her skin was so warm, so silky.

She leaned against his shoulder. "Your devotion need not stop you doing what is natural."

The fountain spluttered and splashed. Fierce yearning spilled over, rushing into every fissure within him. Alina began nuzzling his neck. He closed his eyes and let himself drift.

"Your woman will never know." Her voice was tantalizing, intoxicating.

She lifted his palm to her breast. The fountain's soft patter was suddenly raucous, harsh. He jerked his hand back, his languor dissolving, and he lurched upright. A confused look crept over Alina's face. Cursing himself inwardly, he raked a hand through his hair.

291

"I, ah, I have stayed too long." He gave her a small bow, and she reached for his hand again, pulling herself up, mere inches separating them.

"Let me love you tonight." A plea played in her eyes.

He stared back for a beat, two beats, his mind spinning wildly.

"I am sorry," he muttered. "Good night."

He turned away, locking out her wounded expression. As he headed across the courtyard, he thought he heard a soft sob.

Once behind his door, he secured it, then paced to and fro. He dropped into a chair before the writing table and stared blankly at its polished surface. Oliwia's eyes, like faceted crystals, floated before him. She smiled, and he felt as though the sun came out from behind a steely cloud. Her spirit seemed to enfold him then, as if she reached across the stars to him. The thought she might not still be his lanced him.

I must get home.

He disrobed and slid between the cool sheets, savoring the feel against his bare skin. Would he feel that way the rest of his life, every time he climbed into a clean, soft bed? Folding one arm under his head, he stared at the canopy. His hand idly swept across the mattress, back and forth, as he pictured Oliwia beside him, her exquisite bare skin glowing in moonlight, her dark hair fanned across the white-sheeted expanse. Closing his eyes, he imagined far more, like trailing kisses from her delicate ankles to her perfect, rounded breasts; desire shimmering in her lidded eyes; her dulcet moans; her arching, ivory throat; her rising hips. Rolling to his side, he punched his pillow again and again.

Come to me tonight, Oliwia. Bring me home.

Jacek spotted Alina only once the next day. When she looked up and saw him, she turned abruptly and left. He couldn't fault her, but he had little time to ponder his actions the night before, for he was charged with purpose. Departure for Poland would come tomorrow, on the eve of the vernal equinox.

When morning at last arrived, Gian openly wept as he clasped Jacek to his broad chest. Jacek fought tears of his own. They pulled apart from a fierce embrace and looked each other over.

Gian cuffed his wet nose. "You are welcome to fight by my side anytime."

"As you are always welcome by mine," Jacek said with a bittersweet smile. "And next time we meet, we will be rejoicing at a feasting table with our families."

Gian nodded, then handed Jacek a brown leather bag. It was heavy, and Jacek shot him a quizzical look.

"To remember me by," the dark-haired warrior said.

Jacek loosened the pouch's drawstring and slid out the tubular looker. His eyebrows shot to his hairline, and he grinned as he turned it over in his hand. He slipped it back in its sleeve. "Thank you. I shall make good use of it, and each time I do, I shall think of you."

Then Jacek turned to the women. Rachele hugged him. Alina seemed to have forgiven him, for she gave him a warm embrace. "I wish you much happiness."

"As I do you," he replied and kissed her hand.

Hedwiga kissed him on both cheeks and blushed before Janusz gripped him and pounded his back.

"Thank you. For everything." He surprised Jacek by embracing him ferociously, tears brimming in his eyes. Heat spread to Jacek's cheeks; he was grateful for the whiskers obscuring what surely must have been his red face.

"I wish you a long, blessed life." Jacek cleared his sticky throat. "It has been my honor to call you brother and friend. Stay well."

Jacek's heart was at once heavy and buoyant; they were going home. He mounted his new chestnut and, with Dawid and Pawel, headed out of the courtyard under a cloud-streaked sky. The air was crisp, and the chill frosted their breaths. As they trod Genoa's streets to the countryside beyond, roosters crowed, sheep and goats bleated, and women called to children. The sounds soon faded until naught but the horses' clops and chuffs could be heard. Jacek looked over their gear, gratified, for they traveled light: one gelding apiece, plus a fourth carrying a pack and capacious saddlebags. Though he'd coveted the handsome, strong-bodied

Neopolitans bred by the noble families, he'd settled for unremarkable—and inexpensive—stock.

Jacek felt once more the complete warrior. They were equipped with scimitars claimed from the *Cesaret*, along with daggers, axes, bows, and full quivers. Each man also carried a pair of ornate wheel-lock pistols bestowed upon him as gifts from Genoa's churchmen. Jacek's were inlaid in gold, silver, and ivory. Though he carried powder and shot, Jacek hoped they would have no need to fire the weapons, as much to keep his prized pistols pristine as to avoid conflict.

They crossed the Ligurian Apennines over the La Cisa Pass, into the Po Valley, and followed trade routes and river valleys to Milan, Verona, and Venice, joining clatters of carts and folk moving goods and animals along as they wended their way eastward. They reached the lagoon city in less than a fortnight and lodged in a modest tavern, where they would remain a day to reprovision for their trek through the Eastern Alps to Vienna. The peaks and passes here were lower and broader than their western counterparts, and Jacek reckoned that with a bit of fortune, they could keep the pace they'd maintained thus far. He had always prided himself on his patience, but he was unsure how well he could contain it as the call of home grew louder. He dared not think Oliwia would be aught but unwed and overjoyed to see him.

That evening, as they finished their meal of hemp seed soup, creamed cod, rice and peas, bread, and wine amid the burble of diners and servers, they talked of setting off at dawn.

Pawel was munching a hunk of bread he'd just used to sop up the rest of his meal. "How long do you reckon it will be before we lay eyes on Poland?"

"Barring bandits or blizzards, I expect to arrive in less than three Sundays." *Perhaps before I turn twenty-seven.*

Dawid took a gulp of wine. "And what will you do when we get there, Captain?"

Jacek shrugged, feigning a casualness he did not feel. "Clean up whatever messes have been made during our absence." He drank deeply of his wine and, in an unguarded moment, recklessly added, "Maybe I too will settle down and marry."

Dawid's lips curved up on one side. "The trinket! Have you had a sweetheart all this time, Captain? In Podolia, perhaps?"

Jacek twirled his cup, its uneven metal bottom rocking on the planked table. "Not in Podolia, no. In Biaska."

"Biaska?" exclaimed Dawid, his eyes bright. "Who is she?"

Jacek's eyes narrowed. "I cannot say. Truth is I know not if she is still free."

Dawid laughed. "Now I better understand why you resisted Lady Alina's ample charms."

Jacek snorted and clinked cups with Dawid and Pawel. "To women, God bless them! *Na zdrowie!*"

Chapter 28

Reckoning

olding Adam, Oliwia bounced her way to a tall window. He let out a belly laugh. How she loved those! She swung him in her arms while Anka giggled softly behind them. Peering into his eyes, Oliwia trilled, "What has become of your blue eyes?"

"They are turning, m'lady," Anka said. "I am sure of it."

"Are you going to have your papa's beautiful brown eyes, after all?" Oliwia continued.

A throat cleared, and she whirled to see Henryk behind her, hands extended. "May I?"

She handed Adam to him, laughing inwardly at the sight of him holding a babe. His hands were less sure than Jacek's had been, and his face barely hid his discomfort. Adam yanked his moustache, and Henryk made a fish face at him, causing the boy to squeal. Henryk's eyes met hers, as if to say, "See there? I can be a father to him."

"I owe you a reply." She spoke so softly, only Henryk heard. He inclined his head.

Anka whisked Adam away, leaving Oliwia facing Henryk alone. She gathered her skirts in tight fists. It had been weeks since his proposal, and the Sundays until Easter were disappearing—as were her choices. Antonin had sent two more offers of marriage, each more insistent. The last was accompanied by a threat to dispatch his army to Biaska—with the king's blessing.

Henryk watched her in silence, one hand resting on his hilt.

She drew in a breath. "I am accepting your proposal."

He appeared astonished. "You will marry me?" Or was that terror she saw on his face?

"Yes, Henryk." Bands of guilt and dread constricted about her chest. She squelched the urge to pull in another large breath.

"But this is wonderful news, Oliwia!"

She gave him a mild smirk. "I pray you know what you bargain for in this union. I have grown accustomed to speaking my mind, and I do not plan on changing. If at any time you wish to retract your offer, I will understand and find no fault with you. But if you still wish it, then we'd best make the announcement."

Henryk closed the distance between them. "I will not change my mind." He picked up her hand and held it between both of his. "I know this is not—I am not—your first choice, but together we will make this a happy union."

He drew her to him and laid a full, soft kiss on her mouth, taking her by surprise. She fought the urge to pull away—this man would soon be her husband, after all. As he encircled her in his arms, his scent filled her senses. Masculine, musky. He pressed his body against hers without urgency or insistence; her hands rested lightly on his chest. Deepening the kiss, he lifted her hands to his neck. His breathing accelerated, and his muscled arms tightened, surrounding her in warm male strength. Her body eased, pressing into his. Oh, but it felt good to be held in a powerful, safe embrace again.

What in blazes am I doing?

She broke the kiss and pulled away. Henryk's hazel eyes fixed on her, and for the second time that day, he looked astonished. One side of his mouth hitched up in a smile. Even as delight bloomed on Henryk's face, Oliwia's anguish surged, for soon she would forfeit another piece of herself.

Antonin dripped red sealing wax on a folded sheet of ivory paper, then rocked his ring over the puddled circle. He briskly flapped the letter by one corner while Romek watched him. Two amber pools of light overlapped on the battered desktop, the only points of light in the chamber submerged in night.

"That little bitch just outsmarted herself. The man's nothing but a pretty face and a set of muscles," Antonin sneered.

"Kalinowski's not a bad choice to fortify Biaska's defenses," Romek goaded. "What if you cannot convince the king to override her decision?" Though the turn of fortune could only thwart Romek's plan to regain his family holdings, he was deriving perverse pleasure in Antonin's failure to secure the widow's hand. And he had another surprise coming.

"The king will know what a worthless turd she's picked for a husband." Antonin smirked. "Which plays right into my plan, for I'll have even greater latitude taking the estate for myself—in the interest of protecting the Crown, of course. Whether I take her along with it depends on her."

Antonin's eyes had been darting about the chamber and finally came to rest on Romek, whose arms were now cinched across his chest. Antonin narrowed his eyes.

"What is it, Romek? You look as though you're the cat who's just pilfered the cream."

"Our friend intercepted a very interesting message headed for Biaska." Romek tossed a letter under Antonin's nose and watched his expression as he unfolded the missive and scanned it. The more Antonin read, the wider his eyes grew.

He looked up at Romek. "Do you believe this?"

Romek nodded. "I do. We should prepare for his return in any event."

"I can't believe that bastard is alive! And he sounds positively love-struck. How long do you suppose *that's* been going on?" Antonin's eyes gleamed, and a mad grin split his face. He looked unhinged. Romek wondered for an instant if he was.

Romek shrugged.

"Well, I'll be damned," Antonin continued, as if to himself. "The little vixen's positively a siren. That seals it. Willing or not, I *will* have her—and her late husband's estate."

"What of my lands?" Romek asked.

Antonin began rummaging around his desk. "I've already told you, you'll get your estate, Romek. Now where is my blasted quill?"

"And what of the boy? He still dies?"

Antonin looked up at him and frowned. "What a poor jest, Romek. Of course he dies! I want no living heirs to challenge me for what is rightfully mine. Eliminate her brother while you're about it."

"I will see to it. Do you care how the babe is disposed of?"

Antonin threw out a careless hand. "Slit his gullet, toss him in the river, or feed him to the dogs for all I care. But not a minute before she weds me," he warned.

Romek felt a tingle move up and down his spine, feeding the spark that threatened to explode in a conflagration again. It had been growing, overtaking him, compelling him to hunt prey nearly once a sennight. But as he thought of killing Krezowski's heir, the spark calmed. After all, he was a patient man, wasn't he?

I'll hide the brat in the woods. I'll tell her if she finds him, I'll spare them both. Then I'll make the bitch watch while I carve her little bastard to pieces. Then I'll kill her … slowly.

He could almost hear her shrieks, her tearful pleas. Romek's excitement rose, his breaths shallowing out. He shook himself mentally, realizing Antonin was talking.

"You need to clear out before you are seen. Make sure any other letters from Dąbrowski are intercepted. Lady Oliwia cannot learn he lives. When the time comes, you will stop the man himself."

As you wish, my lord." Romek lifted up his cowl. He bounced on the balls of his feet as he exited the chamber.

"When do you wed Pan Henryk?" Filip perched on a chair in Oliwia's sitting chamber, inspecting the edge of his dagger. The blade had been a gift from Eryk, and she was pleased to see the pride Filip took in keeping it razor-sharp and gleaming.

"Saturday after May Day." Her brother had been elated when she'd married Eryk. Though she had never told him, he would have been even more ecstatic over her union with Jacek. She wasn't sure just what he thought of this new prospect; she was still adjusting to the notion herself. "What do you think of Henryk becoming your brother-in-law?"

Filip shrugged, his eyes still fixed on the blade. "Next to Jacek, he's Biaska's best warrior, but …"

"But?" She looked at him expectantly.

"I, uh, have heard kitchenmaids call him a name," Filip blurted.

"What name?"

Filip darted his eyes everywhere but her face. She grabbed his chin and forced him to look at her. "What name?"

His lips were squished into the shape of a fish's; she relinquished her hold so he could talk. *"Utalentowany uwodziciel."* He looked utterly abashed.

God in Heaven! Oliwia crossed her arms, hiding her alarm. *The gifted seducer.* "Do you know what that means?" she asked evenly.

Filip stammered. "Pan Stefan says … it means … Pan Henryk … Ladies like him. And he likes them. Many ladies. As though they were wives."

"And Stefan spoke to you of such things?" she yelped.

"Liwi! I am a soldier now," Filip squawked indignantly. "I hear *all* the talk in the garrison."

"Not all of it is true," she said feebly. For at least the hundredth time, Oliwia questioned what the devil she'd gotten herself into. *Henryk is the best choice of the lot.*

"But why would Pan Henryk want *you* when he has all of *them*? And where will he sleep? Will *you* become one of his wives, like the others?" Filip's face contorted in a sour look, as though he could not fathom why Henryk would want *any* woman.

She rolled her eyes and threw up her hands in exasperation. "I will be the *only* wife. He will make an oath to … Fidelity is a sacred vow between a man and woman when they wed." *Which Henryk likely will not honor.*

"So does that mean—" Filip continued, but she stopped him.

"Enough, Filip. Time to take your leave," she heaved. When he was gone, she dropped her head in her hands. *I wish to marry no one.* She ticked off the choices in her head—again—and returned to the same dilemma. The king would choose a husband for her, and Adam would lose Biaska. Henryk had promised to keep the estate for Adam; no other suitor had. She knew none of them half so well as she knew Henryk. *He is a scoundrel, but he will keep his word where Adam is concerned.* She would have to adjust. *Jacek, why did you leave?*

Dejected, Oliwia descended the stairs to the great hall, where she spotted Henryk. The space was empty save a few maids, who looked up from their sweeping and smiled at the dashing warrior. He seemed unaware, but perhaps he was showing her a courtesy. He strode to her as though she held his devoted attention.

"Henryk, I must speak with you," she said.

"Of course." He grabbed her elbow and spun her toward the solar. When they were inside, he latched the door and faced her, frowning. "What is it?"

"I know you're a man used to … used to charming many women, and I do not expect it will be a habit easily broken." He arched an eyebrow at her, but she ignored the look and plowed on. "I do, however, expect propriety when it comes to your dalliances and how they relate to me. I prefer you choose your partners with care and discretion. The farther from Biaska, the better. I do not wish to be ridiculed in my own castle or anywhere on my estate. Am I clear?"

With deliberate movements, he took a step back and leaned against the corner of the desk, folding his arms across his chest. "You are abundantly clear."

She suddenly realized she was breathing hard, and she slowed her inhales.

"May I speak?" His voice was calm, his demeanor unruffled.

"Of course." She straightened her shoulders.

"We have been friends far too long, so I will not insult you by saying you are mistaken about my past actions. But you have not yet seen me as a husband who swears fidelity before God and witnesses. No one has. Would you agree I am not an imbecile?"

Puzzled, she agreed.

"I am about to marry the fairest woman in the county. Why would I roam about in pursuit of that which is inferior to what I will have in my own soft bed every night?" If it were possible, his scrutiny was as intense as Jacek's had been. A shiver chattered up Oliwia's spine. She decided against asking him about his intentions when he was away.

Outside, dogs yapped and a child squealed. Horses' hooves clip-clopped over cobbles. Against the clatter, songbirds chirped carefree melodies.

Henryk stood and took one of her hands, leveling his hazel eyes at her. "I will work hard to win your affection, Oliwia. Know that I am earnest in my desire to please you."

301

Though Henryk's measured words were soothing, on close inspection they held no true promise. He brought her hand to his lips and kissed it, then leaned down and kissed her mouth.

He quirked an eyebrow at her. "We'll work on that."

Oliwia sat on Henryk's right, staring at an untouched platter upon impeccable white linen. It was their engagement feast, and the tabletop glittered with brass, pewter, and copper plates, bowls, goblets, and jugs of all shapes and sizes. The contents of those vessels were swiftly disappearing into soldiers' bellies as they laughed and toasted all around. It was an extravagance she could scarcely afford, for Biaska's larders were depleted, yet she could scarcely afford not to hold the small feast, for it would alarm the remaining garrison stalwarts. Dimly aware soldiers raised yet another toast to their captain, she slowly swiveled her head about the glowing hall and was relieved to set eyes on Stefan laughing with Kasimir and Marcin beside Filip. That these loyal men still remained, guarding the estate and her family, was a blessing. Lesław would soon arrive with his Scots to shore up their ragged defenses, although how much that would stave off an attack from Antonin, she knew not. She put the troubling thought away.

Henryk startled her when he leaned into her and whispered, his warm breath falling on her ear. "Are you well?"

Giving herself an inner shake, she turned to him. "Yes, of course. Merely distracted."

Under the table, he took her hand and squeezed it. "I daresay the folk seem to be enjoying the prospect of a wedding." His eyes darted about the space.

Just then, a swirl of green skirts caught Oliwia's eye, and she glimpsed Wanda twirling about the table, waiting on the revelers.

"Wanda!" she called. The girl looked at her, wide-eyed, and hurried over.

"Yes, mistress?" She gave a little dip.

"Why are you acting as a serving maid? You are a chambermaid. *My* chambermaid." Oliwia couldn't keep from frowning.

Wanda dropped her head and her gaze. "With Beata shorthanded, I thought to make myself useful as you're here and not in your chamber needing help in this moment."

Oliwia let out a frustrated sigh. The girl seemed forever in all the wrong places. Yet Oliwia could think of no reason to argue Wanda's logic. Beata *was* shorthanded.

"All right, but see you're in my quarters once the meal is over."

Wanda gave another little curtsy. "Of course, m'lady. Thank you, m'lady."

Oliwia waved her away as she would a buzzing fly and turned in time to catch Henryk's eyes flick away from the maid.

He looked at Oliwia with a guileless smile. "Busy thing, isn't she?"

Oliwia humphed. "Do you think it strange Antonin has said nothing? After Father Augustyn read the first banns, I expected at minimum a scathing letter. The silence is deafening."

"Antonin is a hot gust of wind. Besides, what can he say? You've done what King Zygmunt asked. And now our wedding day is nearly here." Henryk's smile resembled a wan grimace.

Oliwia's stomach gave a little lurch, and she returned her gaze to her platter. She could not force a morsel tonight. In fact, she could barely swallow. *Wedding jitters? Or something altogether different ...*

"Henryk, has there been any more word of the Swedish army?"

Henryk shrugged. "I heard from a merchant the king was misinformed by his spies. Perhaps the army turned elsewhere, divided, or never existed. In any case, the king remains cautious."

"But his caution is forcing me *into marriage,"* she wanted to rail. Two words popped into her head and collided, prickling her neck hairs and interrupting her inner protest. Antonin. Army.

"Henryk, what if there is an army, one led by Antonin, and *he's* been the source of the king's information? Or misinformation?"

A flicker in Henryk's eyes was followed by a nearly imperceptible headshake. He patted her arm. "You give Antonin far too much credit. Do not worry yourself." He might as well have scratched behind her ear and called her a good dog.

Chapter 29

Worlds Collide

A storm raged, mocking Jacek's bullheaded resolve, and as a dark shroud dropped over the afternoon, his frustrations rose. *How much farther to the damned town?* They had passed the night in Langenwang and left at first light for Gloggnitz. When they'd started out, he'd thought surely they would reach Semmering Pass before midday and Gloggnitz before supper—thoughts of eating hot stew before a fire taunted him—but they hadn't even reached the summit yet. They were interminably stuck in Austria, their pace like honey over ice, and they were behind schedule. Spending his birthday slogging through the Eastern Alps had not been Jacek's plan. At times, Gian's laugh had rung out in his head, reminding him he was daft for attempting the journey at the leading edge of spring. Spurred by his eagerness to reach home, Jacek had been lured by the morning's tranquil skies into believing today's destination was easily attainable. But those blue skies had been crowded out by clouds burdened with snow.

He buried his face ever deeper into his fur collar and glimpsed his companions doing the same. Snowflakes caught and covered their horses' rumps and the men's hats, dusting everything white. The wind piled drifts as they continued climbing. He imagined his brothers sullen, grumbling at him for his dogged drive, but so far they had kept their thoughts trapped on their tongues, and he was thankful for it. He was berating himself enough as it was.

A boom rent the air, and Dawid's horse skittered. Jacek tensed and looked up at the sky, then at Pawel and Dawid.

Pawel gentled his horse. "That sounded like thunder."

Jacek swiveled his head and caught a flash in the glaring white veil of snow. Another roar from the heavens, and the veil exploded in bright light, blinding him. A horse screamed, and he felt a tug on his own beast where the pack horse was tied off. Thuds, thrashing, and panicky snorts sounded, dulled by the storm. When Jacek's eyes adjusted, the pack horse was on its side, its hooves flailing.

"What the hell happened?" Dawid yelled, trying to keep his own horse under rein.

Jacek jumped from his saddle and ran to the stricken animal. It reeked of singed hair. He thought steam rose from its hide in places, but before he could reconcile it, another clap rumbled, and he ducked. Dawid's horse jerked, reeled, and pitched Dawid from his saddle.

Muttering a series of blasphemies, Jacek dashed to Dawid's side. "Are you hurt?"

Dawid was reaching for his leg, his face twisted in pain. "Foolish damned beast!"

Jacek helped Dawid sit up, then crouched while Dawid prodded his way down his knee, over his boot, to his ankle. Meanwhile, Pawel grabbed the jumpy animal's reins and hauled it and Jacek's horse in. Jacek gave him a quick nod of thanks.

"That flea-infested, worthless excuse for a horse broke my damned ankle!" Dawid spat.

"Let me take a look." Jacek gritted his teeth, trying to keep annoyance from his voice. "It may hurt like hell," he said when Dawid cursed at his ministrations, "but it's not broken. Nevertheless, you're hobbled."

As night closed in, they limped into Gloggnitz wet, cold, and laden with the supplies the packhorse had been carrying. After securing lodgings, Jacek sat before a smoky fire with Pawel and Dawid and gobbled stew. Though the dish tasted better than he had imagined, it couldn't offset his bitterness over their latest delay.

In fair weather, with all of them fit for travel, Biaska was ten days away. But it might as well have been on the other side of the world for the relentless snow and Dawid's injury. Down one horse, Jacek brooded over how much longer they would be stuck in these infernal mountains, how much longer he had before Oliwia was once again lost to him—if she wasn't already.

Jacek!

Oliwia awoke with a start, breathing heavily as she wrestled with her bedcoverings. She grabbed at shreds of a dream, but they fled her mind's grasp like smoke, and she could only recall one image: Jacek slashing at an enormous white dragon with his sabre while that dragon readied to swallow him whole.

Her nerves bristled, and she pulled herself upright, ransacking her brain for calming thoughts. Unfortunately, her mind turned to her upcoming wedding a fortnight hence. *Soon I will be Henryk's wife.* Dismay waved through her, fresh and cold, as though ice crystallized in her veins. In the early morning light, she threw on her wrap and stepped to the window, where she held back the drape. Trying to cast off the disturbing dream, she stared with unseeing eyes at the fields and the ridge beyond. Movement grabbed her attention. Fixing her eyes, she made out a group of riders cresting the ridge with a familiar banner: a red-crowned eagle holding a serpent in its claws.

"Nadia!" she yelped. "Help me get dressed."

Freshly appareled, Oliwia dashed to the ramparts, scattering panicked pigeons into the pale blue sky, but after the rush of their flapping wings, she was alone in unnatural quiet. *Where are the heralds?* She cast her eyes eastward and gasped. Ropes of smoke, thick and black, rose into the sky.

Merciful God, the village! Why has no one sounded the alarm?

A distant thunder drew her attention, and, peering through an embrasure, she watched in horror as riders—scores upon scores—undulated over the landscape toward the fortress like great armored beetles, spear tips catching the sun, horse hooves churning the moist spring earth and destroying every growing thing upon it.

She streaked from the battlements to the hall, pausing at narrow slits to catch her breath. Horsemen came up fast, unfurling enormous banners as they drew closer. Her heart, already hammering, raced faster still—with fear, with anger. Behind the standard bearers, still more horsemen came. And now men on foot. In the distance, rolling guns, wagons, and contraptions on wheeled platforms lumbered over the ridge.

"Filip!" she shrieked when she caught sight of her brother traipsing through the hall. Three greyhounds who had been snoozing before the hearth snapped their heads up while two maids stopped their sweeping and gawped at her.

"Find Pan Henryk, Stefan, anyone!" she implored, and Filip dashed to the solar. She spied Wanda scurrying toward the kitchens and shouted at her to fetch Anka and Adam. The girl jolted and turned in a frenzied circle before running for the stairs leading to the nursery.

Oliwia ran through the keep's giant oaken doors and paused at the top of the forestairs. A familiar soldier strode the yard with a handful of men-at-arms. They were headed to the guard tower, moving slowly, almost casually, even though the pounding of the army roared beyond the walls.

"Kasimir!" Oliwia hollered. He looked up, surprised. "Thank God you are here! The village is ablaze! Where is everyone?"

He offered an incongruous smile. "Do not be alarmed, my lady. Everyone is safe. I have it well in hand."

"We need to get the villagers inside the walls! We need bowmen on the battlements! What of the men in the garrison?" Her eyes darted to the men surrounding Kasimir. They all seemed to be looking everywhere but at her. She recognized none of them.

"They are arming themselves, my lady." His relaxed manner seemed out of place.

Shouldn't they be armed already? Shouldn't they be running somewhere? Where the devil is Henryk?

She tried to quell her panic. "Have you seen Pan Henryk?"

"Not since he left for Łac last evening. He sought ... He went with the soldiers to the tavern there, and I believe he stayed the night. I have not seen him this morning." He gave her a sheepish look and shrugged, then pivoted away, leaving Oliwia to frown at his back.

"Kasimir!" she yelled once more. He stopped and took his time looking back at her. "Find men to secure the keep." His brows furrowed for a beat, then he nodded and strode away.

Oliwia's eye caught on the bouncing form of Father Augustyn, huffing and puffing across the yard as he hurled himself toward her, a squad of servants in tow. "My lady!" he wheezed. From the other direction ran Feliks, the stable hands behind him. Dimly, Oliwia thought it odd that Henryk had left Biaska; odder still that he'd not returned.

She ordered Feliks, the grooms, and the servants to arm themselves, then she bid the priest follow her. Together, they climbed to the keep. In the great hall, she told servants to secure the keep doors before ascending to the ramparts with Father Augustyn.

Filip caught them up. "I could not find Pan Henryk, Liwi," he panted. "I looked for Pan Stefan without luck. Pan Marcin is gone, on patrol."

Oliwia had little time to register more alarm, for she heard her name being called from far away. Peering over the battlements to the base of Biaska's hillock, her heart dropped. The army seemed to fill the fields against a backdrop of heavy, smudgy smoke carrying embers and ash skyward. A line of mounted combatants was arrayed before the dry moat, and at the very front, covered in armor and mail, wielding a jeweled *budzygan*, was Lucifer himself. Lord Antonin of Wąskadroga. Beside him stood a fearsome warrior outfitted in full hussar battle regalia, impeccable feathers sprouting proudly from his silver helm and his rigid back. In his right hand, he held a gleaming szabla. In his left, a leather officer's budzygan resembling a club. Carts and the odd structures moved on creaking wheels behind them. Horses whinnied, stamped, and champed.

Oliwia stood frozen. All grew eerily quiet until Antonin's voice pierced the silence.

"Lady Oliwia! I have come to offer you one more chance to accept me." He eyed the man beside him. "First, allow me to present the lieutenant of my army. You have met before."

The man pulled off his helmet, and Oliwia narrowed her eyes, taking in his thin, reedy face, his small dark eyes, thin, cruel mouth, and hair the color of faded flax. She gasped, and he smiled, though the smile held no mirth. Only cold malevolence.

"Romek Mazur at your service, Lady Oliwia. I am delighted to see you again," he said smoothly. "Our encounter at Vyatov was far too brief. You have certainly grown up."

Her fear dissolved as a torch of anger quickly caught fire inside her. She gripped her skirts.

Steady.

"I see you have improved not at all," she spat.

Smirking, Romek swiveled his head toward Antonin.

"Enough of pleasantries." Antonin waved his hand. "Lady Oliwia, I give you one hour to agree to my terms. If you do not," he looked around himself, "I'm afraid I will have no choice but to pull down your walls— and I so hate to do that."

"You may have my answer now, my lord," she called back stridently. "Never!"

He shook his head and tsked. "As you wish. But know this: I will not be nearly as lenient with you when I drag you out of there." He said something to Romek; Romek looked over his shoulder and signaled with his budzygan. Men on horseback parted, and foot soldiers began pushing four small cannon into place across the breadth of the field.

"Liwi!" Filip said in alarm. "What do we do?"

Flying down the stairs to the keep, she called over her shoulder, "We ready ourselves."

"And how are we to do that, my lady?" Father Augustyn huffed in panic after her.

"Any way we can!"

A half hour later, Oliwia was still organizing her small corps of fighters. They'd discovered the armory empty and now took up any implement they could find—axes, rakes, knives. Nowhere was Henryk or Stefan, and now Kasimir had gone missing. *Mary, Mother of God, where are they?* Foreboding crept up her neck.

The first *boom* of the guns rocked the castle. Screams rent the air. A rattling report of exploding stone rained down on the battlements and the courtyard, sounding for all the world as though the wall had been torn apart and lay in a ruin of rubble. But when Oliwia peeked out, the wall was solid but for a few bite marks. Beside her, Father Augustyn prayed fervently over a quivering rosary clasped in his hands.

"Add one for Adam and Filip, Father." Oliwia braced herself for the next blast.

Chapter 30

From the Rain, Straight Under the Drainpipe

Poland. Jacek sniffed it in the lumpy clouds overhead and in the soil beneath them as they crossed the border. At last, they had escaped the gripping weather and left Gloggnitz, Vienna, and Brno behind as they headed from Ostrava northeast to Katowice. They'd hunkered down just long enough for Dawid's twisted ankle to mend and make the journey tolerable. In any case, he made no complaint, for which Jacek's jangled nerves were grateful.

Right now, Jacek could not keep from smiling. His head swiveled from the limestone crags to the unfurling oak leaves to the clinging rockfoils as he took it all in. He was home! He nearly wept for being here, really here, and curbed the impulse to jump to the ground and yank up fistfuls of dew-wet grass.

Biaska beckoned.

As he lay in his bedroll that night, drumming his fingers against his chest under the crude canopy held up by three pegged saplings, he wondered that he didn't vault into his saddle and gallop home. Glancing at the snoring frames beyond the small fire, he let out a loud exhale. *Morning will come soon enough. Besides, the horses need the rest for tomorrow's long ride.*

Jacek must have finally drifted, for when a horse's snort roused him, the night's dark easterly hold had given way to the first streaky grays of dawn. He leapt from his makeshift bed and went about preparing for the day's journey. The sky was still dim when he perched on a boulder, hands dangling between his thighs, his gaze fastened on his dozing companions.

Jacek nudged Pawel's foot, and the man sat up on an elbow and scrubbed his eyes.

Then Jacek prodded Dawid, who jerked awake with wide eyes. "Jesus! I thought you a slobbering wolf or a vulture."

"Vultures don't slobber. Get up!" Jacek threw Dawid's boots at him. "Your lazy ass is wasting our precious daylight."

"Yes, sir, Captain, sir," Dawid grumbled.

Pawel yawned, disguising a smile as he exaggerated a stretch and staggered from his bedroll.

Within a half hour, they were underway. Jacek whistled in the crisp morning air that held a hint of an oncoming storm. They entered a thicket and trod over a carpet of moldering needles between tall spruces. Scant light from the watery sunlight pierced the dimness here and there. As they moved through cold shadows, they were slowed by brambled bushes. Jacek leapt from his saddle and walked in the lead as the men wielded axes to clear a path through branches clawing at their clothing. Stealth was not on Jacek's mind as they crashed through the underbrush.

He slowed, held up his hand, and listened.

"What is it?" Dawid grunted.

"What do you hear?" whispered Jacek.

Dawid shrugged. "Nothing."

Jacek's eyes darted through the heavy woods of chestnut, rowan, and pine surrounding them like wiry hairs on a thickly furred dog's back. He heard nothing either—which kindled his growing apprehension. Skin prickled along his arms and neck, and he looked at Pawel just as an arrow whizzed past his ear and slammed into a birch tree trunk. They scrambled, taking cover behind the horses. There was little space for them to move for the encroaching vegetation.

"We make our stand here," Jacek hissed as he transferred his axe and slid his scimitar from its leather sheath. He was in a low crouch. For a moment, the only sound was the blood rushing in and out of his ears. Another projectile cut through the air and glanced off his horse's saddle. The animal whinnied and shied, nearly stepping on him. Gritting his teeth, he rose up and looked over its rump.

I'll be damned if anyone is going to stop me now.

"Show yourself, coward!"

Nothing but the sound of their horses' soft snorts and his companions breathing.

"I said, come out!"

Deadly silence.

Then a rustle so faint it barely registered. Jacek swung round so his back now pressed against the horse. His vision, everything he saw, shrank to the black hole of a barrel aimed at his chest.

A voice, steely and even, came from above the muzzle. "Rather you should drop your weapons." Something about the voice rang a chord, and Jacek looked up into two dark eyes set in a darkly bearded, shadowed face.

Jacek lowered his sword arm and stared. The man stared back. Hauling himself to his feet, Dawid stood beside Jacek, while Pawel remained in a squat. The man holding the pistol shifted his gaze, and, as he looked Dawid over, his mouth dropped open.

"Dawid? Pan Dawid of Biaska?"

Dawid narrowed his eyes. "The same. And who might you be?"

White teeth flashed in the man's dark beard. "Jesus Christ and all the saints! I cannot believe my eyes! Are you not dead?"

Dawid frowned; so did Jacek. "Clearly not," Dawid rejoined. "Why not step out of the shadows so we can see you proper, friend?"

The man lowered his weapon and strode from a tangle of branches, a wide grin splitting his face.

"Lesław!" Jacek and Dawid cried at once.

Lesław opened his arms wide to Dawid, scarcely glancing at Jacek. Just then, a horse whinnied from somewhere in the woods. Jacek looked toward the sound, and a large shape loomed, crashing through the trees, headed right at him. His heart stopped. A horse emerged, gray from the forest's shadows. Jacek blinked. It wasn't the shadows making the horse gray; the horse *was* gray. When it reached him, it head-butted him, nearly knocking him on his backside. He grabbed its leads and its very familiar turquoise-and-brass bridle.

"Jarosława?" he rasped, utterly stunned. As if in answer, she flung her mane, whickered at him, then turned a wary brown eye on him right before shouldering him into the horse at his back. He recovered himself, released the axe, and stroked her muzzle.

Another voice, dripping with malice, came from the woods. "Leave off my horse."

Jacek ruffled the animal's ivory forelock as a hussar materialized, soldiers behind him like wraiths on either flank. The trees were thick with them. Jacek tightened the grip on his blade and glanced at the rider's face. Then he froze and gawped.

"Marcin?" Jacek peered at a soldier clad in armor too big for his angular frame.

Am I looking upon a specter?

The young man's eyes widened into large brown spheres that mimicked the shield suspended from the saddle—a saddle suspiciously resembling one once belonging to Jacek. He wondered if he faced a ghostly horse thief. To Jacek's left, Lesław had released Dawid and now studied Jacek with a puzzled frown. Finally, he said, "Jacek?"

Breaking the silent mutual gawking was Dawid, who paced toward Marcin. "Is this Marcin? You live, you devil! However did you escape? You are a most welcome sight!" Dawid pounded him on the shoulder. Marcin lurched backward, then looked from Dawid to Jacek and back again with bulging eyes. At last, he found his voice.

"Sir?" he choked. "Is it you, Pan Dąbrowski?"

"It is I, Marcin." Jacek regarded his erstwhile dead retainer.

"I did not recognize you, sir!" Marcin cried, his face bright with a smile. "The clothes and the hair." He motioned toward his own kolpak. "And begging your pardon, but your face is much thinner than I recall, Captain." Jacek wondered that Marcin made no mention of the jagged scar running from his left eyebrow the length of his jaw.

"What the devil happened to you, Marcin?" Jacek laughed, though it came out as a bark. "And why do you have my horse? And my saddle? *And my armor?"*

"You … My lord! I can scarcely believe it!" Marcin was hopping and shouting gleefully now, looking around at faces as if to confirm he was not dreaming.

Jacek scratched Jarosława's chin, and in an even voice that belied the twitchiness in his belly, said, "Did Lady Oliwia not receive my letter? Does she know we live?"

"No, Captain," answered Marcin. "We all thought you … Stefan saw you cut down with his own eyes. We have mourned you these many months."

"So she believes me dead?" Jacek's stomach tightened.

313

"Yes, Captain," replied Marcin.

Jacek drew in a sharp breath, still patting his horse, leaning on her to keep himself from reeling. "And how is she? Is she well? Is she wed?"

Dawid threw him a quick glance and arched an eyebrow. Jacek ignored it.

"Jacek," Lesław began grimly, "we've much to tell you. We're encamped close by. Let's retire there so we can talk comfortably."

Jacek clenched his jaw. "Lead on, then."

Camp lay in a small opening in the forest. Fragrant fires drifted up to sullen skies that had yet to spew snow. Jacek was astounded when a small pig-like animal humped its way across camp and latched onto his boot. With its teeth firmly sunk in, it wagged its head back and forth and growled.

Jacek rolled his eyes. "Jesus, Statyw! Why the hell do you still live?"

A lean, dark man with an easy gait ambled over with a smile. "Commander," Florian greeted him. "Saints be praised, I could not believe my ears when the advance guard told us you live!"

As Florian embraced him, Jacek lifted his boot and dangled the three-legged beast. Florian leaned down and obligingly removed the mongrel in an altogether familiar move.

"He's mine now, Commander." Florian patted the dog's head before shooing him away.

"Some things never change, eh, Commander?" laughed another man Jacek hadn't noticed. Benas, the young Lithuanian soldier from Silnyród's garrison, welcomed him warmly.

"'Tis wondrous to see you all." Jacek was suddenly overcome as he looked around at familiar faces. "Even if you are as mangy as that accursed dog," he added with a swipe at his nose. Hell, he didn't even mind seeing the blasted mutt, though he would never admit it outright.

Someone handed him a full cup and plate, and Jacek sat on a barrel, his ankles crossed and his knees splayed wide—because he could.

Twenty-eight in all. Jacek learned most of the soldiers were Scottish mercenaries brought by Lesław to Biaska to fortify the garrison. Besides these men, the group held the hussars and a collection of Silnyród's soldiers, retainers, and servants.

He scraped meat from a cold rabbit leg with his knife. "How is my favorite barmaid, Florian?"

A grin split Florian's face, lifting Jacek's spirits. "Luiza is well, Captain. Much improved since the last time you saw her. She is back in Silnyród with our daughter. Jaromir, I am sorry to say, passed. He never recovered from the deaths of his wife and daughter."

Jacek crossed himself, sadness suddenly stinging his eyes. "My congratulations to you on the birth of your daughter. And my condolences. Jaromir was a good man." He glanced at Statyw, who lay at Florian's feet. It wagged its stubby tail as if recognizing it was the subject of their conversation. "How did you come by the dog?"

"We lost Tymon during a raid. The dog won't tolerate the new stable master, so he's mine now. Won't leave my side, no matter what I do. Does a good job hunting rats."

"Tatars?" asked Jacek as he chewed.

"Them too."

"No, I meant were Tatars behind the raid?"

Florian nodded. "They were. But I did not jest when I said Statyw is good at hunting Tatars. Hates them more than he hates you. Speaking of which, I reckon you may want to congratulate me again." Florian smirked.

Jacek raised his eyebrows. "Luiza is with child again?"

Florian shook his dark curly head and widened his grin wolfishly. "Not yet, though I am giving it my best effort." When the men's laughter died down, his face took on a gritty earnestness. "Do you recall how I said I'd gut that devil's spawn?"

Scar Nose!

"And did you?" Jacek held his breath.

"I did," Florian replied, and his eyes glimmered. "Statyw's the one who led me to him. We were scouting, and I reckon he picked up the scent. We ambushed the bastard and a half-dozen others in their camp. The scum offered us gold, horses, women, anything we wanted when he saw the girth of the log Benas sharpened for him. After we hoisted him up, the bastard begged and screamed more pathetically than his victims ever could have, so I slit his belly and showed him his guts. I threw some to Statyw, but even he wouldn't touch 'em." Florian scratched the dog's ear. "That dark demon's death was neither easy nor honorable."

Jacek held his hand out to Statyw, who sniffed it before dropping his head back on his paws with a snuffle. "No one deserved a more fitting punishment," Jacek said quietly, running his fingers over his scar.

After a few beats, he looked at Marcin. "I've heard how you got away, but now tell me of Biaska. I venture the lady was unsuccessful in building her garrison if she gave you a promotion *and* my horse." He smirked.

Marcin darted his eyes to Lesław, then back to Jacek.

Jacek's neck hairs rose. "What is it?"

Marcin picked up a sliver of wood and prized food from his teeth. "Some I told you on our way here. When all the grain burned up, more men left. Pan Henryk wrote Pan Lesław, who recruited these men here," Marcin said with a nod round, "and just recently, at the enga—" He coughed suddenly, then continued, "Pan Henryk instructed me to take three others and ride out to meet Pan Lesław. Thank God I did."

Marcin stood and cracked his knuckles. "It took no more than a day to locate them. We all headed for Biaska, but our advance guard quickly turned back." Marcin paused and sucked in a huge breath. "The village was gone, burned, and the fortress surrounded by Lord Antonin's army. We've scarcely had time to learn more since."

"What?" Jacek bolted upright, his heart hammering his ribs. Questions bombarded his brain, and he threw a litany of them at Marcin before the young man could catch breath to answer the first.

"All we know," Lesław said evenly, "is that Lord Antonin proposed marriage to the Lady Oliwia time and again, and she refused him. Instead, she consented to wed Henryk. They were to marry Saturday next."

From the corner of his eye, Jacek saw Marcin jerk and heard him mutter something incoherent. Lesław kept droning—something about the king, Lord Antonin, and May Day—but Jacek heard little more than the roar in his head.

A slice of sanity returned to him, and Jacek made his first plan. *When I get my hands on that flea-infested peacock who called himself my friend, I shall flay him alive.*

He looked around; Marcin's and Dawid's eyes were glued to him. Lesław seemed unaware of any change in his demeanor, although he did keep his distance and twitch a bit overmuch.

"So you know nothing of the fate of the family or the garrison. What of the villagers? Have you searched for them? Have you summoned the tenants and their sons to come to Biaska's aid?" Jacek was up now, pacing as he barked his terse questions. "In short, what in blazes are you *doing* to drive Antonin out?"

He battled the impulse to jump astride Jarosława and charge into the army himself. Instead, he found himself embroiled in an interminable war council, where he soon learned he was not in charge. When he wanted camp picked up and moved the long day's ride to Biaska *now*, he was overridden.

"We've marched to battlefields all night and killed enemy all the next day!" he bellowed. "Moving one small camp will not be half so difficult, yet here we sit!"

Lesław pulled him aside. "I know you are anxious to recover the fortress, Jacek, as am I, but I think it would do well to yield a bit. We are one small band against hundreds, and we need the Scots. If we push them, we may lose them."

Jacek dragged a hand through his hair and blew out a great breath. Then he nodded vigorously, not because he was in agreement and wished to show it enthusiastically, but because he needed to do *something*. He stayed back and watched as Lesław calmed Scottish nerves Jacek had frayed. It was here that Marcin found him in a pacing mood as he wore troughs in the dirt.

"I reckon Stefan must have mistaken Andrzej for you, Captain. 'Tis the only way I can figure it. He was the only witness. Everyone at Biaska—and your family, of course—will be overjoyed when they discover you live."

Jacek glanced at him. "Thank you, Marcin. Now tell me about Lady Oliwia and Filip."

"They both looked well enough a few days ago."

"How is her son?" *And has she borne any others?*

"Strong as an ox." A few beats later, Marcin cleared his throat. "So will you be seeking the Lady Eugenia's hand once again, Captain?"

The question caught Jacek off guard, and he let out a wry laugh before he could swallow it. *Eugenia! Jesus, I'd forgotten all about her. Again.* A familiar dread, like stinking mud, oozed through him. "I will work all that out once we are out of *this* mess." Right now, Jacek's thoughts were fixed on the woman who'd filled his head this last long year. And whether she was all right.

The shadows in the forest crept long and dark, throwing a shroud over everything. The brightest lights came from the campfires and torches. Jacek and Marcin stood in silence, and Jacek looked at the sky, wondering if snow would soon fall. A weaving lantern caught his eye. It came toward them, illuminating its handler, Lesław.

Marcin dusted his hands. "Time I checked, ah, things." He walked away briskly.

"So, Lesław," Jacek offered with a small smile, "tell me what has happened to you and Silnyród this past year." Looking his friend over, he added, "Have you recovered from your injuries?"

"Injuries?" Lesław started, as if he'd been lost in thought. "Oh! Yes, I recovered rather quickly."

Lesław began fidgeting, causing the lantern to bob and throw jerky patterns of light on the foliage. Jacek took it from him and hung it on a nearby branch. When he looked back at him, Lesław was chewing his nails, darting his eyes about, and muttering something.

Jacek frowned and cocked his head. "What was that?"

Lesław looked at Jacek squarely and let out a long exhale. "I took a wife."

"But that's wonderful!" Jacek's wide grin puckered his scar. "Who is the unfortunate woman? Anyone I know?"

Lesław now shifted his weight from foot to foot. "Well, as a matter of fact, yes."

Jacek waited expectantly, but Lesław said nothing. Just rocked. "Come, man! Who is she? Not one of Henryk's whores, surely," Jacek blurted, his eyebrows inching up his forehead.

His comment earned him a murderous look—a most unusual expression for Lesław. "She's no whore!" Before Jacek could appease him, Lesław snarled, "She's a noblewoman."

Never a talkative man, Lesław began speaking so fast Jacek could scarcely catch a word. But he did catch the word "Eugenia."

Jacek lurched and gripped Lesław's arms, seeming to frighten the man out of his wits. "Say that again?"

"I said, I … Lady Eugenia … we both thought you dead, she was inconsolable, so I … visited, called … she … her father … we …" he stammered.

"Did you say you wed her?"

A worried look on his face, Lesław nodded.

"My blessings to you both!" Jacek nearly whooped, clapping him on the shoulder.

Lesław's eyes widened. "You're not going to kill me?"

Jacek shrugged, the movement more of a body twitch. "I'm disappointed, naturally," he lied. "But how can I be angry when two people I care about have made a life together?"

Lesław seemed to ease and ventured a smile. "Just like Henryk and Lady Oliwia!"

Before he could stop himself, Jacek gave Lesław a hard shove.

"Are you not happy for Henryk?" Lesław was obviously confused.

Jacek growled something altogether incomprehensible.

Had he not been so vexed as he lay down that night, he might have found it humorous that one of his best friends had taken the woman he didn't want, while the other had taken the one he did. Instead, he turned from the battle in his heart to the battle at hand and did what all good soldiers do. He dragged his mind through every strategy he could devise— looking at it backward, frontward, and from every facet imaginable—to drive Antonin and his army from Biaska. What he refused to ponder was what would happen to Oliwia if Antonin should succeed before Jacek could stop him.

Leaving Pawel in camp, Jacek rode with Dawid, Marcin, Florian, and Benas to Biaska's familiar ridges late the next afternoon. They had ridden ahead, driving their mounts hard. Now as he sat upon Jarosława, he edged along the southwestern boundary of the estate. He'd grown prickly, impatient. What he longed for was so close, but what would he find when he got there?

They climbed a ridgeback of limestone, and as they crested it, Jacek got his first glimpse of the castle on its knobby rock perched in the distance. Though they were as yet far away, his heart thudded, alternately lifting and seizing, excitement roiling with fear. Catching his breath, he shaded his eyes from the late-day sun.

"There it is, lads." Jacek jerked his chin at the outcropping rising out of the fields.

The five men stood in silence, side by side on their mounts. The day was bright and clear, and Jacek could see across the meadows bordered by sweeping forests and ridges. As he peered at the scene, he spotted a dark smudge surrounding the land at the foot of the castle's hillock. It seemed to crawl. Reaching into his saddlebag, he extracted the looker and brought it to his eye, scanning back and forth. He drew in an audible breath.

"I see hundreds of tents and horses. Men are moving about, though I cannot make out any uniforms. I count six supply wagons, two ordnance wagons, and what appear to be siege catapults. At least two. They have light guns—three or four." With a furrowed brow, Jacek lowered the tube and handed it to Dawid.

"Do you see the holes and scarring along the south and east walls? Those weren't there before. It looks as though they've been hit, though I see no breach," Jacek said in an even voice.

"Nor do I," Dawid replied. "But I do see earth mounds. They may be tunneling, Captain."

Eyes still on the horizon, Jacek nodded and absentmindedly patted his mare's neck as Dawid handed the instrument to Marcin.

"Your plan, Captain?" Florian asked.

"We begin with Benas," Jacek answered with a nod toward said soldier, "who will deliver our appeals for aid to Kraków and Matejko Manor. Then we scout and meet up with Lesław and the rest of his troop. For the remainder of the afternoon, we seek villagers, merchants—anyone who knows what's taking place inside that fortress. When it's dark, Dawid and Marcin go to the village while Florian and I visit Łac. Christ, I hope no one recognizes me."

"*I* didn't recognize you. I doubt patrons in their cups will remember you *or* that great brawl you started two years ago," Marcin chimed helpfully.

"Tomorrow, you and I visit Oławieża," Jacek said to him.

"The tower? Why?" asked Dawid.

320

Jacek flicked his eyes at Marcin, who suddenly brightened. He grinned at Jacek. "You're thinking of the old tunnel, Captain, yes?"

Jacek had meant to have his whiskers shaved off and his hair cropped but was glad now he hadn't. With his dark beard and long blond hair, he would be harder to recognize, especially if he stooped to hide his height. After discovering virtually nothing from the villagers taking refuge in tenants' homes—many had fled before Antonin's army descended—they reunited with Lesław's men and encamped in a thick wood several leagues from Biaska.

Under Statyw's curious gaze, Jacek adjusted garments he'd traded for as they'd moved about the countryside throughout the day. In exchange for his fine Naples garb, he'd acquired a simple żupan of deep emerald wool that was too small in the shoulders and too short everywhere else, brown trousers, simple black boots, and a blue kolpak with two vulture feathers. Better to wear ill-fitting Polish clothes than the costume of a Spanish dandy. He wore no armor but carried scimitar, dagger, and a *czekan*—a war hammer with an axe blade in place of the hammerhead. He resembled his former self once more, and he set out for Łac with some of his old swagger.

For nearly three-quarters of an hour, he sat at a scarred table nursing a tankard of piwo in Łac's dim, grubby tavern. The place had scarcely changed. Next to him were Florian and one Ensign MacDonald, a black-haired soldier they'd brought along from the Scottish squad. MacDonald spoke passable Polish, and though Scotsmen weren't unusual in these parts, this one was more boisterous than Jacek cared for. They were, after all, trying *not* to draw attention.

So far, they'd learned nothing from the patrons or maids, but that was all about to change. A man approached them, shouted at MacDonald and clapped him on the shoulder. All eyes turned their way. Jacek dropped his head and grumbled.

Scots, it seemed, had a knack for picking one another out—at least in crowded taverns in Łac—and the stranger, Machjeld, had recognized a fellow countryman and rushed to meet him. They spoke loudly and unendingly about their villages and families, trying to trace their lineage to discover a common ancestral thread. Jacek lost interest and returned to studying the patrons. When the two Scots finally gave up trying to match ancestry, they began talking of their travels. Machjeld ordered a round of wodka and several jugs of piwo, for which he generously paid.

"I fancy you're a soldier," Machjeld said to MacDonald as he raised a toast. MacDonald said he was, that he had left Podolia and was working his way across Poland.

"Maybe I can join you and your squad!" Machjeld roared as he looked around the table. Then he dropped his voice conspiratorially. "I *was* a soldier until today, when I walked out. Got tired of going without pay. Started out well enough, but I got naught but drivel the last six months." Machjeld rolled his eyes, his hand mimicking a mouth opening and closing. "Hell and damnation, if I'd stuck to me old work as a carpenter, I'd be far richer now. The lord had been giving us food, a place to stay, plenty o' ale and women, and promises the pay would come, but then we march off, and the food, ale, and whores are gone! He says 'forage for yourselves.' Miserable bastard," he growled right before tossing back his wodka.

Jacek's every muscle tautened, and he shoved his still-full wodka cup across the table to Machjeld. "Have mine," he invited.

Machjeld raised his cup in thanks and gulped it down. Jacek summoned the tavern maid.

"Another round, m'lord?" she asked.

Jacek slipped coins into her hand and gave her a wink. "Bring the bottle."

She returned with the bottle and began to pour. Jacek inclined his head, and she kept filling Machjeld's cup until it was nearly running over its sides.

During the course of the following thirty minutes, Machjeld spun a weaving tale during which they learned he was related to other Machjelds who were part of Wąskadroga's army, though he'd arrived at it late.

"My third cousins—or are they fourth cousins?—well, they were recruited more'n four years back, and they're big men now. They run the settlement—call themselves elders—and if that weren't fancy enough, they and their sons are part of the lord's trusted troops. His inner circle. And they've been well paid for it. Not like now," he laughed.

"So what is it like now?" Jacek raised his mostly full cup to his lips.

322

"Four years ago, the lord rewarded loyalty well. The last eight months or so, he really built up his force—for this very mission, I reckon. So now his troops are roughly four hundred I'm told, though some might be camp followers. I never was good at timing things right." He frowned.

Four hundred. Jacek checked his surprise.

Four hundred warriors to feed, Machjeld said, was why the lord claimed poverty and told them to fend for themselves. When they were victorious, he pledged, their reward would come with the sacking of Biaska.

Between greedy gulps of wodka, Machjeld went on to say they'd gotten some booty from plundering the village, but that the lord and his lieutenant had taken the largest share—including gold and silver from the church.

"You sacked a church?" asked MacDonald, astonished. Jacek gave him a warning scowl.

Machjeld seemed to notice neither MacDonald's reaction nor the ensuing silent exchange. "I weren't there for that bit of dirty work." He shrugged.

"If the army's on the castle's doorstep and you were about to collect your reward, why'd you leave?" asked Jacek mildly as he balanced the bottle on the rim of Machjeld's cup. He dribbled in more wodka.

Machjeld hiccupped, then looked at Jacek and grinned. "I got my share of the spoils and decided it was time to go." *And spend it all on drink.* Then Machjeld tapped a blocky finger to his temple. "'Sides, I overheard some things I weren't ought to, and I know *no one's* getting paid. I ain't laying down *my* life for naught. Takes a canny one to fool old Machjeld."

Jacek raised his cup and feigned a swallow. "So what did you hear? Must've been serious to cause a bright man like you to leave."

Florian and MacDonald kept their mouths shut and their eyes fastened on Jacek and Machjeld. Machjeld puffed his chest and snorted. He drew close and cupped his mouth to Jacek's ear. Jacek held his breath to keep from inhaling his foul stench. In a loud whisper easily overheard by Florian and MacDonald, Machjeld said, "Lord's randy for the young widow, and he's got someone on the inside's been chasing off the garrison so's they ain't got many left to fight. Them guards are all locked up—or dead now, mebbe—and he's gonna let him in sneaky-like. Once he's in, he takes *all* the riches." Machjeld nodded. "He don't need the damned army for nothing but show. 'Twill make anybody think twice if they be thinking to rescue the bitch he's looking to rut. He only needs that sour bastard Lieutenant Mazur and a few of his finest."

Out of the slurry of disconcerting thoughts sloshing through Jacek's mind, one flashed like a beacon.

Mazur?

Jacek ran his finger over his chin as if lost in thought. "So he's looking to take the Lady of Biaska's riches?"

Machjeld waggled his eyebrows. "More'n that. Never seen her myself, but I hear she's a fine thing, and Lieutenant don't hide the fact the lord's looking forward to riding her. The bastard might even marry her—would make taking her lands easier, now wouldn't it? He was all fired up to get there afore she could marry some other whoreson. Once Lord Antonin's in, he's flying his banner. You watch. When he hoists that banner, means he's hoisted her skirts and humped her good." Pounding the table, he added, "Way he talks, mebbe she won't walk again!" He nearly fell over laughing.

Jacek drew in a sharp breath but hid it. "I hear everyone is loyal to the lady. So who might the lord's inside man be?"

Machjeld half chortled, half hiccupped and looked at Jacek blearily. "Could be a woman. But I dinna hear that part."

Jacek knew the man would soon topple over, so he learned what else he could. The army—an undisciplined bunch that fought amongst themselves, Jacek gathered—was led by a professional unit under Lieutenant Mazur, and Mazur was a hussar.

"So this lieutenant—Mazur, you said?—I grew up with a Mazur. What did you say his first name was, and where's he from?" asked Jacek.

Machjeld appeared to reel in his seat. "Huh?"

"Tell me about Mazur," Jacek repeated.

"Uh ..." Machjeld swiped at his nose and missed. "He, uh ..." Florian snaked in a hand and started to pull Machjeld's cup away. "No, wait! Uh, Romek. Romek Mazur. From Sandomierz, I think." Florian returned the cup, which Machjeld drained. Then Machjeld slurred, "A real sonuvabitch, that Mazur. Touched, I think. Caught him cutting up one of our whores one night. She weren't doing nothing wrong; just working her trade, trying to keep the men happy. He cut her bad. For no reason! Hadn't even tried poking her. And if that weren't bad enough, he took the poor girl's shoes. Wouldn't give 'em back."

Jacek sat up straight, feeling as though ice spread throughout his body.

Before he could ask more questions, Machjeld's eyes rolled back in their sockets, and his face crashed onto the table. He shot up as if someone had pulled his hair, then lay his head back down on his arm, sighed, and promptly went slack. Several beats later, he began snoring. No amount of rousting could bring him back, so Jacek put a few more coins on the tabletop before they left. He set aside the disturbing discovery of Romek Mazur for now. Instead, he let himself feel hope as he pondered cracks to be exploited.

As they mounted up, he heard two owls hoot in quick succession, and a fresh chill ran down his spine. He crossed himself. *The devil's cries.*

When they returned to camp, Dawid and Marcin were waiting. They'd found camp followers rummaging through the village debris, but other than grumbling, they'd overheard little of value. As they'd left the village, they stole close to the edge of the enemy encampment under cover of the nearly new moon. What they observed bolstered Jacek's theory about Antonin's tattered assemblage, for many a drunken jig was being danced and many a sotted soldier's lusts were being satisfied about blazing fires in that camp.

But then they reported something Jacek was altogether unprepared to hear, and his heart plummeted to his knees.

Wąskadroga's blood-red eagle banners brazenly flapped from each of Biaska's four towers.

Chapter 31

Every Stick Has Two Ends

Oliwia was startled awake by loud pounding on her bedchamber door. Nadia leapt from her pallet. It was yet dark, and the large chamber was lit by feeble candlelight from several tapers, one of which Nadia now held. Just as Nadia reached the barred door, Oliwia heard a desperate voice on the other side.

"Liwi! Liwi! Let me in!"

Oliwia nodded when Nadia looked over her shoulder, and the maid slid the bar and opened the door to a breathless Filip shifting from foot to foot in the passageway. He pushed his way into the room, and Nadia swiftly turned, barring the door behind him.

"What is it?" Oliwia's pulse raced as she sat up.

"The Wąskadroga banner hangs from our towers." Filip sprinted across the room to a window. "Come, Liwi! Look!"

She slid from beneath the counterpane as icy tendrils rushed through her veins, stockinged feet sinking into the carpet. She had slept fully clothed in a simple woollen gown and now pulled on her boots, slipping a small knife inside one.

Upon her insistence, Filip had moved from the garrison to a chamber one door away. In the lord's chamber adjoining Oliwia's, which had once been Eryk's, slept Adam along with Anka and Wanda.

Filip pressed against the wall, hands resting on the stone sill as he peered out, and Oliwia joined him there. Morning was close, and she reckoned it would be a clear, bright day, though not a cheerful one, no matter the sky's brilliance. Not since the arrival of Antonin's army. They had pummeled the walls for hours that first day, and though stone that had stood for hundreds of years had crumbled in places, Biaska's walls had held defiant and impenetrable. Though Antonin had not breached the castle walls, the fright he'd instilled in folk barricaded within the keep had been breathtaking. So Oliwia had, without much of a telltale quaver, shouted down to Antonin to come and get her. For not the first time, she wondered at the prudence of provoking him.

When the guns quit, they did not start up again. Perhaps he'd merely been testing her *and* his guns. The quiet had implanted a new dread that crept through her; she reckoned Antonin had simply put aside that strategy for one more covert, one she couldn't see, couldn't fight.

In the two days since the army's arrival, a vast encampment resembling a noisy village had unfolded itself outside Biaska's walls. Nighttime was illuminated by a multitude of bright fires, and within the shadows was constant movement, as though great beasts prowled the spaces between the light. She'd been unable to make out hard forms, but raucous shouts and laughter had caught on the wind and waved into her chamber.

Yesterday, she thought Antonin's men had begun digging tunnels. Perhaps it explained how someone had managed to hang Wąskadroga's flags that she now looked upon. Henryk had vanished, as had Stefan and Kasimir, and last night she'd been unable to find Feliks. It made no sense. Where had they gone? And there was no sign of Marcin or Lesław and the Silnyród soldiers. For a fleeting moment, she considered that the guns had scared them off, but then she remembered who these men were. They did not flinch at peril; they embraced it.

As Oliwia stood beside Filip and peered into the fading night, she felt terribly small and dreadfully alone. She shivered involuntarily. Her brother's brows were drawn together in a fierce scowl. When she looked at his profile, she not only glimpsed Jacek's determination but also the man's face Filip would one day wear. In that instant, he did not resemble the boy he still was.

The two stood side by side and watched a banner catch and flail in the breeze. Below, tents covered the slopes and fields surrounding Biaska. Wagons were lined up, catapults and guns arrayed, breastworks had been carved from the ground, and smoke rose from cookfires. War had come to Biaska, uninvited, unwelcome, because of another man's greed. Oliwia wanted to shake her fist at the sky and rage at the injustice of it all. But her impotence dragged her down instead. She gritted her teeth and pressed her lips in a hard line as she asked herself the well-worn question: What could be done?

Turning from the window, she padded down the private corridor to the adjoining chamber. When she opened the door, an unsettling quiet greeted her, and her heart sank like a rock hurled from a cliff into a cold pool. She ran to the bed and tore apart its coverings, frantically crying out Adam's name. Nothing. The gloomy space was empty.

Filip appeared in the doorway. "Liwi, what is it?"

Holding back the bile rising in her throat, she cried, "Adam is gone! So are Anka and Wanda!"

Filip's huge eyes blinked. She tore back to her chamber, Filip on her heels, then whirled toward a stricken Nadia. "Nadia, you and Filip will remain here. Bar the door, do not let *anyone* in until you hear from me."

She flew through the door before they could protest, pausing in the dim hallway until the bar stuttered into place. Then she threw herself down the steps, ducking into the solar with the frenzied hope Henryk would be there. The room was as still as a graveyard at dawn. She scurried through the cavernous hall, her footfalls echoing as she scanned pillars, the dais, the banked hearth. Then she turned to the kitchen, sure kitchenmaids were laying fires. She could almost hear Beata scolding them while she worked her doughs for the morning meal.

When Oliwia entered the kitchen, it too was cold, too empty. She hugged herself. *Where is everyone?* She heard a strange sound from the buttery and pivoted. One double door was closed, the other ajar. She stepped in, surprised to find the space lit. Darting her eyes about, she froze when they caught on something to her right. She gasped. Splayed on her belly was a maid lying in a pool of blood the color of chestnut shells, thick and shiny as jelly on the stone floor.

Oliwia drew closer. Strawberry-blond hair.

"Wanda?" Oliwia croaked. *Where is Adam?*

Her mind areel, she jumped when a large shape loomed from the shadows. As the shape's features emerged, she saw an unfamiliar soldier in unfamiliar garb. He slid a knife from his belt and leered at her, revealing broken, gapped teeth. Oliwia spun, but he caught her arm, yanked her to him, and held the knife to her throat. The point dug into her flesh.

"There now, what's a pretty thing like you doing wandering about? Let me help you find whatever you're looking for, love," he mocked. The reek of his rank ale breath engulfed her. Oliwia wriggled from his grasp, but he lunged for her and caught her by her arm, dragging her backward. Her shoulder burned where he pulled, and she cried out.

Another figure materialized in the doorway, growling and cursing at the man who had hold of her. The man who held her shoved her into the other man's arms, and as she glimpsed him, relief flooded her.

"Kasimir!"

Kasimir grasped her arm; his eyes flicked over Wanda's body.

"What the hell are you doing in here?" he shouted at the other man.

Sheathing his knife, the man calmly replied, "Looking for piwo. We're thirsty."

"You're supposed to be at sentry, you halfwit!" Kasimir snapped. "And don't let me catch you touching Lord Antonin's woman again lest you want to suffer at Lieutenant Mazur's hands. Better yet, I'll kill you myself!"

It took Oliwia's addled brain a moment to understand Kasimir meant her when he spoke of Lord Antonin's "woman." *Am I dreaming?* With surging dismay, she realized she was not.

The other man's eyes widened. "I didn't know. She came busting in here, and I thought she was just another kitchenmaid. What happened to that one?" He jerked his head toward Wanda.

"She became a bit too troublesome," Kasimir replied, looking at Oliwia pointedly. "Come quietly, *my lady,* lest the same should happen to you."

"Where are you taking me? Where is my son?" she spluttered as he hauled her away.

Kasimir grinned, the look more frightening by far than the sneer had been. "Lord Antonin is anxious to see you."

Realization bashed her over the head. Kasimir, a Biaska soldier before her arrival. Eryk's oathman. Stefan's best friend. How could he betray them all? Suddenly, she understood why the garrison was half-empty, why the wrong banners flew.

"Where's Henryk? Where's Stefan?" she demanded. If she kept talking, kept asking, maybe it would tamp her rising panic, but Kasimir said nothing. Instead, he dragged her into the solar, which had been empty mere minutes before, and shoved her roughly toward a figure with his back to her. Antonin turned from a window and faced her.

"Ah! There you are. You're looking lovely as always, my dear." His gleaming weasel eyes looked her over rapaciously.

"What are *you* doing here?" she hissed.

Antonin reached for Oliwia's hand, and she recoiled. He scoffed. "Kasimir was good enough to show me in. I mean you no harm, my dear. Quite the contrary. I want nothing more than to please you." His words slid out of his mouth like eels slithering over slimy river rocks.

Oliwia fought back her nausea and folded her arms across her chest. She flexed her calf, reassured by the hardness of the knife in her boot.

"If you want to *please* me, my lord, then leave at once and take this rubbish with you," she ground out as she jerked her chin at Kasimir, who flashed her another hideous grin.

Antonin feigned offense. "After going to all this trouble to get in here? Why, I've already replaced all your late husband's tattered banners. Surely you can offer me some hospitability?"

She gave him a stony look. "Where's my son?"

He sighed loudly. "I see you are incapable at the moment. Well, no matter," he said cheerfully. "The fact is, though I wish to accommodate you, I simply cannot leave right now."

"And why is that?"

"Because I am in charge here." He waved grandly about the chamber. "Oh yes, and there is one other small matter keeping me here." When she arched an eyebrow at him, he added, "Our wedding, of course."

"I am already engaged to marry another." Jutting her chin out, she mustered as much conviction as she could. Then she began calculating her chances of whipping the knife from her boot into Antonin's neck. *A small target. His chest? It could glance off ribs. His groin?*

"Yes, about your betrothed … He has been, shall we say, *removed* and can no longer uphold his pledge." Antonin gave her a downcast look.

Oliwia's eyes widened, alarm bells clanging in her head. "What do you mean, 'removed'? What have you done to him?"

Antonin had been pacing off short steps and now came to stand before her. She backed up. He took another step toward her.

"Do not be distressed, my dear. It was not by his own choice. No, no, no. I am sure he would much rather be here with you—such a lovely thing." Antonin ran a finger along Oliwia's arm. She stood her ground and suppressed a shudder. "It took some doing—slowed us down, in fact,"

Antonin continued, "but he is alive. For now. *Your* behavior will affect what I do with him and his men. So you see, sadly, no one will be coming to your aid, and you would do well to understand you hold their fate in your hands. Your hands alone." He gave her an oily smile and scratched his chin.

Oliwia's mind flashed to Wanda's corpse, and her stomach clenched. "I still will not marry you." Her voice was steadier than she would have thought possible.

His face sharpened, all charm—real or feigned—completely gone. "And I say you will. If you want to see your lover and your son alive again, that is."

Oliwia's mouth fell open as panic waved over her. Antonin laughed.

"There is no greater love than that of a mother for her child. I knew I could count on it." He wore an ugly, arrogant smile.

Oliwia gathered up her skirts and turned to run, but Kasimir blocked her path.

"Let her go," Antonin said indifferently.

Oliwia tore for her apartments, Antonin's chortles ringing in her ears. "Go ahead, my dear. By all means, go look for your boy. You will not find him."

Jacek sat on his bedroll, scratching his nape. Yawning, he looked around the murky interior of the tent. He had slept little for shutting out all the images of what might be happening to Oliwia and her kin throughout the long night. By the time he set foot out of his tent, the camp was buzzing, and the first streaks of a bright dawn illuminated the horizon. A half hour later, he was riding toward Maławieża with Dawid, Marcin, and Florian.

They swung west and approached cautiously, keeping cover in the trees surrounding the village and watchtower. Marcin dismounted and led his horse—the one Jacek had ridden from Genoa—at an easy gait to the inn. Jacek and the others watched from a thicket as he ducked inside. Marcin soon emerged and bobbed a quick nod, and they advanced toward him. Jacek dismounted.

"Few are here, Captain. Most have fled," Marcin said.

Jacek nodded grimly, fiddling with his stirrup. "The army that eats wins. Let's breakfast while we're here." He'd always enjoyed eating, but since his time in captivity, it had become rather an obsession. The thought of going too long without food in his belly spurred him to eat anytime he could.

When they stepped into the cramped, wood-ceilinged chamber, Jacek took a moment and let his eyes adjust to the gloom. The place was dark but neat, clean but worn, and held one innkeeper, one server, and two patrons. They had their pick of tables. As they scoffed beetroot soup, cheese, and bread, the few folks told them they'd not seen Biaska's inhabitants since Antonin's army rolled in.

"Anybody living in the tower?" Jacek asked casually, sopping a hunk of bread in his soup and stuffing it in his mouth.

The innkeeper shook his head. "Just the caretaker, his family, and staff. The owner hasn't been by in a long while now. He has bigger estates to look after."

"What do you know about the old tunnel?"

Frowning, the innkeeper twirled his moustache while the serving girl filled their cups with piwo. "Don't know of any tunnel."

Florian looked at Jacek, a question on his face. "'Tis an old tale I heard once," Jacek began, "of twin brothers. One lived at Biaska, and the other at Maławieża. They were great friends and dug a tunnel connecting their two fortresses, and there they stowed a vast treasure. The brothers went to war—"

"Only one brother went to war," an old man, one of the two patrons who'd had his back to them, piped up as he looked over his shoulder. He narrowed his eyes at Jacek. "Tell it right."

Jacek waved his hand at him, inviting the elder to pick up the telling, and he did. "When they put the treasure in the tunnel," the man said," they also put a witch in there to guard it. *One* brother went to war and came back with a beautiful girl." The man paused to hold his hands up reverently, as if making an offering to the ceiling. The innkeeper and serving girl had stopped what they were doing. "She was so beautiful that the brother who brought her home suspected his twin had fallen in love with her, so he locked her up in the tunnel."

Florian pursed his lips. "If he was worried his brother loved her, why put her where he could get at her? Why not lock her up in his chamber or—"

"Shh!" the old man scolded.

Jacek raised his eyebrows at Florian, who leaned back and folded his arms across his chest, a smile quirking his lips.

"When he locked the girl up in the tunnel," the old man continued, shooting daggers at Florian from beneath his heavy brows, "he told the witch to guard her. One day, he came home and discovered the witch had left her post, and when he ran to the tunnel, he found the girl in his brother's arms."

"What happened?" asked Florian.

"He slew his brother and walled the girl up. Of course she died, and now she haunts the place. She is called the 'White Lady,'" the man said with a twinkle.

"So there *is* a tunnel?" asked Marcin, crossing himself.

"Perhaps."

"Is there a treasure?" added Florian.

"Will you show us?" Dawid threw in.

"Perhaps."

Jacek nodded at Marcin, who extracted a leather pouch and jingled it in front of the man. Thereafter, a peculiar procession of four warriors, two wizened men, one innkeeper, and one serving girl arrived at the outer wall of the fortress. Soon the caretaker, his family, and a small flock of servants joined in, caught up in the hunt for the tunnel's entrance.

"I must go find more men," Jacek told Marcin after putting him in charge of the search. "Make sure they stay on task. There's only a whisper of a chance, but still, it's a chance, and I'll grab any I can."

Jacek rode off with Dawid and Florian. They traveled several miles into the woods northeast of Maławieża on their way to one of the larger villages where Jacek reckoned he might recruit a half-dozen men. He stopped abruptly and held up his hand, cocking his head. "Horses headed our way."

The men readied weapons and took cover upslope on a nearby hillock. Whatever was approaching, it did so with thundering urgency. With his looker, Jacek spied eight horses and seven riders in the distance, riding full-out, kicking up large clouds of brown dust that hung in their wake. The eighth horse carried a bulky brown sack across its saddle.

"Six are men astride fine mounts, and the seventh rider is a woman carrying something." Jacek motioned the others down the slope, where they stopped before a bridge, barring the riders' path as they clattered onto it. Jacek gripped the scimitar in one hand and the czekan in the other; Dawid and Florian flanked him with drawn bows. The riders came to an abrupt halt.

The lead man seemed familiar. He held up his hand and scowled at the trio while his companions unsheathed sabres. "Gentlemen," he said warily, "we are on urgent business."

"What sort of business?" Jacek asked coolly, placing the man's face. It was Radek, Antonin's second from Wąskadroga, whom Jacek had met five years ago when he'd visited the stronghold with Lord Eryk.

A wail erupted from a sling across the woman's chest. Though she was at the back of the caravan, Jacek saw her face clearly. Her eyes widened, then she dropped her gaze. The brown lump they carried over the saddle seemed to move. Jacek thought it grunted.

Jacek pointed at the bundle. "What do you carry there?"

Radek bristled. "It is none of your affair."

"And where did you say you're from?" Jacek repeated, though he knew full well.

"That is not your affair either. Now let us pass!" Radek urged his mount forward, but Jacek headed him off.

Jacek kept his tone even, and his grip on his swordhilt tightened. "Not until you answer my questions." Radek had not yet recognized him. The woman lifted her eyes and darted them between his face and the bundle in her arms.

Radek reined in his horse. "By whose authority do you impede us?" he growled.

"By authority of Lady Oliwia of Biaska."

Radek let out a derisive laugh. "Lady Oliwia? She *has* no authority in these parts—not any longer."

"And why is that?" Jacek replied.

"Because she is Lord Antonin Wąskaski's wife, and *he* holds the authority." Radek smirked.

Jacek nodded so slightly that Antonin's men didn't notice. Dawid and Florian loosed their arrows, striking two riders right away, then blistered two more.

"Get the child!" Radek bellowed at his companions.

One of those companions took an arrow in the thigh, crying out as he grabbed at it. Chaos erupted. Dawid and Florian sizzled their blades from their sheaths and lunged into the fracas. The woman turned her horse and headed in the opposite direction. Radek's man wheeled in pursuit. Jacek surged into Radek, swinging the czekan, catching him in the shoulder with the axe's edge. It sank into flesh, crunched bone, and Radek screamed and swayed. Jacek seized his injured arm and wrenched him from his saddle. He hit the ground hard and screamed again.

Horses danced around one another, kicking up dirt clods. Riders weaved and crashed steel together.

The fight ended almost as soon as it started.

Jacek lit after the rider now struggling with the woman. The man was trying to pry the bundle from her arms, but she kicked out as she clutched it to her. Then he turned, saw Jacek, and urged his horse into a gallop. Dawid took off after him like the very devil on his tail. Jacek halted Jarosława beside the woman and grabbed her reins. The bundle shrieked.

"Lieutenant," the woman gasped. "It is lieutenant, yes?"

"Pan Dąbrowski will do." He narrowed his eyes at her. "Is this your babe?"

"No." She began soothing it, even as it howled. Then she jerked her head toward the pack horse. "There's a woman wrapped up in that cloak."

Jacek nodded at Florian, who jumped down and hefted the lump to the ground.

Dawid rode up and stopped his horse beside Jacek. "Got him."

"Did you finish him?" Jacek asked.

"Yes."

"Good. Guard him," Jacek instructed with a nod toward Radek, still writhing on the ground.

"You still serve Biaska?" the woman asked, snapping Jacek's attention back to her.

"I do."

She held her bundle out to him. "Then you'll be wanting him."

He took it from her. Just then, Florian unwound the cloak to reveal a disheveled young woman, bound and gagged. Terrified, she shook her head vigorously. Jacek peered at her, recognizing her when Florian pulled her to her feet and removed her bindings.

"Anka?" Jacek looked from her to the babe in his arms. "What the devil is going on here?" he bellowed and quieted immediately when the child howled anew.

Anka ran toward him, and Jacek handed the baby down to her. She looked up at him, and her mouth swung open. "Captain? But you're dead!"

"Not yet," he remarked blandly.

"It's Krystiana, yes?" Jacek asked the woman on the horse, a maid from Wąskadroga Castle whom he'd dumped to the floor once when she sat in his lap uninvited. She nodded, and he backed his mare. "Why are you out here, and who's baby is this?"

"The baby belongs to the lady you serve," she replied.

"Lord Adam?"

"Yes!" both women cried, then began speaking in fits and starts, interrupting and talking over one another in rising voices.

He held up his hand "Stop! Florian, take them to shelter."

Jacek walked Jarosława to where Radek sat on the ground clutching his left shoulder, Dawid's scimitar at his throat. "You ruined my arm!" Radek snarled. Blood stained his sleeve and hand, and sweat slicked his face.

"And I'll ruin the other one if you don't tell me what I wish to know," Jacek drawled as he dismounted. "What is your mission?"

Radek's eyes darted to the czekan Jacek hefted. Jacek raised his eyebrows expectantly, then began circling him. He prodded his back with the butt end of the war hammer.

"Dawid," Jacek said in a low voice, "straighten his right arm."

Radek jerked his head to the side, his eyes seeking the czekan.

"We were to take the boy to Wąskadroga Castle. For safekeeping," Radek rasped.

"Safekeeping?" Jacek scoffed. "You mean to bend the lady's will, yes?" He rested the axe edge on Radek's right shoulder. The man twitched; now sweat rolled from his forehead.

"I don't know Lord Antonin's plans," Radek blurted. "He only confides in Lieutenant Mazur, the man in charge of his estate troops."

Jacek drew himself up before Radek, the blade still in place. The man seemed to shrink into the dirt. "How many troops?" Jacek asked, his voice calm.

Radek glared at him. Jacek pressed the blade into his shoulder, then stepped on his thigh, digging his spur into the meat below Radek's groin.

"Dawid, have you ever seen what spurs do to a man's flesh?" Jacek asked casually.

Before Dawid could answer, Radek's mouth exploded. "Eighty trained warriors are inside Biaska Castle with Lord Antonin. They were let in a few at a time until the entire garrison was neutralized. Lord Antonin controls Biaska from the *inside*. Them outside are more rabble than army. The estate troops inside are the bigger threat."

Jacek leaned in, rocking his weight to the toe of his boot. "And Lady Oliwia?"

Radek clenched his jaw. "Mmmph. Jesus!" he panted. "He will wed her."

"But he hasn't yet?"

Radek shook his head and began to groan. "That's all I know."

Jacek lifted his foot, and Radek exhaled. Then he slid the axe slowly off Radek's shoulder.

"You shouldn't have taken her child," Jacek said evenly. With scorching speed, he brought the axe blade crashing down on Radek's crown. Radek's caving skull let out a *crack,* followed by a *squish.* A strange sort of mewling sound escaped Radek. Jacek wrenched the axe free and kicked him in the chest, sending him sprawling backward.

After they dragged the bodies out of sight, they made their way to a derelict one-room cottage Florian had appropriated. The women sat at a broken-down table; Adam babbled contentedly in Anka's lap, his bright eyes tracking Jacek. Jacek felt confined in the small space, closed in, and he paced back and forth in snappy strides, pivoting on his heel for turn after turn.

He stopped, pulled a hand through his hair, and pointed at Anka. "Tell me what's been happening within castle walls."

The maid swallowed. "I'm not sure I know, sir. My mistress had us moved into the lord's chamber. As we slept, men came and dragged Wanda, the little lord, and myself away. I did not see my lady. The beasts kept Lord Adam and I hidden in the smithy's until they spirited us away a short while ago."

"Did you recognize the men who seized you?"

"Only one, sir."

Jacek raised an expectant eyebrow. With a stutter, Anka said, "'Twas Kasimir, lord. Wanda let him in, but I do not know what became of her."

Kasimir? Jacek smacked his fist in his palm. *Son of a bitch!*

He urged Anka on.

"Kasimir tried to take Lord Adam, sir, but the child fussed so." She gave Adam a little squeeze and stroked his silky brown hair. "Kasimir said I should go too. He ordered them to bind me in that cloak, then told the men to hurry to Wąskadroga and keep us out of sight until Lord Antonin sent word. I fret for m'lady, sir. She is at the mercy of a blackguard."

"Has Lady Oliwia *any* guards?"

The maid shook her head. "I don't know, lord. Pan Henryk disappeared when the siege began, as did others who watch over m'lady. Kasimir remains, but he's the devil himself! M'lady is all alone."

"What of Filip?" Jacek quelled his growing alarm.

"He was in the chamber beside hers, but I know nothing of him." Tears welled in Anka's eyes. "What will become of them, m'lord?"

"I think I know where Lord Henryk and the others might be," offered Krystiana.

Jacek swiveled his head to her.

"I believe my master had them locked up, at least Lord Henryk. He plans to keep him alive for now, to use him against the lady."

"How the devil did Henryk let himself get captured?" Dawid asked of no one in particular.

"'Twas that scoundrel Kasimir! He tricked him, I'm that sure of it," Anka said tearfully. "Lord Henryk would not have left m'lady's side willingly. They were to be married, you know," she sniffed. Dawid darted a glance at Jacek.

"Yes, I know," Jacek muttered. He turned to Krystiana. "What was Antonin's plan for Adam?"

She looked at him sullenly. "Like what she said about the lady's lover," she nodded at Anka, "to use him against the lady." Jacek bit back the urge to shout that Henryk was *not* the lady's lover.

Krystiana added, "But he only planned to keep the child alive long enough to force her, and then he meant to kill him. No heirs, he says."

Anka gasped and covered Adam's ears. The child gave Jacek a toothy smile as he shook a wooden soldier. He began gnawing on it.

"And why are you telling me this?" Jacek asked Krystiana, watching her closely. He hadn't been surprised by what she said, but that she had said it. He was looking for the trap.

"I am not for kidnapping and killing children."

Jacek grunted.

Krystiana shifted in her seat and raised her gaze to him. "When I accosted you at Wąskadroga Hall, it was because he made me. He … he made me do many things, and I did them because I thought he loved me. He promised to marry me." Tears rimmed her eyes. "But then I learned he's been using me, all these years … he had no plan to wed me, ever." She cast her eyes to her lap and sniffled.

"And now you will betray him?"

Krystiana's face suddenly twisted with anger. The tears spilled freely, as did her spiteful words. "He's taken a fancy to a new servant girl—she's twelve! She doesn't even have tits yet! After all I've done for him, he throws me out for that little slut, and she's not the first. There have been many others, and I've abided them, even while he told *me* he loved *me*. It was all lies! He *laughed* at me when I reminded him of his promises. I would have tolerated his marriage to Lady Oliwia because he planned to kill her after he had control of her holdings, like he did the others. But then he takes that little whore to his bed!" She cried miserably.

Hell hath no fury … Now this makes sense.

"So he plans to wed Lady Oliwia, then kill her?"

Anka gasped again. Krystiana nodded, her bottom lip quivering.

"How do you know all this?" Was Jacek dealing with a rancorous woman, a treacherous one, or an unhinged one?

She sighed and looked at him as though he were an oaf. "I have been his mistress for many years. There is much a man will divulge in bed, especially if he is full of drink." Snuffling, she rubbed her nose, leaving a trail of sticky wetness on the back of her hand. "For instance," she mumbled, "Lord Antonin arranged to be the king's eyes and ears on the western border, but all he fed him were lies about a Swedish army. There was none. He made it up so the king would order the lady to marry him." She mopped her eyes and looked around the room, suddenly panicked. "You're going to kill him, aren't you?"

"I am not yet sure what I'm going to do." *First, I have to get into the damned castle!*

And to do that, he needed more men … and a miracle.

Chapter 32

Passage

Icy fear coiled in Oliwia's gut. Adam was gone. Anka was gone. She tried to convince herself Anka was with him, wherever that was, and that they were well. But then she remembered Wanda's body and shuddered. Kasimir had betrayed them all, and Antonin was helping himself to her castle. Amid her despair, she fought the panic that threatened to seize her and rip her apart, willing herself to keep a clear mind.

Oliwia walked into the kitchen, easing in Beata's presence, even as the sentry who'd accosted her stood guard and leered at her. One of the kitchenmaids sniffled and darted fearful glances at the lout. Oliwia felt heat rising from her toes to her crown, and she gathered the girl to her while Beata watched blearily.

"Why don't we see if Nadia needs your help?" Oliwia soothed, walking the girl upstairs. After checking on fidgety Filip—"I forbid you attacking Antonin's guards," she'd told him when he'd threatened just that—Oliwia descended once more and gazed out a solar window, scratching her nails on the ledge as her mind whirred.

"Ah, there you are, my dear." Antonin crossed the threshold as though he owned the place already. She'd not seen him come in, and she jumped. Clenching her jaw, she turned and braced her hands on the sill. A man lurked behind him, blocking the door.

"I trust you've had a chance to search for your son and anyone else you are concerned about?" Antonin's voice dripped with sarcasm as he slinked toward her, revealing Romek Mazur.

Shudders danced up her spine. Antonin must have noticed, for he laughed and eyed her, saying, "You would do well to heed Lieutenant Mazur, my dear. You *and* your staff. He is my second here, and he suffers no fools."

The lieutenant came into full view. He was a good-sized man, about Henryk's age, with pale blond hair cut short on the sides and long and limp on top. Under a heavily ridged brow were malevolent eyes that sharpened on her with profound hatred. He might have struck some as handsome, but she saw nothing attractive. Rather, he had an unhinged quality about him. Twitching, he cracked his neck and swiveled his head, his gray eyes darting everywhere. She blinked to dislodge the image of a glossy black tongue flicking from his tightly pressed lips. Time had not improved the look of her would-be-kidnapper from Vyatov.

Antonin was dressed in mail sleeves and skirt. His leather vambraces were well-worn, as was his brown belt that bristled with blades. His divoted face and oily hair were well-worn too, both lanky and gray. His beard was unkempt, and he wore a dingy, smug smile. Oliwia drew herself up regally, thrusting her chin at him.

"What do you want, Antonin?"

"My, but that haughty look you affect so well excites me," he sniggered. He spread his hands wide, as if in appeasement. "I have come to tell you the details of our wedding tomorrow, my dear."

"I have not agreed to a wedding."

He rolled his eyes extravagantly. "Oh, my dear, do you not yet understand? No, of course not—you're just a helpless, feeble-minded thing," he tsked. "Let me explain, and I will say the words slowly so you can follow along. I hold your only child. I hold your sweetheart. *You* hold their futures. Now, to show how eager I am to please you, I allow you the choice of time. Would you prefer a midday wedding or an evening affair?"

"Father Augustyn cannot perform a wedding on such short notice," she retorted.

He pursed his lips and scratched his chin. She was certain she saw something crawling in his whiskers. "Ah. The priest. Yes, well, you see, he said the same thing, so I called for my own priest. He will arrive in time for the ceremony tomorrow."

"Where is Father Augustyn?" she cried, looking from Antonin to Romek and back again.

"I had no use for him, so Romek sent him to his reward," Antonin shrugged.

Dear God, no! Blood drained from her face, and her heart squeezed when she thought of the kindly, dough-faced priest.

Antonin held up a finger. "Oh. And should you do aught but cooperate, the same fate will befall your loved ones. Where have you hidden your brother?"

Oliwia caught her breath, her heart hammering with fear. "If I am to agree," she stammered, "I want to see Adam and Henryk. I want to know they're alive."

With a snort, he said, "I anticipated as much. Romek? Indulge the lady."

Romek pulled out a wad of linen half the size of her hand and as big around as a staff. He placed it in her hand.

Antonin grinned wolfishly. "Open it. It's a gift."

As she unwound the strip of cloth, each layer grew more saturated with a red-brown stain. When she at last pulled the bundle apart, she stared, her mind rejecting what she saw. With a gasp, she flung a severed finger from her hold. A ring encircled it, and when the digit hit the floor, it landed with a small, sickening *thwack* and the sound of metal clinking stone. She squeezed her eyes shut and covered her mouth to hold back the vomit propelling itself upward.

"Oh, you dropped it," Antonin said, as though she'd spilled her pudding. He picked up the finger, carefully threaded it through the ring, and thrust it at her. He spoke about the color of the skin and blood, how fresh it was, telling her Romek had only just removed it from Henryk's left hand.

"And the ring. Do you see it?" He beamed.

She did see it. A gold ring with a blood-red garnet, identical to one Henryk always wore. A loud buzzing reverberated in her head, as though angry bees swarmed between her ears, and she was sucking in air. *The knife.*

"Romek selected this one, you see," he prattled on, "because it is your former lover's ring finger, and he no longer needs it, does he? But perhaps you'd care to keep it as a memento?" he mocked as Romek looked on, stony and still.

"You're the devil's spawn," she hissed.

Antonin wagged his head. "I'm really quite pleasant when you get to know me. And tomorrow, you will have your chance. Now if you remain

342

obstinate, I will gladly add another finger to this one so you may begin a collection. Perhaps your son's pudgy toe would cheer you. Oh, wait." He handed Romek the finger and fumbled in his żupan.

Aghast, Oliwia drew in another sharp breath, shaking her head. "No!" she shouted.

"Ah! Here it is." Antonin extracted a small paper packet and held it out to her. "I thought you might like something of your baby's."

She staggered backward and caught herself on the window ledge. Antonin had begun unfolding the paper. She braced herself. He stepped to her and grabbed her hand roughly, shoving something soft into it.

"There now," he crooned. "What mother doesn't want a lock of her baby's hair?"

She dared a glimpse at her open palm, and let out an enormous breath, for her hand held a fine, dark brown curl. Trembling now, tears sprang to her eyes. She crumpled against the ledge; it was all that held her up. The two men began laughing riotously. Antonin couldn't speak for laughing so hard, and tears ran down his cheeks.

"Oh, my dear," he gasped, "the look on your face!" And they set to howling again.

He straightened at last, mopping his tears, and said in a voice that sounded like two stones grinding against each other, "The wedding is when the sun is at its highest tomorrow, and I will have your full cooperation. My priest will see a woman ready to marry, not one coerced. Do you understand?"

Numbly, she nodded, her cheeks wet. A dreadful ache welled in her, fracturing her heart. She yearned to cuddle her small son, to be far away from this wickedness.

Antonin withdrew, and as he did so, he flashed a lecherous smile. "I expect a grand feast afterward, for I will need all my strength for what I expect will be a very long, very gratifying wedding night. Prepare yourself, and get your lazy cooks busy." She crouched and slid her hand to her boot, her outstretched fingers not quite reaching it.

"Search her," Antonin snapped at Romek before banging the door shut behind him.

She straightened as Romek came toward her, cracking his knuckles, one side of his mouth curved in a sneer. She recoiled. To her horror, he dropped to his knees, startling her more than his monstrous presence

343

already did. Quickly and expertly, he loosened the laces on one side of her boot and slipped the knife out. "Thought so," he said quietly, tucking it in his belt.

Her only remaining defense was her guile, which in that moment was in tatters.

So predictable. After extracting the knife, Romek took his time undoing the rest of the boot. His pulse raced as he worked it slowly, stroking the smooth leather as he went. She flinched as he ran his hands over the shoe, obviously discomfited, and it made the spark in him flare a little higher.

"Has anyone told you how your husband died?" he asked, not bothering to wait for her answer. "He was a sniveler to the end, crying for his worthless life before I put him out of his misery."

He heard her gasp and stiffen, and that fed the spark too. He would have to check himself—it was too soon.

She drew in a sharp breath. "You're the one who killed him?"

Romek put aside an image of Eryk's flashing brown eyes, defiant and hate-filled. When he'd taken his life, Eryk did cry out, but he cried his wife's and son's names in agony before loosing a raging curse at Romek. But this bitch would never know.

"Some of my finest work, your late husband," he went on as he slowly caressed the other boot. "I caught him right after he'd spent the morning rutting his other whore." He raised his eyes to hers and was disappointed to see a blank look. He wanted pain, shock, so he continued. "He enjoyed her immensely, I daresay. It's her he whined for when I sawed off his balls."

When he looked up this time, he was rewarded by the sight of her holding back a heave.

He smiled.

Maławieża was a stone fortress smaller than Biaska Castle and shaped altogether differently. Like Biaska, it rose from a limestone formation and perched on high ground. One large, round turret emerged from a formidable wall of stacked stone, giving the castle its title as a watchtower. But Jacek had no interest in what soared above—he only cared about what lay below. Time was slipping away, and he sent Dawid to the village to find help while he guided the rest of their party back to Maławieża.

Right now, Jacek followed the old man dubiously as he led them from one dungeon to another. The cellar had been searched but revealed nothing. As Jacek's impatience grew, he began to suspect he was being led on a merry chase for one old man's amusement. Weaving through the dark, dank corridors, Jacek ignored the reek of urine and decay and the sounds of dripping water and rats scrabbling over stone. The flickering torches' light seemed to be swallowed up in the gloom, and he stayed close to the others should one be left behind in the labyrinth winding below Maławieża.

They'd been at it for hours. By his stomach's grumbling, Jacek reckoned the sun was just past its zenith. As he considered calling off the foolish plan and climbing out of the stinking, murky depths, the old man let out a whoop. He stood in a hollowed-out chamber with a heavy door that hung drunkenly by one rusted barrel bolt, peering at a pile of stones on the floor.

"There!" he pointed cheerfully.

"Where?" asked Jacek.

"Right here." The old man rested a foot on the stones.

"The latrine?"

"That's no latrine," the man scoffed. "They *had* no latrines. Just pissed where they lay, shackled to the walls. This is the entrance to the tunnel."

Jacek looked at him skeptically. "This pile of rocks?"

"Put your ox's brain to rest and your ox's back to work pulling them out, and you'll see," the old man said with a twinkle. Jacek didn't know whether to leave him there or throttle him.

But he proved right. When they cleared the pile away, they squeezed through an opening to a chamber below piled with rubble. At first, Jacek thought it a pit, but after squeezing around the pile, they stepped into a large chamber almost high enough for Jacek to stand without hitting his head. Spreading his arms, he could just press his fingertips to the walls. The chamber stretched into unending darkness, clogged with stones or fallen blocks in places, but not such that they could not pass. So they ventured about a hundred paces, leaving the Maławieża folk behind. Jacek was buoyed, and he and his men ventured another hundred paces—and hit a heap of rock blocking the passage.

They returned to the surface, and Jacek dragged in fresh air, trying to expel the stench in his nose. More curious Maławieża folk had gathered and now stood about expectantly.

"We encountered a rockslide," he said stridently. "Who here will help us dig it out?"

No one answered. They coughed or mumbled or shifted their weight foot to foot.

"No one?" he asked, astonished.

"The White Lady." The caretaker crossed himself. "We will bring you shovels, picks, and torches, but I for one will not set foot back in that tunnel."

"Did you *see* the White Lady?" Jacek snapped, exasperated.

"No, but she's down there, lord, with a witch no less. 'Tis an evil place. I felt the devil tapping my shoulder." He made the sign of the devil's horns and crossed himself again.

Jacek suppressed a roll of his eyes. After arguing fruitlessly for another precious five minutes, he threw up his hands and tromped to the stableyard, where he mounted up. He would find men willing to dig and men willing to fight. Meanwhile, Marcin and Florian headed back to the tunnel to pull down the rubble wall. It was a pathetic plan, but it was the only plan, and they were agreed.

I need a miracle.

As he made his way through the fortress gate, he saw movement in the distance and stopped in his tracks. Emerging from the trees to the southwest came a large party of armed soldiers yet several furlongs distant, heading straight for Maławieża.

Merciful God! We have been discovered.

Oliwia tore from the solar, the sound of Romek's dark chuckle behind her. Searching under her skirts, in her bodice, up her sleeves, he'd ignored her humiliated protests and manhandled her as he went, chattering of unspeakable deeds. He'd dug his grubby hands into her flesh until she'd cried out; she was no doubt covered in bruises and welts. He made her skin crawl. It was only when Kasimir entered that Romek had stopped his sadistic groping. Rounding into the great hall, she spotted guards—not hers—posted at the main doors. Though bootless, she strode brazenly toward them as though to exit, and they crossed lances, hindering her.

"I am the lady here. I wish to visit the stables," she declared.

A burly guard looked at her. "No one leaves, and no one enters without Lord Antonin's accord, my lady. He has given strict orders for you to remain in the keep."

"You should know, my dear," came Antonin's sickly sweet voice from behind her, "that they also have orders to lock you up if you try."

She whirled to see his unctuous smile. He gave her a head dip. She ran to her quarters, getting as far from him as she could. When she reached her sitting room, she banged the door shut and slammed down the bar. Nadia jumped up. So did Filip.

"Liwi! I would speak with you," Filip said.

Oliwia leaned against the secured door, a stitch in her side, as she caught her breath. "Has either of you seen Adam or Anka?" Lamentably, but not surprisingly, they had not. "Nadia, fetch me a pair of shoes. Filip, where have you been hiding?"

Ignoring her, he raced on excitedly. "I think they have Pan Henryk in the old dungeons."

She blinked. "What makes you say that?"

A broad grin split his face. "Have you ever been down there, Liwi?"

"No. Are they not walled off?" Oliwia looked at Nadia, who had just come in with the shoes, little more substantial than slippers.

Filip's eyes lit up. "They are. At least the entrance you know of. But there's another way in, through an old cellar storeroom. One of the other boys showed it to me. The kitchen sentry guards neither the kitchen nor the cellars—he guards the dungeon! I know because he thought I was a servant, and I snuck past him. From the cellar, I stole into the connecting corridor, and I heard voices!"

Details of Filip's foray into the bowels of Biaska spilled from him in an animated, hurried flurry of words. Nadia's pebble eyes had grown to the size of river stones.

Oliwia plopped into a chair and pulled on the shoes. "Who else knows this way in?"

"Many of the old guards. Like Kasimir," Filip said triumphantly.

She grabbed Filip's hand. "Could you make out the voices? Are they our men?"

"I don't know, but somebody's down there."

A flare of hope dispelled some of her despair, and she tapped her finger against her cheek as her mind began to whir.

"Filip, do you think you can get back in there?" When he bobbed his head, she rushed on. "First, I will need you to deliver a message to Beata. I've a plan."

Jacek pulled out the spyglass and surveyed the oncoming soldiers, then he sprang Jarosława forward and headed for them. Reining in his mare, he awaited the vanguard. Three men rode forward.

He greeted Dawid with a nod before turning his eyes on the other two. "Benas, you will have to tell me the secret of your swift travels. Pan Klemens, my God, you are a welcome sight!"

Tears streaming down his face, Klemens said nothing. He just drew close and threw his arms around Jacek in a fierce embrace, pounded his back, and kissed his cheeks.

"All this time, Pan Jacek, we thought you lost," Klemens choked out between tears and laughter. He wiped his eyes. Jacek found himself dabbing at his own.

"I met him heading this way, Captain!" Benas grinned. "And look who he has brought!"

"Kapitana Kamen-Holova!" came a shout.

"Sweet Jesus! Is that Ataman Ivan Humansky?" Jacek shaded his eyes and peered into the group of soldiers.

The Cossack leader from the Wild Fields rode forward, his solo hank of hair hanging from beneath his cap. He grasped Jacek's forearm and pulled him close, pounding his back, belting out a laugh.

"You need help, Kapitana, and we are ready for a fight. Life has been boring on the steppe."

Jacek pounded him right back. "You are a long way from home, Ataman, and I thank God for it!"

"There are more, Captain, mobilizing the camp with Lesław," Dawid added.

"What brings you to this outpost?" Jacek looked from Humansky to Klemens.

"I learned Biaska's garrison was depleted when Lady Krezowska called for Silnyród reinforcements." Klemens cuffed his nose. "Pan Lesław had just departed with the Scots when I received your letter from Genoa. Spirit of God! After I got up off the floor from my shock, I decided it was time to travel—to see an old friend, and to see how best to help the lady. I owe you at least that much." Jacek knew he spoke of Eugenia.

Jacek clasped Klemens's beefy shoulder. "Your daughter found a good man, and I am pleased for you all."

Klemens gave a quick nod and cleared his throat. "This whoreson you fight may not be a Tatar, but he's just as bad. Possibly worse. Our own countryman! We're spoiling for the fight!"

Jacek scanned the men behind Klemens. "How many are with you?"

"With the Ataman's men, we are one hundred, plus a score of hussars. Enough to make those devils run!"

We are one hundred and forty-five. Not enough to overpower them and get inside.

"The whoreson is inside the castle walls and holds the lady hostage, so we must tread carefully. We managed to recover her son, though she does not know it. Before we can attack, we have to get her out."

"How do we get this lady out?" asked Humansky.

"Through a tunnel we've yet to clear." Jacek withheld the ghost story.

With a jolly gleam in his eyes, Klemens said, "And so we dig. Lead on."

Jacek's spirits rose a few rungs as he led them inside Małowieża's walls. The tunnel could only hold so many, but Klemens's men and Humansky's Cossacks bustled like determined ants in their colonies. The *chink-chink-chink* of their tools against stone became a sweet melody in Jacek's ears. They sang, they laughed, they insulted one another. He took in the energy like lightning crackling and popping in his bloodstream. He was charged, excited. At long last, he felt as though they were getting somewhere.

And they did get somewhere, for they dismantled the piled rock, only to go another fifty paces and run into another obstruction. They worked diligently, cautiously, for timbers had been crushed in the rock fall, and the ceiling was so low here that Jacek could only walk in a crouch. He left men far more accomplished in the art of tunneling to calculate how best to dislodge the stone and returned above ground to gather a war council. Lesław and Pawel had arrived; the new camp was being set up halfway between the two fortresses, secreted in Biaska's thick woods.

"I have scouts and sentries in place," said Lesław, "and so far we've encountered no patrols. Lord Antonin is overconfident."

"Because he holds all the advantages." Jacek paced in the open air of the courtyard. "When we make our way in, we will use stealth and surprise to nullify Antonin's estate troops. And neutralize them we must. They're the best of the lot, and they're inside that castle." He paused. So much depended on their breaking through the tunnel, of the tunnel being what he prayed it was. Everything hung on that one thin hope.

A few village women had set up tables of food and drink in the watchtower's courtyard for the men, but Jacek's appetite had long ago fled. The day was warm and clear, and the late afternoon sun gilded leaves and grasses in golden light. Daylight was dwindling; twilight would close in fast.

He pivoted at the end of a track he'd worn in the dirt. "Should we find no way in …" And on he went, outlining a strategy he himself could not yet accept, for it surely meant Oliwia's and Filip's deaths.

"Captain Dąbrowski!"

Jacek looked up to see one of Klemens's men running at him. A small crowd gathered round, hindering him.

"Let that man pass! Get him a drink!" With Dawid and Marcin flanking him, Jacek strode briskly toward him.

"We did it, sir!" The soldier was hauling in breath. He turned and pointed to where he'd just emerged; a Cossack escorted a scruffy soldier. The soldier looked as though he might expire at any moment, dropping to his knees, gasping. The women sprang toward him.

"Who's that?" asked Jacek, bewildered.

"One of our garrison, Captain!" shouted Marcin.

Jacek walked over to the man, who sat on his heels, choking down water and air. "Where did this man come from?"

"The lady," the man wheezed as he looked up at Jacek. "Lady Oliwia set us free."

Chapter 33

The Darkest Hour

Relief and confusion flooded Jacek in alternating waves. "The lady lives?" His throat had clogged, and his question came out in a choke he masked with a cough.

The raggedy man nodded. "She must, m'lord. This was her doing."

"We found the garrison—over a score!—locked up just as Lady Oliwia's servants were trying to free them," Klemens's man said. "We're bringing them up as we speak, but it may take a while yet. Some are in bad shape."

Jacek's brows furrowed.

The Biaska soldier tried to stand, wobbled, and dropped to the ground on his backside, looking altogether like a defiant, listing sack of grain. "We're thirsty and hungry," he croaked, "but madder than blazes and eager to cut those bastards down."

The Cossack who had escorted the soldier above ground went on to explain they had broken through the tunnel, and that he'd been the first to wriggle through the aperture, finding himself in a cell. He'd crept through a maze of fusty dungeons, where he'd discovered the prisoners behind a heavy door in a single cell. He'd advanced to a larger chamber he reckoned was the guards' station, for it held chairs and a table littered with cards, wine bottles, and cups, but no guards. Puzzled, he'd inched closer and found four guards sprawled on the floor by the table, unconscious, two small figures rifling their persons.

"'Twas a kitchenmaid and a boy—said he was the lady's brother and that the cook had brought down a concoction—poppy seed tea mixed with wine, I believe. Anyway, the boy said the Lady of Biaska had ordered the potion, for she meant to free her guard. It did its work and sent them to sleep like babies. The two panicked when they heard something above, and I told them I would finish the job, so they scrambled upstairs. I found the keys, dragged the guards to a nearby cell, slit their gullets, then unlocked the prisoners. We should have them all out before the changing of the prison guards," he said as a few more bedraggled men appeared in the courtyard. Hailing them, Marcin ran their way.

"So the lady's brother knows help is on the way?" Jacek asked the soldier hurriedly.

"I can only assume, sir, for I told him there was a force gathered here, and that we'd just opened up a tunnel. There was little time for details."

Jacek's frown deepened. His eyes darted to the growing ranks of disheveled men, looking them over in the gathering dark as they were fed and watered by the women and interrogated by Marcin. Though he recognized none of them, his heart was gathering speed.

"Captain, shall I ask after Pan Henryk?" Dawid asked quietly.

Jacek snorted. "I hope he lives," he muttered. "First, I will shove his head through a palisade, then I shall skewer him with one of the posts."

Dawid's eyes went round. "Surely you don't intend ... We need Pan Henryk. Besides, he didn't know—"

And then there he was. Pan Henryk himself.

"What is it?" Antonin said tersely when Romek entered the solar.

Romek smirked. "You look rather comfortable in that chair."

"It fits me well," agreed Antonin. "Now what do you want? I have a serving maid I wish to get better acquainted with. Lovely little creatures here at Biaska. Such treasures, each and every one."

"The men are restless for worrying there will be nothing left to pillage once the estate troops have had at it."

Antonin slapped his hand on the desk. "These are *your* men, Romek. You should demonstrate better control over them."

"They have not been paid in—"

Antonin rolled his eyes. "Yes, yes, I know. You do nothing but vomit the same rubbish daily, and I'm tired of the endless whining—theirs *and* yours."

A cold fire rose to Romek's crown.

"Tell me, Antonin," he said harshly. "Who put you here, where you now sit?"

Antonin snapped his head up and narrowed his eyes. Romek had never called him by his first name before.

"I put myself here, and you would do well to remember it," Antonin retorted.

Romek brought his hand down savagely on the tabletop, making Antonin jump. "You would not be sitting here right now, thinking with your cock instead of your head, if I hadn't found, trained, and convinced all those men what a great and generous lord you are and how worthwhile their time serving you would be. I've paid them out of my own pocket, and now *I've* nothing left."

"That's not my concern," Antonin sniffed. "And maybe *you* should try thinking with your cock for a change. Might take some of the vinegar out of you. But I forget. You don't care for women."

Romek clenched his fists.

Antonin rubbed his finger over his chin and regarded Romek. "Everyone has vices, so tell me, Romek, what are yours? Girls? Boys? Goats? Did you hump your own sister while she lived? Your mother, perhaps. I've yet to figure you out. Perhaps it's men you prefer?"

Fuming, Romek stood stock-still and scowled at Antonin. Antonin erupted in a laugh and clapped his hands, then pointed his finger at him. "That's it, isn't it? You're a filthy sodomite who buggers his own men."

Romek gritted his teeth. "How I ever deluded myself that following you was a sound choice is inexplicable."

Antonin aimed his thumb at his own chest. "Because you fancied me, is that it? Did you really think me keen on such depravity? With *you*? Oh my God, you are indisputably repulsive! You wallow in the dung heap of humanity!"

Then he laughed. And laughed. And laughed so hard he could scarcely catch his breath. Romek saw him for what he truly was in that moment, and he despised him for it.

What a fool I've been, putting my faith in this lewd, arrogant whoreson who fell out of Satan's ass!

"You've no intention of giving me back my estate, do you?"

Antonin gave him a hard look. "You have been a good lieutenant, Romek, a good lapdog, so I will forgive your insolence, but only this once. I have told you, repeatedly, that I will divide up the spoils once I've secured Biaska. Now get the hell out of here before I have you taken out and flogged."

As Romek let himself out of the solar, he heard Antonin mutter, "Sodomite."

Oliwia paced the width of her chamber, her skirts rustling about her as she walked to and fro. The constant swishing mirrored what coursed through her. The chamber door opened a crack, and the sound of raucous laughter drifted in with Nadia's slight form as she balanced a tray of food in her arms. She darted in and set the tray down.

"You must eat, m'lady, and keep your strength up."

"And you must hide, Nadia. Besides, I am not hungry." Oliwia's stomach was bunched in knots, and anything she took in would simply come right back up again. "It sounds as if Antonin's men are about to enjoy the meal Beata has prepared for them," she added.

"Yes, m'lady, and the best mead from our cellars," the girl replied with an edge to her voice.

"Have you seen Filip?"

Nadia shook her head. "Not yet, m'lady, but Beata pledged she will let nothing befall the young master."

Oliwia drew in a long breath and let it out slowly as she wrung her hands. *Dear God, let this plan work.* Her timing was off, but opportunity was everything, and she'd taken it when she could. Now she prayed the garrison would be freed and storm the great hall when Antonin's troops were well in their cups. She continually turned over two discomfiting thoughts: Would Biaska's soldiers be capable of fighting, and what weapons could they use? There were only so many knives to be had in the kitchens. With a jolt, she sent a prayer heavenward that she was not sending men to their slaughter.

A knock sounded at the door, and both women exchanged furtive glances.

"Liwi! It's me. Open up!"

Nadia quickly unbarred the door and Filip slipped in, nadziak in hand. Oliwia's eyes widened.

"Filip! Where did you get that? I thought they had taken everything."

Filip grinned. "I hid it in the canopy above my bed. But that doesn't matter—"

"Did it work? Did you get them out?"

"I don't know. That is, the potion worked, but a soldier was there, said he'd just come through a tunnel in the dungeons from Maławieża, and he says there's a force gathering there to help us," he said excitedly.

"What?" Oliwia exclaimed.

"We had to get out, but the soldier said he'd free the garrison. Then they'll come for us."

Dumbfounded, Oliwia looked at Nadia to make sure she wasn't dreaming, then sat down hard, trying to quell the laughter about to erupt from her. "They must be Lesław's men come at last. We need only wait here until we are freed."

Just then, loud pummeling rattled her chamber door, startling all three.

"Lady Oliwia! Unbar your door!" Antonin bellowed.

Hope fled as she realized far more faced them than waiting for rescue.

Jacek watched Henryk stumble into the courtyard, his left hand held to his chest. It was wrapped in a bloodied shirt. A tangle of emotions snaked through Jacek all at once. Happy to see his friend lived, he nonetheless wanted to pull his throat from him.

"Ah, here staggers my oldest, dearest friend. Marcin! Have we a cup of something for the valiant captain of the Biaska garrison?" Jacek said mirthlessly.

Henryk reeled, shaking his head as though casting something off. He looked dazed, stupefied as he stared at Jacek.

"Jacek!" a voice boomed. That voice belonged to Stefan, who stood in a cluster of garrison soldiers being tended. He hobbled toward Jacek. "Is it truly you? Saints be praised! I never thought to see you again!"

Stefan embraced him with an iron grip. "How are you not dead?"

"'Tis a long story, and one I promise to tell. Right now, we've more urgent matters."

Stefan looked him over, and tears welled in his eyes. "My God, this is nothing short of a miracle! You have no idea how overjoyed I am to see you. Welcome home." He thumped him soundly on the back.

"Jacek?"

Jacek turned his gaze to Henryk. "You do not look upon a ghost, Henryk. It is indeed I, returned from the dead."

"But how? I buried you myself! Where the hell have you been?"

Ignoring the question, Jacek jerked his chin to Henryk's hand. "What happened to you?"

"I lost a finger to that son of a bitch Romek. Remember him? He's here." Henryk returned to gawking at Jacek.

While the men ate, Jacek told them what he knew of the siege and the plan to recover Biaska. They hammered him with incessant questions about his capture and escape, so he filled them in with scant details. Henryk watched him—sullenly, he thought—the entire time.

"I wrote letters, but it seems only Pan Matejko received one." Jacek shot daggers at Henryk.

An old healer fussed over Henryk's wound, muttering her hope he would not suffer fevers. "Nasty places, dungeons," she said, tying off his bandage. He winced.

Torchlight danced in the courtyard as Jacek climbed the ramparts and looked toward Biaska, but he saw nothing through the deeply shadowed vegetation. As he clambered down, he felt Henryk's eyes on him, and he gave him a quick nod.

"Henryk, walk with me."

"Can it wait? I'm still famished."

Jacek snatched up an earthen jug of piwo and a loaf of bread. He tossed the bread to Henryk and kept the drink, then led him to a quiet corner

357

behind the stables. Jacek pivoted, and Henryk sidestepped. Setting the jug down, Jacek leveled his eyes at Henryk.

"You were to wed Oliwia. Did you touch her?"

His mouth full of bread, Henryk stopped chewing and glowered, dropping his head as though he might charge.

Jacek's eyes sharpened, and he asked the question again, growling this time. "Did you touch her?"

"What do you think?"

"I think you're a brigand and a scoundrel, and that you touched her and then some."

Henryk laughed derisively. "Stop being so sanctimonious, Jacek. You somehow overlooked telling her—or me—that *you* were to wed someone else. You played both ends of the practice field."

Jacek felt as though he'd been slapped, and he flinched.

"That doesn't concern you," he said truculently.

"But it concerns *her,* and what concerns her, concerns me," Henryk threw back.

"A fine job you've done taking care of her concerns! This," Jacek waved about himself, "happened on *your* watch!" He felt control slipping from him like water through his fingers.

Henryk pinned him with a threatening glare. "You, my friend, *were dead!* I was the one who had the misfortune of telling her. I bore her wails and her tears, and it fell to me to care for her."

"By putting your filthy hands—and God knows what else—on her? And now she's captive in her own castle at the whims of that despicable piece of sheep dung!" Jacek barked, then heaved in two great breaths. He *knew* he should have thrashed Henryk long ago.

"Did you expect everyone to carry on as if you were going to come back from the grave I myself placed you in?" Henryk retorted. "She was supposed to remarry—*you* insisted upon it. Just listen to yourself!"

Jacek bristled, and his brows knotted together as he lowered his own head. "I never expected her to marry *you*! It didn't take you long, did it?"

Henryk scoffed. "You weren't here, so I did what I thought best. For *her* sake."

"To hell with you!" Jacek yelled.

"No, *back* to hell with *you!*"

Jacek threw the first punch, which Henryk deflected with his forearm, though the effort didn't keep him upright. He thudded to the ground, cursing as he held his injured hand to his chest.

"Jesus Christ, you mare's ass! You can't even fight fair," Henryk spat.

Then he threw himself at Jacek's legs and hauled him down. They grappled and grunted and scrabbled and cursed, rolled in the dirt, thumped, pummeled, thrashed, grabbed, and swung at each other. Jacek was dimly aware stable hands and servants had gathered round and picked sides. He thought he heard wagers being made. He definitely heard cheers and jeers. Then he heard the boom of Lesław's voice.

"What the devil are you doing, scrapping like children over a toy?" Lesław kicked them both, then pulled Henryk off Jacek. They sat on the ground, huffing, sputtering, panting, while Jacek glared at Henryk and he glared right back.

"You split my lip, you bastard!" Henryk prodded said puffy lip.

Jacek wiped blood and dirt from his knuckles. "You earned it, goat turd."

Lesław stood between them, looking from one to the other.

Henryk glanced up at Lesław and casually said, "We're fighting over a woman."

Lesław's expression transformed to one of alarm.

Jacek finally caught his breath and looked at Henryk. "Your finger hurt much?"

Henryk's chest was still heaving. "I don't have a finger, you stupid son of a bitch, and yes, it hurts like hell!"

"Good!" In a milder voice, Jacek asked, "Do you love her?"

Henryk shrugged.

"Does she love you?"

Henryk shrugged again.

"She promised to wed *me*," Jacek groused.

"And you were already engaged to marry someone else!" Henryk said hotly. "Moreover, we both thought you dead. One does not uphold a promise to a corpse."

Lesław frowned, looking utterly befuddled.

The crowd dispersed. Some argued as they walked away. "Neither one won, you imbecile! I owe you nothing!" Or, "The big blond one was clearly the winner. Now pay up!" And then, "The dark-haired one landed more blows, so he won the bout. Both of you pay up!" And on it went.

"Are we done here?" Lesław asked. "We still have a real enemy to battle."

Jacek lurched to his feet and held out a hand to Henryk. Henryk warily accepted, and Jacek hauled him up.

"You fought well," said Jacek, "for a cripple."

Henryk shook his head and smirked. "At least it's not my head that's crippled. You never could keep a sane thought when it came to her, and clearly death has changed nothing." Then he thumped Jacek on the back, a little too hard. "Christ, it's good to see you!"

Jacek grabbed Henryk's nape and banged their heads together. "I'm glad you live."

"Kasimir is mine," growled Henryk. "So's Romek."

"And Antonin is mine. Now let's recover Oliwia. Why'd they hack off your finger anyway?"

The pounding continued, growing louder. "*Oliwia!* Open this door! I know you're in there!" Antonin boomed as he battered the door.

"My lady is occupied, m'lord. She will see you on the morrow," Nadia called in a quavering voice.

An impact juddered the door, shaking it in its frame. A great splintering noise followed. Then came another blow.

"She will admit me *now*, or I will have this door hacked down. Do you hear me?"

"Filip! Go! Go!" ordered Oliwia, pointing her finger at the private corridor. She let out a relieved breath when, without protest, he scurried through the doorway, bringing the overly large war hammer with him, and slid the bar in place behind him. The chopping resumed.

"A moment, my lord," Oliwia called between blows, her pulse racing.

She gathered her skirts, dropped into an armchair in front of the fire, and picked up her sewing. Her hands trembled, and her breaths came rapidly. *Breathe!* Inhaling deeply, she nodded to Nadia. The maid slowly raised the bar, and before she had finished, the door banged open with such force that it flung her against the wall. Oliwia stood abruptly to confront a seething, intoxicated bull.

Breathe!

"There you are! I expected you beside me at dinner. What the devil are you doing up here?" He dismissed the axe-wielding servants with a curt order.

Oliwia cleared her dry throat. "I did not realize I was to dine with you. I have no appetite."

His beady eyes darted to the still-full tray on the table.

"I don't give a damn if you're hungry or not. You *will* eat with me." Then his voice took on an eerie, singsong quality. "It's our engagement feast."

Fluid as quicksilver, his tone changed to a roar. "And for God's sake, get out of that drab gown and put on something gay, something that shows your bosom. It's a celebration, woman!"

He stomped to one of her trunks, and as he rifled through the garments, she exchanged a quick glance with Nadia. Oliwia thought the maid shook.

"Here!" He yanked out a gown and tossed it across the bed. "And I want your hair down!" He stood, his arms folded across his chest, his toe tapping the thick carpet with an impotent swishing sound. From below floors, the rising racket caused Oliwia's heart to sink. She doubted the laced mead was having its effect, for where she expected quiet merrymaking as men dropped off, the revelry was riotous, debauched. A shrill scream punctured the air, followed by explosive laughter. Oliwia ran her hands up her arms; she was chilled even though she stood an arm's length from the fire. This monster had Adam. What choice did she have but to play along until rescue came?

"May I have some privacy so my maid can help me dress?"

"I give you five minutes, or I'll rip the damned gown off myself and drag you downstairs naked!" He snapped his fingers, then marched into her sitting room. She couldn't decide which Antonin was worse: the oily one or the fulminating one.

Oliwia splashed her face with bracing water. Nadia helped her into the gown Antonin had selected—a low-cut burgundy velvet bodice with an overskirt trimmed in gold braid. Oliwia arranged a lace collar over her décolletage. Her hair was loosely brushed back, and she wore no jewelry save her cross, which she slid back and forth along its chain before tucking it away.

Without so much as a knock, Antonin stormed back into her chamber. He ogled her chest but said nothing. Instead, he astonished her by yanking down a velvet cord that held a bed curtain in place, tying a loop knot on one end and threading the cord through. He inspected his work and, seeming quite satisfied, dropped the assembly over her head before she realized what he'd done. As she started to protest, he tightened it around her neck and cut off her air. Nadia gasped. Antonin looked at Oliwia and smiled as he held the cord taut. She clawed at the binding but got no purchase, and she was soon on her knees.

"Good wives," he said in that spine-chilling voice, "like good dogs, heel to their masters. You will learn to obey me. You are a woman, so your stupidity is excusable, but I expect you've enough sense to comprehend what I am telling you, yes?" She nodded, light-headed. He nodded back deliberately. "Good. Now show me what a good girl you are and take that blasted collar off." She scrabbled at the collar and tore it away; he slackened the line. Coughing, gasping, she grabbed at her throat as she drew in sweet air.

Still holding the cord, he looked her over, amusement on his face. "That's much improved. A splendid bosom like yours should be flaunted proudly."

She stood and began loosening the cord, but he stopped her with a wagging finger. "No, no. For your defiance, the rope remains in place."

Her eyes widened. "You mean to lead me about on a leash?"

"Yes, just like any other slave. Or bitch." Hardness glinted in his eyes. "I advise you to remember who holds the end of it and do as you're told. Come now." He laughed as he tugged on it. "I've worked up quite a thirst and am anxious to show off my prize."

Sucking in a deep breath, she followed him into the passageway, staying close to slacken the restraint. Her cheeks burned with humiliation. When would the force from Małavieża come?

What if they do not come?

Her cheeks flared hotter, anger overcoming her shame.

Then I will kill him myself.

Chapter 34

Rage of Achilles

The moon had risen, though it cast no light. Jacek had been contemplating running through the tunnel into Biaska's belly, finding Oliwia, slinging her over his shoulder, and dashing out to safety. But that was his heart talking. His far more rational head told him even if he could get to her without endangering her, she would never leave without Filip, Nadia, Beata, and every other person in the keep, so he pounded down the impulse. If he *could* rescue her, who would she run to given the choice—him or Henryk? If Henryk knew about Eugenia, certainly Oliwia did. Jacek's duplicity, no matter the good intention that had spawned it, had come home to roost, and the thought leveled him. So he rammed it deep down the same dark hole as the impulse.

Now he occupied himself with what he knew best. He prepared for battle. Marcin had returned his armor and now helped him into it. Despite cinching the buckles, it hung a bit loosely. Still, it felt good.

The guard room at Maławieża doubled as their war room. He stood before a crowd of men pressed shoulder to shoulder. Klemens, clearly superior in rank, deferred to him, as did everyone else. This campaign was now his to command.

"Take us through it one more time, Pan Jacek," Klemens urged.

"The enemy has two forces: the larger, the one encamped outside castle walls, is three hundred strong. The smaller, roughly one hundred, is stationed inside. Though they're one-third the size, they are Antonin's estate troops and will be the hardest to fight. They're trained, disciplined.

As long as they remain there, they have the advantage. They can attack from the small spaces, take cover, hide. We must draw them into the great hall or outside.

"We will assume the drawbridge is down and all gates are open, meaning either force can come to the aid of the other. We must cut them off, keep them apart. Pan Lesław and Pan Matejko will have one hundred and twenty in the trees, ready to strike the encampment on my signal."

He paused and took a sip of piwo. Not one man moved.

"Pan Henryk and I will lead fifty through the tunnel. That force goes first. Once inside, we nullify Antonin's guard and secure the keep. Then we take the guard tower and the gates. That's when the signal goes out to our men in the trees.

"When we enter the keep, surprise is everything. We hammer the bastards before they know what's hit them. Does everyone understand his part?"

Nods all around.

"We begin here." He stabbed at a crudely drawn map, continuing to outline the plan as men, already packed together, drew closer.

The time for talk had ended. Jacek paced, though it did not dispel the lightning sizzling in his bloodstream. He needed to stay calm, needed to keep his rage harnessed. Striding to the chamber occupied by Anka and Adam, he stopped momentarily to check that Krystiana was still under guard. She regarded him blandly. When he found Adam sleeping soundly in Anka's arms, he eased his shoulders. Removing a glove, he ran a finger along Adam's chubby cheek. The boy's fine curls brushed his neck and the tops of his ears, and his dark lashes lay perfectly splayed against his smooth skin. His mouth was slack, and he drew deep, even breaths between rosy lips. Jacek cupped the boy's face before meeting Anka's anxious gaze.

"You know what to do?" he asked her.

"Yes, m'lord. I leave with two of your men, we ride to Łac pretending to be husband, wife, child, and husband's brother traveling to Lelów. We are to remain at the inn until we receive word from you. If we have no word by midday tomorrow, we ride on to Toruń and seek Lord Eryk's kin, Lady Maria and Lord Teodor."

Jacek nodded. "Good." He handed her a coin pouch. Tears brightened her eyes. "It will end well, Anka," he lied; he was not so confident. He aimed to bolster himself as much as her, refusing to think of all that could go wrong.

Seated beside Antonin, Oliwia looked around at the rabble and struggled to keep rage—and fear—from overtaking her. The great hall was unrecognizable. Where lush tapestries had covered the walls, exposed limestone stood stark and cold. Rich burgundy velvet curtains hung askew, or were missing entirely, and had been strewn about the stone floors, where revelers fornicated, vomited, or relieved themselves on them without a care. Centuries-old heirlooms that had hung on walls or had been displayed on ornate credenzas were gone, as were family shields and coats of arms. Furniture was overturned, wrecked. Where there had been orderliness and grace, chaos was in full swing. And there was naught she could do about it.

"Drink some mead, my dear." Antonin handed her an overflowing cup. She shook her head, and he rolled his eyes. "Oh, come now. It's very good."

And it's tainted.

He swallowed a large mouthful, then turned to her, beaming. He wiped his mouth on his sleeve. "Delicious. Now have some, I insist." He waved the cup under her nose, and she shook her head again. *I need my wits.*

He swiftly stood and wrenched her binding. She cried out. He forced her mouth wider and poured the liquid down her throat. She choked and spluttered.

"Ah! There's a good girl," he snickered. The drink went down her gullet, her chin, her chest. He didn't stop pouring until he'd emptied the cup. His men howled, chanted, pounded the tables.

"Here, let me help you." He swiped at the liquid on her chest to whistles and bawdy remarks.

"I don't believe I got it all." He reached down her bodice and began squeezing her breasts. His soldiers cheered, urging him on. Chortling, he handed the lead to Romek and began licking the mead off her skin. He laved a slobbery path down her throat, over her chest, darting his tongue in and out of her cleavage as he pinched her nipples. Appalled, revolted, she tried to push his smelly head away, but Romek tightened the lead. She felt her eyes bulge and her face fill with blood as her world dimmed.

"Don't kill her, for God's sake! I'm not through with her yet!" Antonin yelled and jerked the leash from Romek.

She gulped in air. When she caught her breath, Antonin handed her another full cup and grinned obscenely. "Drink up, my dear."

She downed her own poisoned drink, praying she wouldn't pass out.

Jacek dropped through the dungeon floor into the tunnel, his left hand gripping his czekan. He rubbed the hilt of his still-sheathed scimitar. Habit. He glimpsed Henryk. Despite the finger, a pummeling from Kasimir before being imprisoned, and lack of food, water, and sleep since, Henryk was the best damned fighter Jacek knew, and he was grateful to have him. A feral smile spread over Jacek's face as he thought of Henryk's revenge on Kasimir—he hoped to witness it. As they ran through the tunnel, Henryk's story replayed in Jacek's head. Kasimir had lured Henryk to the deserted dungeons on the pretext of capturing and holding some of Antonin's men, and just as Henryk had grown suspicious, Kasimir had pounced.

Now they crept into those same dungeons—Biaska's dungeons!—and Jacek drew his scimitar when they entered the cell. Loud voices echoed from beyond a partly open door. At his silent signal, the group pressed itself into the cell's shadows. He inched forward, Henryk, Dawid, and Marcin beside him. He stopped, muttering a curse. Two guards stood beside a table.

"Where the devil are they?" groused one, swiveling his head about.

The other laughed gruffly. "They're upstairs enjoying the feast, you idiot! That's where *we* should be right now."

"Lord Wąskaski will not be pleased they've abandoned their posts."

"What's the harm? We'll get four more down here. The castle is secure inside and out, and those miserable bastards aren't going to escape. Come on, I want to get above floors before the drink and the women are gone."

Footsteps and talk receded as the guards moved away, and the space went as still as a tomb. Jacek released the breath he'd been holding and motioned to his men. They moved briskly, furtively through the cell, past the empty guard station, and up the stairs into a storeroom. Jacek steadied his steps and his breathing, craned his head, and entered a darkened corridor. He listened. The sounds puzzled him. Henryk, Marcin, and Dawid followed as he crept through the passageway. When he neared the steps ascending to the main kitchen, he cocked his head.

What in blazes ...

What he heard brought to mind a tavern brawl. Thuds, crashes, yells, screams, wood splitting, crockery breaking, and men's furious voices rebounded off stone walls. He tiptoed up a few steps and raised his head. He saw the first of Antonin's revered guard: a pair of black boots, whose tops were covered by the hem of a żupan, scuffling with a skirt and brown leather shoes. Jacek took the next step up. His sight was immediately blanked by another, more voluminous skirt, and he soon heard a thud, a grunt, and Beata's angry voice.

"Hell-spawn!" she spat. A girl began crying.

The skirt moved, and Jacek saw a soldier on the floor, facedown, grabbing the back of his head where blood leaked between his fingers. He let out a loud groan. The maid screamed—Jacek thought she screamed at the prone man—but instead she was pointing at *him*. Beata whirled with a pair of wicked tongs that she swung at him, and he ducked. Just in time.

"Beata!" he hissed. "Wait!"

Marcin streaked past him, nearly stepping on him, and grappled with Beata, whose red eyes were wild with fury. Jacek was astounded to see a smile splitting Marcin's face even as Beata tried to kill him. Marcin was talking to her, and at last she stopped her battling. "Master Marcin?" she asked, sounding befuddled.

Just then, the soldier began slithering away, and Jacek pounced, driving the wind from him. He fisted the soldier's hair and yanked his head sideways. His left arm was cocked above his shoulder, and he brought the axehead down, hacking into the man's neck so hard the edge struck stone. Blood pumped onto the floor and quickly spread into the cracks. Still holding the head yet attached to the man's shoulders, Jacek stayed on his back until the man stopped twitching. Catching his breath, he jumped up. Eyes were riveted to him.

"Hello, Beata," he said with a head dip. "I regret the mess."

The old cook's eyes bugged, and her mouth dropped open. She stood frozen while Jacek quickly surveyed the wreckage in the kitchen. Bodies lay partly in and out of the buttery and scullery amid crockery, iron pots, metal utensils, barrels, and food.

"You've been busy, Beata. They could use you in the garrison."

"Captain?" she croaked, crossed herself, then continued staring in astonishment.

"Yes, Beata, it is I. Tell me what you can. We've no time."

More of his men filled the kitchen. Two pairs took up station at the kitchen's entrance. Henryk was beside him when Beata ran through Oliwia's plan to drug all of Antonin's men during the feast.

"It partly worked, lord."

"'Partly' explains the clamor in the great hall," said Henryk bleakly.

"They are tearing the place apart, looting, drinking, attacking our girls," she spat, putting her arm around the maid who'd been wrestling with the soldier. The girl was trembling, staring at the body, her eyes huge and glassy.

Jacek motioned Dawid over. "Take the men into the hall. You won't be recognized. Act indifferently, like you belong among them. Then dispatch them." He turned back to Beata. "Where is your mistress now, Beata?"

The anger left Beata's face, replaced by a gloom that dragged it down, making it far more dog-like than it already was. Alarms clanged in Jacek's head.

"Lord Antonin forced her above floors, m'lord, dragging her by a leash like a dog. None could stop him." She glanced at Henryk.

Explosions teemed and burst inside Jacek's head. His vision went black, vivid red, lightning-white. He gripped the czekan so tightly he might have snapped the haft in two. Drawing in a long breath, then another, he quelled his fury. He exchanged looks with Henryk, and both men sprinted for the great hall only to stop in their tracks. Antonin's soldiers, stupid with drink and revelry, were being cut down by Dawid's force. Many already lay in a bloody sprawl across floors and tabletops. Incredibly, some still celebrated, oblivious to the fight around them.

Jacek checked himself from growing heartened. *Focus. Don't divide the skin while it's still on the bear.*

"There he is!" Henryk growled beside him. Jacek looked up and saw what Henryk saw: Kasimir, slinking toward the doors leading to the gardens and escape.

"Get Oliwia. Go!" Henryk urged as he dashed toward his quarry. "Kasimir," he bellowed, "you maggot-riddled coward! I'm going to kill you!" Kasimir jerked and ran.

Jacek turned for the stairs, but his attention was hauled back to a pair of Antonin's men running at him with murder in their eyes and sabres in their fists. His vision clear and wide, he obliged them the fight, hefting the czekan as if he were splitting wood. He thrilled at plying it, driving them back, ending the bout quickly and badly for them.

More now blocked his path. Antonin's men seemed to be rousing, awakening to their danger. Urgency coursing through him, Jacek's warrior mindset grabbed hold. Wheeling and dancing, sparing steps, he sliced and hacked with unrelenting brutality, a blur of motion. A surge tore through him, and he heard himself roar as he cleared men out of his way, like a crazed Norse marauder of old.

It felt good.

Woozy, Oliwia staggered as Antonin hauled her along the shadowy passageway. He wrenched her bedchamber door open. Nadia yelped.

"Get out!" he thundered. Nadia froze. He dropped the leash, took two strides, and struck her. She fell to her knees with a sob; he lifted his hand to strike again. "I said *get out!*"

Nadia darted her eyes to Oliwia; Oliwia gave her two quick nods. Nadia picked up her skirts and scampered through the doorway while Oliwia shucked the fetter and drew breath. Beads of sweat dotted her forehead. Antonin slammed the heavy door, turned, and stalked toward her with a wolfish smile, his eyes gleaming as they traveled over her. He looked utterly mad.

Oliwia inched backward to the hearth, searching for the fire iron but finding none. She blinked, trying to cast off her haze. The table holding the food tray from earlier stood nearby; she picked up a platter and hurled it.

Next came goblets and bottles. They hit him, slowing him little and enraging him mightily. Fighting her dizziness, she stumbled for her desk and grabbed up the dainty chair that sat before it. She swung it at his head. Antonin ducked, and the chair glanced off his back. With a snarl, he gripped it and threw it aside in a clatter. Her hands closed around a box, a writing set, books, and she threw those too as she scurried for a door. She had hold of a quill. Antonin's anger was erupting from him like deadly lava flows, coloring his pitted face purple.

"You little whore!"

He came at her, and she stabbed the quill in his cheek. Another vicious snarl, and he jerked his head back. The quill flew from her hand. Blood ran in a straight line into his beard. With a grunt, he hurled himself at her, driving her to the floor, expelling the air from her lungs. He pinned her and straddled her, putting all his weight on her midsection. She couldn't breathe. Then he slapped her so hard that her head whipped to the side. Pain exploded behind her eyes, taking her to the brink of blackness. He hit her again, backhanding her other cheek. His hand was like an iron mallet, and he wore studded leather armguards. A boss split her skin; her face went numb.

Her head felt as though it were stuffed with wads of cloth. Shaking herself, fighting stupor, she looked up at the madman atop her through watery eyes. He held her down, spittle flying from his mouth, dribbling into his beard, mixing with blood as he bared his teeth and cursed her, his eyes like smoldering coals. His damp hair clung to his forehead, spilling to his shoulders in greasy hanks.

"You promised me a wedding with a priest," she wailed lamely.

"You'll get your wedding, you little bitch, but tonight I get what I want. I want to see if you're worth the trouble."

"Please, my lord, not here. On the bed," she begged tearfully.

Antonin slid off her, fisted her hair, and pulled her to her feet. He dragged her to the bed and heaved her onto the mattress. She tried to scrabble away. He leapt on her. She groaned and bucked under him, bringing her knee up, but he was ready for her. He cocked his fist back. She squeezed her eyes shut and braced herself, but rather than unleash the blow, he chuckled malevolently.

"We can do this the hard way or the easy way. I care not."

Astride her again, he forced her legs apart as he rucked up her skirts. Oliwia wriggled, worming her way toward the headboard as he busied himself pushing her skirts out of his way. Still in his armor, the mail skirt proved an obstruction he struggled to overcome in his frenzy. He paused and let fly a frustrated curse. Just then, the door thudded open, and he turned his head and erupted in laughter.

"What do you want, little man? Have you come to learn a few things? Pull up a chair and watch, then."

Oliwia looked to the side and gasped as she beheld Filip, his back pressed to the wall, his eyes wide. His expression quickly transformed from shock to anger.

"Leave her alone!" he cried, hefting the nadziak.

Ignoring him, Antonin wrestled the mail coat and shed it onto the floor. It landed with a metallic thud. His patience seemed to stand on a knife's edge, and he wasted no time loosening his breeches and wedging himself between Oliwia's bare legs as she continued struggling. With a cry, Filip ran at him. Antonin's weight was gone for an instant. She heard a crack, a moan, and a dull thud. She shot to the bolsters, but Antonin was back, trapping her, his reek descending on her.

"Don't worry. I didn't kill him. Yet." He grinned.

Squeezing her eyes shut, Oliwia stretched her right hand beneath the pillows, inch by inch, while he groped her. Heaving in breaths, she shut out the smell of his fetid breath. Her heart thumped so wildly she thought it might jump from her chest. Sweeping her hand under the bolsters, straining, reaching, her fingers brushed something solid, knobby. Atop her, Antonin frantically thrust, missed, then cursed and grunted like a boar. Closing her eyes, she drew in one long breath and with it, a vision of what she was about to do.

She snapped her eyes open.

In one motion, she pulled the dagger from its hiding place and wrenched the scabbard off, sending it clattering across the floor. Antonin looked up, his muddy eyes staring at her dully through a curtain of greasy hair. Her hands tight around the hilt, she brought the blade up and punched it into his side with a primal yell. It bit into flesh. She drove the point in until the quillons stopped her. Antonin jerked sideways. His eyes bulged, and his mouth stretched wide in a grimace. She twisted and sawed and dragged the knife out, then plunged it in again. It was slicked in blood, and her grip slipped.

Antonin howled furiously. He flailed at the blade, trying to wrangle it from his back. She'd struck him, and struck him well, but she hadn't killed him. She rolled out from under him, but his weight pinned her leg. He groaned so loudly that she barely heard a door opening.

Antonin juddered and flopped face-first on the mattress. She caught the glint of a blade as it was torn from his body. The blade sizzled a ghostly silver trail through the air, sweeping upward and swiftly back down, striking the back of his head with a sickening *thunk*. A sound that was part-moan and part-hiss escaped him in one long, last gasp. She cleared the bed just as a man's silhouette emerged from the darkness. Light revealed his face. She swallowed and wiped her cheek.

"Come," he beckoned in a lilting voice. "I know where your son is. Let me take you to him." He held out his hand, and her eye caught on gleaming armor. Hussar armor.

She looked at Filip's crumpled form. "But my brother—"

"Will die if you don't come now. I'll slit his gullet."

Just then, Filip rolled to his side and moaned. She leapt up and looked into Romek's dusky face. He handed her a cloak, and she let him lead her away, stealing one last glance at Filip.

They fled along the corridor. She heard thuds, grunts, shouts, and metal ringing—sounds of men bashing each other—from below floors as she ran, and she prayed the men from Maławieża were killing Antonin's troops, that they would save her brother and everyone she held dear. Down a back set of stairs they flew, and out into the empty courtyard.

Soon they straddled Romek's mount, wending their way through a campfire-dotted sprawl of tents. He was breathing down her neck, holding a dagger to her side under her cloak. The few men awake hailed Romek. The earth was soft and muddy, churned up by so many men, horses, and wagons, and they picked their way carefully. Once they cleared the camp, Romek pointed his horse north and urged it into a gallop. They were soon swallowed up in the pines and the dim dawn.

372

Jacek dodged blades, crashing fists, falling bodies, and all manner of debris as he leapt to the stairs. His troops were winning the fight. He charged above floors two, three steps at once. Pausing a beat to wipe blood from his hands and hilts, he peered through an arrow slit, and his eye caught on two people atop a horse that threaded its way through the enemy encampment below. He flew up the stairs, landed hard on the third floor, rounded a corner, bolted down the passageway. The door to Oliwia's sitting room stood ajar; he slid in. The space was empty. Her bedchamber door was also ajar, and he tilted his head, hearing voices and scuffling on the other side. Checking his grip on czekan and scimitar, he crept toward the opening.

"Come away now, Master Filip," Jacek heard Nadia say. This was followed by unintelligible muttering.

Jacek peered through the gap, his heart thundering, his eyes sweeping the chamber. It was wrecked, the rumpled bed soaked with blood that trailed to a man's body lying facedown. A knobby, bloody hilt protruded from his lower back. Several paces from the body, Nadia bent over Filip, who sat on his rump, rubbing the back of his head. Grasping the door, Jacek eased it open until Filip flicked his eyes to him. Using Nadia's shoulder like a fulcrum, Filip scrambled to his feet and presented a defiant scowl.

"Who the devil are you, and what in blazes do you want?" he squawked.

"An old friend, Filip," Jacek replied. "What happened here? Where is your sister?"

Filip's eyes narrowed, then flew wide. His mouth dropped open and closed several times, as though he were a carp scavenging the bottom of a river. Nadia stood, and a violent shudder rolled through her small frame. Teetering, she crossed herself.

"Captain Dąbrowski?" she choked.

Filip at last recovered, emitting a shriek that seemed torn from his lungs. "Pan Jacek!" A grin split Filip's face ear to ear.

Jacek gripped Filip's shoulder. "Where is Liwi?"

"I don't know. Lord Antonin had her. He struck me, and when I came to, he was dead," the boy gabbled, pointing to the corpse. "My nadziak was gone, and so was Liwi."

"She must be in the keep somewhere," Jacek said more to himself than to Filip. He walked over to the body and stabbed his scimitar into it. Dead.

Good. To Nadia, he said, "Take Filip to shelter. Not the hall. If you see your mistress, tell her Adam is safe." He wiped his sword on Antonin's clothing and sheathed it, stuffed his czekan into his belt, and grasped the dead man's legs. He dragged him into the passageway. Filip gawked at him.

"Go, Filip!" Jacek ordered.

"What are you doing?"

"Ending this," Jacek called over his shoulder. Then he swung the door shut and hauled the body to an alcove. There, he chopped the czekan down on Antonin's neck. It took another blow to separate head from body. He seized his hair, gore oozing, spattering on the floorboards, and descended to the first landing above the hall. Men still fought in clusters. He held the head up.

"It's over!" he shouted. "Antonin is dead!"

Men turned toward him, their eyes startling wide when they looked upon what he held. His men cheered. A great clamor rose from outside, and he ran through the hall, past men, bodies, and rubble. He stopped at the top of the forestairs. Below him in the courtyard, armed men were running in a disorderly jumble. He spotted Henryk astride a dancing horse, and he dashed down the stairs.

"Antonin's dead?" Henryk glanced at the head in Jacek's grip.

Jacek nodded, looking around at the growing chaos. "What's happening here?"

Jerking the horse's reins, Henryk steadied it. The animal kept one huge eye fixed on Jacek. Amid men's shouts, drums began to beat outside the castle walls.

"Antonin's army is marshaling to attack."

"It sounds as though they've already marshaled," Jacek said. "We charge them first."

Henryk looked at him quizzically, but Jacek was already running for the stables. "Find Dawid, Marcin, and Florian, and have a servant find me a kopia," he yelled after him.

Jacek soon led a sally through the gate. Dawn was glowing on the eastern horizon, and the air was damp and chill. Steam rolled off men and horses in rhythmic puffs. In his right hand, Jacek hefted a kopia affixed with Biaska's pennon. Stuffed on its metal tip was Antonin's head. He carried it like a standard as they clattered across the drawbridge and arrayed at the edge of the dry moat. Before them, torches burned brightly, lighting up the field where rows of foot soldiers stood facing them with pikes, swords, war hammers. Their cavalry was behind the front lines with archers lined up beyond them. Jacek could see the gleam in their smiles as they calculated how long it would take to wipe out his small band.

Twenty against three hundred. More, if their camp followers joined in. *They won't bother with the cannon.*

The enemy's drums beat out a thundering tattoo. Warriors raised swords, shook axes and war hammers, jabbed spears at the sky, clanged metal, and shouted insults, but they did not advance. Jacek, mounted on Jarosława, stood with his men as they listened to their foes' uproar. Breathing in, breathing out, he kept his eyes fixed on the field. Drew in and released another breath. The cacophony faded, replaced by the sound of blood rushing in and out of his head. One foe advanced a few paces and hurled a pike, drilling it harmlessly into the soft earth. Jacek waited. Why they did not loose their arrows, he could not figure, but he'd been in enough battles to know overconfidence bred poor decisions. The standoff seemed to last hours yet was mere minutes. Then he saw what he waited for and planted the kopia in the ground beside the drawbridge. He drew his scimitar and rode along his thin line of men, clattering it against their lances and swords as he bellowed what, he could not remember. His men raised their weapons and belted out war cries. The enemy army began a slow advance, screaming about killing, blood, and victory.

One ragged line of twenty before an entire army.

Jacek raised his sword. *"Uderzaj!"* he roared. *Attack!*

They surged forward.

Arrows flew across the morning's twilight sky, thick, swooping like sharp-beaked kites as they landed among the army, felling some, confusing many. At the same time, guns fired into the enemy, unleashing thudding reports and great clouds of white smoke. A beat before Jacek and his men impacted the front line of foot soldiers, unearthly war cries and thundering erupted from the trees behind the army, and wings shuddered in the morning air. The enemy was herded before the savage blades of Klemens's winged hussars, Lesław's mercenaries, and Humansky's Cossacks. The slaughter had begun.

Jacek struck his first man in the neck. Whether he killed him, he knew not, but he saw him go down. The man had been facing him, dazed, as if disbelieving what he saw.

Jacek hacked and slashed at soldiers' backs as they ran. Men scuttled everywhere, scattering like cockroaches exposed to light. The enemy cavalry had turned, but panic waved through their horses. They had no room to maneuver and so, overwhelmed and overrun, became fodder for Biaska's blades. Those horsemen grimaced and screamed as they fought desperately for their lives. Their confident smiles were gone.

The battle ended quickly, lasting barely longer than the hussars' charge. Over half the foemen surrendered at the outset; they'd not been paid enough for the fight, they said. Some had run away; others had joined Biaska's side. Many lay dead or wounded. Women and children wailed amid smashed tents, broken wagons, and other fragments in the bloody camp.

Jacek rode to Henryk and Lesław, who sat on their mounts surveying the carnage. Klemens and Paweł gave him a wave from the tree line, and Humansky whooped a "Kapitana!" It was over. Jacek felt fatigue seep into his bones.

Marcin hailed him and trotted over, wings shuddering on his back, three men in tow.

"Marcin," Jacek said. "You are unhurt, yes?"

"I am, thanks to these men." Grinning, Marcin nodded toward the trio. "They turned against their commanders and helped me when I was surrounded. I wish no harm to come to them."

Jacek nodded at the grim faces. "So it shall be." To Henryk, he said, "Kasimir?"

"I sent him to the devil," Henryk spat, then grew puzzled. "But I have yet to find that whoreson, Romek Mazur."

"The lieutenant?" one of Marcin's three piped up. "He left before the battle broke out. With a woman. We thought she was his, that he was taking her to safety."

Jacek came to full alertness, fear driving out his fatigue. He tried to quell the panic rising in his chest. "Describe her."

The man frowned. "Well, it was still dark, but I saw her face. Very pretty. Fair-skinned, dark hair. Light-eyed."

"Which way did they go?"

"They headed north, but I could not say if they stayed the course."

Jacek urged Jarosława. Henryk made to hold his reins. "It might not be her, Jacek."

"She's with Romek," he ground out, his pulse racing furiously. "He's the one who's been butchering the women these many years. I have to stop him."

Jacek turned his horse, maneuvering around the small clog of soldiers. A tic jumped in his bunched jaw muscles.

"We're coming with you," exclaimed Lesław, echoed by Pawel. Behind them, Dawid and Florian were nodding. So was Marcin.

"Lesław, I need you in command of the keep while Klemens secures the field. Pawel, Florian, you're not familiar with the terrain, so you'll be of more use here. Dawid and Marcin, search the woods around Małylas where Lord Eryk was killed. Henryk is with me, and we go to Łac."

Without a word, Henryk fell in beside him. As they picked their way through the camp, he asked, "Why Łac and Małylas?"

"Romek is from Sandomierz, where most of the murders happened. There have only been two near Biaska—Łac and Małylas. And I know why the tavern maid's body was recovered at Małylas. He spent a lot of time there scouting, and he slaughtered that girl right before he was to kill Eryk and leave the place for good. Right now, he's in a hurry, so he will not go all the way back to Sandomierz. He has no time to search out a new killing ground, so I'm counting on him going to—"

"Go someplace he's been before, someplace he's familiar with, and of the two, Łac is the closest," Henryk finished for him. "Makes sense. I pray you reckon right."

"As do I."

"Jacek, when we find her, I will not stand in your way. I will release her and rip up the contract."

Jacek turned his head sharply. Henryk continued with a shrug. "She never wanted me, and I only asked her because ... well, I thought it the right thing to do."

Jacek nodded.

When they cleared the camp, they broke into a gallop.

"Now let's find her!" Jacek yelled.

Chapter 35

We'll Catch a Pig and Dance a Jig

The sun's first rays brightened the forest. They'd been riding in the woods, covering miles of uneven ground, for over an hour. The horse had slowed considerably despite Romek spurring it. Now Romek pulled up. Oliwia shivered against him, praying he was not taking her to Adam, for she had not yet worked out how she could protect her son from this madman.

"Are we close?" she asked.

Her head throbbed, the skin on her cheek was shredded, her legs hung numbly on either side of the horse, and the parts of her backside she could feel ached. During the ride, exhaustion had crept through her entire body, and her arms felt leaden.

"We're going through there." Romek ignored her question and pointed to a thick coppice where a tangle of dwarf birch and brambles crowded together unhospitably.

"In there?" Her neck hairs prickled.

"There's a hut just there. That's where your son is." He cocked his head. "Do you hear that?"

"No. What?"

"I thought I heard a baby cry. Might have been a lynx mewling." He shrugged.

He urged the horse through the undergrowth along a game track that led through another thicket and disappeared. The animal went reluctantly. The thorns clawing at Oliwia's clothing must have been tearing at the poor horse. She looked around herself, wondering how she would ever find her way out of this jumble of trees and shrubs. When she glanced over her shoulder, something light caught her eye and she realized a piece of chemise had wound up on a raspberry bush. Though the fabric was soiled and gray, its starkness stood out against the forest's murk. She tore at more bits of raggedy lace, the ripping masked by the snap of limbs, and dropped them as they went so she could retrace her route.

Romek didn't notice. He was singing—an eerie, high-pitched nasally sort of sound—sending fresh chills along her spine. He sounded almost jolly.

Jacek and Henryk headed north, riding full-out. Jacek had found a muddy track no wider than a horse that weaved in and out of the underbrush with fresh hoofprints, but they were too mashed to tell apart. Second-guessing himself the entire way, he grew more fearful, more frustrated, and more infuriated the farther they went.

What if I've guessed wrong and she's not here?

What if I can't get to her in time?

What if he's hurting her right now?

And on it went. Though he could not see the horizon, the sun had crested and sent brilliant shafts of light that trapped swirling motes resembling bright pinpoints of fire. The day was clear but damp, and drops of dew slid off leaves and needles onto ferns and creeping green leaves. A few hit his cheek and neck. Behind him, Henryk's horse chuffed and snorted. The tranquility shattered when the horse screeched and reared, stumbling as it landed, nearly throwing Henryk. Two blackbirds squawked at being disturbed and made a racket leaving their perch.

Jacek turned Jarosława. "What happened?"

Henryk cradled his left hand against his chest with a grimace, muttering and cursing. "Something in the underbrush frightened him. I saw it dart out. Maybe a snake or a mouse. Ah, Christ!" he snarled and dismounted.

"What is it?" Jacek held his breath as Henryk ran his good hand over the horse's forearms, knees, and fetlocks.

"He won't put weight on his left leg." Henryk ducked around the horse's other limbs. He looked up at Jacek with a pained expression. "I'll catch you up. Go!"

With an exhale, Jacek turned and kept moving.

Romek halted in an open space that could scarce be considered a clearing, for it was little more than two horses wide.

"Is this it?" Oliwia squinted at a jumble of bare, twiggy bushes among a palisade of tree trunks. Nothing resembling a structure stood in her line of sight. "I thought you said there was a hut nearby."

As if he hadn't heard her, Romek dismounted and tied the horse off to an alder. Whistling now, he came toward her, slid off her shoe, and mildly asked, "Do you recall the ambush some five years ago right after Krezowski took you from me in Vyatov?"

The act—coupled with the question—was so peculiar as to be unreal. She shuddered involuntarily.

He continued as if speaking to himself. "He shouldn't have done that. Well, I arranged that little attack, but it didn't end as I'd planned." He chuckled, ambling to the other side of the horse. "That was yet one more time I learned one cannot rely on others to see a job well done."

She tried not to let her shock show and closed her mouth.

"I could have recovered you then if I'd done it all myself. Of course, I should not have been forced to try in the first place ... Well, that's past. And now, after five years, I must admit the reward is very sweet." He smiled up at her dreamily, then grasped her other foot and slipped that shoe off too.

"My shoes!" she yelped.

"Your son's nearby, my lady. So very close now," he said with unnerving glee.

"My shoes!" she repeated. Her face and hands were clammy, cold.

"I will keep the shoes safe. They are precious to me, much like a shield or a lance becomes a treasured war trophy. Come now, and we will find your son." He reached up for her.

She recoiled and grabbed at the reins. Regarding her with a grotesque half smile, he grasped her leg and yanked viciously, nearly dislocating her knee as he pulled her from the saddle. She landed hard on her tailbone, and pain jolted her lower back, numbing her toes.

"What are you doing?" she cried.

He carefully placed her shoes in his saddlebag, then pulled out a game knife. He gazed at it lovingly, as one might look upon a lover. "Such sharp edges," he said in his singsong voice. "We'll soon find out just how sharp, yes?"

She'd pulled herself to her knees, a rush of power surging through her. He lifted his boot, braced it against her upper arm, and shoved her on her side. She expected him to attack, but he just stood there, regarding her with amusement. His face transformed from mild to evil and back again.

"What are you doing?" she repeated, getting her feet under her in a crouch, readying to spring. "Where's my son?"

He pressed his thumb pad against the point of the knife and drew blood. "Sharp." He sucked his thumb, then glared at her with unbridled hatred, his face turning dark.

"Here are the rules. I am giving you a quarter hour to try and escape me," he said icily. "You may run as far as you like wherever you like. When your time is up, I will hunt you like a rabbit. And when I catch you, I will clean you like one too. First, I will split you open and take out your heart and entrails and all those disgusting parts that make you female." He grimaced. "Then I will skin you. I'm quite artful with a knife. Your husband certainly came to understand what a master carver I am. As for your son, well, he's in hell with your husband, where they both await you." His shoulders twitched and his face ticced, changing his expression from a grimace to a hideous grin.

Oliwia willed the bile back into her stomach and the terror out of her mind. *Deep breath. Keep your wits.* "How can I give you proper chase without shoes?" She flicked her eyes over the tired, tethered horse, over the ground, all around her.

"That is for you to solve, isn't it?" He shrugged. "Now if I were you, I would stop asking questions because your time has already begun." He leaned against the horse and crossed his arms.

She'd been shaking, and now she used all that tautness to spring into a run, like an overwound coil whipping loose. She vaulted between two trees, heading the way they'd come. Locking out the jabs of sharp stones, dry needles, twigs, branches, and roots on the soles of her feet, she searched out the fabric bits. Whipping branches scored her hands, her face, her neck as she ducked, shifted, calculated. An opening here, a blocked way there, was that lace over there? *I don't see it. I am off course! I don't have time to look. I must get away!* Puffing, panting, she bounced off tree trunks and squeezed through places where no creature should be able to fit.

How long have I been running? Which way am I headed?

Her dark gray cloak caught on a bush, and she yanked it free. She thought to unfasten it, but then she gathered it tightly, and, rather than a way out, her eyes sought something different.

How much time is left?

Where do I hide?

Her feet were ragged, and she knew she couldn't keep going. And then she saw a juniper bush and she stopped, feeling eyes on her. Her chest was heaving; she cast about the ground. She gathered up rocks, sticks, and branches, which she clutched to herself before diving under the bush. Frantically, she rearranged her body and looked out from under low branches; she realized she'd left a clear trail. She shimmied out and raked dead leaves with her hands, covering her tracks as best she could. Tucking the cloak around herself, she backed under the bush and waited for her racing heart to quiet. Then she clawed through the rocks and picked one, gathered up her branches and selected the stoutest. She lay on her belly, her legs curled under her, her neck raised, her eyes constantly darting out of her hole while she scraped the rock over the end of the first branch, back and forth. That one broke, and she let out a frustrated growl. She picked up the next one and began anew, trying to still her shaking hands.

The good thing about Łac—the only good thing—was that it was forested on only one side. So Jacek's search went from utterly impossible to nearly impossible. He did not know the exact spot where Romek had left the tavern maid from so long ago, but he reckoned she would have lain on either side of the southerly road. It was this road Jacek and his companions had followed when they'd left Lac's tavern the night the girl died. So he pushed north, sweeping branches and bushes out of his way as noiselessly as a fully grown man upon a horse could. He wound through vegetation, listening, craning his neck, but heard only the cawing of blackbirds, the occasional warbler's tune, or the skittering of squirrels up and down bark.

The woods grew thick, so he tied Jarosława off and stepped lightly through shrubs, swiveling his head, czekan to hand. Just as he pivoted back to the horse, his eye snagged on something light caught on a branch, and he plucked it off. Cloth. Lace, specifically. He spotted another bit farther away, and he followed.

He thought he heard the faint scraping of wood, and he froze. It was gone—or maybe wasn't there to begin with. Creeping in that direction, the sound came again, followed by a snap from a different direction. He stopped. Nothing. No birds chirped, no squirrels chattered, no small things rustled and scrabbled through the carpet of leaves. No movement. The woods were still. Unusually quiet.

Slowly, silently, he slid his scimitar out of its scabbard.

Tiny movement caught the corner of his eye, and he darted his gaze to a large juniper. One of its low branches fluttered. *Could be the breeze. But there is no breeze.* Cautiously, quietly, he slunk toward the bush, his eyes scanning the entirety of it, trying to pierce it, unable to get a clear look into the heart of it. He took in a scant depression on one side; a pile of turned-over leaves was mounded higher than anything around it. Moving ever so deliberately, he stole toward it. He crouched and peered under the branches.

Dear God, go away, go away, go away! Oliwia hunkered where she'd been the better part of a half hour, trying not to breathe, cursing herself for startling when a creature—likely the one whose home she'd invaded—had darted in and back out again. It had been a small movement, but Romek had seen it, and he had come stealthily. His boots stood just outside her lair—she could practically hear him breathing.

But Romek's boots were red, not black.

Just then, he sank to the ground and peered in, right at her, and she sprang from her hole, knocking him sideways, driving a stubby, sharpened branch into his neck. He vaulted to his feet, tossing her off with a grunt as though she were no more than a sack of peas. He swiftly snatched her wrist, hauling her up, and she realized she'd missed and plunged her crude weapon into the meat of his shoulder. He hissed a curse. In her free hand, she held another stick. She cocked it back and brought it down with all her might. He threw up his forearm, blocking her. It felt like smacking iron. As the blow juddered up her arm, her stake fell from her grip, useless, into the bed of dead leaves.

"Jesus Christ!" he huffed.

He had hold of both her wrists, his fingers encircling them and then some. He drove her backward, even as she dug her heels in.

This was not Romek.

She stared into a bearded face crowned in golden hair with wide, deep blue eyes.

"Liwi?" the face said, looking altogether astonished—and familiar. His deep voice was also familiar.

She eased her tautened legs, and his momentum carried them in a backward, sliding stumble. Something crashed into his back, flattening him and her beneath him. He groaned. The wind had fled her lungs. He was on his feet, moving, diving, grabbing at something in the leaves while she lay flat on her broken back, her heart, lungs, and belly exposed, ready for something to stab into them and rip her apart. She recovered her breath and the feeling in her body and scrambled backward. Her back smacked against a trunk.

Before her, two men faced off. One was the strange man she'd struck. He reached over his shoulder and yanked out the stick, seeming to wince. Her heart dropped when she recognized the second man.

Romek.

He taunted the golden man with a thin, curved blade. "Looking for this?" His voice sounded feverish. Then he hurled the sabre, and it crashed through the woods.

"I can smell the stink of fear on you," Romek snarled.

She didn't notice the sabre in Romek's hand until he lunged. The other man dodged and parried the blow with an axeheaded war hammer, but he seemed to wield it slowly. He hefted it to his left hand.

"You call yourself a hussar, you hapless coward?" Romek smirked.

The stranger said nothing. He kept his eyes riveted on Romek.

Romek sliced at the man's midsection, but the man swung at the same time. Metal clanged on metal, the sword glancing off the axehead. The stranger tried to wrangle Romek's blade with the axe's hook but missed. Both men were breathing fast, moving in a slow circle around each other in a near-crouch. The stranger seemed to favor his right arm, holding it bent against his body.

"Your foolish lord never should have let me go in Vyatov," Romek laughed, flourishing his sabre in one hand and the hunting knife in the other.

"On this we agree," the stranger replied.

"And now I send you to join him in hell," Romek jeered.

The two men danced backward and forward, lunging, dodging, and blocking as if rehearsing a series of dance steps. They came together suddenly, steel on steel, and she could not tell who held what. They grappled, muscles taut and trembling, like drawings she'd seen of ancient Greek wrestlers. But this was no game.

The stranger had hold of Romek's wrist, the one holding the knife. Neither man had room to swing sword or axe. They strained and shoved, shoulder to shoulder, heels digging, trying to gain purchase as they pushed against one another. The stranger threw his head back and smashed it into Romek's forehead, but he slipped in the damp leaves and went down. Though he reeled, Romek was still on his feet. He seemed to recover himself and rushed at the stranger, who was pulling himself up. The stranger ducked swiftly, burying his shoulder in Romek's hip, and Romek flipped end over end, landing hard on his back with a *whomp* and a moan. Somehow he still held both weapons. The stranger jumped on him, and the men wrestled again, fiercely locked together.

Oliwia leapt to her feet, wincing as she waded into the bushes, looking, kicking leaves, searching, searching, now on her knees, scattering foliage. The men struggled behind her, their grunts and yelps coming in bursts. Her knee hit something solid, and she tossed leaves aside. A gleam, a glint. She snatched the blade. She hobbled back—just in time to see Romek astride the stranger, bringing the knife down on his neck. But the stranger shot a powerful forearm up and stopped him. With his free hand, he punched Romek hard, sending him backward, blood bright and glossy red on his mouth and chin. The stranger scrabbled to his feet, heaving in breaths. He was unarmed.

She dashed in, shoving the blade's hilt at him. "Your sword!" His gaze still fixed on Romek, he took the blade and double-fisted it. He brought it up, crashed it down. But Romek flung himself away, and the blade struck dirt and broke, leaving a jagged length beyond the hilt shorter than a dagger. Romek was on his feet, lunging. The stranger raised the swordless hilt and deflected the sabre even as he jumped back, dodging the dagger coming for his underarm. Transfixed, Oliwia watched as the men circled slowly again with spare steps. Romek chopped his sabre at the stranger's shoulder, but the stranger nimbly stepped back and avoided the bite of the blade. And the dance continued.

Though her mind was thick as a fog bank, it occurred to her that the stranger's size and fluid movements mimicked Jacek's. But that was impossible. Unless, of course, she was already dead. Before she could reconcile what she saw with what she knew, the stranger yelled at her.

"Run, Liwi! Now!"

I must *be dead!*

Oliwia shook her head as if the motion would waken her from her delirium. He sounded and moved like Jacek, but this man lived, breathed. Nothing made sense.

Romek darted a step toward the Jacek-like man and retreated, but the man did not flinch. Instead, he sidestepped smoothly in one long, flowing movement, like a dancer. He gripped the hilt in his left hand. Romek darted again, spitting insults, snarling like a rabid wolf, thrusting with the sword. The stranger deflected and took a step back, still seeming to favor his right arm. Romek dashed at him, scything his sabre as though slashing the heads from ripe wheat. The stranger dodged, but not quickly enough. The blow caught the inner part of his forearm, and he dropped the broken sword. A rent in his żupan darkened as blood soaked into the cloth. Smirking, Romek advanced. The stranger was flagging; he backed up, continued backing away. Oliwia held her breath.

Romek attacked, missed, and recovered in a crouch. He thrust his knife frantically. The stranger kicked high from the side, dislodging the dagger, sending it into the underbrush. Now he moved in a blur, curling away, stooping, grabbing, whirling, kicking Romek's knee with the other foot. The strike hadn't seemed hard, but it knocked Romek off balance, and he wobbled. The stranger continued advancing in liquid steps. He was cat-quick—quicker than Romek—and he now held the war hammer.

Romek's eyes fixed on the weapon. The stranger lunged at him. Romek raised his sabre and crashed it down, but the stranger pulled back, dodging the strike. The blade whistled through air even as the stranger hooked Romek's ankle with the czekan. Romek didn't fall, but he staggered. The stranger whirled the war hammer and drove its spike end into Romek's breastplate, piercing it. Romek looked down, stunned, took a step back, sinking to his knees as he held the hole in his armor. Blood leaked through his fingers, and he looked at the wound with detached curiosity. The stranger gripped the axe in both hands and brought it up. Romek let out an unearthly cry. The stranger powered the weapon across his body in a savage swing, striking the base of Romek's neck. Romek thudded to his side and writhed on the ground, moaning and mewling. The stranger turned to her, extending the haft of the war hammer. His breathing was ragged.

"This man slaughtered your husband. He was prepared to butcher you. Do you wish to finish him?"

She shook her head, the throb returning to her temples, then watched as the axe, bright with wet blood, rose and fell time and again. She sank to the ground. The stranger stood for long minutes, looking down at the bloody mass at his feet. It never crossed her mind to run, to defend herself. At last, he looked over his shoulder at her. Blood trickled thickly down his face, into his beard.

His chest still heaved. "Are you hurt?"

She blinked and stared at him. Was she hurt? She had little idea. He came toward her, the war hammer still to hand, and squatted before her.

"Liwi, are you all right?" His voice was kind, like that of a tender lover. He laid a warm hand on her neck. His thumb caressed her cheek. What an odd feeling it was.

She looked into his face and saw nothing but his eyes—his sapphire eyes.

"Have you come for me?" she heard herself ask.

"Yes, I've come to take you home."

"I shall see my mother, then. My father too. Will Eryk be there? And Adam?"

A frown came and went on his chiseled, grisly face in the space of several heartbeats.

"Liwi, Adam lives. He is with Anka, and he is safe."

She nodded, uncomprehending. Then her mind whirlpooled into a dark ocean, warm and deep, and her eyes rolled backward, her body following. He caught her shoulders and pulled her to him, easing her against his breastplate, where he cradled her in his strong arms. The smell of him was familiar, comforting, and she let herself go.

Oliwia had been staring at him as though her soul had fled her body, and for a panicked moment, Jacek thought it had. She was bloodied everywhere, but he knew not where every wound was nor how bad. Then her eyes rolled back and she wilted like a plucked corn cockle. He caught her and pulled her to him. She breathed. Relieved, he stroked her hair; tears welled in his eyes and slid down his face. He let them come and carve wet tracks over his cheeks. As he held her, he rocked her; he knew not if it lasted minutes or hours. He was vaguely aware of the throbbing in his forearm and shoulder. It was peaceful there in the woods. A light breeze had picked up and ruffled leaves in high canopies. A bee raiding pollen buzzed about. The birds had resumed their bright choruses, ringing him with song from high atop branches. And Oliwia breathed. Deeply, rhythmically.

At last, she stirred and sat up. Her hand flew to her head, and she winced. She looked at him with a puzzled frown. He tucked wild strands of sable hair behind her ear.

"Let's get you home," he said softly.

They struggled up together, trudged to Jarosława, and mounted laboriously. He turned the mare and retraced his path.

The sun had climbed in the cerulean sky, a cheerful spring day, and jaunty wildflowers in blues and yellows seemed to wave at them. She shivered against him despite her cloak, which he'd wound tightly around her small frame. With one hand on her and the other loosely clutching the reins, he guided the mare with his knees. Oliwia did not speak as they rode.

They'd been underway for a while when a familiar figure came into view, walking beside a hobbled horse.

Jacek cantered to him. "Henryk!"

Henryk looked over his shoulder and stopped. Oliwia seemed to brighten. He scanned them both, a small smile playing across his face. "You found him," was all he said.

"I found him," Jacek replied.

"Henryk," Oliwia said excitedly, reaching out her hands. Henryk took a step back and darted his eyes at Jacek. He must have decided Jacek wasn't going to pummel him, for he approached and took her left hand in his good one.

"I am so pleased you're all right. I thought you lost. Are you well?" she chattered animatedly. "Oh! What has happened to your hand? I've so much to tell you. Romek told me he knew where Adam was, and that he would take me to him, you see, and that I'd best come or he would kill Filip. How is Filip? Have you seen him? Well, what choice did I have but to go, really? Then, of course, Romek didn't take me to him because he was lying. He's a wicked man."

Jacek exchanged surprised looks with Henryk.

Oliwia had only paused for breath. She started back up, babbling, words tumbling out of her like frothy brook water over mossy rocks. Her eyes shone like bright jewels, lending her a slightly mad look. "He led me into a deep part of the wood—oh, the horse is still there! That poor horse! He whipped it. We must get it back."

"We will," Henryk assured her.

"Well, there he took my shoes—so odd, isn't it—then told me to run, for he was going to hunt me and skin me like a rabbit. I didn't wish to be gutted and skinned, so I ran. It was hard with only stockings, but I kept going until I could no longer—did you know it was Romek who ambushed us on our journey from Vyatov?—then I hid under my bush, and that's when this man," she lifted her hand to indicate Jacek, "came to be by my hiding place in the bush, and—"

"Oliwia," Henryk said gently, squeezing her hand, "this man is Jacek."

She glanced at Jacek, her dark brows drawn together. "I knew someone by that name. He was a dear friend." Then she looked back at Henryk. "Wasn't he, Henryk? The dearest friend." Glancing at Jacek once more, she added, "I am sorry for stabbing you, especially as you saved me from being flayed. I hope your shoulder will be all right." She paused and shivered, then rushed on, "Henryk, this Jacek says Adam is safe." Her small shoulders had twitched the entire time she prattled, and now she stilled and began smoothing her skirt.

Jacek kept his mouth from dropping open. Henryk opened his only to close it again. He took a deep breath and placed her hand back on her lap, patting it. "And so he is, Oliwia."

"Shall I ride with you, Henryk?" she asked.

"You cannot ride with me. My horse is lame. Stay as you are. Jacek will see you safe."

She twisted her body then and studied Jacek as if seeing him for the first time. Her expression went from curious to dazed to shocked. Jacek shot Henryk a questioning look, and Henryk's shoulders lifted to his ears as if to say, "I have little idea."

Then she reached up and ran her fingertips along Jacek's scar, shifting her gaze from the scar to his eyes and back again. He bit his lower lip.

Suddenly, her eyes filled, and tears spilled down her cheeks. "Merciful God. Am I dreaming?" she whispered as she cupped his face.

Jacek shook his head, then kissed her palm and covered her hand with his. "I am real, Liwi. I've returned."

Astonished, she looked at Henryk. "He is real," he confirmed.

Her eyes flew back to Jacek's, and she clutched his biceps, surprising him with her strength. Then she threw her arms about his shoulders. He dropped the reins and pulled her close, splaying his hands over her back. She kissed the base of his neck and breathed, "I love you so much," sending shivers through him.

In a voice thick with emotion, she said, "If I am dreaming, never wake me."

Chapter 36

And the Truth Will Rise

J acek awoke with a start to an unfamiliar noise. He had no idea where he was. Every bone in his body ached, and that every bone let him know it. Squinting, he peered through a small window at watery daylight. The rest of the room was shrouded in shadow. He lay on his stomach, an unusual position for him, and when he rose on his elbows, he went back down again with a groan. Bandages covered his forearm and his back; the back ached worse than the arm. Memory flooded him.

Merciful God, at least she did not have a proper weapon.

"My lord," a voice called tentatively, "I beg your pardon, but the healer is here. May I bring you anything?" A swish of drapes being pulled back, and the room brightened.

"What time is it?" Jacek asked the servant.

"An hour past sunrise, sire," the man said.

"No wonder my stomach is rumbling," he complained. The mattress beside him sank, and a woman's thin-skinned, gnarled hands began probing his forearm while she clucked.

"The Lady Oliwia …" he began.

"Has asked that you come to her," the manservant finished.

"So she is well this morning?" Jacek had had to relinquish her to healers and servants the afternoon before and had not glimpsed her since.

The healer clucked again. "I'll be tending her as soon as I've done with you, lord, so you'd best fill that empty stomach before seeking her out."

"Is she well?" he repeated. *Is she daft?*

"She's like a sapling, that one, already springing back. Long as she stays off those feet and doesn't get the fever, she'll be right enough."

"A sapling perhaps, but a stubborn one. Best tie her to her chair," he muttered in a perfectly serious voice, belying the joy rising up inside him.

The crone shot him a scowl from beneath bushy gray-black brows and leaned in to his face, her onion-and-cabbage breath hitting him full force. "That will not be necessary, sire."

Soon he was in clean linen undershirt, black trousers, and peacock-blue żupan, his waist swathed in a sash woven with threads of red, ivory, and black. He went in search of a meal; Henryk found him first.

"You look as though you could use some food," his friend said cheerfully.

They ambled to a table, where a serving maid brought cups of wine and a plate of hard bread and cheese. Jacek tore off a hunk of bread and cut a wedge of cheese, then looked around.

"The walls and windows are bare, there is less furniture, and chunks are missing from pillar bricks, but otherwise everything seems as it was," he remarked. A greyhound raised its head and chuffed as if agreeing with him.

Henryk nodded. "Castle staff, tenants, villagers—everyone has been working tirelessly."

"How is she?" Jacek popped the cheese in his mouth and washed it down with a gulp of wine.

"She has all her wits. Of course, that may change when she sees you again."

"So she wishes to see me again?" Jacek chuckled as he reached for more cheese. "I wonder. I rush to save her, and she spears me and reaches for you."

Henryk rubbed a finger over his chin. "I daresay she was glued to you so tightly in that saddle I could not tell where she began or you ended."

But did she know who I was? Did she believe Henryk held her?

Jacek cleared his throat. "Tell me what you know of Kasimir."

"He did Antonin's bidding, and Romek's. He was drowning in gambling debt and was promised large sums, prestige, and land once Antonin controlled Biaska. Kasimir was a horrible gambler, but he was sly—more than I ever thought possible. The bastard told Romek everything about the garrison and Biaska's doings. He was also responsible for destroying our

392

entire shipment of grain from last year's harvest, putting Biaska in dire financial straits."

"How was he able to gather so much information?" Jacek frowned.

Henryk signaled to the serving maid, and she topped off their cups and left the jug when he winked at her. "Through Oliwia's maid Wanda. He seduced the girl, all the while promising to marry her. She believed him and told him everything. He led him along like a dog on a rope."

"How did you find out?" Jacek sliced his third chunk of cheese, this one bigger than the last two.

Henryk exhaled. "She told Beata. When Kasimir came for Adam, Wanda tried to stop him. She followed him to the buttery, where she pleaded with him. Told him she was carrying his child. Seems that made him angry, so he stabbed her in the belly. Beata found her before she died." Henryk paused. "Mangy whoreson," he hissed.

"He's roasting in hell's fires now."

"Small consolation," Henryk replied.

"I want to see Oliwia."

Henryk arched his eyebrows. "Who's stopping you?"

Jacek rose but was waylaid by Marcin, Dawid, Pawel, and Lesław, Filip in their wake.

"It's good to see you all." Jacek grasped their arms with his good one. He sat back down and listened to the routing of Antonin's army, with glorious embellishments already decorating the tale.

"And Filip," Henryk indicated with his thumb, "went after Antonin with a nadziak taller than he is. Never mind that he ended up on top of it. He still slowed him down." Filip reddened and nodded, curls bobbing as he did so. Henryk ruffled the grinning boy's hair.

"Did you get it back?" asked Jacek.

"Yes," the boy replied, "but Romek broke it."

"We'll get you a new one, a good one that won't break," Jacek smiled. "Where is Pan Matejko?"

"Encamped outside. Said to come find him when you got your lazy ass up," Lesław chuckled. "Humansky's there too."

"When does everyone return?" Jacek asked.

"One Sunday hence."

"We will feast before you go. A celebration of victory, of thanks. I am forever in your debt," Jacek said.

"No need. We are square now," said Lesław sheepishly.

"Jacek, I leave after the midday meal for Wiesław's estate and home. You will accompany me?" Pawel said solemnly.

Wiesław. Something tore inside Jacek. He didn't want to go; he had to go. "We will deliver the sad tidings to our fallen brother's family," he explained to the puzzled group.

Each man bowed his head. The silence was broken moments later when two serving maids delivered flagons of wine and three platters of salted fish, bread, cheese, and dried plums.

Filip snatched a handful of plums. "I want to hear how you killed all those heathens, Pan Jacek." His eyes gleamed.

"Later, Filip," Henryk said, then poked Jacek's chest. "Should you be someplace else?"

Jacek left them and made his way briskly up two flights to Oliwia's temporary quarters. He knocked on the door and stepped back, pulling in deep breaths. He ran his hand through his hair, fingered his scar, and straightened his żupan. Nadia's small head poked out, her pebble-round brown eyes larger than usual as she scanned him from boot to crown.

She smiled and in a squeaky voice said, "Captain. My lady has been asking after you. Please come in."

Oliwia sat in an armchair before a window, her glossy hair waving down her back and her feet propped on a cushioned stool. Her body was twisted toward him, and a smile lit her face. Her light blue eyes were clear, and her face resembled polished ivory, except for a crusted red gash on one cheekbone and blotchy purple bruises. The sight made him seethe, made him want to hack Antonin's and Romek's corpses anew. He stood frozen in place and realized he was staring, so he stepped into the chamber while bowing, feeling altogether like a waddling goose with a broken shank.

"Jacek." She held out her hand.

He took it. "You will not faint?"

She let out a little chuckle. "I will not faint, although I may still believe myself dreaming. You will forgive me if I reach out and touch you from time to time."

Touch me all you like, he wanted to say but stopped himself. He rubbed his scar self-consciously.

She reddened. "Sit with me, please."

Tentatively, he sank into the armchair beside her and released her hand—it was akin to letting go of a lifeline, and he suddenly felt adrift. *Close yet so far.* He fastened his eyes on her. The bruising aside, her skin was a becoming creamy shade of pink, and her lips were a vibrant stain, like a ripe strawberry he longed to nibble. She had grown thinner but was otherwise as he remembered—as she'd appeared in his frequent reveries when he'd been lashed to the oar.

He dragged a hand through his hair. "How are your feet?" He pointed at said stockinged feet.

"Sore, but 'tis merely a nuisance. And you? What of your injuries?" She accepted a metal cup from Nadia and handed it to him.

He unconsciously reached for the shoulder. "I'd forgotten it," he lied. Oliwia smiled contritely, and he gave her a sidelong glance. "Just another scar." He sipped, watching her over the rim of the cup. Her blush grew a little deeper, and he itched to pull her into his lap but reined in the desire. Instead, he said, "Stefan and a squad are escorting Adam and Anka home. You'll soon see for yourself your son is unharmed."

"I do not believe I have thanked you yet—for him, for me."

He waved her off. "Not needed."

"Henryk has told me a little of your ordeal," she said softly. "I can scarcely imagine it."

"Yet you have endured your own hardships."

She smiled sympathetically. "They pale by comparison."

"I was most pleased to see you made good use of the Turkish knife. Antonin would have died from that wound had Romek not been eager to finish him. Well done." He didn't hide his admiration.

She arched her eyebrows. "Truly?"

"Truly." Jacek took another sip and stared out the window. A hawk screeched as it circled, heedless of a trio of birds haranguing it. In a far pasture, a small figure drove a flock of sheep, like jolting little clouds, over an emerald blanket. The tang of dung mixed with rich, moist earth wafted through the window, brought there by a stiffening breeze.

"Would you tell me about it? About what happened to you?" Her voice was hesitant.

He drew in a long breath and blew it out. Haltingly, he unearthed the ordeal, reliving it as the morning waned.

When he'd finished, he stole a glance at her. She tugged something from her bodice, slipping it along a chain. The glint caught his eye, transfixing him. He reached over and slid it from her grasp. Astonished, he turned it in his fingers and studied a small stamp on the back, a lopped off letter *S*. In his hand, he held the cross she had given him on the eve of his departure a year ago. Her family cross—the Sewell cross—that had been taken from him during the ambush.

The breath rushed out of him. "Where did you get this?"

"When we got word of your—of the attack, Henryk led men there … where the killing happened. He found it on the body he thought was yours. Stefan believed he'd seen you struck down. When Henryk brought back the necklace, brought Jarosława back …"

Oliwia plucked the cross from his open palm and dropped it down her front. She twisted her hands in her lap and continued. "It never occurred to me that you survived. Had I the faintest idea, I would have searched for you, tried to bring you home." In a hush, she said, "I would not have stopped looking. I would never have abandoned you." Tears spilled down her face like an overfilled basin.

Yet she'd agreed to marry Henryk. Jealousy jabbed him. "Did you grieve?" he blurted. It was a stupid question, but he so needed to hear the answer from her lips.

"Merciful God, yes." Gazing out the window, she swiped at her cheeks. "I died that day," she breathed. She began drumming her fist against her chest. "My heart was shattered. I was bereft. Devastated."

"God must have had another plan for me, Liwi. I wish … I wish … Dear God, I wish so many things had been different. I should have known better, done better. All those men, their families … they depended on me … And you … And this …" He swept a hand around him. Tears sprang up, and he pressed his thumbs into his eyes.

The hawk circled in the opposite direction, now pursued by five frantic birds. The shepherd, along with his flock, had disappeared over a rise. In the distance, the lake shimmered like beads of quicksilver where it shone through gaps between drab tree trunks. The breeze had become a spring wind that chased shredded clouds across the sky, so he dragged their chairs, with her still seated in one, before the hearth, admonishing her when she tried to clamber out.

"What are your plans now?" she asked as they settled before a fiery hearth leaking tendrils of gray smoke.

The question thumped him. He had had only one goal, one dream that had fed him, had kept him alive, and here he was at the end of that long, improbable journey, suddenly unsure how to complete the mission. He cleared his throat. "I leave for Boronów midday."

"But you just got back!" she yelped. "What is so important that pulls you there?"

Her reaction surprised him, and he stammered. "The man I told you about, Pan Wiesław, has … had an estate close by. His widow and two daughters do not know he is dead. Pawel and I will bring whatever comfort we can, and—"

Frowning, she threw up her hands. "And no one else can do this? How I wish I were one of your soldiers!"

He stared at her, searching for an answer but finding none.

She dropped her head. "I am sorry, Jacek. It's just … I'm just—"

Nadia and another servant appeared with trays holding the midday meal and deposited them on the table separating Jacek and Oliwia. As he lifted a bowl of steaming chicken soup to his lips, Oliwia fidgeted. The room was quiet save the sound of a maid pouring out drinks, the rustle of Oliwia's woollen skirts, Nadia's squeak when she asked if she could get them anything more.

Oliwia chewed her nails more than anything on her plate. Jacek stood and scratched his nape, poked at the fire, and plopped back down. Nadia was out of hearing range.

Sucking in a breath, he leveled his eyes at Oliwia. "Liwi, I … I must take my leave, but before I do, I would explain about Lady Eugenia."

"You were not truthful with me." Her eyes remained riveted on the flames.

A sinking feeling seized him. One misstep after another propelled her from him. "No, I was not, and for that I am sorrier than I can say. I had agreed to marry her before Eryk's death, before it ever occurred you might be … I wanted to tell you before I left, so many times, but I feared you would not marry me."

"Do you love her?" she asked evenly.

He shook his head "No. God help me, I never did. The ink was not yet dry on the parchment when I realized my error."

397

They sat for long moments, the blaze popping occasionally, cascading a sizzle of embers onto the hearth. Jacek crossed and uncrossed his ankles, tapped his fingers on his thigh. Nadia picked up the tray and left.

"If I'd told you I had signed an engagement contract, what would you have done?"

She frowned at him. "I'm not sure I underst—"

"Would you have agreed to marry me?" he prodded.

She shook her head slowly, once, twice. "Of course not."

"Right or wrong, that is precisely why I chose not to tell you. Not until I had undone my error. I planned to break the contract as soon as I reached Silnyród."

"Were you ever going to tell me?"

"Yes, but not until I returned and wed you, when you could not bolt from me. I would have done anything to keep from losing you again, Liwi."

Nadia poked her head in. "The healer is back, m'lady."

Jacek rose and brushed his thumb over a cross affixed to the hilt of his new szabla, one he'd lifted from the battle booty. Then, with an awkward head dip, he turned and left.

In stunned silence, Oliwia watched Jacek's retreating back. As the healer scrutinized her wounds, Oliwia's mind reeled and blanked simultaneously, leaving her wanting for a coherent thought. *My love, my life is back.* With joy came wretchedness. *But everything has changed.*

His eyes were exactly as she had remembered them, intense sapphire blue fringed in thick, dark lashes. Eyes she could lose herself in. She'd stopped herself from tracing her fingers along the raw gash running the length of his cheek, the scar that made her heart weep for the suffering he'd endured. Despite it and the deeper lines on his face, he was more handsome than she'd remembered.

She'd been moved at least a dozen times to reach out to him during his tale—to touch his solid shoulder, his sinewy arm, his gaunt face—but he'd seemed unreachable, as though he'd shielded himself behind a stone wall.

Oliwia's heavy heart lifted when Anka brought Adam into the chamber. She picked her precious baby up, his chubby feet—with all ten toes—kicking at her lap. He laughed his infectious laugh as she held him aloft.

"I'll keep him a while, Anka." Oliwia pressed Adam's solid body to her chest and drew in the smell of his skin and hair. Tears pricked her eyes on the wings of a fresh prayer of thanks, and she realized she held him too tightly when he began wriggling.

Henryk tapped on the door. "May I come in?"

"Yes, of course." Oliwia bounced Adam on her leg.

Henryk's left hand was bandaged and resting in a sling. With his other hand, he held the door for Anka, and she squeezed by.

Oliwia signaled him to take the chair beside hers. "Why do you look that way?"

"What way?" He dropped into the seat.

"As if everything that happened is your fault."

"But it is," he said derisively.

She tilted her head and sighed. "You could not have known a man you'd fought beside and trusted all these years would betray you, betray us all."

"I should have seen it," he said bitterly.

"It was impossible to see, Henryk, unless you are a divine angel with the sight."

He chuckled. "There is no danger of that, is there? A divine angel and I being confused with one another."

"I hope you know how grateful I am, and always will be, for everything you have done and have given up for Biaska, for me." She glanced at his hand. He nodded. Then she looked at him squarely. "Henryk, I release you from your pledge."

He feigned surprise, but his relief was evident. "You do not wish to marry me, after all?"

"I could not endure so many broken hearts. I fear the maids' tears would cause the rivers to rise and flood," she teased.

"You will go to Jacek?"

Her attention was drawn to the window, where swallows darted across the pallid sky. A thin column of smoke swirled lazily and disappeared into wispy, unformed clouds. In the distance lay tilled, moist brown soil that would soon burst with verdant down. The world should be right.

"I'm not sure he wants me, Henryk. He has me muddled."

He dropped his head and looked at her from under his brows. "Of course he wants you! Jacek did not claw his way out of the pits of hell and drag himself over hundreds of miles because he missed my company or Beata's cooking. Nor did he do it to marry Lady Eugenia."

Her throat clogged, and she swallowed hard. Tears threatened to spill. "I know," she whispered. "But he seems so distant. And now he's gone again."

Henryk continued softly. "Give him time, Oliwia. He needs to find his way, to know where his place is. Jacek has always kept himself in control, so he may never tell you what you long to hear. You may need to be the one to say it all. But know *you* are the reason he survived."

Now the tears did come, gently, like a soft, pattering rain, and she let them. Henryk brushed them from her cheek. "Life is short, and it is brutal. You've both been given a miracle. Recognize joy when it comes and take it where you can—even if you have to bash him over the head with it."

She half laughed, half cried as she looked into his sympathetic hazel eyes.

"And no, he doesn't know I'm here." He grinned. "He would likely lop my head off and stake it beside Antonin's if he knew I sat this close to you." They both laughed, and more tears leaked from her eyes.

She leaned over and planted a soft kiss on his cheek. "Thank you."

Chapter 37

Refuge

J acek stood with Pawel in the stableyard, ready to mount up. He narrowed his eyes and watched two crows squawk from the ramparts as they unfurled their great black wings. A breeze lifted leaves and jiggled bushes at the edge of the yard. The air was damp and brisk, and he pulled it into his lungs, along with odors of woodsmoke and stables. Feliks handed him his reins.

What the hell am I doing?

He passed the reins back to Feliks. "I am not going." He turned to Pawel. "This is where we part ways, my lord-brother. Dawid will accompany you in my stead." Pawel gave him a knowing nod.

After hunting Dawid down and exchanging good-byes with Pawel, Jacek saw the men off and returned to the keep. He found Oliwia in the kitchen garden, her back to him as she sat on the edge of a planter box of herbs. Here was her refuge, her sanctuary, and he was not surprised to find her alone. In fact, he'd counted on it.

The late afternoon sun dazzled as it sank below the garden's parapet, bathing the walls with shimmering pale light while violet shadows encroached. Oliwia didn't know he was there, so he watched her, taking in her narrow shoulders, the soft curve of her hips, and her thick curls bound against her creamy neck. She hummed, singing out an occasional word. She had not been entirely truthful when she told him she could not sing a note, though she would never be mistaken for a songbird. Despite his attempt to rein it in, his heart sped up. He let out a nervous cough, and she stood and whirled, her big eyes glittering in the gathering twilight.

"Jacek!" she yelped. "I thought you had left."

He removed his gloves and grasped them in one hand. "I sent Dawid instead. Should you be on your feet?"

She shrugged and wiped her hands on her apron. Her face was flushed with a rosy glow, a sheen of perspiration on her polished cheeks. Drawing the back of her hand across her face, she streaked her nose with dirt. He stared at her, so many thoughts spinning in his head.

"What of your duty?" she asked.

"My duty," he sighed. "My duty lies here. Will you forgive me my mistakes, Oliwia?"

She frowned. "There is nothing to forgive, Jacek." Her throat rippled with a swallow. "I, uh, might ask you the same. You know I was to wed Henryk, yes?"

"I do know, yes."

"If I had known you lived, I never would have … Jacek, I would not have betrayed you."

"There was no betrayal. You didn't know." He smacked his gloves against his open palm. "Do you love him?"

Her mouth opened and closed wordlessly. "I do love him," she finally said in a small voice. He felt a band tighten around his chest. She let out a little huff and gave him a sweet smile. "But as a dear friend. Not as a lover. Not as a husband. We shared one kiss. That's all." She reached out and touched his arm. "No one can ever replace you in my heart, Jacek."

He nodded, words failing him. How he could conquer a galley, an army, yet be utterly helpless in the presence of this slip of a dark-haired, blue-eyed girl escaped his comprehension.

He began rummaging in his żupan. "I have something for you."

Her eyes remained fixed on him as he pulled out the burgundy velvet pouch, loosened its drawstring, and spilled its contents in his palm. "I thought to give you this, to replace the one I lost." With stiff fingers, he picked up a gold chain made of slender links. At the end of the chain was a golden cross the length of his index finger. At each edge and in its center were rubies of deep crimson, while in between the stones were petite lustrous pearls. It was a delicate thing, and he held it up, silently seeking her approval to put it on her. She looked from it to him, then bent her neck forward, and he slipped it over her head.

Even as her fingers twiddled it, he shook another object from the pouch—a band of gold, with a dazzling ruby at its center, surrounded by dainty pearls and diamonds. He offered it to her. Her hands flew to her mouth, stifling a sob.

Alarmed, he placed the ring on a planter box beside him; the metal thudded on wood.

Her eyes—wide, glistening like liquid crystals—blinked, and she drew in shuddering breaths. "They are beautiful, Jacek," she choked. "So you still … Does this mean …"

"My desire to be with you has not wavered, Liwi. If anything, it has grown stronger." He paused. "These are my wedding gifts to you … if you'll still have me."

She seemed to laugh and cry at the same time. Confused, he did the only thing that came to him and took a stride, closing the gap between them. He cupped the back of her head. She let out a little cry that he stifled when he took her mouth. Her lips softened and parted, and he moved his mouth hungrily over hers. She wrapped her arms around his neck, and he crushed her to him, letting her herbal-citrus fragrance wash over him. He pulled back, catching his breath.

"I don't give a damn about Henryk or anyone else," he rasped.

A chapel bell rang and set the hounds to howling, followed by the crash of crockery and Beata screeching. It startled them both, and they flew a foot apart. He was still breathing hard, chilled where her body had heated his mere moments before.

"I feared your feeling for me had changed." She bit her bottom lip.

"Liwi," he said quietly, "when I'm with you, I'm reduced to a gabbling fool who cannot express what's in his heart. But know you are all I want and ever have been." He reached out and brushed the dirt from her nose. "When I'm not with you, my arms ache and my heart grieves." *I cannot live without you.* He picked up the ring and offered it to her. "Say you will still marry me."

She launched herself at him. He caught her just as her mouth landed on his. Heated minutes later, she broke the kiss and laughed.

"I will marry you, my lord, for I feel the urge to compromise your virtue overtaking me."

Delight lit him up inside. He slid the ring on her finger and twined his hand in her hair. "It might interest you to know I have new scars."

She flicked her eyes over him. "Where?"

"Beneath my clothing. Everywhere. And of course this hideous mark on my face." He drew in a breath. "Can you bear looking at it?"

She reached up and feathered her fingertips over his scar. He suppressed the urge to flinch as she studied his face. One more delicate trace from temple to jaw, and she cradled his cheek. "I rather like it on you. It gives you an air of … danger. Jacek, you have always been a beautiful man, and now you are positively roguish." She winked. "I don't see how I'll be able to keep my hands off you."

He thought to make a rejoinder, but she'd rendered him speechless once more. For a moment, all he could do was stare at her as though he were halfwitted. Then he raised one eyebrow and dropped the other in a show of skepticism. "Beautiful?"

"Mm-hmm. As for these other scars, I shall need to see for myself, yes?"

"I am counting on it." He covered her hand in his, resting his furry cheek in her palm. "Dear God, I adore you."

"And I adore you, scars and all."

Firelight gilded the polished mantel. The rest of the room was plunged in indigo shadows dotted by candlelight, and here Oliwia paced, her heart beating like dragonfly wings. Ever since dinner, when Jacek had whispered he wished to spend time alone with her tonight, she'd expected him at her door. But it was late, and he hadn't come. Was he awaiting her in his chamber? On the ramparts? Perhaps she'd misunderstood.

She stopped and cocked her head. Were those footsteps? She ran her fingers through her hair and settled her wrap on her shoulders. *Please be Jacek, please be Jacek.*

When a knock came, her heart fairly leapt from her chest. She opened it a crack only to discover Nadia wearing a tentative smile. "Checking your fire, m'lady."

Oliwia threw the door open, and the maid peeked in. "It's fine, Nadia. In fact, I've no need of you the rest of this night." A look of surprise crossed the girl's face before she curtsied and pivoted. Oliwia leaned into the passageway and glanced one way, then the other. Except for the maid's retreating footsteps, nothing stirred. Oliwia leaned against the door with a sigh but couldn't close it completely. She pressed a little harder; it held. She shoved; it shoved back. Startled, she looked up to see Jacek grinning at her as he slipped through the opening.

"May I come in?" He was already in and latching the door behind him.

"Where did you come from?" she squeaked.

"A cupboard. I've been hiding like a common thief, dodging your army of servants."

She was overcome with giddiness that quickly transformed to shyness when she glanced down at her two layers of clothing. The silk mantle and linen chemise could only be deemed appropriate for the bedchamber and were far too thin—and far too presumptuous. She wrapped her arms about herself and headed to the hearth; he fell in behind.

"I cannot picture a cupboard big enough to hold you."

"It wasn't."

She lowered herself into an armchair. He stood beside her like a sentinel and leaned his arm along its back. She sat forward. Where was her boldness from mere hours ago?

"Um, you said you wished to speak with me?"

He looked at her, bemused. The firelight sparkled in his deep blue eyes. "I did?"

"Yes. You said you wished to be alone to … I thought to talk."

In one fluid move, he lifted her up, slid into her seat, pulled her into his lap, and wrapped his arms around her. "I thought we made rather a good job of talking already today. Have you more to say?" He ran a gentle fingertip over her bruises and her cut cheek. Anything she might say was frozen—on her tongue as well as in her brain. Her face and neck blazed, but not from the fire. She resisted the urge to squirm as she perched on his long, solid thigh bones, noticeably hard even through the thickness of his wool trousers and linen żupan.

"Does it hurt?" He frowned.

"What?"

He skimmed his thumb over the cut. "This."

She shook her head. Her breathing gathered speed.

He cradled her face in one big hand and pulled it to his. He kissed the wound, his touch feather-light. "Even bruised, you're still the most beautiful thing I've ever seen."

She flinched involuntarily.

"Do you wish me to go?" he asked.

"No! I ... I'm ... Your arm! Does it not hurt?"

One side of his mouth quirked; he continued holding her face mere inches from his. "My arm is fine. But if it makes you feel any better, my heart will shortly gallop out of my chest. I may have to run after it." His eyes lowered to her mouth.

She let out a nervous snicker that came out as a snort, and they both broke into laughter that shook them until tears ran down their cheeks.

He grabbed her hip to prevent her sliding to the floor, and when he caught his breath, he said, "You're all bone. We must fatten you up."

She ran her hands over his angular shoulders, suddenly filled with tenderness. "And you," she murmured. She fingered the long golden strands that brushed his jaw, then glided her fingers over his scar. "What they did—"

He placed his finger on her lips. "Shh, sweet. It's over. My prayers have been answered. I'm here with you." He pulled her to his chest, and she rested her head on his shoulder with a sigh. He swept his hand the length of her thigh, up her arm, and back again. Her body tingled with every warm caress.

He kissed her throat, inching up to her ear. "I was daft to consider leaving today," he mumbled. Her entire body was covered in gooseflesh.

"I'm so glad you stayed." She unfastened the top of his żupan and his undershirt. Kissing the base of his neck, she breathed him in.

"Are you going to examine my scars?" His soft voice sounded hopeful.

Like magnet to metal, their lips drew together. He kissed her deeply, fully, his tongue languidly exploring her mouth. Moans rose in her throat, echoes of the heat rising in her body. She wanted his hands on her, his skin on hers, wanted him deep inside her. She broke the kiss.

"Do you want me to examine them now?" she breathed.

"You have no idea how sorely," he whispered back.

He arose and carried her to the bed, and she clung to him, safe, protected. Loved.

A fortnight later, Jacek floated in sleep's oblivion, exhausted and contented as he held Oliwia beside him. Their bodies had drifted apart during the night, and he startled awake, in a cold sweat, not knowing where he was. He panicked, thinking himself aboard the *Cesaret*; it was a familiar nightmare. But then he saw Oliwia, and he eased his head on the bolster. In the faint glow of one guttering candle, he watched her sleep. She was so tranquil. So beautiful. He studied the curve of her cheek, her milky throat, her smooth skin glistening just above the counterpane. Her dark hair lay in a jumble between them, and he picked up a lock and brought it to his nose, inhaling her fragrance as he slid it over his lip, catching it on his stubble. *This is real.*

Leaves quaked in the breeze while frogs sang in a croaking chorus. The sounds of a peaceful, late-spring night surrounded and soothed him. But thoughts bobbed along in his mind like petals caught in a stream, eddying, swirling. Tomorrow was their wedding day. No longer would he skulk in the dark to her bedchamber. Not that he cared about being discovered, but she did, and that he did care about.

Come morning, he would ride with her to Maławieża's church, surrounded by his lord-brothers, his family, and his friends. The banns had been waived and the troops persuaded to linger—it was bound to be a grand celebration. And after they spoke their vows before God and the congregation, he would gain a wife, a son, another brother. They would become *his* family to cherish, to protect. To grow.

Oliwia stirred and turned her face to him, her eyes still closed. As he studied her, his mind wandered back to how he'd gotten here. Mere months before, he'd languished in despair, shackled to a wretched life of slavery. Now he was free, and he was home. At times, he was uncomfortable in Biaska's familiar flurry and found it unbearable, like a man lowering himself into a scalding spring. In the end, he would grow used to it and let it cleanse the dirt and pain.

He ran the back of his hand over Oliwia's hair, her bare shoulder. Her lips curved in a little smile, and she soughed and sank into the mattress. Slipping his hand under the coverlet, he stroked the soft skin between her thighs, skimmed his fingers over the dip of her belly, to her breasts, caressing each one. Would lying with her, like eating after starving for so long, be an insatiable hunger that drove him constantly?

Her eyes fluttered open, and she pulled herself to him, warm, soft, yielding, her hums like a melody in his ear. She draped her arm over his shoulder and ran her hand in his hair, kissing him slowly, deeply, whispering his name in the dark, whispering that she loved him. Sparks kindled and ignited a blaze inside him once more, engulfing him, chasing away all thought. He entered her, and her hips rose to take him in, to move with him. They found their rhythm together, fusing. When they were done, he buried his face in her hair, and he wept. She cradled him, rocked him, comforted him in her arms, and she wept with him.

"All is well," she murmured. "You are here now. You are home, Jacek."

And he realized that was why he wept. He was home.

Oliwia bounded from her empty bed, her eyes flicking over the depression where Jacek's body had been. With a smile, she thought of his protests when she'd pushed him out of bed. He'd shrugged on his undershirt and kissed her, his tousled hair flopping in his eyes. In that moment, like so many before, sweet warmth had flooded her until her heart nearly burst. She'd resisted pulling him back into bed with her, instead watching the door after he'd gone.

Soon she was dressed in a shimmering aquamarine gown adorned with lace and ribbons. About her waist was a belt of silver-and-gold thread that held the pink-bejeweled Turkish dagger. Her hair was loosely woven with white roses and blue forget-me-nots—no maiden wreaths for her this day, nor would she endure another shearing and capping ceremony. At her throat were her silver necklace and Jacek's ruby-and-pearl cross. She had given him his own cross of rich gold suspended on a simple chain, which he wore beneath his garments.

He awaited her beside his parents at a table in the great hall. His large frame had filled out, and today he wore a żupan of deep blue silk lined in crimson. A fringed sash encircled his trim waist. His golden-brown hair was neatly trimmed and his face clean-shaven, the scar a faded, pallid pink. Truthfully, she'd stopped noticing it.

Together they kneeled on cushions before his father and mother. In a ritual usually discharged by the bride's parents, Oliwia gave them her thanks, and they gave her and Jacek their blessings. Her heart galloped so much she only recalled bits of what his mother said as she sprinkled them with holy water.

"May God bless you ... Always be strong together ... Faithful to one another ..."

Oliwia remembered none of what his father said. In fact, she remembered little of the ceremony, save Jacek's warm hand holding hers and his rumbling voice as he recited his vows and prayers—punctuated by a crack that made them both snicker and made the priest frown. That frown recalled kind, pudding-faced Father Augustyn, for he would have snickered too; her heart squeezed.

They left the church and entered a shower of grains; a pair of collared doves took wing. "A good sign," Jacek said as she clung to his arm.

"As is the wedding bread," she replied.

His eyebrows inched to his forehead. "No cracks?"

"Not one." *Intact bread, intact marriage.*

"I had no doubt." He gave her a beatific smile.

Guests were greeted with salt and bread as they entered the great hall. Soon Oliwia sat beside Jacek at the head table upon the dais. Many a toast was raised—and drowned out by the boisterous merrymakers—while servants deposited platters of pork sausage, stuffed capon, and venison in white mustard sauce amid bowls of sweet cabbage, carrots, and peas.

Among the toastmakers was Humansky, who had outshouted Henryk and Klemens. Even Filip's squawk couldn't overcome him. "Kapitana Kamen-holova," he cried, "Even the happiest of marriages know ups and downs. May all yours be in the bedroom—her toes up and yours down!"

Oliwia's hand flew to her mouth to hold in an embarrassed laugh while Jacek sputtered wine. He recovered himself and managed to raise his goblet aloft.

"Thank you, my friend," he croaked and took a long swallow.

Humansky continued standing as though preparing yet another toast. Wide-eyed, Oliwia cringed when he opened his mouth. "The sultan never blessed us with a reply."

"Then it worked!" Jacek exclaimed, helping himself to more food.

Relieved when Humansky sat back down, Oliwia crinkled her eyebrows in a silent question directed at Jacek. He leaned to her ear. "Ataman Humansky helped me rescue Silnyród's folk, and I helped him, ah, correspond with the sultan." He shoveled in a helping of carrots.

Oliwia gawked at his heaped platter. "You will be sick if you eat all that, Captain Rockhead!"

Henryk must have overheard her, for he pulled away from two buxom companions, obviously suffering no ill effects from their broken engagement. "A stallion needs plenty of fuel if he's going to run all night, Oliwia."

Jacek stopped chewing long enough to down his wine and wink at her. She gave them both her most scandalized look and stymied the giggles bubbling inside her.

The musicians began to play, adding to the din of voices and countless *"Na zdrowies!"* Jacek leaned back to her ear, lightly brushing his lips against it, sending a delightful shiver through her. "What happens next?"

"We've sweets yet, and dancing, and then …"

"And then? Tell me what happens." He waggled his eyebrows over half-lidded eyes and gave her a few sidelong head jerks, all while the hint of a mischievous smile curved his lips.

"You are wicked!" She swatted his arm. "And impatient."

"Impatient?" he laughed. "I have been the most patient suitor I know."

The music and clapping swelled, and she was soon whirling in a wheel of women's bright skirts. She danced with the menfolk, and Jacek promenaded and twirled the ladies. The final dance arrived, and she finished in her husband's arms. Where she belonged.

Henryk held up his hand and shouted for quiet. "The groom has something he would say to his bride."

Jacek took Oliwia's hand and kissed it. She felt a tingle in every nook of her body and was sure her face was the color of the beets upon the table. As she looked at all the faces surrounding them, each one held a smile.

Jacek cleared his throat. "The vow of love which thou didst make, I pray that thou wilt never forsake. Bring it and thy sweet self to me. No other gift I wish from thee."

"I believe that is the groom's well-dressed way of telling his bride 'tis time they retire to the wedding chamber," Henryk hooted.

The crowd clapped, whistled, and howled ribald toasts that sent a fresh flush up her throat. She and Jacek soon climbed upstairs, moved along by the wedding party as though they were fish in a school swimming upriver. Henryk burst into the chamber and invited the entire party to jump upon the bed. Oliwia remembered the last time her marriage bed had been seasoned. She had been burdened with a heavy heart and a heaving stomach and had been horrified by the ritual. Tonight, as Jacek's sisters, Filip, Henryk, and the groomsmen capered and tossed pillows at one another, she laughed until her side cramped.

"Jump harder! We must ensure it will hold up," Henryk yelled.

She stood with Jacek, the two of them like one mind, one heart, as though apart from the merrymaking party. She rose on tiptoe and whispered in his ear, "Perhaps we should find another chamber to sleep in tonight."

He grinned. "If they don't leave momentarily, we shall." Then he gazed at her tenderly, his eyes the color of a calm ocean. "I care not where we sleep, my sweet wife. Wherever you are, then there shall I be."

Jacek and Henryk seemed to exchange a silent message, and Henryk halted the party. Oliwia was taken to her chamber and undressed, then draped in fluttering silk. A half hour—an eternity—passed before she was reunited with Jacek. Now, as he stood before her in the candlelit quiet of their wedding chamber, she drank him in; her stomach danced as though a swarm of butterflies rose to the sky. His mantle draped carelessly over his broad shoulders, revealing his sculpted chest adorned with the gold cross. He was tall and straight, lean and muscled, and he was hers. Her heart nearly burst. If she told him how much she loved him every minute of every day for the rest of their lives, it would never express the breadth of her adoration.

Soon Jacek would leave her to lead men to battle. Peace was ever short-lived, enemies always threatening. And she had married a warrior. There were armies to fight, to vanquish. But as he closed the door softly and barred it that night, as he gathered her in his arms, that world was locked out … for a little while.

The End

Thank you!

Thank you for reading *A Hussar's Promise*! Reviews are crucial for indie authors, so if you enjoyed the story, please consider leaving a review on Amazon, BookBub, or GoodReads.

It doesn't have to be long to make all the difference, and I would be so very grateful!

Glossary

Buzdygan *'Booze-de-gun'* – mace, usually wielded by a higher-ranking officer

Cham – a peasant, a lowborn person; calling a Polish nobleman a cham was an insult

Castrum doloris – Latin for "castle of grief;" a decorated structure within a church that shelters a bier and holds candles, flowers, epitaphs, coats of arms, paintings, allegorical statues to honor the deceased

Chorągiew *'Ho-rongev'* – company, banner, usually between 100-200 men

Chorągiew Husarka – a hussar banner or company

Commonwealth – short for Polish-Lithuanian Commonwealth; a term that refers to the United Kingdom of Poland and Duchy of Lithuania

Crown – the Kingdom of Poland

Czekan *'Check-on'* – a war hammer with an axe blade on one side and hammer claw on the other

Dożynki *'Doh-jin-kee'* – harvest festival

Elear – a member of a regiment that rode for the adventurer Aleksander Lisowski; also known as "Lisowczycy," meaning lost men, forlorn hope

Gorget – metal neck piece; armor worn at the neck

Heavy lancers – see husaria

Hetman – general

Husaria *'Hoo-sah-reeah'* – heavy cavalry; Polish winged hussars

Husarski *'Hoo-sahr-ski'* – another word for husaria

Hussar – another word for husaria

Kolpak – aka 'calpac;' a man's fur hat

Koncerz *'Kone-sesh'* – a tuck; a thin four-foot blade with a triangular or square cross-section used like a short lance to punch through armor

Kopia – long, hollow lance wielded by a hussar, between 13-20 feet long

Muscovites – Russians

Muscovy – Russia

Na zdrowie! *'Nahz-drov-eeah* – To your health!

Nadziak *'Nahd-jack'* – war hammer with a hammer head on one side and a claw on the other

Namiestnik *'Nah-mia-sneek'* – placeholder; an officer/lieutenant who fills in while the regular is away

Pacholik *'Pahk-ho-leek'* – a retainer or squire; serves a towarzysz

Pałasz *'Pa-wash'* – a hussar's broadsword

Pallash – see pałasz

Pan – Lord, sir; title for a nobleman

Pani – Lady; title for a noblewoman

Pauldron – shoulder armor

Piwo *'Pee-voh'* – beer, ale

Poczet *'Poe-chets'* – retinue; 2-5 men (servants and retainers) who serve the towarzysz/hussar

Porucznik *'Poh-rootz-neek'* – a commander's second, the lieutenant

Starosta – mayor, official in charge of security

Suka – type of fiddle

Szabla Husaria *'Shah-blah hoo-sah-reeah'* – a hussar's sabre; highly valued and prized. Next to the kopia, the favored weapon of a hussar

Szlachcic *'Shlahth-cheets'* – Polish nobleman

Szlachta *'Shlahth-dah'* – Polish nobility

Szlachcianka *'Shlahth-chiankah'* – noblewoman

Szyszak *'Shu-shahk'* – lobster-tailed pot helmet

Towarzysz *'Toe-vah-jez'* – literally a "companion" in Polish; a hussar; a nobleman of wealth, with his own armor, horses and retinue. Knight class

Towarzysze – plural of towarzysz

Winged hussars – heavy hussars; heavy husaria; heavy lancers

Wodka – vodka

Złote *'Zwah-tay'* – plural form of basic Polish monetary unit

Złoty *'Zwah-tee'* – basic Polish monetary unit

Zupa rybna *'Zoopah rebnah'* – fish soup

Żupan *'Jzo-pahn'* – a man's outer garment; resembles a long coat with a high collar; buttons down the front; normally worn over trousers and a shirt

414

Name/Place Pronunciation Guide

Biaska *'Bee-aska'* – fictional estate and village

Bilicki, Witold *Be-licky, Vee-told'* – deputy starosta to Mikołaj Zebrzydowski; fictional character

Boronów *'Boh-roh-noff'* – a real village in Poland

Brenna *'Bren-nah'* – a real village in Poland

Dąbrowski *'Dom-brov-ski'*

Eryk *'Eric'*

Filip *'Fee-leep'*

Jacek *'Yaht-sek'*

Jacuś *'Yaht-sosh'* – diminutive of Jacek, used for a boy

Jarosława *'Yah-ro-swah-vah'* – combination of "powerful" and "glory"

Katarzyna *'Ka-tar-zayna'*

Kobietasklep *'Kohbia-tah-sklep'* – a fictional town

Łac *'Wahtz'* – a fictional town

Lesław *'Less-wahf'*

Lisowski, Aleksander Józef *'Lee-soff-ski, Alexahnder Yo-zeff'*

Liwi *'Lee-vee'* – diminutive of Oliwia

Machjeld *'My-helled'* – Polonized version of MacLeod

Małavieża *'Mah-wah-vee-ay-jah'* – fictional fortress one mile from Biaska

Małylas *'Mao-wish'* – fictional manor house belonging to Pani Zofia

Marcin *'Mahr-cheen'*

Oliwia *'Oh-lee-vee-ah'*

Romek *'Roh-meck'*

Sosnowski, Michal *'Sose-novski, Mee-hal'* – fictional character who acts as deputy to Jan Potocki *('Poe-toet-ski')*, a historical figure who died at Kamieniec April 22, 1611

Stanisław *'Stah-nee-swahf'*

Wąskadroga *'Vohn-ska-drogah'* – fictional castle belonging to Antonin Wąskaski; means "narrow road"

Wąskaski *'Vohn-ska-skee'*
Zebrzydowski, Mikołaj *'Zeb-je-dovski, Mee-ko-why'*
Żółkiewski, Stanisław *'Jeull-kevski, Stah-nee-swahf'*

Author's Notes

1. The Polish-Lithuanian Commonwealth came about as the result of the Treaty of Lublin, signed in 1569, which united the Kingdom of Poland and the Grand Duchy of Lithuania. The Commonwealth was one of the richest, most powerful, and most populous countries in Europe at the time. It existed until the Third Partition of Poland in 1795.

2. Poland was one the great powers and a center of culture in Eastern and Central Europe for two hundred years. Memories of its former greatness were methodically erased during the Partitions of Poland in the eighteenth century. Russia, Austria, and Prussia carried off Poland's books and treasures and disseminated propaganda that its might and influence had never existed.

3. Golden Freedom, or Golden Liberty, refers to privileges enjoyed by the Polish nobility (the szlachta). It conveyed religious freedom and declared all nobility equal, regardless of rank or status. It also gave the nobility extensive legal rights, including assigned private jurisdiction, protecting them from being arrested or having their property seized without a conviction from a court of law. In addition, it limited the monarchy's power. The szlachta made up the two-chamber legislature/Parliament: an appointive Senate and an elected Sejm. The king was chairman of the Senate. The szlachta filled the legislative seats, wrote the laws (often for their benefit), and elected the king. In short, they wielded a great deal of power. The *Liberum Veto* conveyed the power of veto on a single member so, quite literally, one man could bring voting to a halt.

4. With the advent of the Golden Liberty, formal titles were banned. All noblemen were to refer to one another as "Pan" ("Sir" or "Lord"), whether they were a lowly noble or a powerful magnate. Loopholes did

exist, however. For instance, noblemen who signed the Union of Lublin with their titles were allowed to keep them.

5. Noblemen were granted the right to bear coats of arms. However, coats of arms worked a little differently in the Commonwealth. Noble families adopted those belonging to others, fitting themselves under an "umbrella," if you will. While there were over forty thousand noble families, there existed approximately seven thousand coats of arms (and variations). Thus it wasn't uncommon for two noble families to share the same coat of arms.

6. During the time the novel takes place, Poland was fighting Muscovy, Sweden, and the Ottoman Empire. The conflict with Sweden was a series of intermittent wars that spanned two centuries. King Zygmunt III Vasa was Swedish and had been King of Sweden until his uncle, Charles IX Vasa, who had been ruling in Zygmunt's place, took the crown for himself. Zygmunt was deposed in 1599 but never gave up his claim to the Swedish throne.

7. At times, Poland was allied with Sweden against Muscovy, and at other times with Muscovy against Sweden. For instance, Poland and Sweden signed a truce in 1611 that lasted until 1617, when full-on war broke out again between the two countries over, among other things, possession of Livonia and domination over the Baltic Sea.

8. The conflict with Muscovy arose during Russia's Time of Troubles (1598-1613), when that country was in the midst of a leadership crisis. The conflict has several names, including the Dymitriads, the Polish-Muscovite War, the Polish Invasion, and the Polish Intervention. The conflict ran from 1605 to 1618, though Poland's real involvement began in 1609 when Muscovy and Sweden signed a treaty, with Sweden pledging some of its military force to Muscovy. Poland had been seeking to federalize Muscovy and saw this union as a threat. The King of Poland acted, marching on and besieging Smoleńsk with a small army. The Commonwealth would eventually take Smoleńsk in 1611. Poland did take Moscow in 1610, occupying it until 1612. The king's son, Prince Władysław, was elected tsar by the boyars in 1610, but the king sought to change the terms of the agreement with Muscovy, and

the boyars became alarmed. The agreement unraveled, Władysław did not take the throne, and the conflict continued.

9. To the south, the Ottomon Empire and its vassals, the Crimean Tatars, threatened the Commonwealth and Christianity. The Commonwealth was often referred to as the "Bulwark of Christendom," and indeed was a deciding factor in turning the Ottomans back when they were set to capture Vienna in 1683. Of the two, the Tatars were deemed the greater threat because they raided annually, pillaging, burning, and carrying off countless captives to be sold in Turkish slave markets. It is estimated that in all, the Tatars took over one million Poles captive. Their raiding was equally, if not more, devastating in surrounding countries, such as Muscovy.

10. The Moldavian Magnate Wars were a series of conflicts spanning from the late sixteenth century to the early seventeenth century. Amid ongoing cross-border raids by Cossacks into the Ottoman Empire on one side and Tatar raids into the Commonwealth on the other, a semi-permanent war zone existed. In this hotbed, magnates from the Commonwealth began interfering in Moldavia's affairs in order to extend the Commonwealth's influence, which upset the Ottoman Empire. Wallachia, Transylvania, Hungary, and the Habsburgs were also part of the mix. Stefan Potocki, a powerful magnate, sought to re-establish the head of Moldavia and led an army of seven thousand into battle against Moldavia and the Ottoman Empire. He was defeated in July 1612 and taken prisoner. He later died a captive in the notorious Fortress of the Seven Towers (Yekidule Fortress). Months after Potocki's defeat, Żółkiewski negotiated a treaty without further bloodshed. However, the conflict would continue until the Battle of Cecora in 1620, where Żółkiewski lost his life.

11. The Thirty Years' War began as a war over religion. The conflict lasted from 1618 until 1648 and involved the Holy Roman Empire and nearly all of Europe. For the most part, the Commonwealth stayed out of it, aiding the Holy Roman Empire indirectly. For instance, Zygmunt III sent ten thousand cavalrymen to help the Habsburgs. A number of hussars, perhaps adventurers, are said to have joined the fight on the side of the Holy Roman Empire, hiring on as mercenaries. Sweden's

engagement overlapped its war with the Commonwealth, teaming up with Muscovy, who sought to recover Smoleńsk.

12. The main character, Jacek Dąbrowski, is a captain, but he would have actually been a lieutenant (the porucznik), and his friend and subordinate, Henryk Kalinowski, would have been the deputy or second lieutenant. Hussars did not use ranks that translate to those we are accustomed to. Since they were equals, they were all designated "junior officers" under their commander. For the sake of facility, the designations of lieutenant, captain, and colonel (pułkownik) have been applied to this story.

13. There were two top generals in Poland: the Crown Grand Hetman and the Crown Field Hetman, with the Crown Grand Hetman being the highest ranking of the two. Both were offices assigned for life. Lithuania had its own separate, equivalent designations for generals.

14. The main character fights with a nadziak, a war hammer with a hammer head on one side, and a claw on the other (also known as a horseman's pick). The distinctive term "nadziak" wasn't yet established at the time this novel takes place. It might have been called a "czekan," which was a catch-all term for war hammers. Later, the term czekan would be used to distinguish a war hammer with a hammer head on one side, and an ax blade on the other.

15. The layout of Biaska Castle is loosely based on Ogrodzieniec Castle in the Eagles' Nests fortifications in the Polish Jura. Its geographical position would, however, more closely resemble that of Bobolice Castle.

16. The Eagles' Nests fortifications are a series of castles along Poland's western border that King Kazimierz the Great (Kazimierz III Wielki) ordered built in the fourteenth century to secure Poland's western border against its aggressors. As time went on, the fortifications were no longer necessary, and many fell into disrepair.

17. The tale of the Cossacks penning the letter to the Sultan is real, although it's thought to have been written in the mid-1600s. Interpretations of the Sultan's letter to the Cossacks, and their reply, can be found on line and are quite entertaining to read.

18. Women were indeed money lenders, most popular in Gdańsk, where they loaned funds to merchants and businessmen.

19. The Tatar commander, Bater Beg, was a real commander who led tens of thousands of Tatars into Russia in 1614. His real name was Bogatyr Giray Diveev, and Bater Beg was the name the Polish used for him.

20. Khadjibey is the present-day port city of Odessa in southern Ukraine. The notion that slave trade took place there is purely the author's invention.

21. The story of Jacek's escape from the Cesaret is based on the real-life tale of a Polish nobleman, Marek Jakimowski, who was captured by the Ottomans at the Battle of Cecora in 1620. He was sold into slavery and bought by an Ottoman admiral and governor, Kassym Beg. Marek served aboard Kassym Beg's lead galley in a fleet of four merchant ships. His adventure was first printed in Rome in the 1600s, then in several other countries and languages.

22. Maływieża is loosely based on Mirów Castle, a watchtower one mile from Bobolice Castle. The two are located in the Eagle's Nest fortifications and are said to have been connected by a tunnel. The tale of the twin brothers, the treasure, the witch, the girl, and the "White Lady" is based on a ghost tale about Bobolice and Mirów.

23. Miles used are English miles, not Polish miles, which were longer.

24. The novel uses a variety of English and French terms. While perhaps not historically accurate for the story's place and time, I chose terms I felt would be easily recognizable to the modern reader.

25. A number of historical locations and figures were referred to by different names and had various spellings. Where possible, I opted for names recognizable today, in their Polish spellings.

𝕳istorical 𝕵igures

Batory, Stefan

King of Poland, Prince (or Grand Duke) of Transylvania, elected King of Poland and reigned from 1576 until his death in 1586. Batory was responsible for forming the winged hussars in the iteration for which they became famous.

Karwacki, Jan

Leader of one of the most notorious *konfederacjas* (a semi-legal rebellion practiced in the Commonwealth). The mutiny was mounted in 1612 by unpaid Crown troops and was considered one of the largest and worst konfederacjas in Commonwealth history because the soldiers preyed on their own countrymen for recompense. The rebels were finally defeated at the Battle of Rohatyn in 1614. Karwacki was captured by future hetman Stanisław Koniecpolski and sent in chains to Koniecpolski's mentor and future father-in-law, Grand Hetman of the Crown Stanisław Żółkiewski. Karwacki was later executed, while the rest of the soldiers received their back pay.

Lisowski, Aleksander Józef

A Lithuanian nobleman and soldier who led a konferacja (a semi-legal rebellion practiced in the Commonwealth) for unpaid wages. He also took part with the rebels against the royalists in the "Zebrzydowski Rokosz" (Zebrzydowski Rebellion) in 1607-1609. Lisowski eventually became the leader of a band of mercenaries that fought on behalf of the Commonwealth. They took their pay in the form of pillage. Lisowski and his men were opportunistic, often preying on their own countrymen. Because they were skilled, fearsome fighters, the Crown looked the other way. Lisowski's men adopted the name "Lisowczycy," which means lost men, forlorn hope, or chorągiew elearska (company of elears), after his death in 1616. They were eventually hunted down and executed and later officially disbanded by the Sejm (the lower house of Polish Parliament).

Potocki Family

Powerful, influential Polish magnate family. Stefan Potocki was part of the Moldavian Magnate Wars and was defeated with his army July 1612. He later died in Ottoman captivity. Hetman Stanisław Żółkiewski wrote in his memoirs that Jakub Potocki (Castellan of Kamieniec) was ordered by the king to prepare ladders for the assault on Smoleńsk and became one of the first men up on the great fortress's wall before it was breached and taken by the Poles on June 11, 1611.

Szujski, Dymitr

Brother to the tsar, and commander of the Russian army at Kłuszyn. Captured and died in Poland 1613.

Szujski, Tsar Wasyl IV

Tsar of Muscovy from 1606 to 1610. Stanisław Żółkiewski delivered Wasyl IV to the King of Poland in Warsaw after the Battle of Kłuszyn in 1610. Wasyl IV died in Poland two years later.

Vasa, Władysław IV

Son of Zygmunt III, was elected Tsar of Russia July 27, 1610 at the age of fifteen. Because Zygmunt coveted the throne for himself and consequently lost the support of the boyars who elected his son, Prince Władysław never assumed the throne, though he held the title until he relinquished it in1634. Władysław followed in his father's footsteps and became King of Poland/Grand Duke of Lithuania from 1632 until his death in 1648.

Vasa, Zygmunt III

King of Poland elected in 1587 and reigned until his death in 1632. Zygmunt was born in Sweden to King John III and his wife, Katarzyna Jagiellonka of Poland, while his parents were held captive. He was raised Catholic and remained so throughout his life. He held the title of King of Sweden until 1599 when he was deposed by his uncle, King Charles IX Vasa, though he would not give up his claim to the Swedish throne. In fact, he went to war with Sweden to reclaim his crown. The Polish-Swedish War would continue intermittently until 1629 (the term "Polish-Swedish Wars" is a broad term that includes a series of wars between the two countries from the sixteenth century until the eighteenth century). Zygmunt III was criticized for his Swedish ambitions at Poland's expense. He was also criticized for warring with Muscovy (the Polish-Muscovite War, also known as the "Dymitriads") during his reign.

King Zygmunt attempted to institute a number of reforms which the Polish nobility (the szlachta) viewed as a threat to their power and their "Golden Freedom." Conflict between the King and nobility led to the Zebrzydowski Rokosz (Zebrzydowski Rebellion).

Zebrzydowski, Mikołaj

A Polish magnate from Sandomierz and the Palatine of Kraków. He led a rebellion of nobles against King Zygmunt III known as the "Zebrzydowski Rokosz" (Zebrzydowski Rebellion) in 1607-1609, in which Aleksander Lisowski also participated on the rebels' side. The rebellion stemmed in part from the king's attempts to expand his power, which the nobility viewed as an erosion of their own power. The rebels were defeated at Guzów by the king's forces and later pardoned without suffering loss of privilege or assets. The conflict was deemed a stalemate, with neither side making any advances. The rebels were unable to wrestle power from the king, and the king was unable to usurp any of the nobility's power over the monarchy.

Żółkiewski, Stanisław

A Polish magnate and diplomat who was lauded as one of Poland's most brilliant generals, best known for victories such as the Battle of Kłuszyn. He served as Crown Field Hetman, and in 1613, the king appointed him Grand Hetman of the Crown, Poland's highest military ranking and a lifetime position. Żółkiewski had an uneasy relationship with the king (many thought he should have been awarded Grand Hetman of the Crown far sooner than 1613 and that the king withheld it from him purposely). Żółkiewski had negotiated an agreement with the Muscovite boyars and entered Moscow in 1611 prepared for King Zygmunt III's son, Prince Władysław IV, to take the throne. The king thwarted this plan, which ultimately lost Poland the opportunity to gain Muscovy's throne. Żółkiewski penned his memoir, *Expedition to Moscow*, explaining events as he experienced them—some say in an attempt to tell his side of the story. Żółkiewski would continue his brilliant military career engaged in numerous campaigns on the Commonwealth's southern and eastern borders, eventually losing his life at the Battle of Cecora in 1620. He was in his 70s.

Timeline

Date	Event
Jul. 1, 1569	The Union of Lublin treaty is signed, forming the Polish-Lithuanian Commonwealth
Jan. 28, 1573	The Confederation of Warsaw is instituted, granting religious freedom throughout the Commonwealth
May 1, 1576	King Stefan Batory is crowned king, reforms army, and organizes the husaria
Apr. 17, 1577	Battle of Lubieszów, the first of many hussar victories
Dec. 12, 1586	King Stefan Batory dies
Aug. 19, 1587	Zygmunt III Vasa is elected King of Poland
1593	The Moldavian Magnate Wars begin
1595	Fire breaks out in Wawel Castle (Kraków), destroying the royal quarters
1596	King Zygmunt III elects to move his court to Warsaw
1598	Death of Fyodor, Tsar of Muscovy; beginning of Muscovy's Time of Troubles
1600	Beginning of Polish-Swedish War
1605	Beginning of the Dymitriads, the rise of false claimants to the Muscovite throne
1605	King Zygmunt III marries Austrian Archduchess Constance, sister of his late wife
Sep. 27, 1605	Battle of Kircholm, a hussar victory over Swedish forces
1606	Zebrzydowski Rebellion begins
Jul., 1607	Battle of Guzów, where the Zebrzydowski rebels are crushed

1608	Zebrzydowski Rebellion ends
1609	Polish-Muscovite War begins
1609	Siege of Smoleńsk by Poland
Jul. 4, 1610	Battle of Kłuszyn, led by Field Hetman Stanisław Żółkiewski, a hussar victory over combined Muscovite and Swedish forces
Aug., 1610	Field Hetman Żółkiewski marches into Moscow; Poland begins its occupation
Aug. 27, 1610	Muscovite boyars sign a treaty wherein King Zygmunt III's son, Prince Władysław, is elected Tsar
Jun., 1611	Smoleńsk falls to Poland
Jun., 1611	King Zygmunt III sends Field Hetman Żółkiewski to Moscow to relieve the Polish garrison
Aug., 1611	Field Hetman Żółkiewski is driven off by the Muscovites; returns to Poland
Sep., 1611	King Zygmunt III moves into the Royal Palace at Warsaw
Oct., 1611	Field Hetman Żółkiewski presents deposed Tsar Wasyl IV to King Zygmunt III
Jul., 1612	Magnate Stefan Potocki leads his army into Moldovia where he is defeated and taken prisoner
Oct. 22, 1612	The Polish garrison is driven out of Moscow
Oct., 1612	Field Hetman Żółkiewsk reaches agreement on behalf of the Commonwealth with Ştefan II Tomża of Moldavia
Feb., 1613	Michał Romanov, founder of the Romanov Dynasty, becomes Tsar; the end of the Dymitriads
1613	Żółkiewski given title of Great Crown Hetman
Oct. 7, 1620	Great Crown Hetman Żółkiewski dies at the Battle of Cecora in Moldavia; end of the Moldavian Magnate Wars

Acknowledgments

To Eryk Jadaszewski of Polish Hussar Supply Plus, a fountain of knowledge who shared it so freely, and to Joan Karasinski, the gracious queen who welcomed me into her court and allowed me to hang out in her tent during the reenactment of the Battle of Jasna Góra.

To all the living history reenactors who teach us about Poland's storied past and keep its memories vibrant. I'm honored to have been so warmly welcomed by all of you and humbled by your knowledge and your passion. Never stop. Na zdrowie!

To Sophie Hodorowicz Knab, who so patiently answered my questions about Polish traditions and customs.

To the countless history professors, whose knowledge can be found woven into the details.

To Jenny Quinlan, editor extraordinaire, whose expertise, honesty, and belief in the story helped get it to the finish line.

To fellow author, Liz St. John, for her unfailing patience, support, and generosity.

To my Scribophile critiquers, Janet, Andrea, TZ, Wendy, Kurt, and Paul, for sticking with the story and helping me craft a better one.

To Francisco Cordoba of HippoCampus Publishing, for his input and attention to detail.

And especially to my family. Kyle, Matt, and Ryan, my wonderful cheerleaders whose enthusiasm encouraged me to keep going. To my husband Tim, who sat and listened to the story as I reeled it out of my head one night over pizza and beer, and whose spark made me believe. Whose support never wavered. Who was the first to slug through my rough early chapters. Who shared his knowledge of period-specific weaponry, and who voluntarily researched the details that weren't stored in his memory banks. Who gifted me with some of those weapons—best presents ever! Who lived with all my characters, even when things got crowded. Who participated in infinite plotting sessions when I got stuck. We killed many a good bottle of wine to get here, and we made it!

Connect

Want to know about character and historical insights, exclusive bonus content, and upcoming releases? Be the first to find out by signing up for my email list at www.griffin-brady.com.

Other ways to connect:

Facebook: https://www.facebook.com/AuthorGriffinBrady
Twitter: https://twitter.com/griffbrady1588
BookBub: https://www.bookbub.com/profile/griffin-brady
GoodReads:
https://www.goodreads.com/author/show/20675881.Griffin_Brady
Website: www.griffin-brady.com
Or email me! griffin@griffin-brady.com

Also by this Author

The Heart of a Hussar, Book One

Available through Amazon in
Kindle version:
https://www.amazon.com/dp/B08HJQBHP2
or paperback version:
https://www.amazon.com/dp/1735455814

*Writing as G.K. Brady, award-winning contemporary romance author
of* The Playmakers Series

Book 1 - *Taming Beckett*
Book 2 - *Third Man In*
Book 3 - *Gauging the Player*
Book 4 - *The Winning Score*
Book 5 - *Defending the Reaper*
Book 6 - *No Touch Zone*
Book 7 - *Twisted Wrister*
Book 7.5 – *Puck the Halls* (coming Nov. 2021)

About the Author

Griffin Brady is a historical fiction author with a keen interest in the Polish Winged Hussars of the 16th and 17th centuries. She accidentally stumbled into their world while researching another novel and was hooked, falling in love with their rich history of nobility, discipline, and valor. She is a member of the Historical Novel Society and Rocky Mountain Fiction Writers.

The proud mother of three grown sons, she lives in Colorado with her husband. She is also an award-winning romance author who writes under the pen name G.K. Brady.

Made in the USA
Coppell, TX
12 December 2021